PING

Hareta and Piplup's great adventure in search of the Legendary Pokémon Dialga begins! Their boundless energy and strong friendship will guide them past countless obstacles. So c'mon, everyone, let's go! Come travel with us to the land of Sinnoh! I challenge you!

—*Shigekatsu Ihara*

Shigekatsu Ihara's other manga titles include *Pokémon: Lucario and the Mystery of Mew*, *Pokémon Emerald Challenge!! Battle Frontier*, and *Dual Jack!!*.

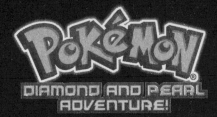

POKéMON
DIAMOND AND PEARL ADVENTURE!

Vol. 1
VIZ Kids Edition

Story and Art by SHIGEKATSU IHARA

Translation/Kaori Inoue
Touch-up Art & Lettering/Rina Mapa and Steve Dutro
Cover Design/Hitomi Yokoyama Ross
Editor/Leyla Aker

Editor in Chief, Books/Alvin Lu
Editor in Chief, Magazines/Marc Weidenbaum
VP of Publishing Licensing/Rika Inouye
VP of Sales/Gonzalo Ferreyra
VP of Marketing/Liza Coppola
Publisher/Hyoe Narita

First published by Shogakukan Inc. in Japan as
"Pokémon D • P Pocket Monster Diamond Pearl Monogatari"

Printed in the U.S.A.

Published by VIZ Media, LLC
P.O. Box 77010
San Francisco, CA 94107

VIZ Kids Edition
10 9 8 7 6 5 4 3 2 1
First printing, April 2008

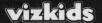

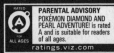

Pokémon®
Diamond and Pearl Adventure!

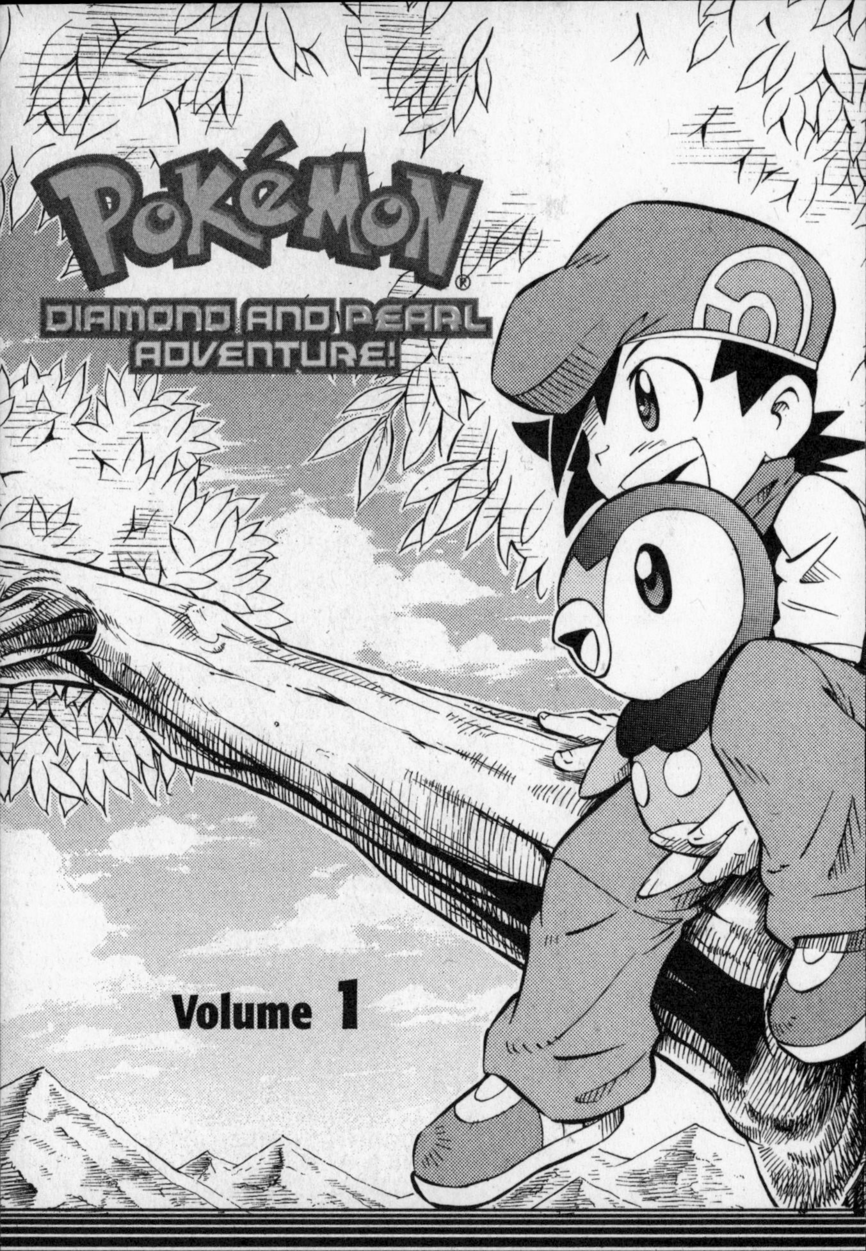

Volume 1

Story & Art by
Shigekatsu Ihara

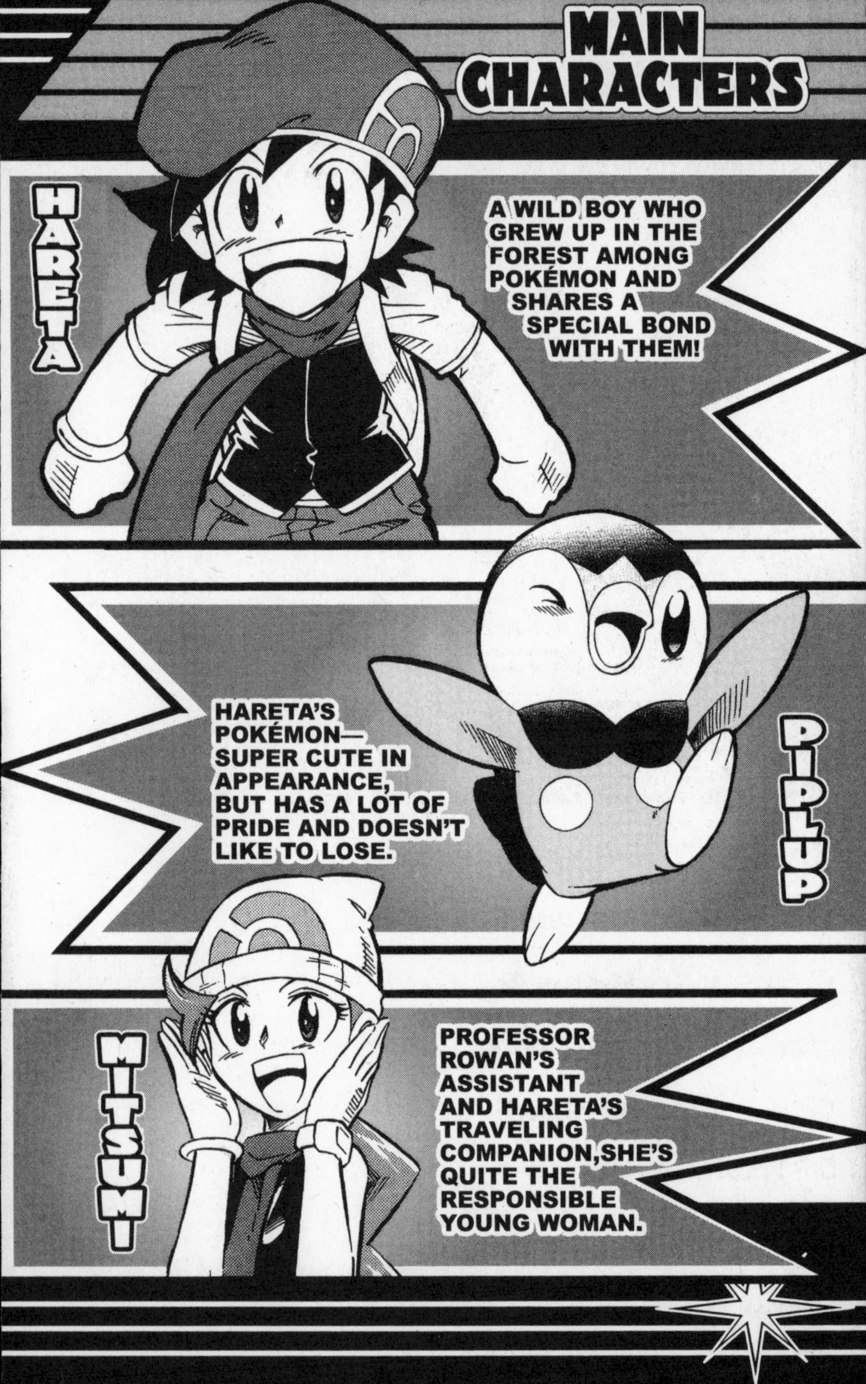
MAIN CHARACTERS
HARETA
A WILD BOY WHO GREW UP IN THE FOREST AMONG POKÉMON AND SHARES A SPECIAL BOND WITH THEM!
PIPLUP
HARETA'S POKÉMON—SUPER CUTE IN APPEARANCE, BUT HAS A LOT OF PRIDE AND DOESN'T LIKE TO LOSE.
MITSUMI
PROFESSOR ROWAN'S ASSISTANT AND HARETA'S TRAVELING COMPANION,SHE'S QUITE THE RESPONSIBLE YOUNG WOMAN.

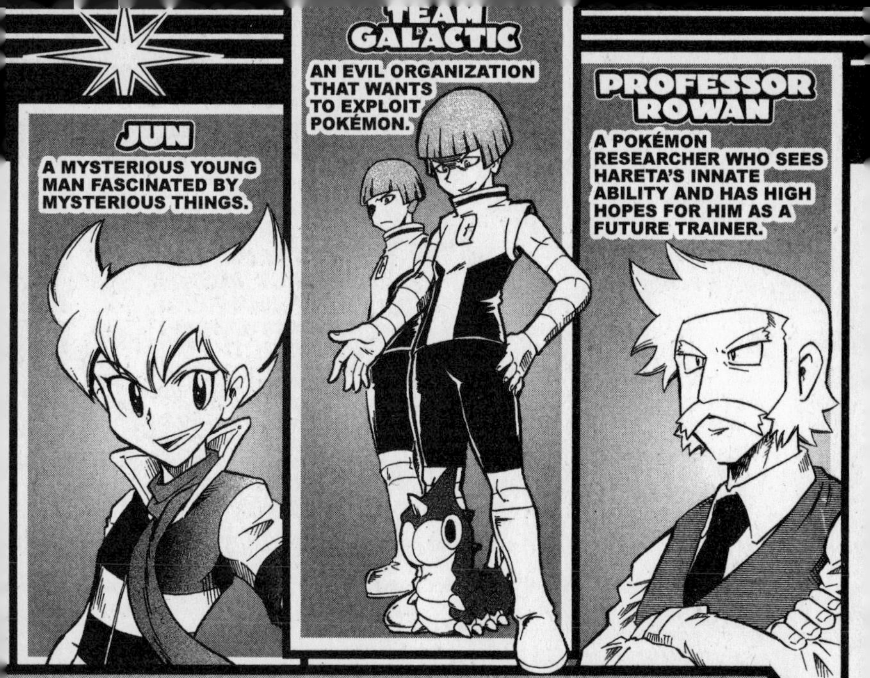
PROFESSOR ROWAN
A POKÉMON RESEARCHER WHO SEES HARETA'S INNATE ABILITY AND HAS HIGH HOPES FOR HIM AS A FUTURE TRAINER.
TEAM GALACTIC
AN EVIL ORGANIZATION THAT WANTS TO EXPLOIT POKÉMON.
JUN
A MYSTERIOUS YOUNG MAN FASCINATED BY MYSTERIOUS THINGS.

CONTENTS

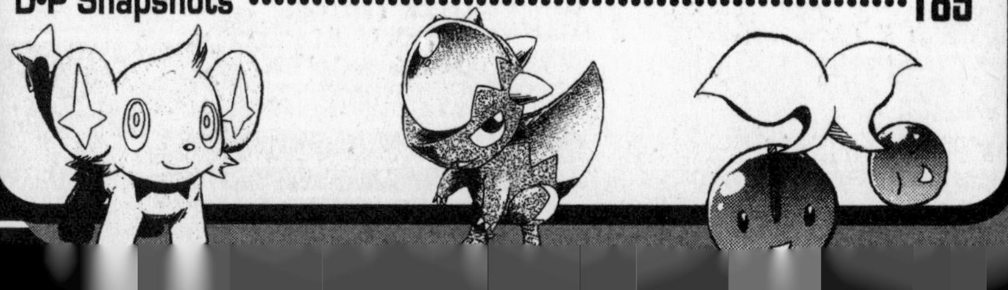

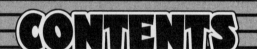

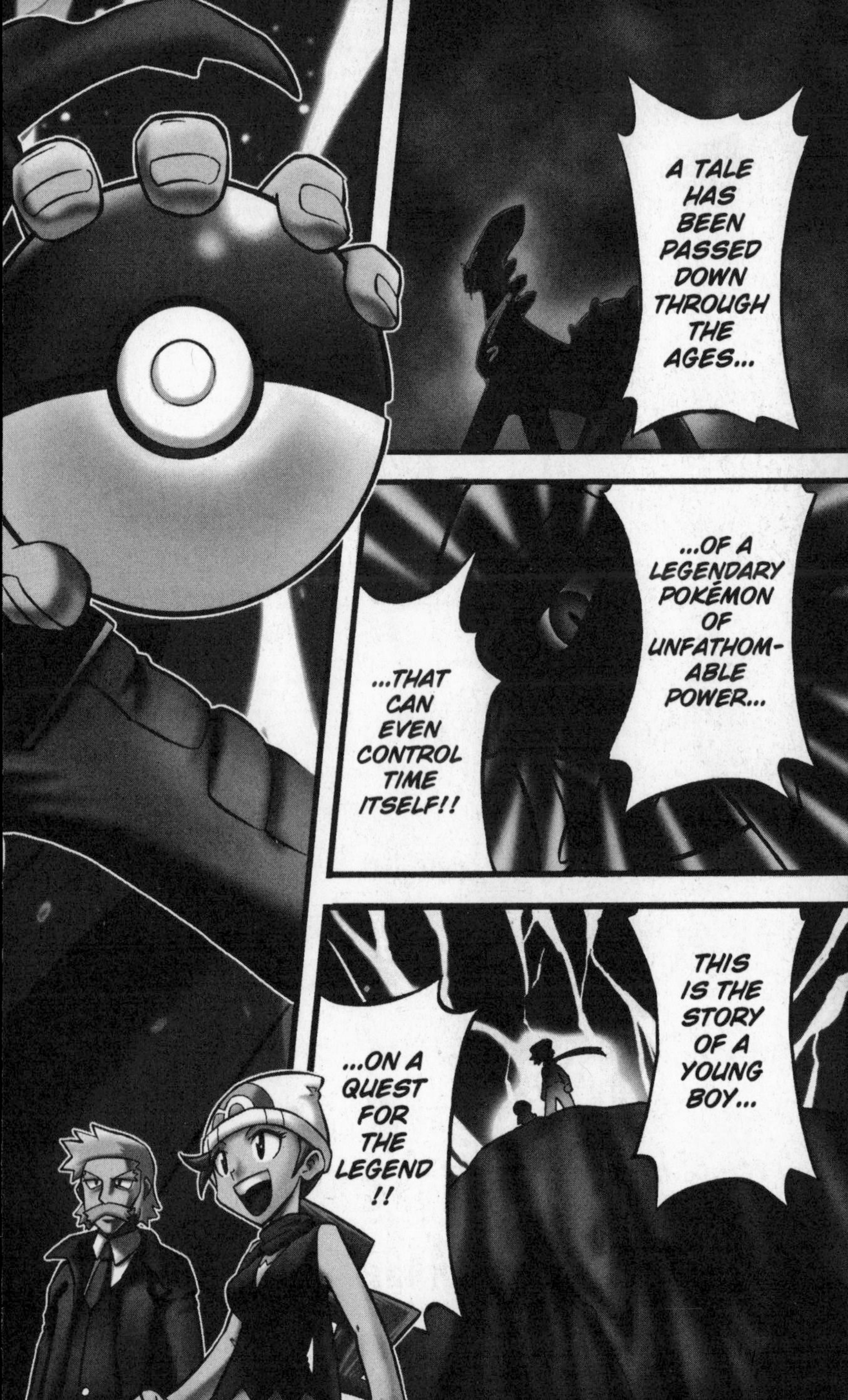
A TALE HAS BEEN PASSED DOWN THROUGH THE AGES...
...OF A LEGENDARY POKéMON OF UNFATHOMABLE POWER...
...THAT CAN EVEN CONTROL TIME ITSELF!!
THIS IS THE STORY OF A YOUNG BOY...
...ON A QUEST FOR THE LEGEND!!

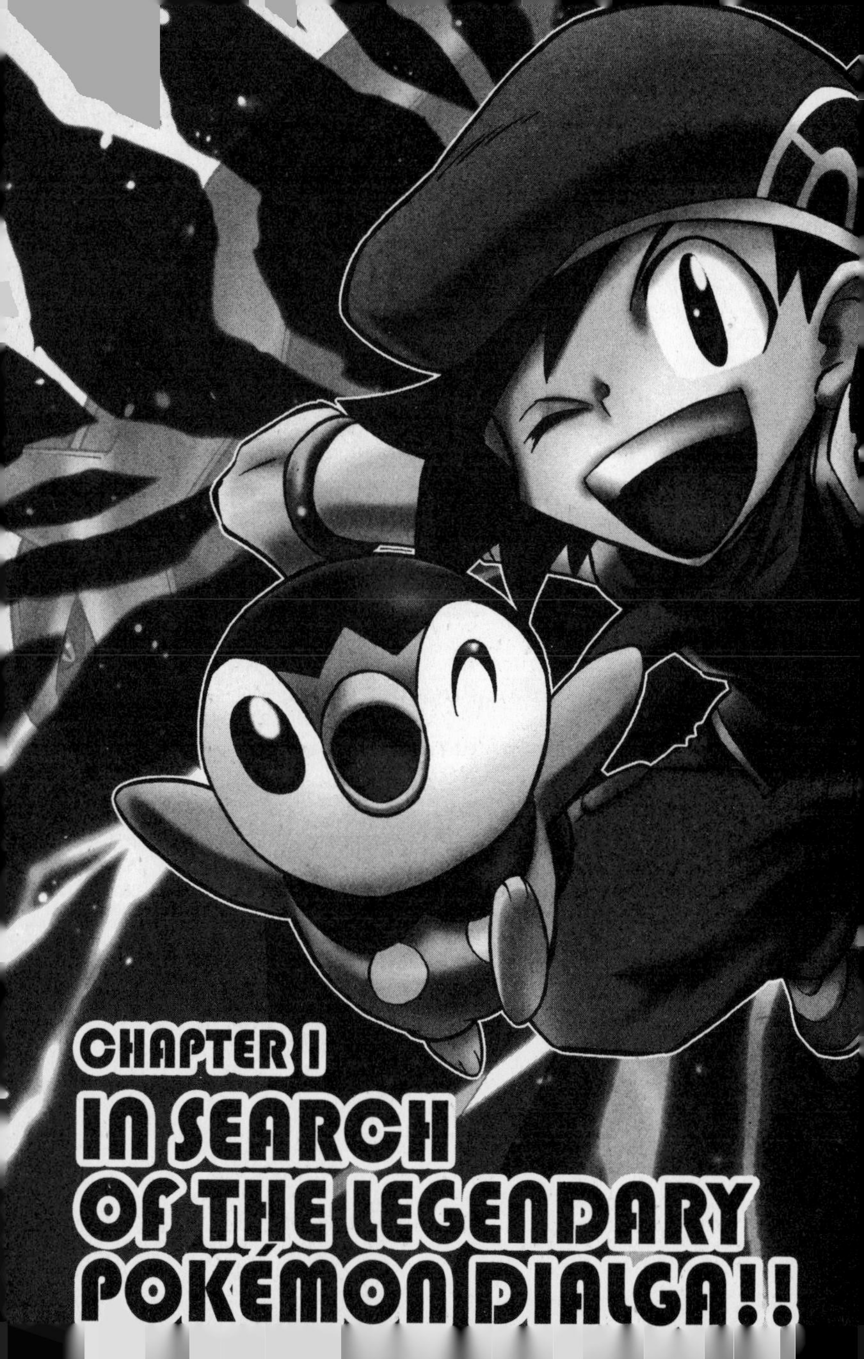
CHAPTER 1
IN SEARCH OF THE LEGENDARY POKÉMON DIALGA!!

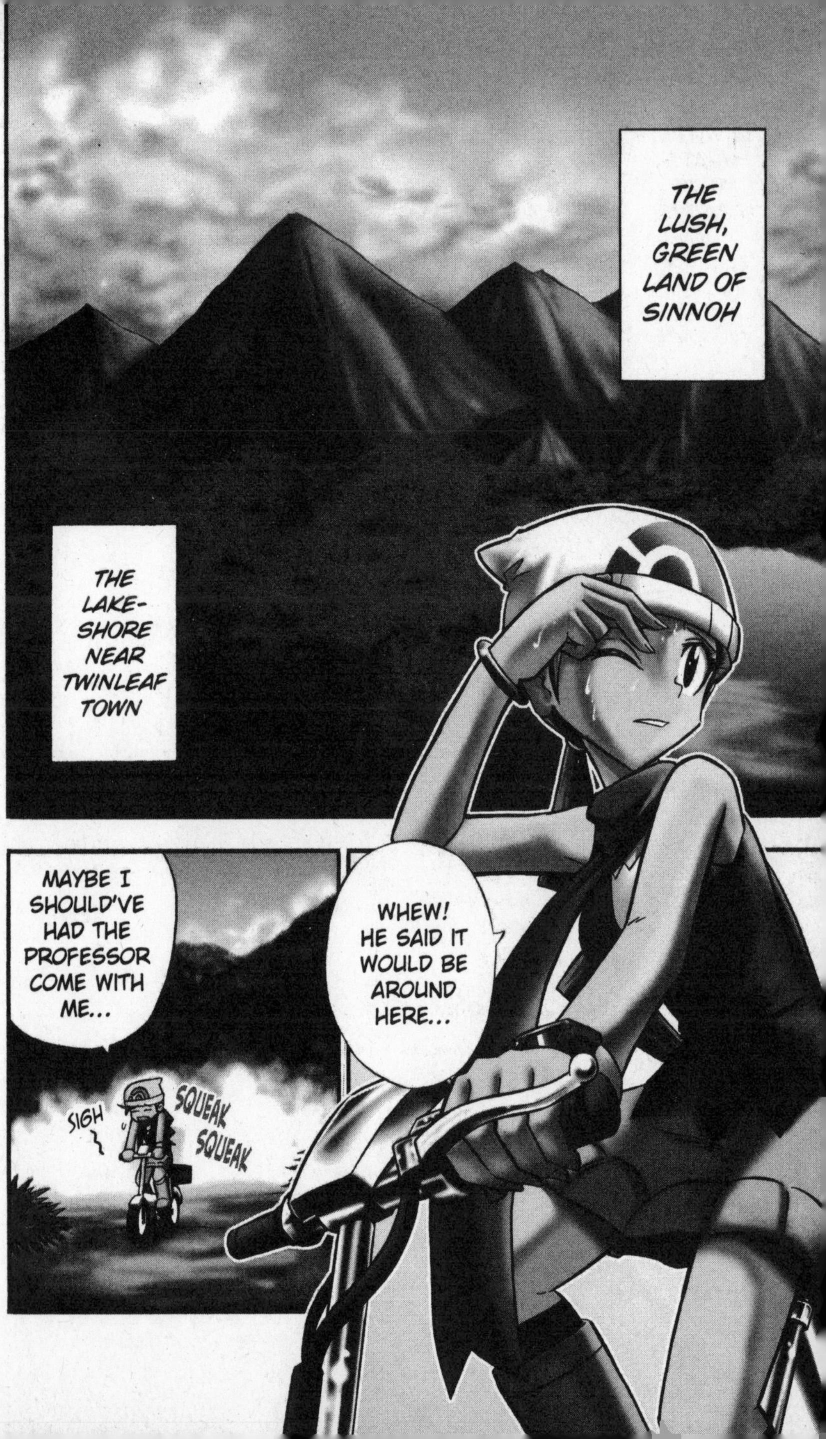
THE LUSH, GREEN LAND OF SINNOH
THE LAKE-SHORE NEAR TWINLEAF TOWN
WHEW! HE SAID IT WOULD BE AROUND HERE...
MAYBE I SHOULD'VE HAD THE PROFESSOR COME WITH ME...
SIGH
SQUEAK SQUEAK

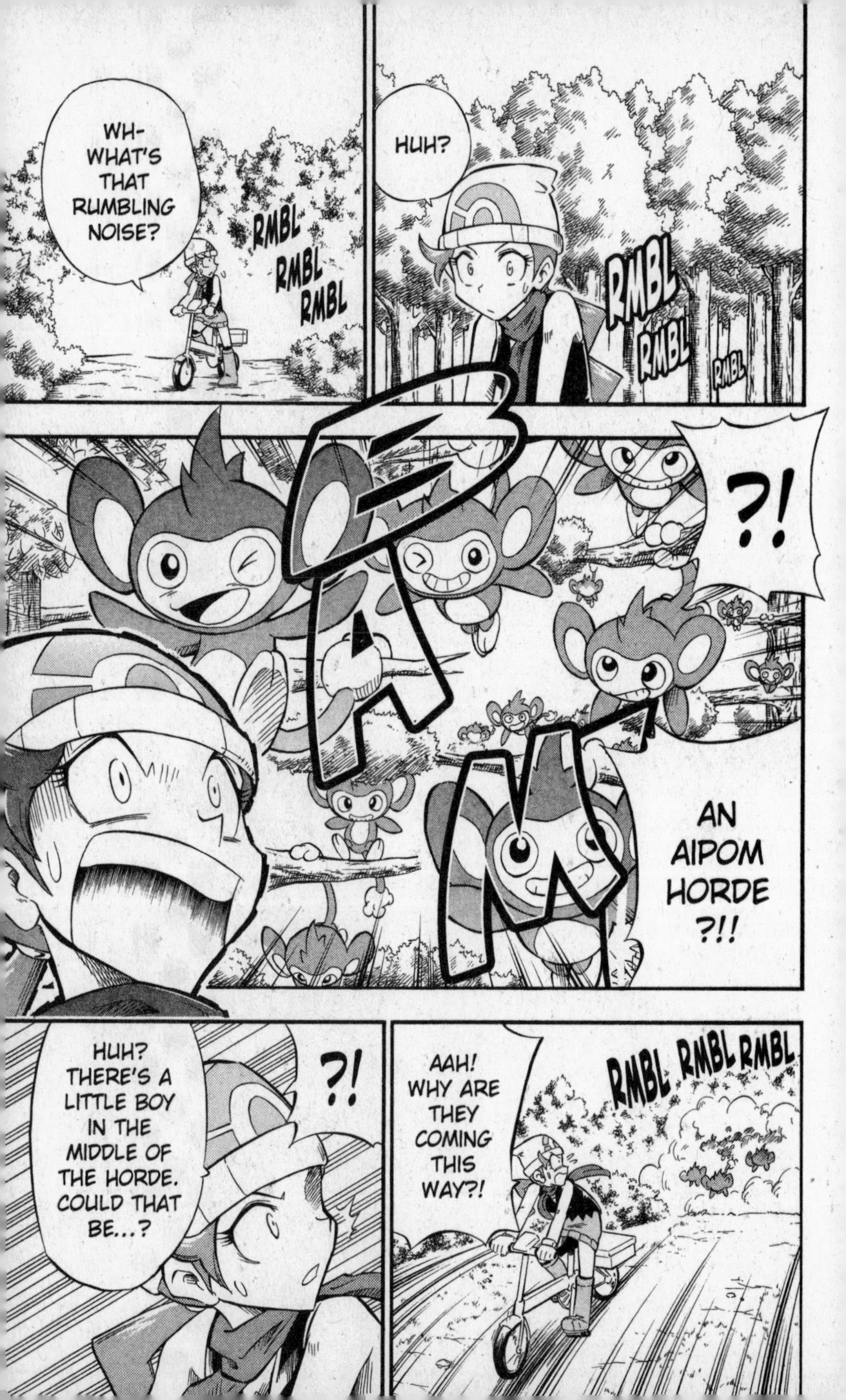
HUH?
RMBL
RMBL
RMBL
WH- WHAT'S THAT RUMBLING NOISE?
RMBL
RMBL
RMBL
?!
BAM
AN AIPOM HORDE ?!!
RMBL RMBL RMBL
AAH! WHY ARE THEY COMING THIS WAY?!
?!
HUH? THERE'S A LITTLE BOY IN THE MIDDLE OF THE HORDE. COULD THAT BE...?

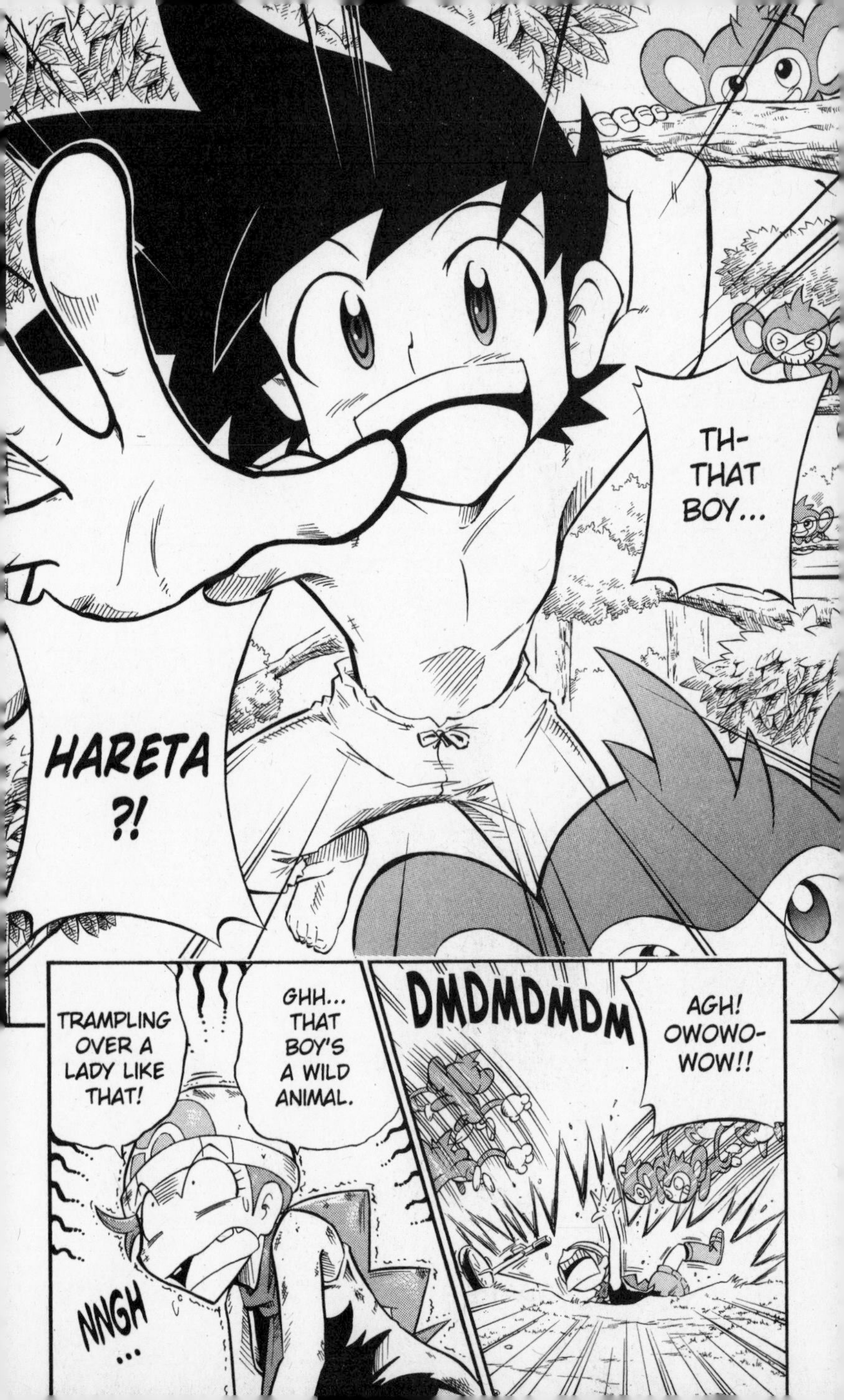
TH- THAT BOY...
HARETA ?!
AGH! OWOWO-WOW!!
DMDMDMDM
GHH... THAT BOY'S A WILD ANIMAL.
TRAMPLING OVER A LADY LIKE THAT!
NNGH ...

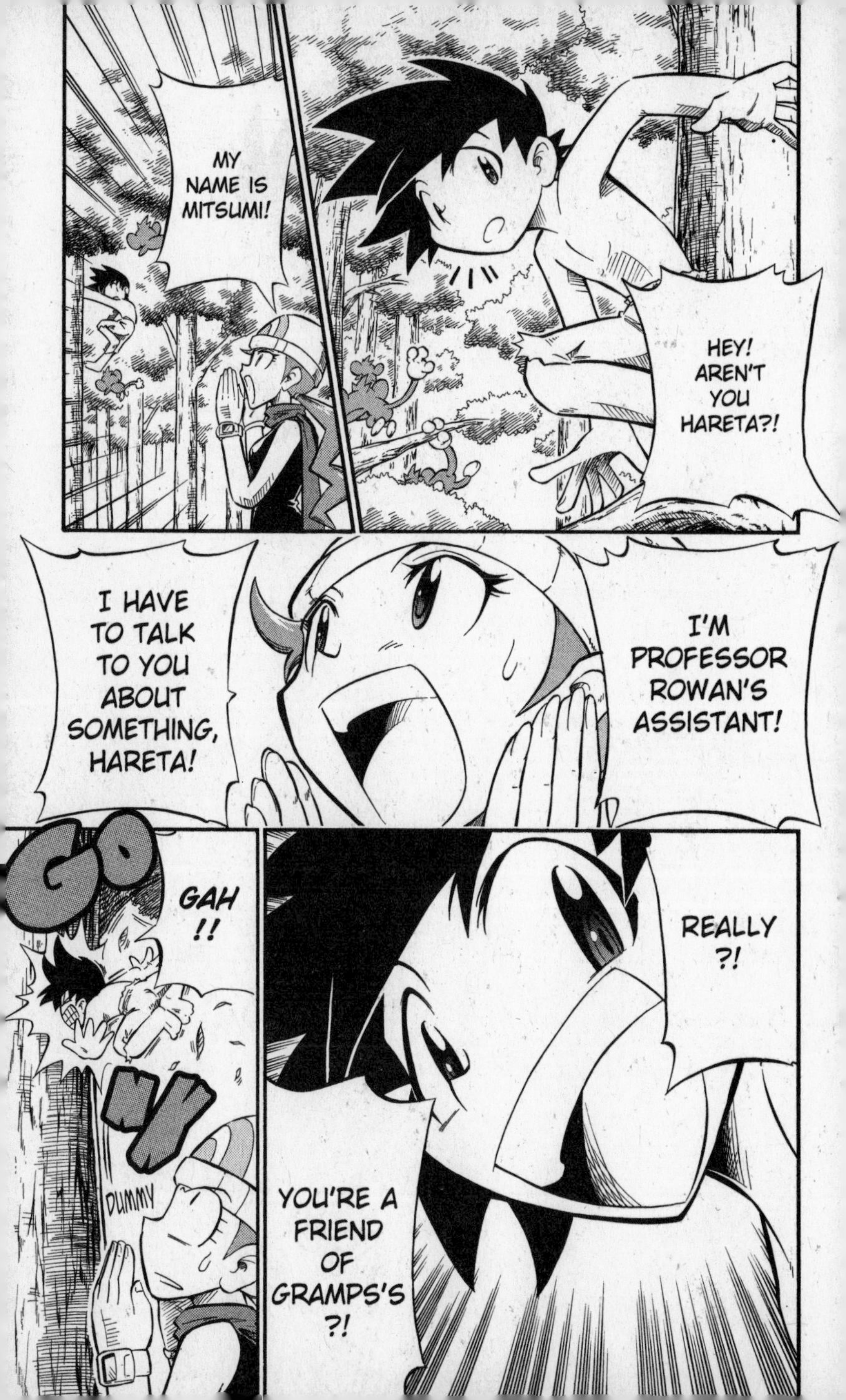
HEY! AREN'T YOU HARETA?!
MY NAME IS MITSUMI!
I'M PROFESSOR ROWAN'S ASSISTANT!
I HAVE TO TALK TO YOU ABOUT SOMETHING, HARETA!
REALLY ?!
YOU'RE A FRIEND OF GRAMPS'S ?!
GO
GAH !!
DUMMY

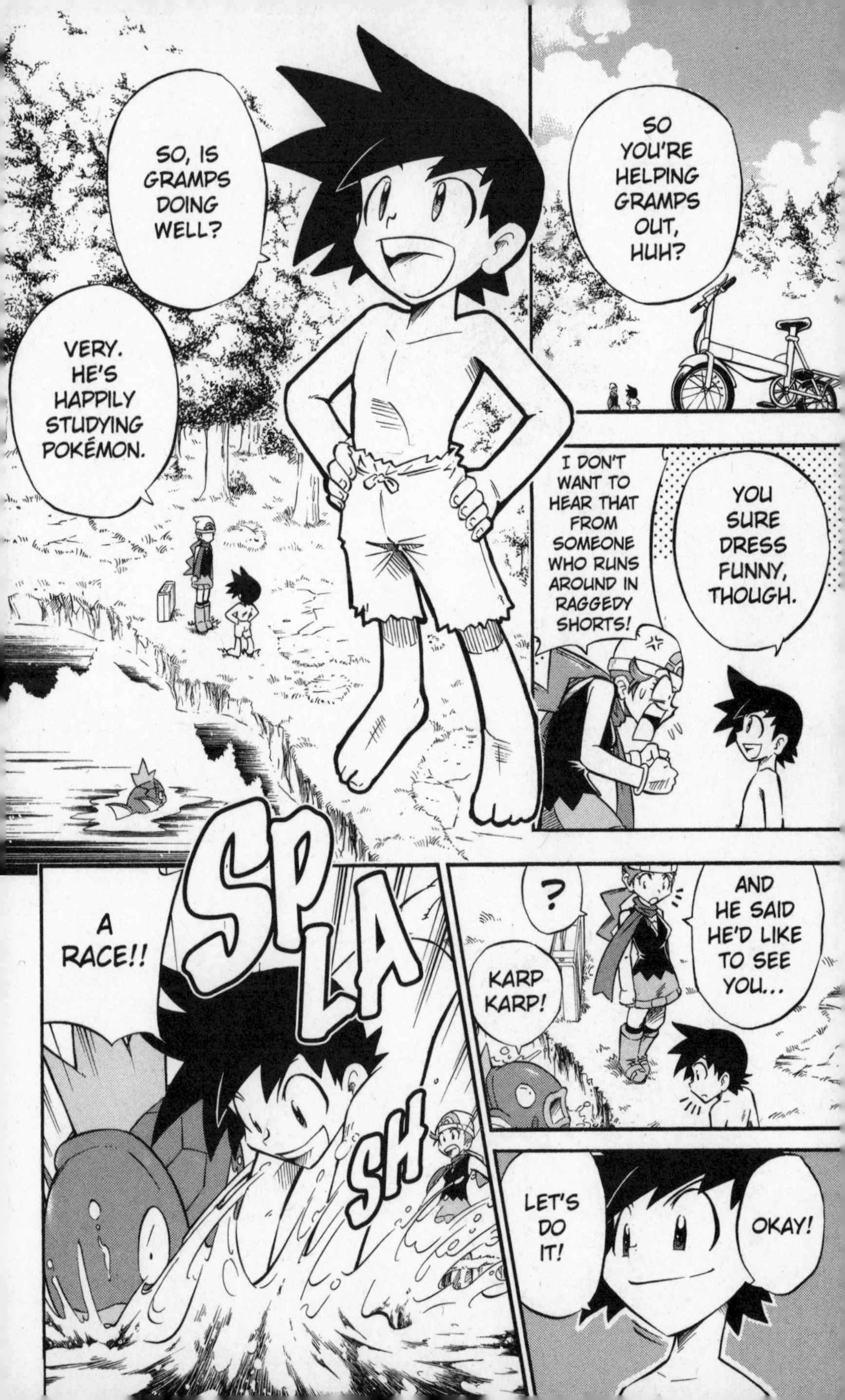
SO YOU'RE HELPING GRAMPS OUT, HUH?
YOU SURE DRESS FUNNY, THOUGH.
I DON'T WANT TO HEAR THAT FROM SOMEONE WHO RUNS AROUND IN RAGGEDY SHORTS!
SO, IS GRAMPS DOING WELL?
VERY. HE'S HAPPILY STUDYING POKÉMON.
AND HE SAID HE'D LIKE TO SEE YOU...
?
KARP KARP!
OKAY!
LET'S DO IT!
A RACE!!
SPLASH

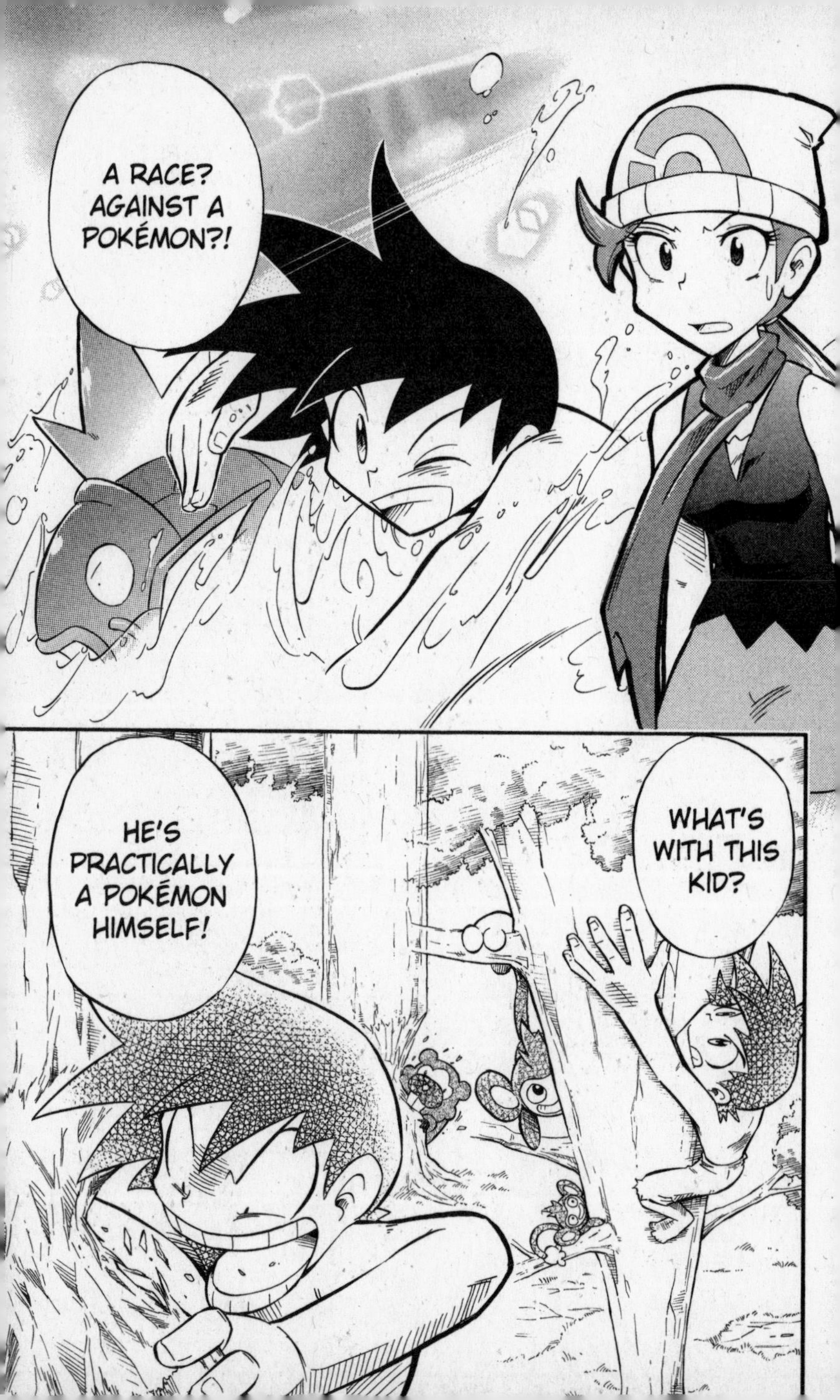
A RACE? AGAINST A POKÉMON?!
WHAT'S WITH THIS KID?
HE'S PRACTICALLY A POKÉMON HIMSELF!

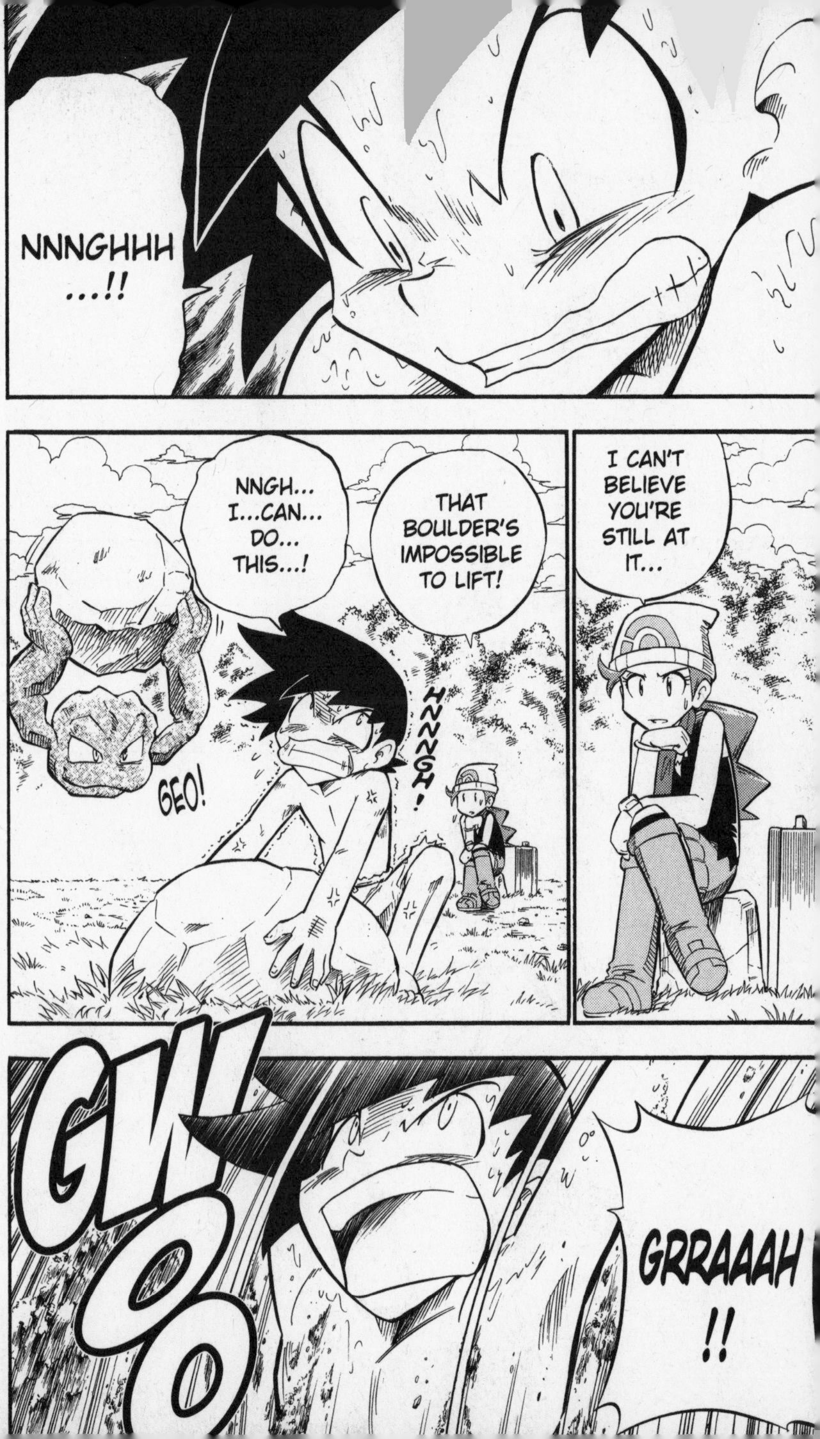
NNNGHHH ...!!
I CAN'T BELIEVE YOU'RE STILL AT IT...
THAT BOULDER'S IMPOSSIBLE TO LIFT!
NNGH... I...CAN... DO... THIS...!
HNNNGH!
GEO!
GRRAAAH !!

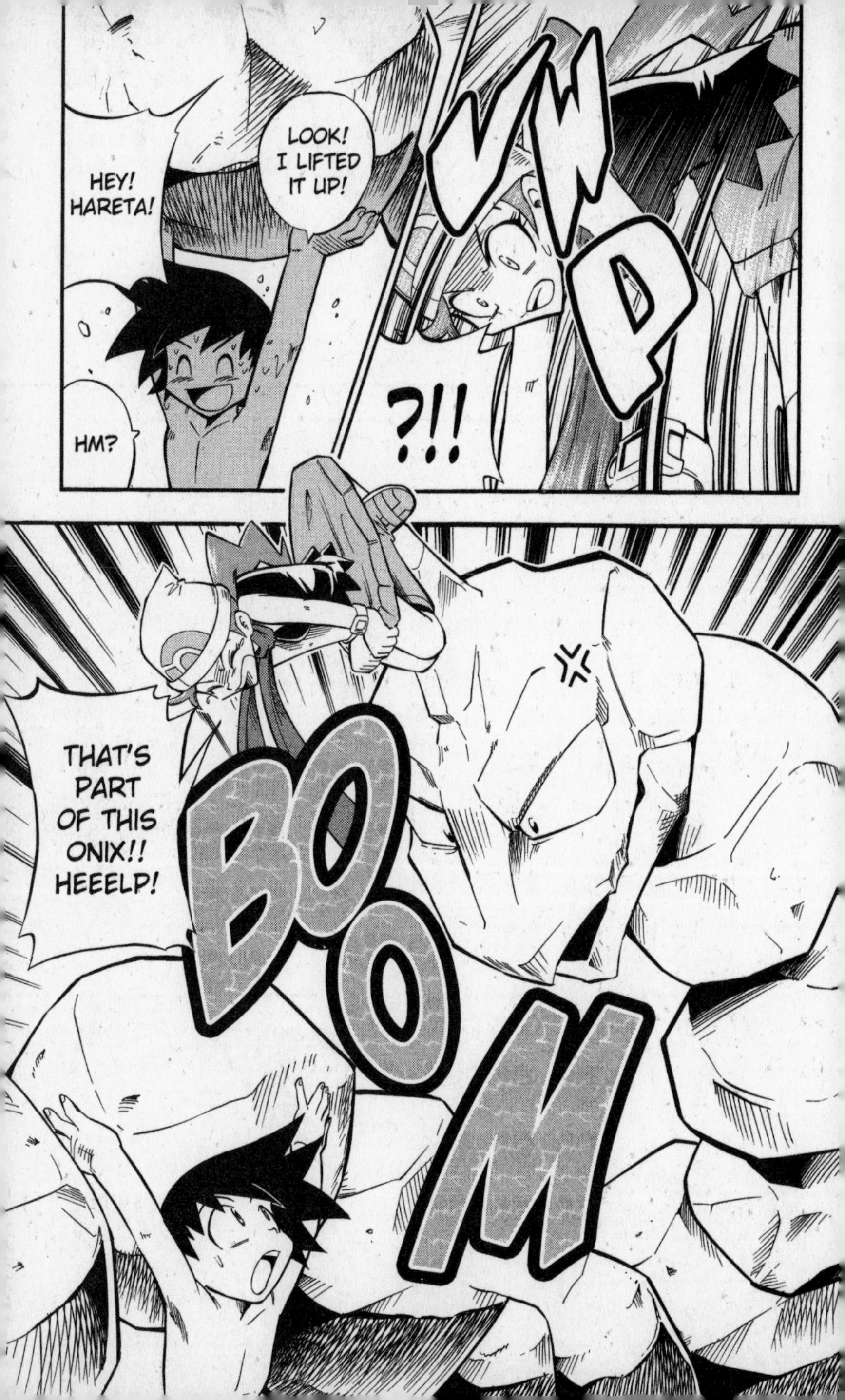
?!!
LOOK! I LIFTED IT UP!
HEY! HARETA!
HM?
THAT'S PART OF THIS ONIX!! HEEELP!
BOOM

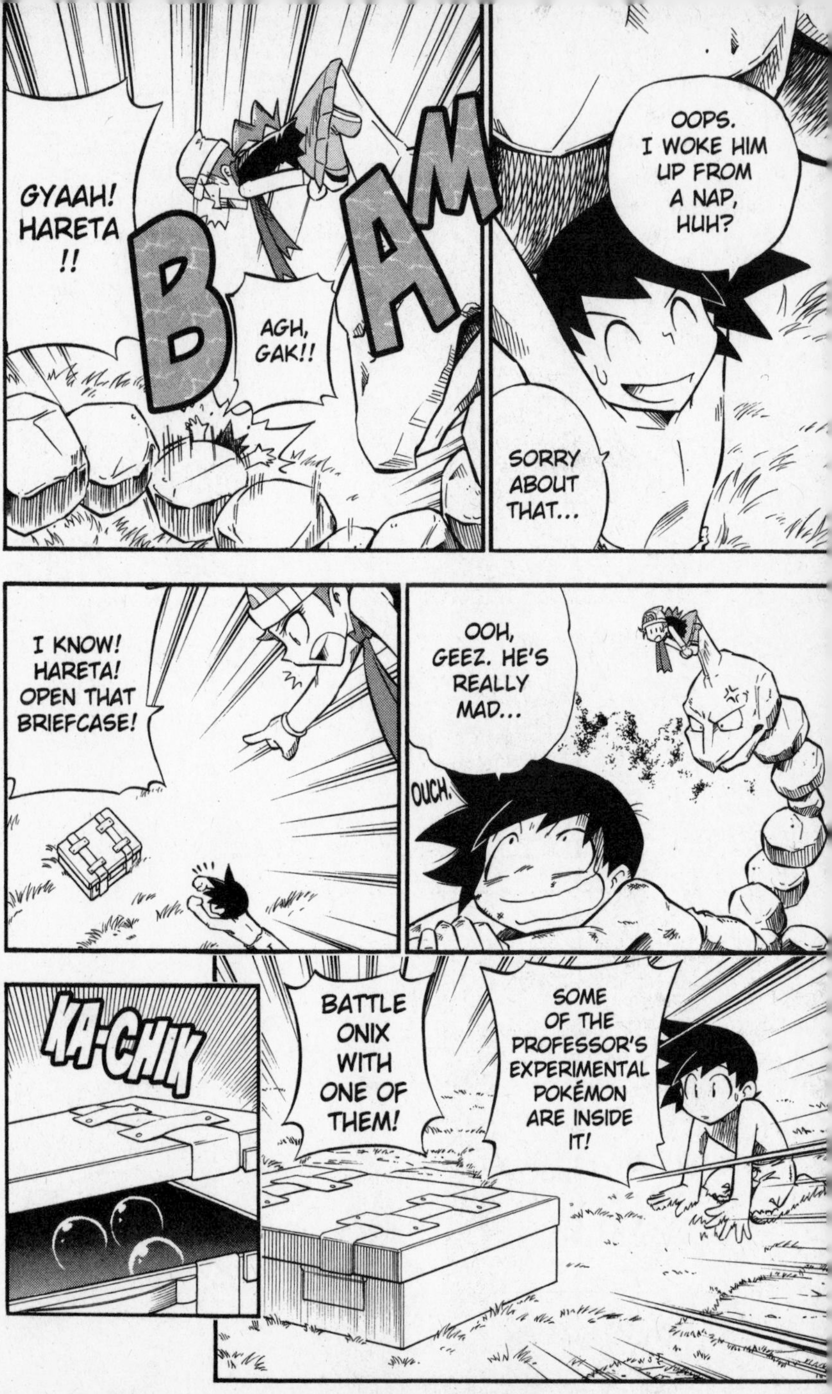
OOPS. I WOKE HIM UP FROM A NAP, HUH?
SORRY ABOUT THAT...
GYAAH! HARETA !!
BAM
AGH, GAK!!
OOH, GEEZ. HE'S REALLY MAD...
OUCH.
I KNOW! HARETA! OPEN THAT BRIEFCASE!
SOME OF THE PROFESSOR'S EXPERIMENTAL POKÉMON ARE INSIDE IT!
BATTLE ONIX WITH ONE OF THEM!
KA-CHIK

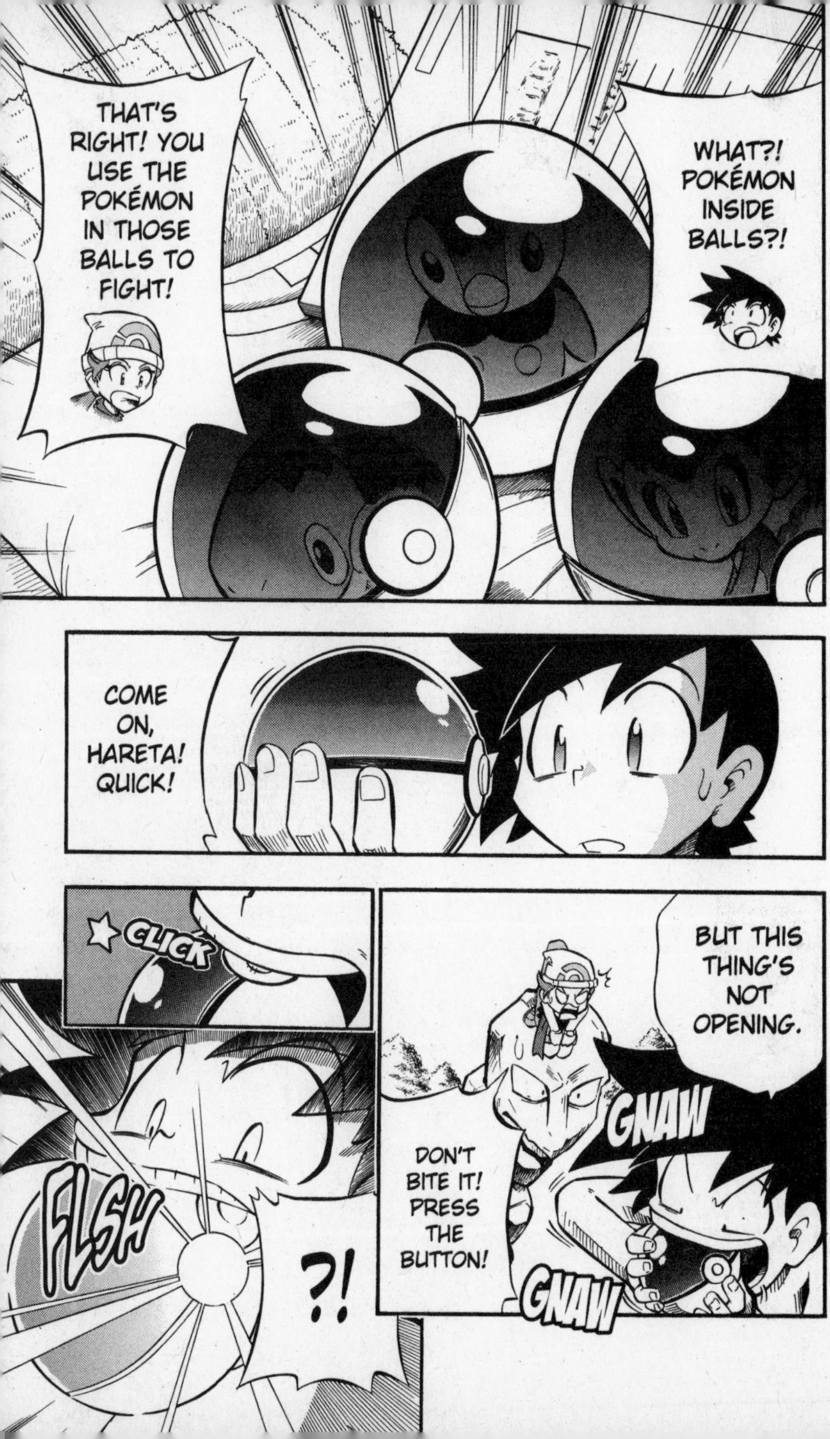
WHAT?! POKÉMON INSIDE BALLS?!
THAT'S RIGHT! YOU USE THE POKÉMON IN THOSE BALLS TO FIGHT!
COME ON, HARETA! QUICK!
BUT THIS THING'S NOT OPENING.
GNAW
DON'T BITE IT! PRESS THE BUTTON!
GNAW
CLICK
FLSH
?!

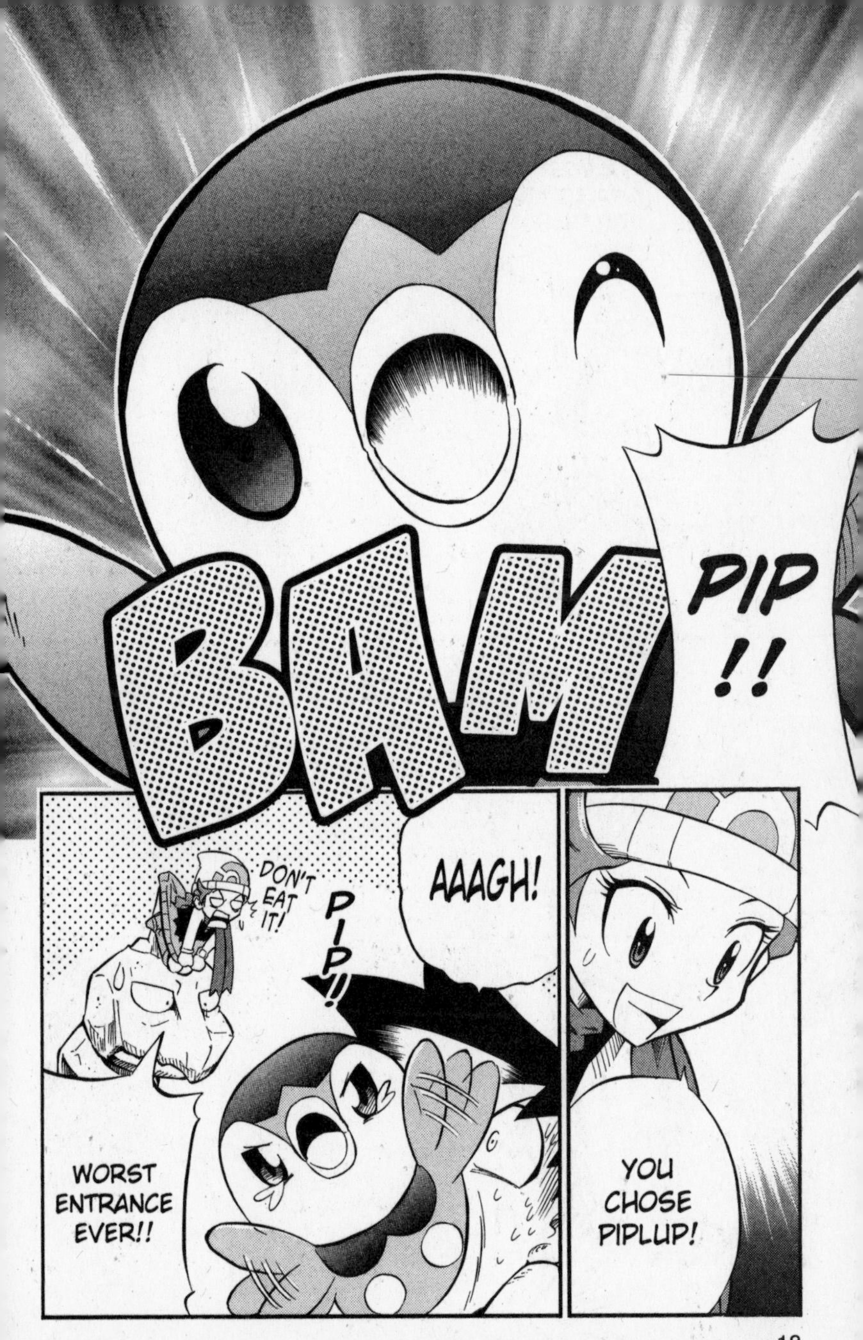
BAM
PIP!!
YOU CHOSE PIPLUP!
AAAGH!
DON'T EAT IT!
PIP!!
WORST ENTRANCE EVER!!

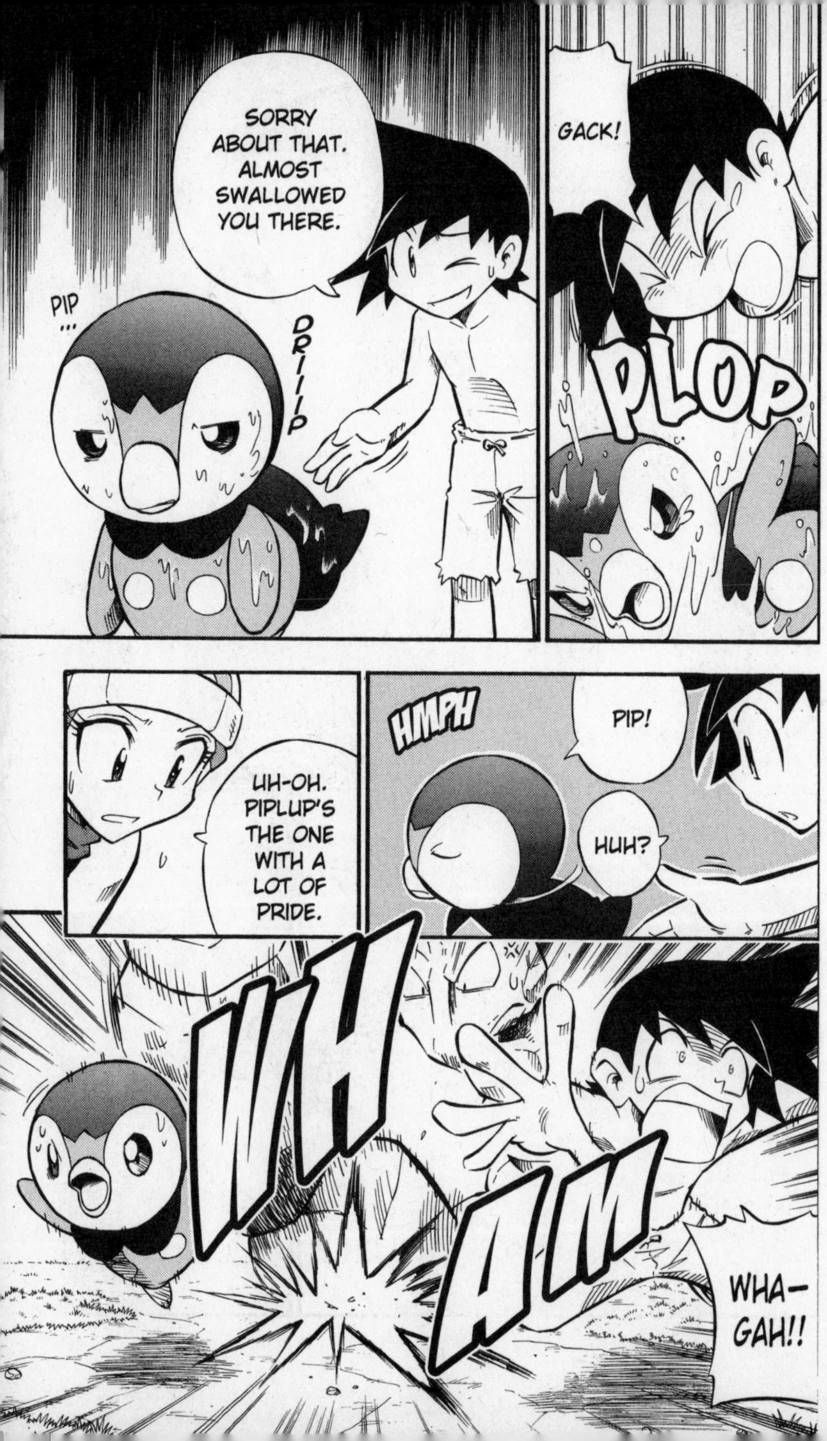
GACK!
PLOP
SORRY ABOUT THAT. ALMOST SWALLOWED YOU THERE.
DRIIIP
PIP...
HMPH
PIP!
HUH?
UH-OH. PIPLUP'S THE ONE WITH A LOT OF PRIDE.
WHAM
WHA-GAH!!

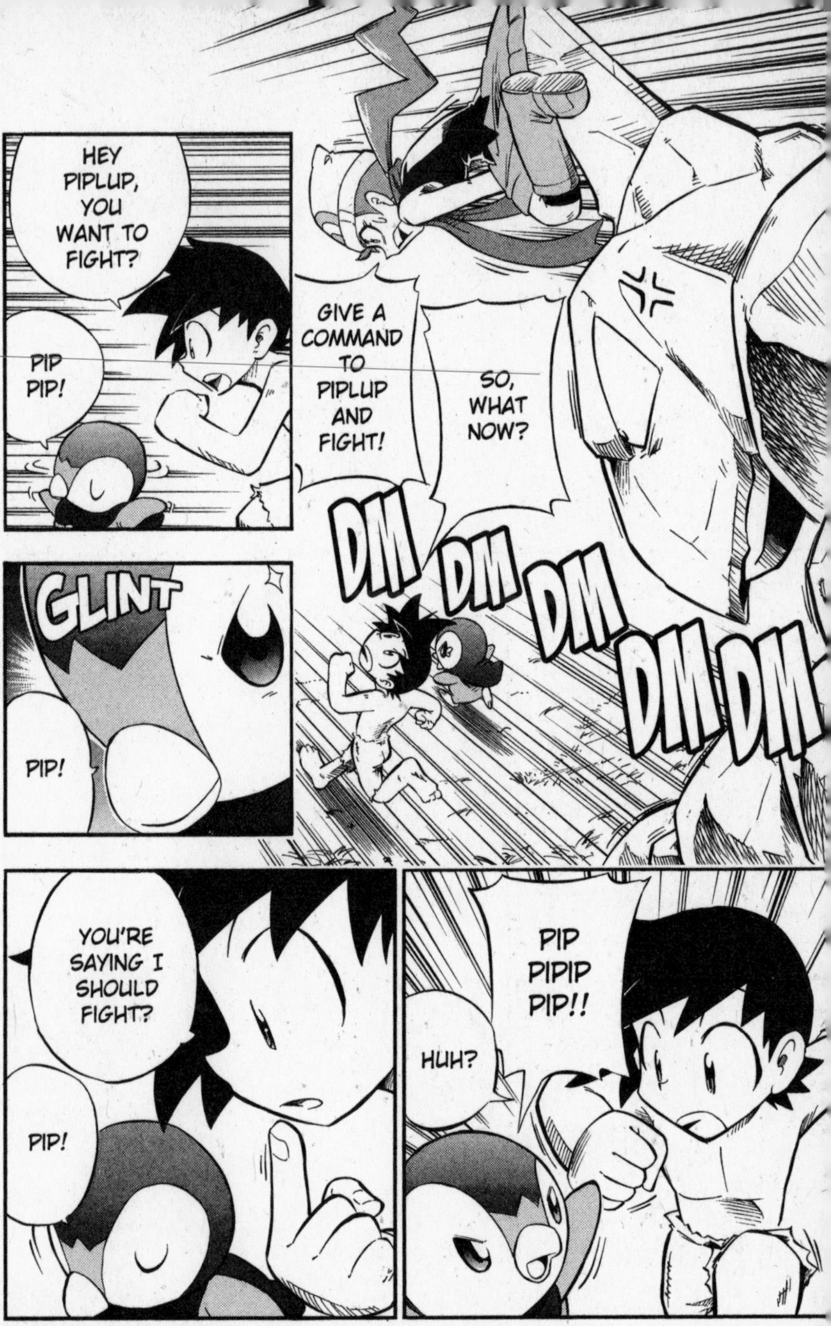

SO, WHAT NOW?
GIVE A COMMAND TO PIPLUP AND FIGHT!
DM DM DM DM DM
HEY PIPLUP, YOU WANT TO FIGHT?
PIP PIP!
GLINT
PIP!
PIP PIPIP PIP!!
HUH?
YOU'RE SAYING I SHOULD FIGHT?
PIP!

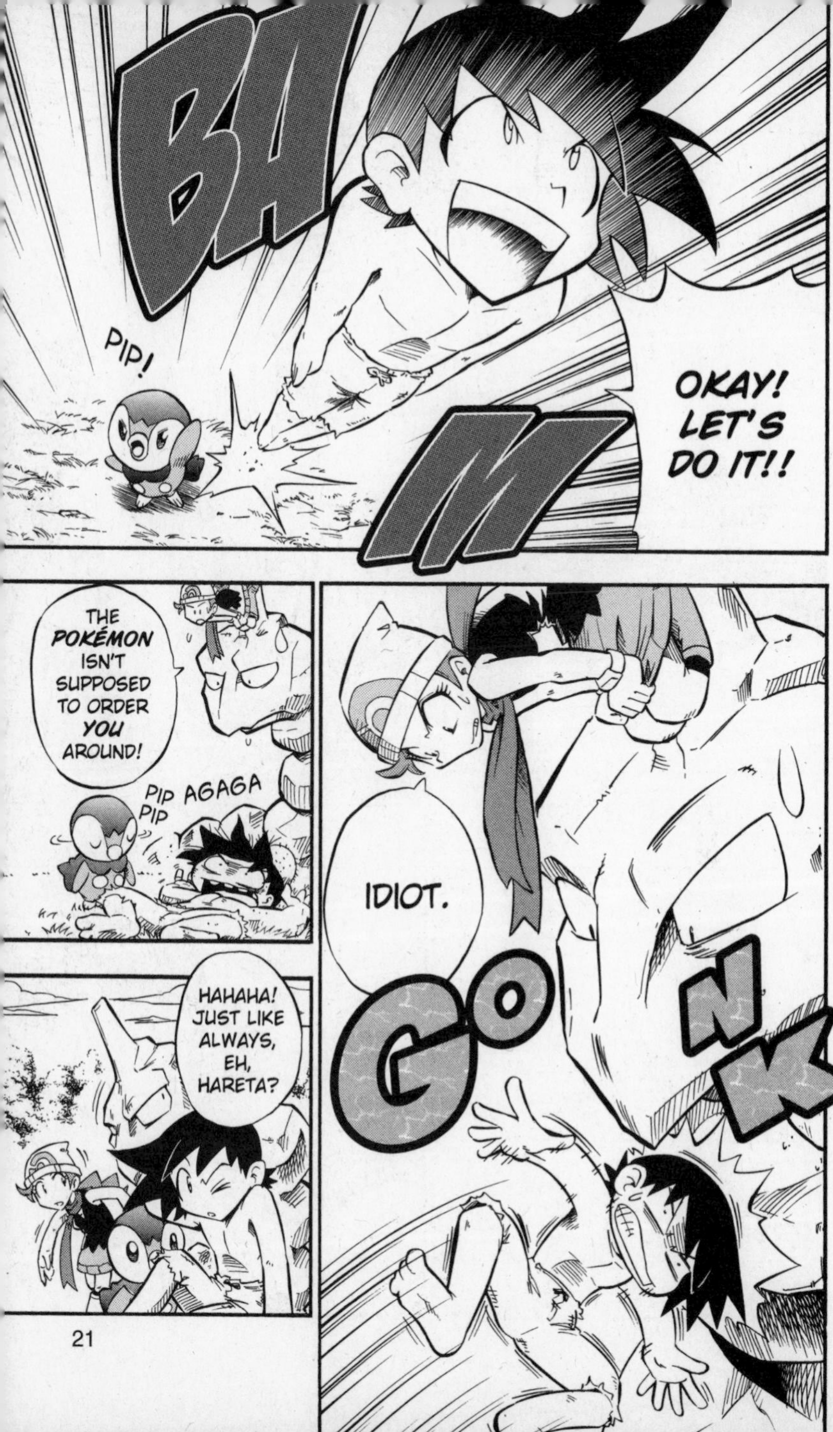

BAM
OKAY! LET'S DO IT!!
PIP!
IDIOT.
GONK
THE POKÉMON ISN'T SUPPOSED TO ORDER YOU AROUND!
PIP PIP
AGAGA
HAHAHA! JUST LIKE ALWAYS, EH, HARETA?

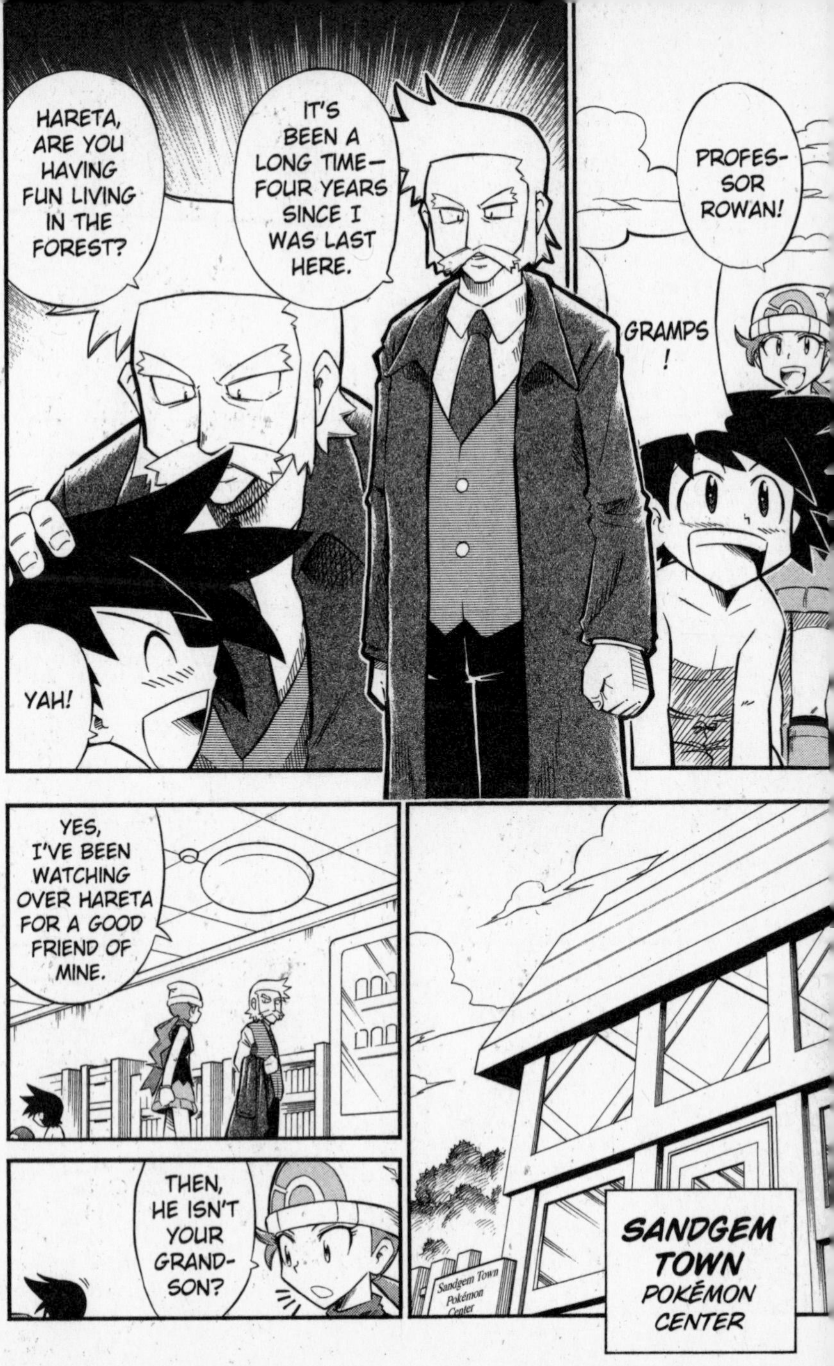
PROFESSOR ROWAN!
GRAMPS!
IT'S BEEN A LONG TIME—FOUR YEARS SINCE I WAS LAST HERE.
HARETA, ARE YOU HAVING FUN LIVING IN THE FOREST?
YAH!
SANDGEM TOWN POKÉMON CENTER
Sandgem Town Pokémon Center
YES, I'VE BEEN WATCHING OVER HARETA FOR A GOOD FRIEND OF MINE.
THEN, HE ISN'T YOUR GRANDSON?

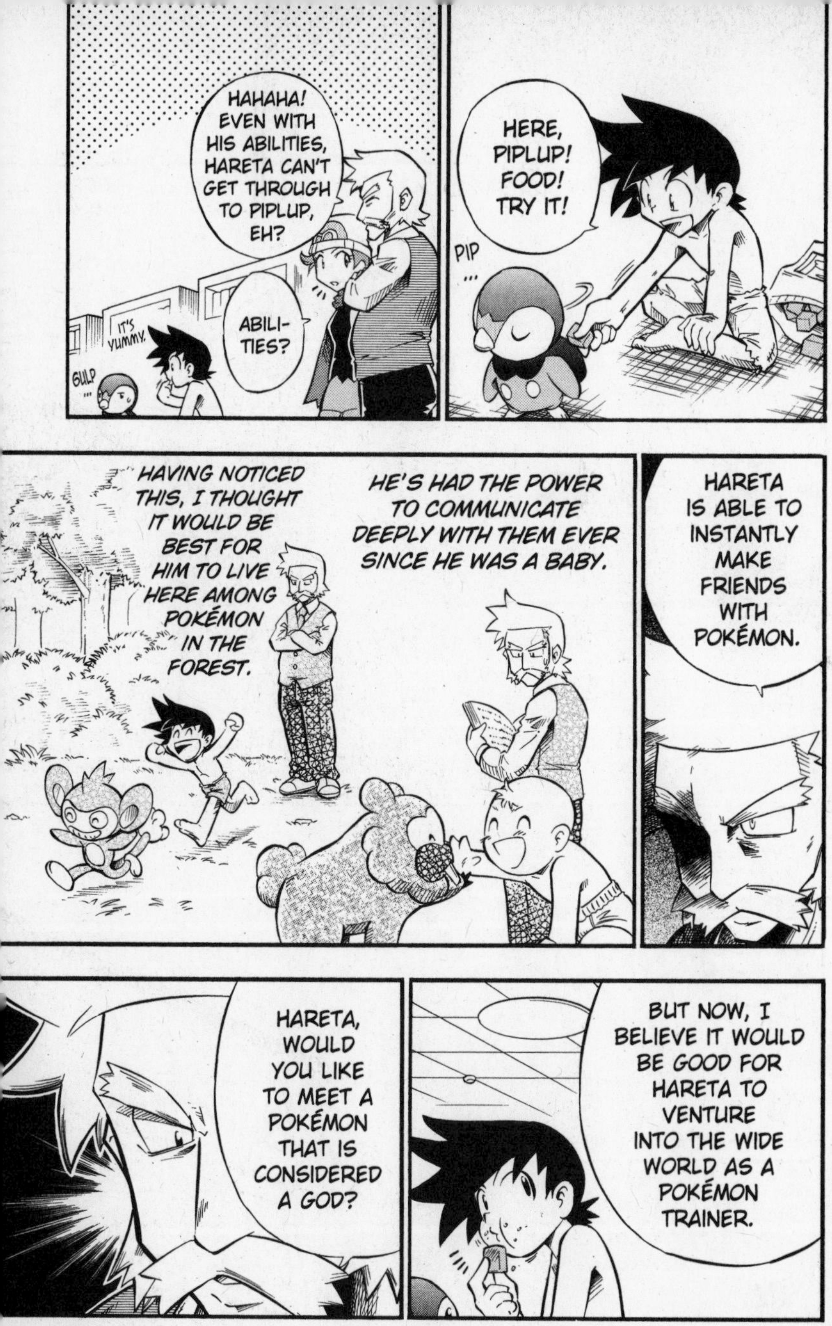
HERE, PIPLUP! FOOD! TRY IT!
PIP ...
HAHAHA! EVEN WITH HIS ABILITIES, HARETA CAN'T GET THROUGH TO PIPLUP, EH?
ABILITIES?
IT'S YUMMY.
GULP ...
HARETA IS ABLE TO INSTANTLY MAKE FRIENDS WITH POKÉMON.
HE'S HAD THE POWER TO COMMUNICATE DEEPLY WITH THEM EVER SINCE HE WAS A BABY.
HAVING NOTICED THIS, I THOUGHT IT WOULD BE BEST FOR HIM TO LIVE HERE AMONG POKÉMON IN THE FOREST.
BUT NOW, I BELIEVE IT WOULD BE GOOD FOR HARETA TO VENTURE INTO THE WIDE WORLD AS A POKÉMON TRAINER.
HARETA, WOULD YOU LIKE TO MEET A POKÉMON THAT IS CONSIDERED A GOD?

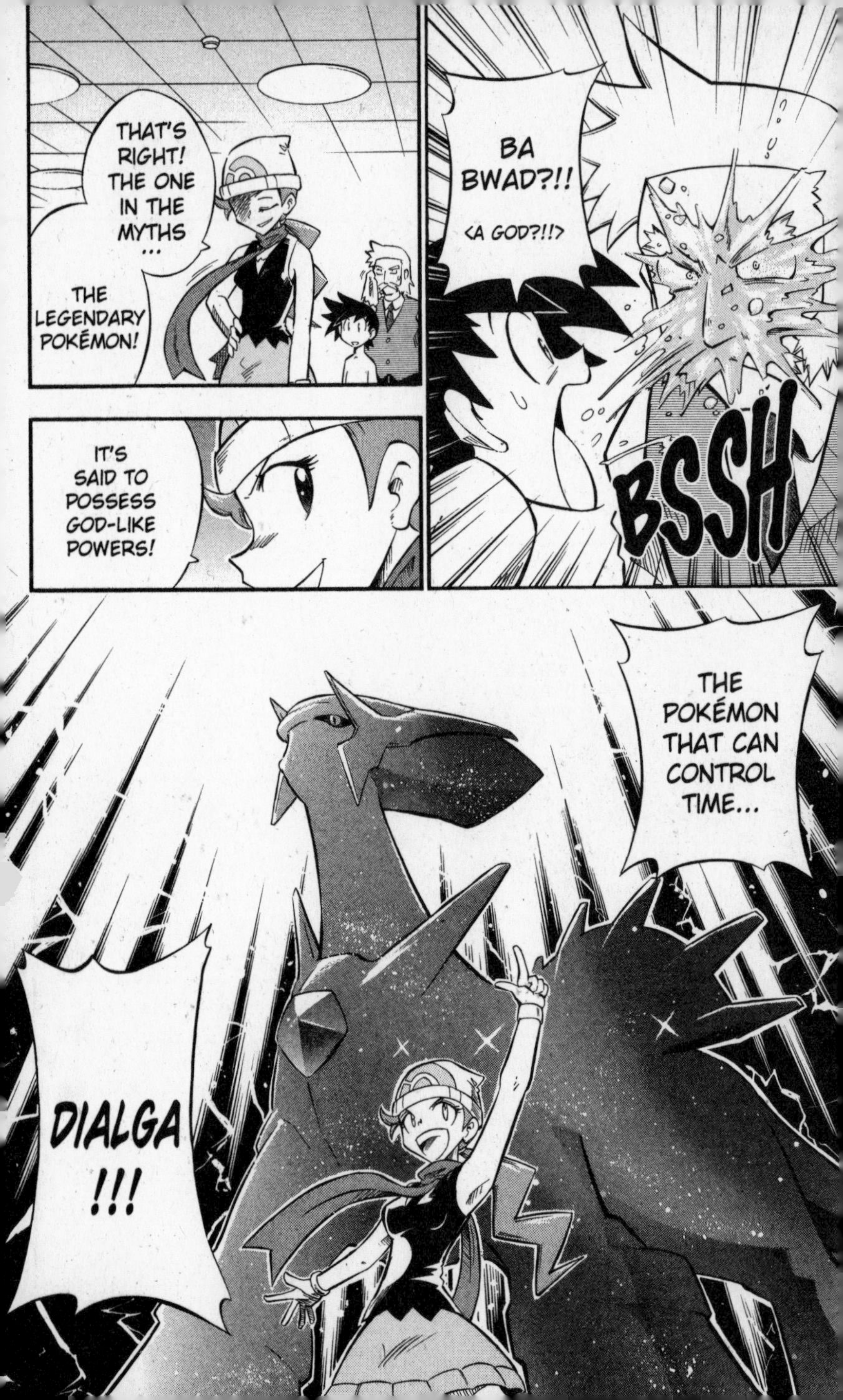
THAT'S RIGHT! THE ONE IN THE MYTHS ...
THE LEGENDARY POKÉMON!
IT'S SAID TO POSSESS GOD-LIKE POWERS!
BA BWAD?!!
<A GOD?!!>
BSSH
THE POKÉMON THAT CAN CONTROL TIME...
DIALGA !!!

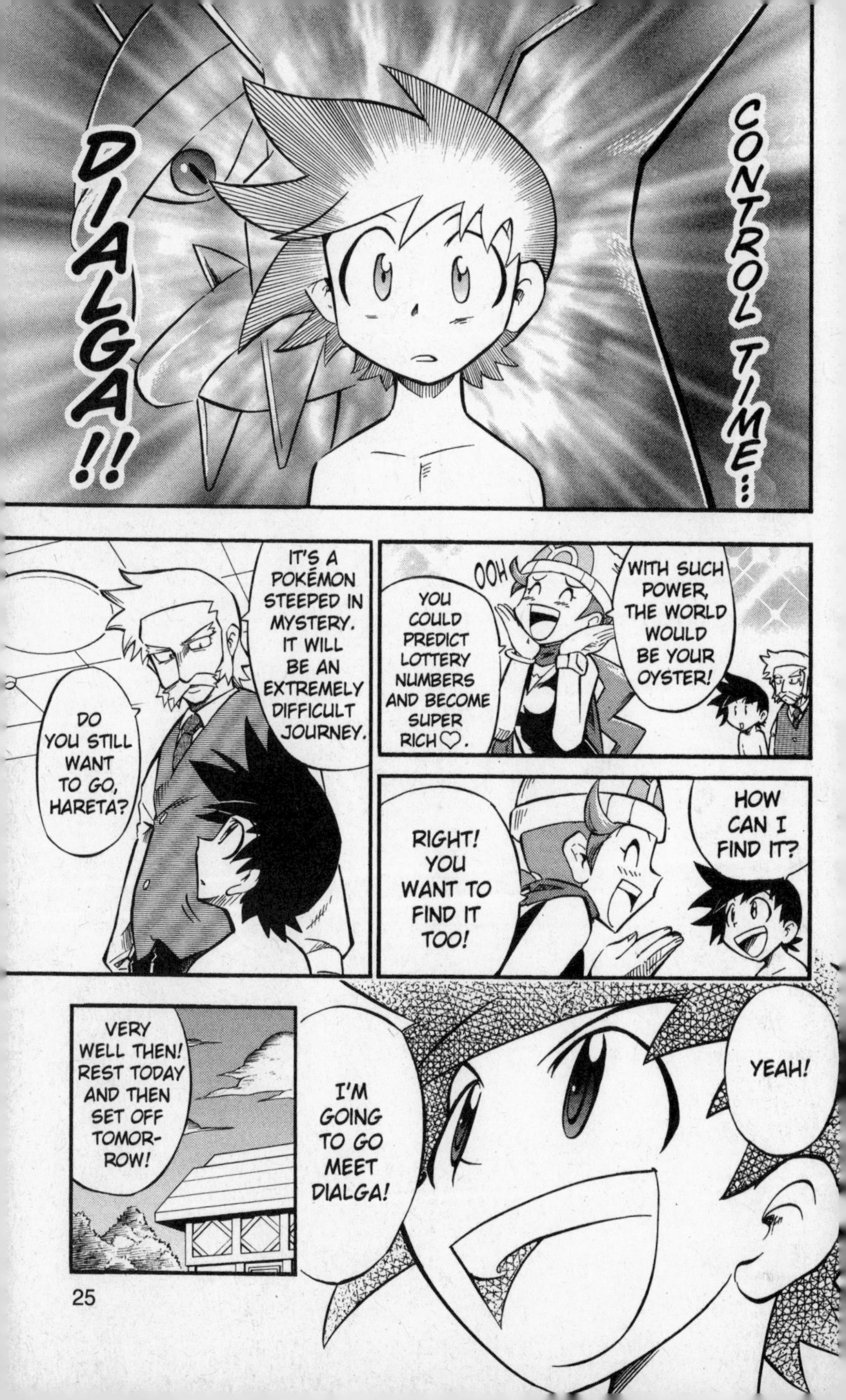
CONTROL TIME...
DIALGA!!
WITH SUCH POWER, THE WORLD WOULD BE YOUR OYSTER!
OOH
YOU COULD PREDICT LOTTERY NUMBERS AND BECOME SUPER RICH♡.
HOW CAN I FIND IT?
RIGHT! YOU WANT TO FIND IT TOO!
IT'S A POKÉMON STEEPED IN MYSTERY. IT WILL BE AN EXTREMELY DIFFICULT JOURNEY.
DO YOU STILL WANT TO GO, HARETA?
YEAH!
I'M GOING TO GO MEET DIALGA!
VERY WELL THEN! REST TODAY AND THEN SET OFF TOMOR-ROW!

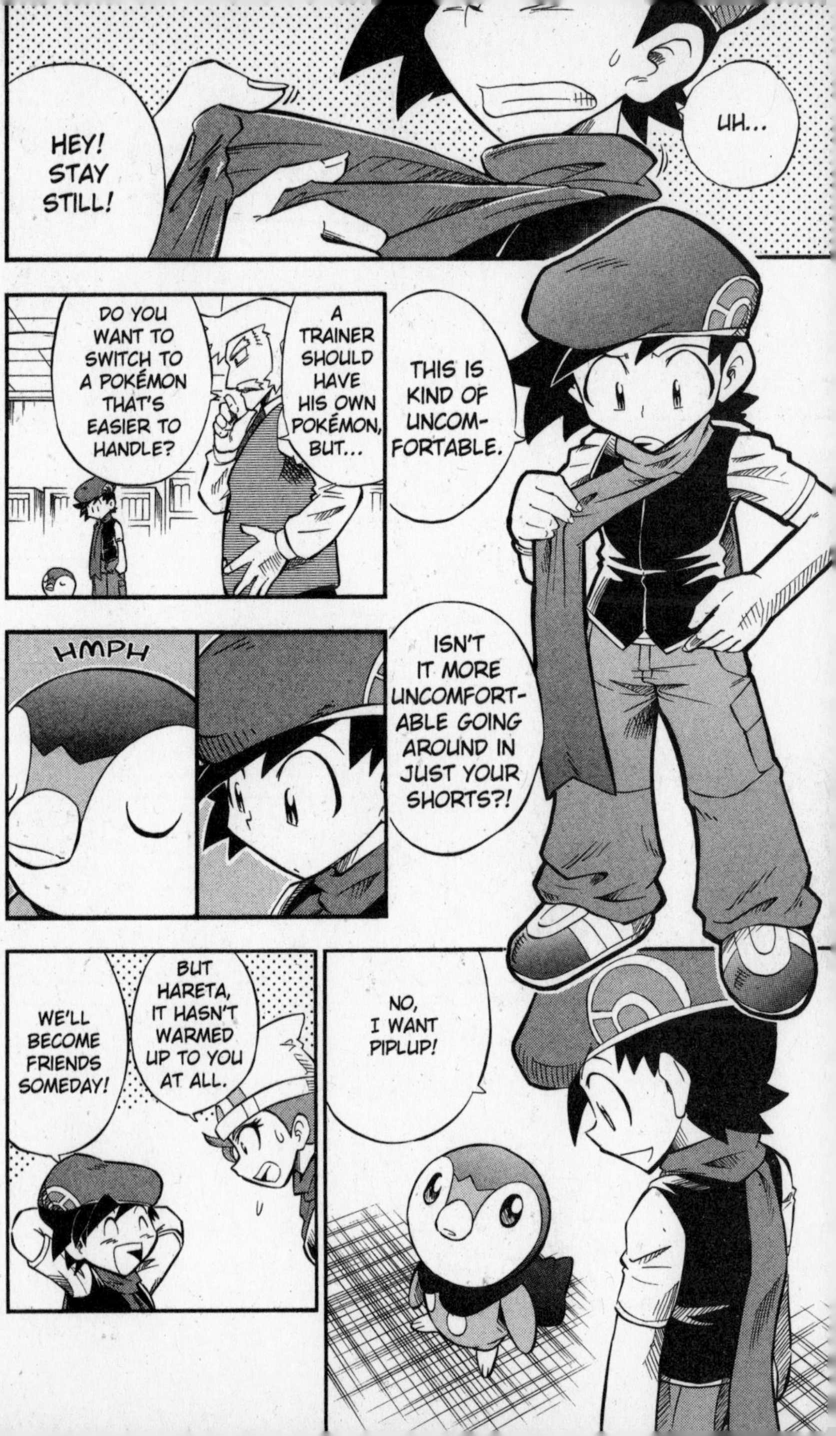
UH...
HEY! STAY STILL!
THIS IS KIND OF UNCOMFORTABLE.
ISN'T IT MORE UNCOMFORTABLE GOING AROUND IN JUST YOUR SHORTS?!
A TRAINER SHOULD HAVE HIS OWN POKÉMON, BUT...
DO YOU WANT TO SWITCH TO A POKÉMON THAT'S EASIER TO HANDLE?
HMPH
NO, I WANT PIPLUP!
BUT HARETA, IT HASN'T WARMED UP TO YOU AT ALL.
WE'LL BECOME FRIENDS SOMEDAY!

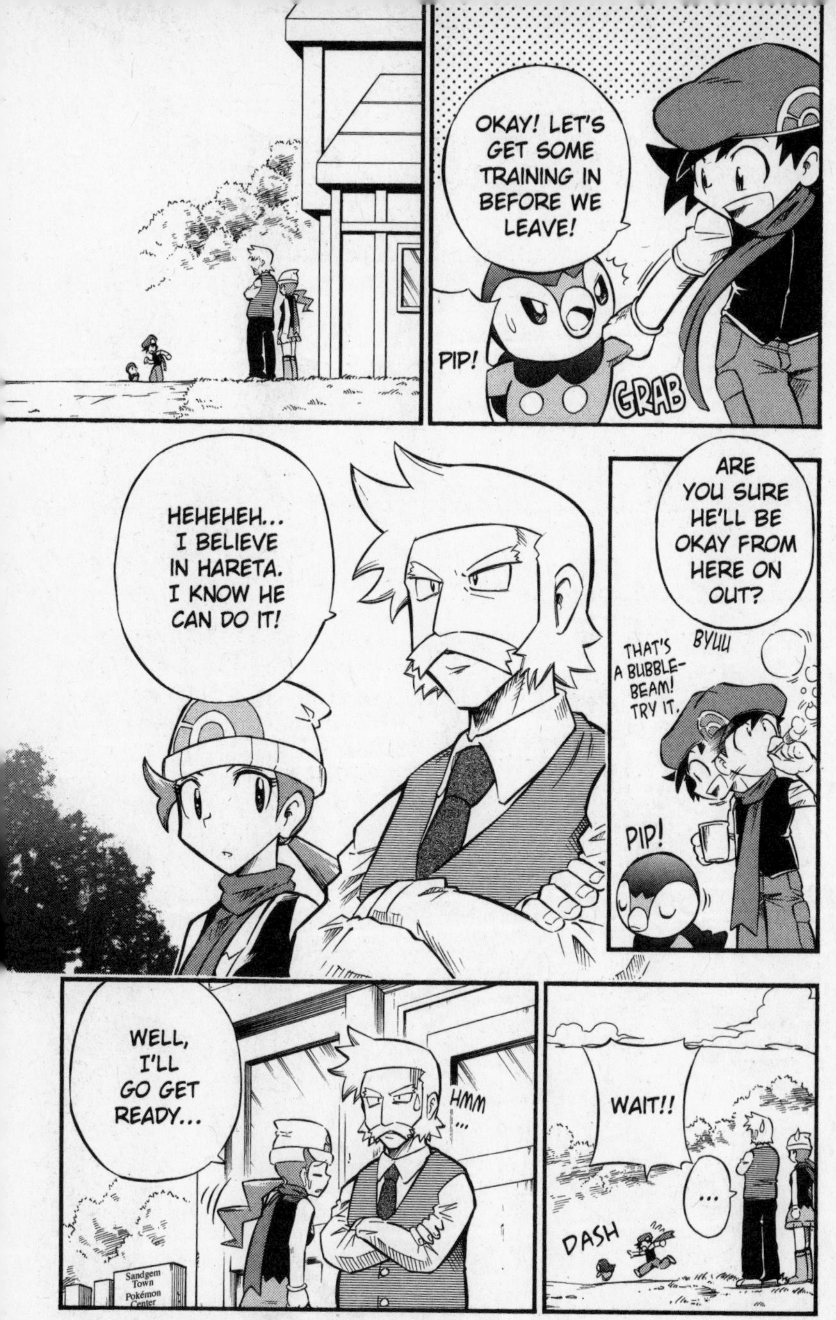
OKAY! LET'S GET SOME TRAINING IN BEFORE WE LEAVE!
PIP!
GRAB
ARE YOU SURE HE'LL BE OKAY FROM HERE ON OUT?
BYUU
THAT'S A BUBBLE-BEAM! TRY IT.
PIP!
HEHEHEH... I BELIEVE IN HARETA. I KNOW HE CAN DO IT!
WAIT!!
...
DASH
WELL, I'LL GO GET READY...
HMM ...
Sandgem Town Pokémon Center

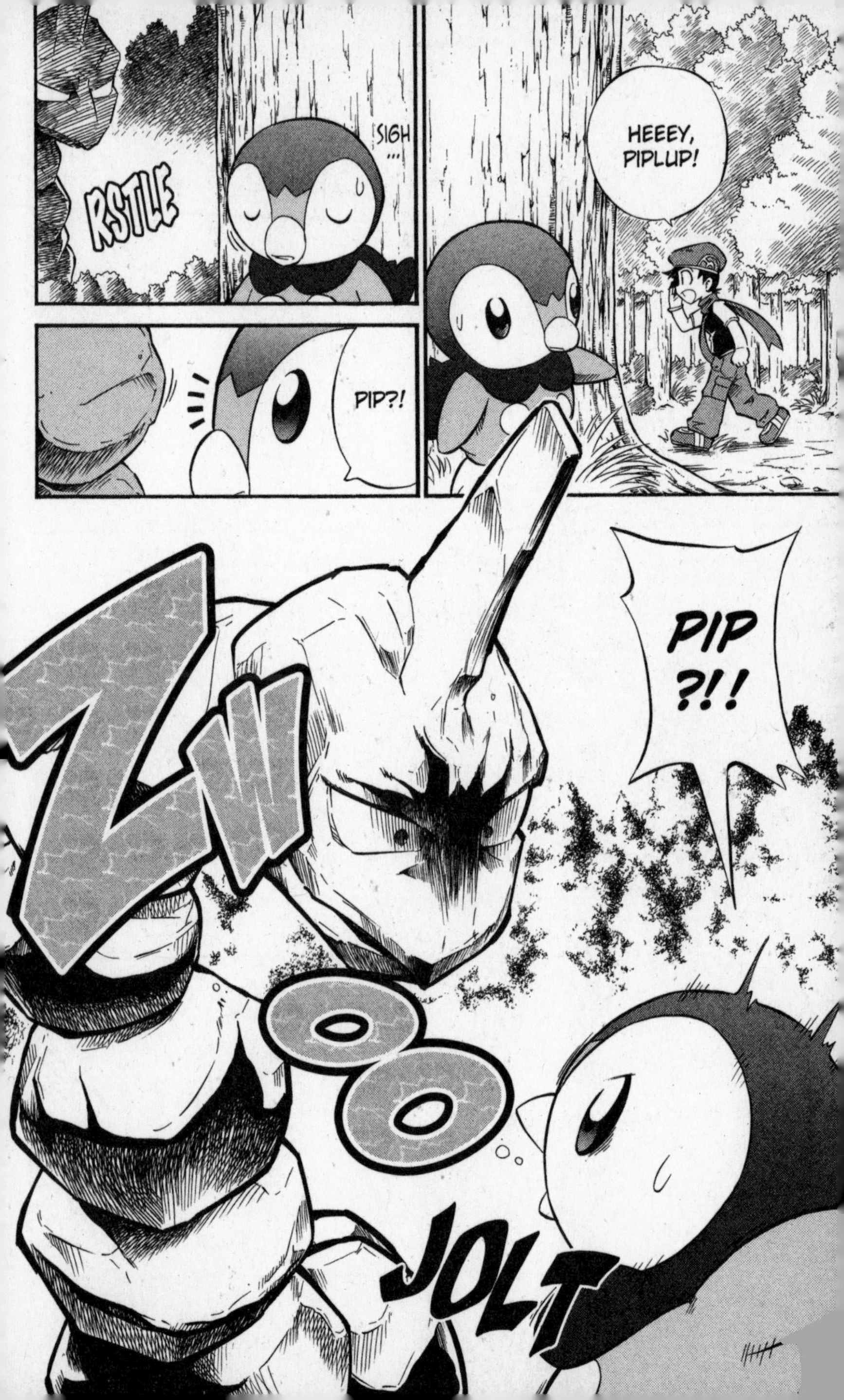
HEEEY, PIPLUP!
SIGH ...
RSTLE
PIP?!
PIP ?!!
ZWOO
JOLT

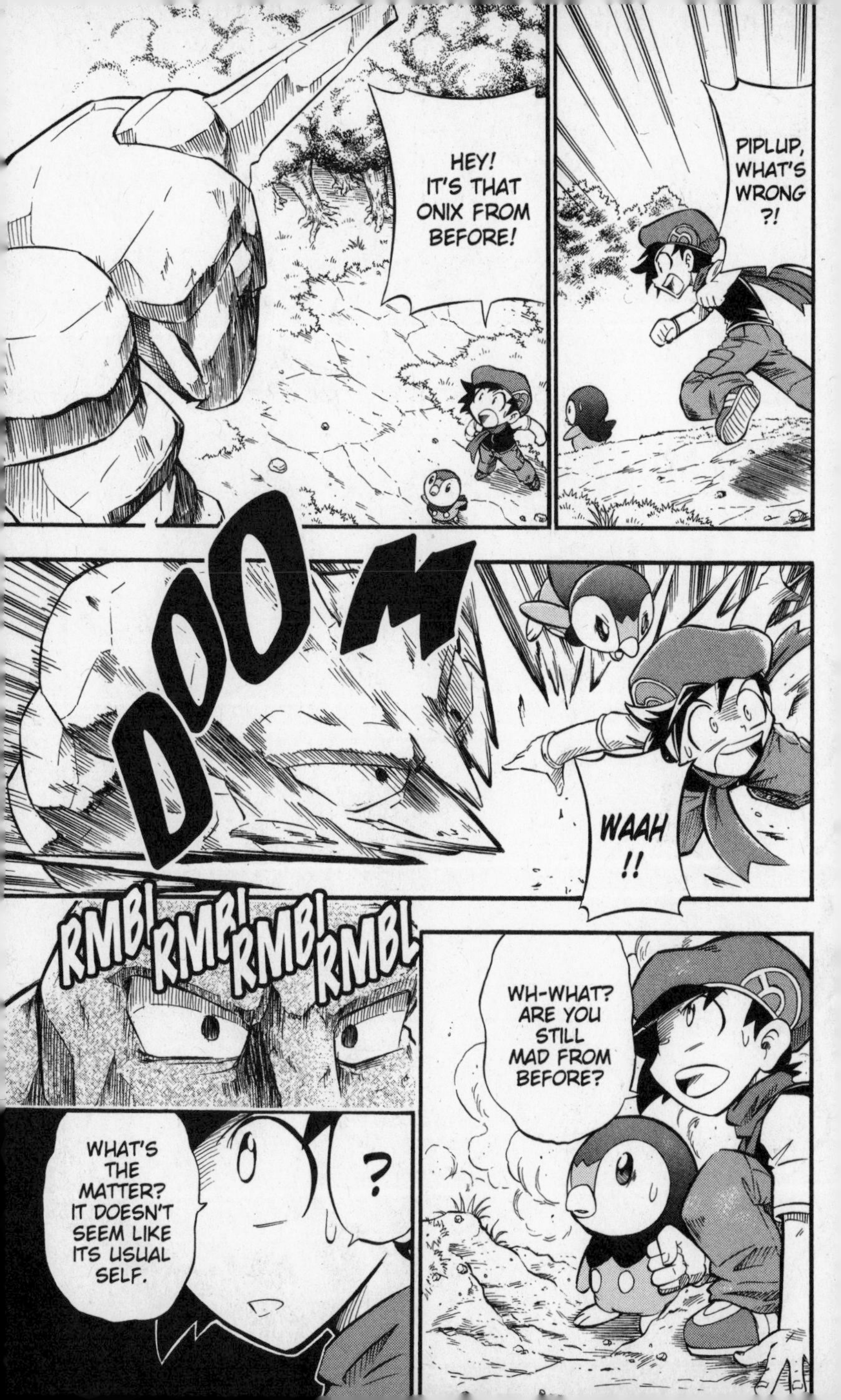
PIPLUP, WHAT'S WRONG ?!
HEY! IT'S THAT ONIX FROM BEFORE!
DOOM
WAAH !!
WH-WHAT? ARE YOU STILL MAD FROM BEFORE?
RMBL RMBL RMBL RMBL
WHAT'S THE MATTER? IT DOESN'T SEEM LIKE ITS USUAL SELF.
?

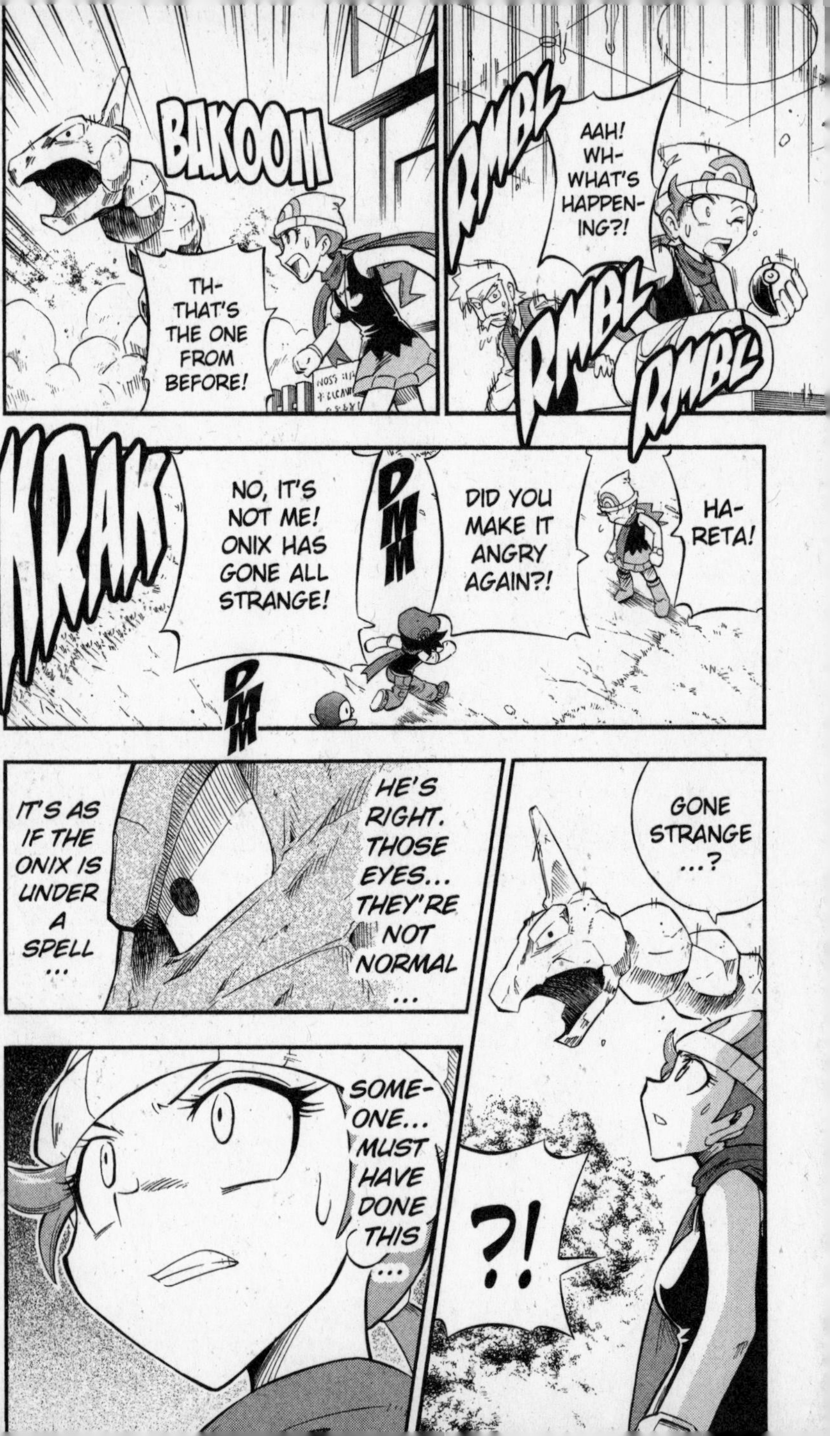
RMBL
AAH! WH-WHAT'S HAPPENING?!
RMBL
RMBL
BAKOOM
TH-THAT'S THE ONE FROM BEFORE!
HA-RETA!
DID YOU MAKE IT ANGRY AGAIN?!
DMM
NO, IT'S NOT ME! ONIX HAS GONE ALL STRANGE!
KRAK
DMM
GONE STRANGE...?
?!
HE'S RIGHT. THOSE EYES... THEY'RE NOT NORMAL...
IT'S AS IF THE ONIX IS UNDER A SPELL...
SOME-ONE... MUST HAVE DONE THIS...

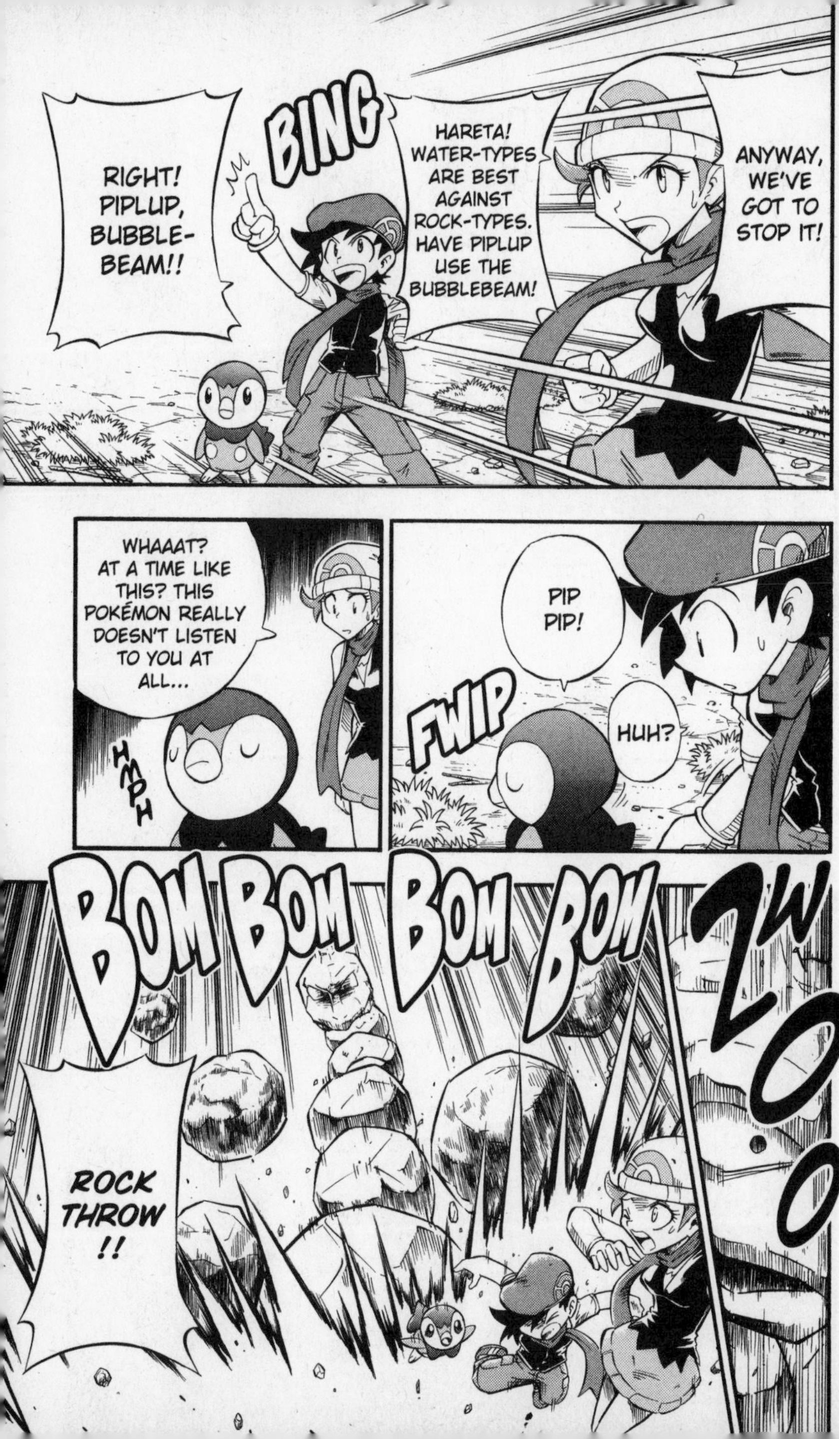
ANYWAY, WE'VE GOT TO STOP IT!
HARETA! WATER-TYPES ARE BEST AGAINST ROCK-TYPES. HAVE PIPLUP USE THE BUBBLEBEAM!
BING
RIGHT! PIPLUP, BUBBLE-BEAM!!
PIP PIP!
HUH?
FWIP
WHAAAT? AT A TIME LIKE THIS? THIS POKÉMON REALLY DOESN'T LISTEN TO YOU AT ALL...
HMPH
ZWOOO
BOM BOM BOM BOM
ROCK THROW!!

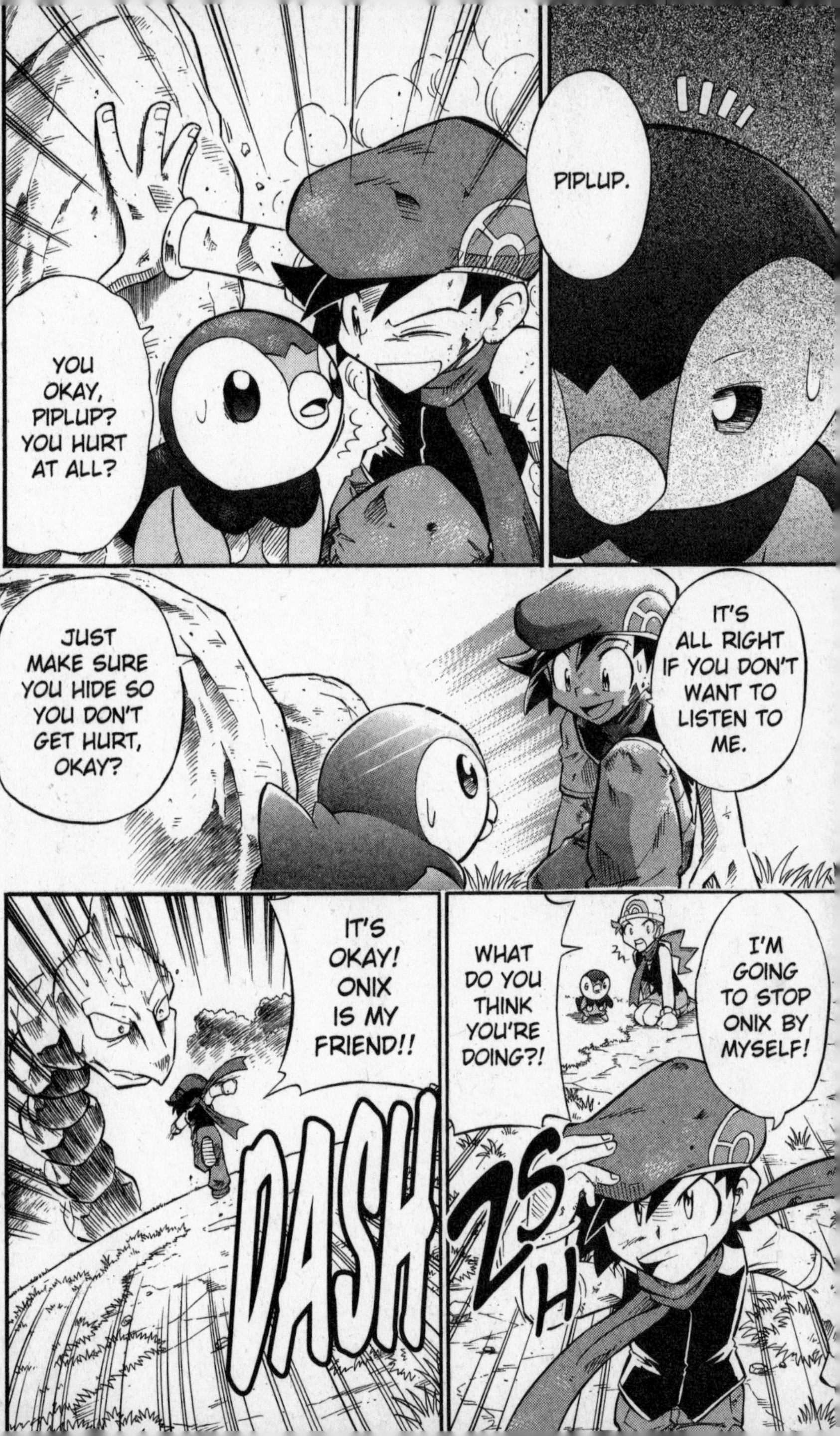
PIPLUP.
YOU OKAY, PIPLUP? YOU HURT AT ALL?
IT'S ALL RIGHT IF YOU DON'T WANT TO LISTEN TO ME.
JUST MAKE SURE YOU HIDE SO YOU DON'T GET HURT, OKAY?
I'M GOING TO STOP ONIX BY MYSELF!
WHAT DO YOU THINK YOU'RE DOING?!
ZSH
IT'S OKAY! ONIX IS MY FRIEND!!
DASH

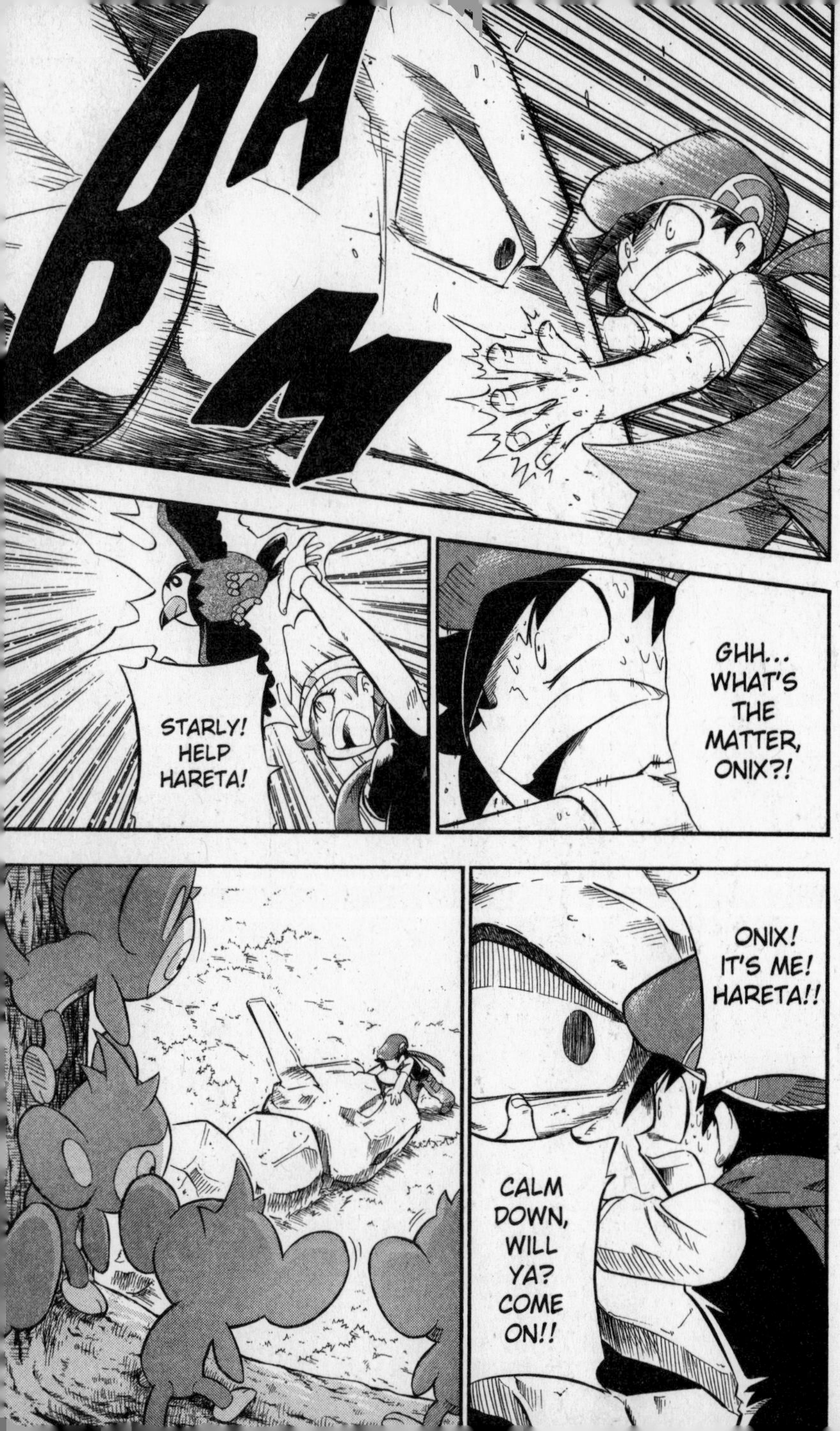
BAM
GHH... WHAT'S THE MATTER, ONIX?!
STARLY! HELP HARETA!
ONIX! IT'S ME! HARETA!!
CALM DOWN, WILL YA? COME ON!!

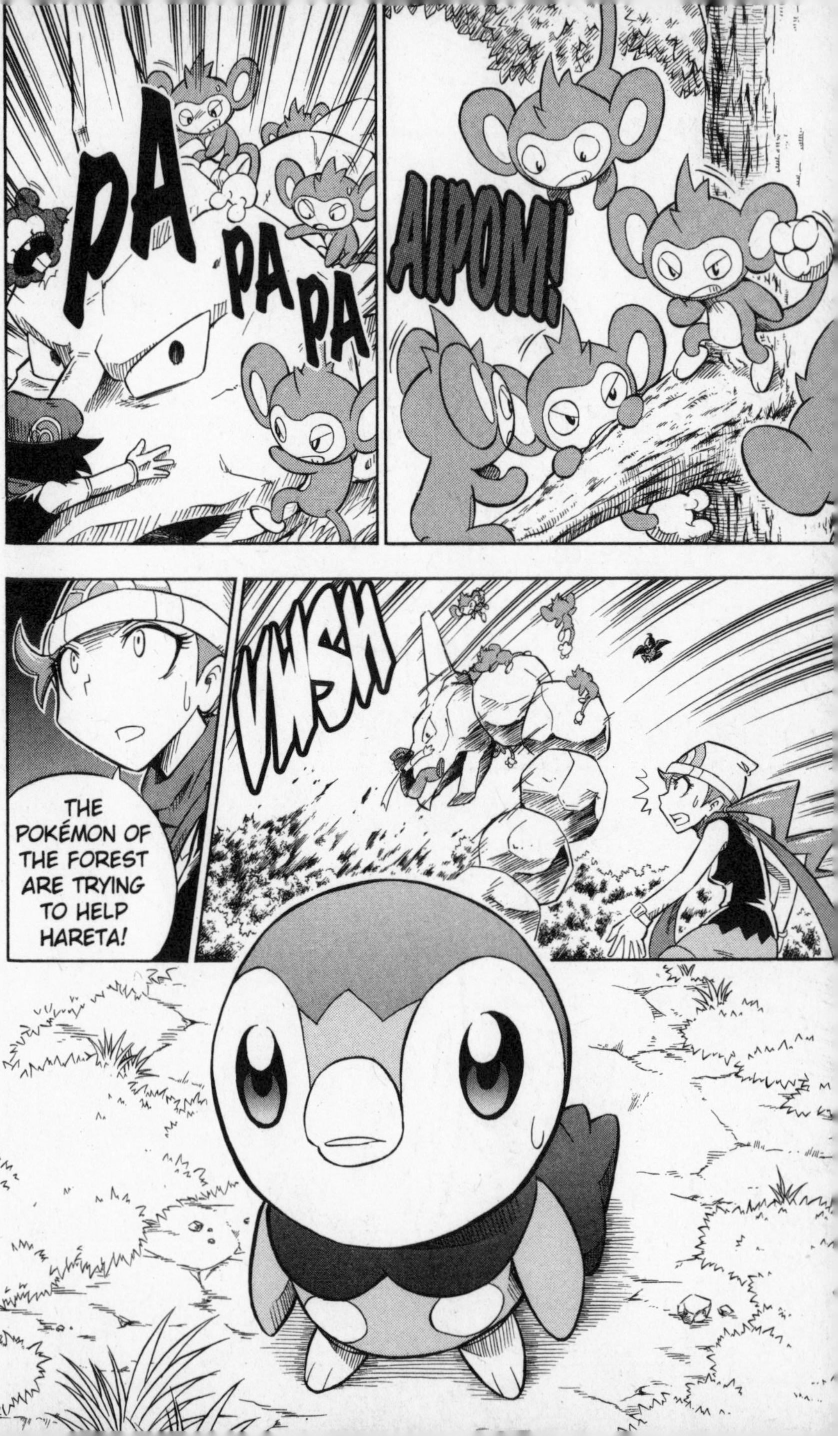
AIPOM!
PA
PA
PA
PA
VWISH
THE POKÉMON OF THE FOREST ARE TRYING TO HELP HARETA!

GROARR!!

VWOOSH

GHH...

BAM

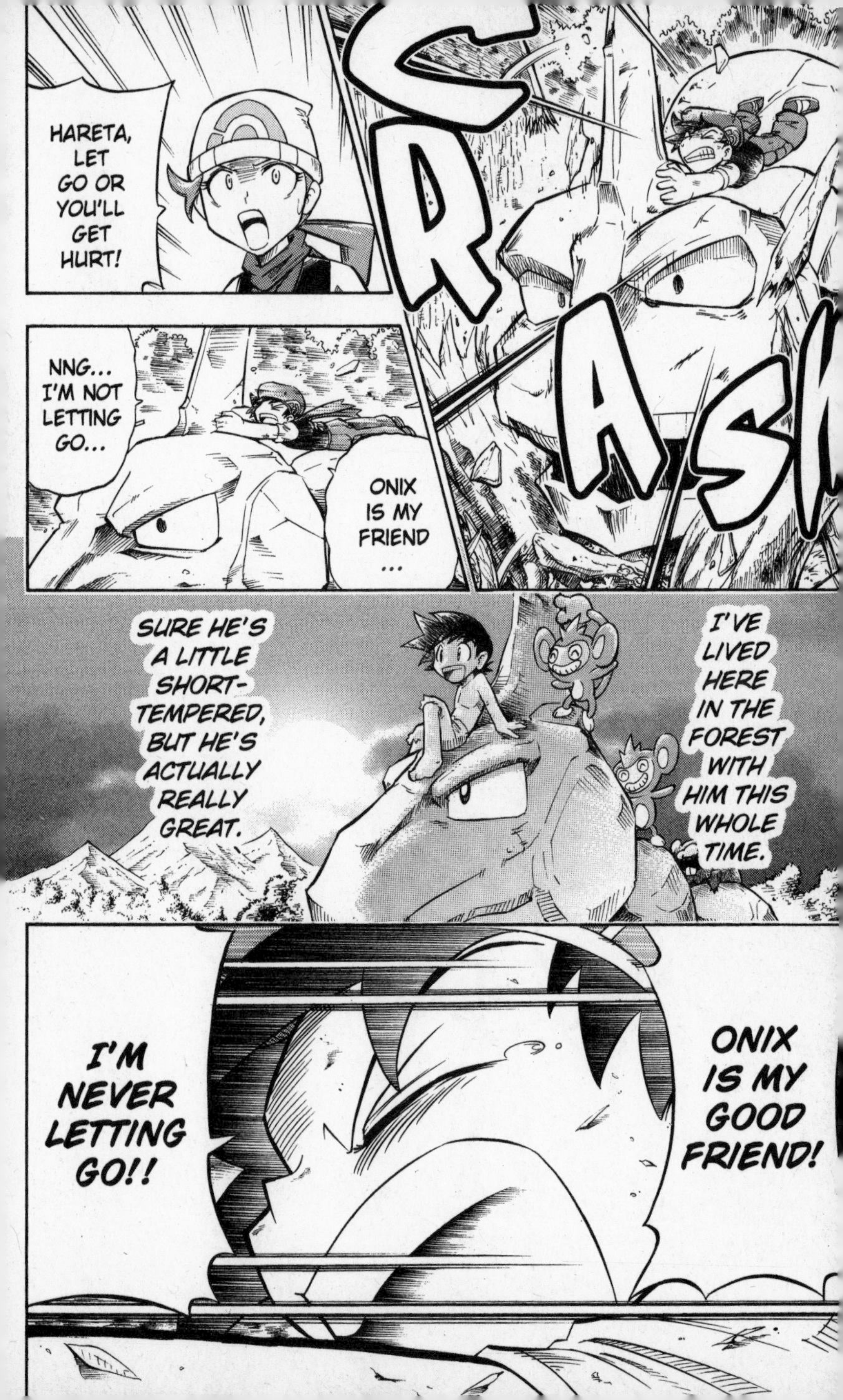
CRASH
HARETA, LET GO OR YOU'LL GET HURT!
NNG... I'M NOT LETTING GO...
ONIX IS MY FRIEND...
I'VE LIVED HERE IN THE FOREST WITH HIM THIS WHOLE TIME.
SURE HE'S A LITTLE SHORT-TEMPERED, BUT HE'S ACTUALLY REALLY GREAT.
ONIX IS MY GOOD FRIEND!
I'M NEVER LETTING GO!!

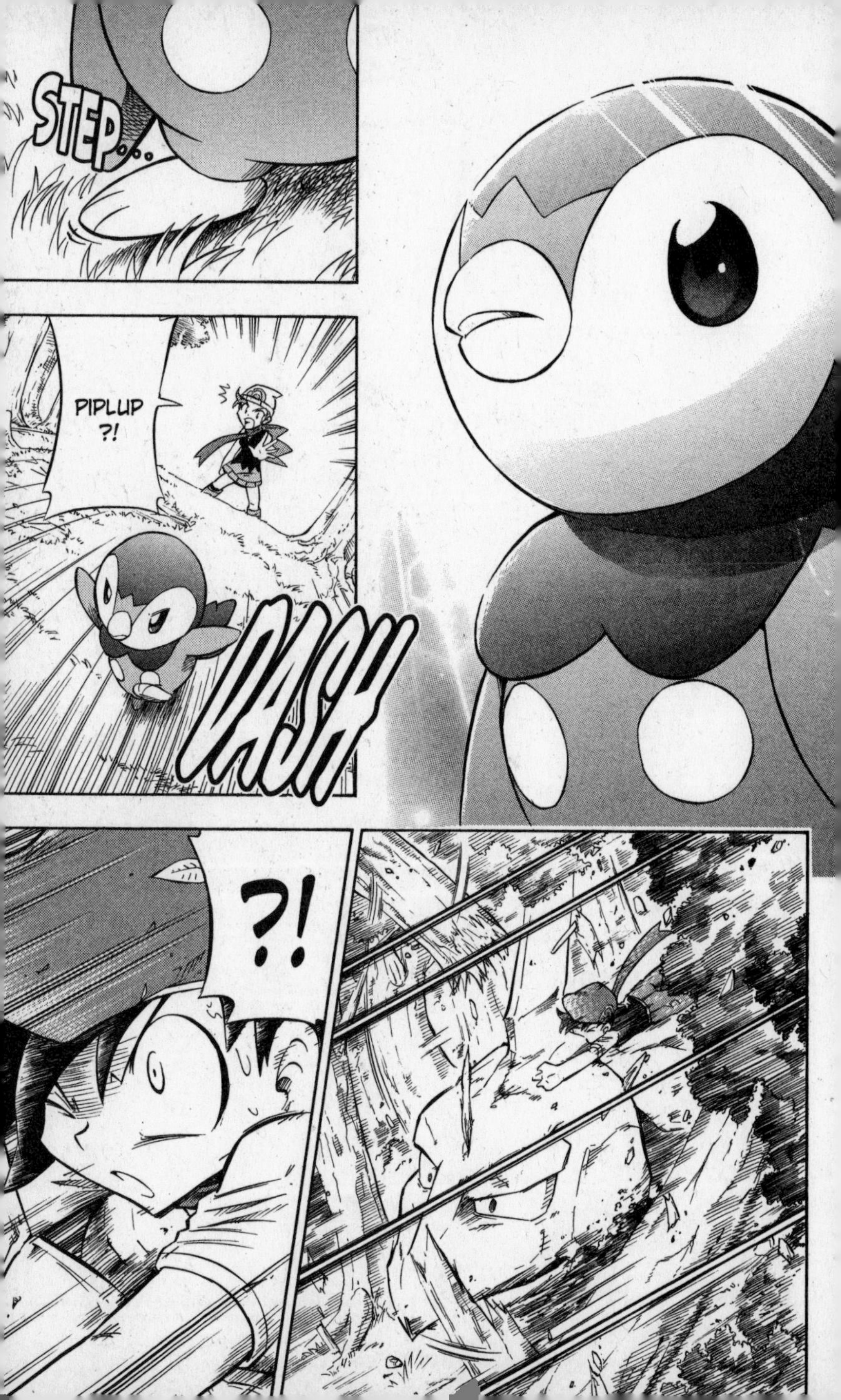
STEP...
PIPLUP ?!
DASH
?!

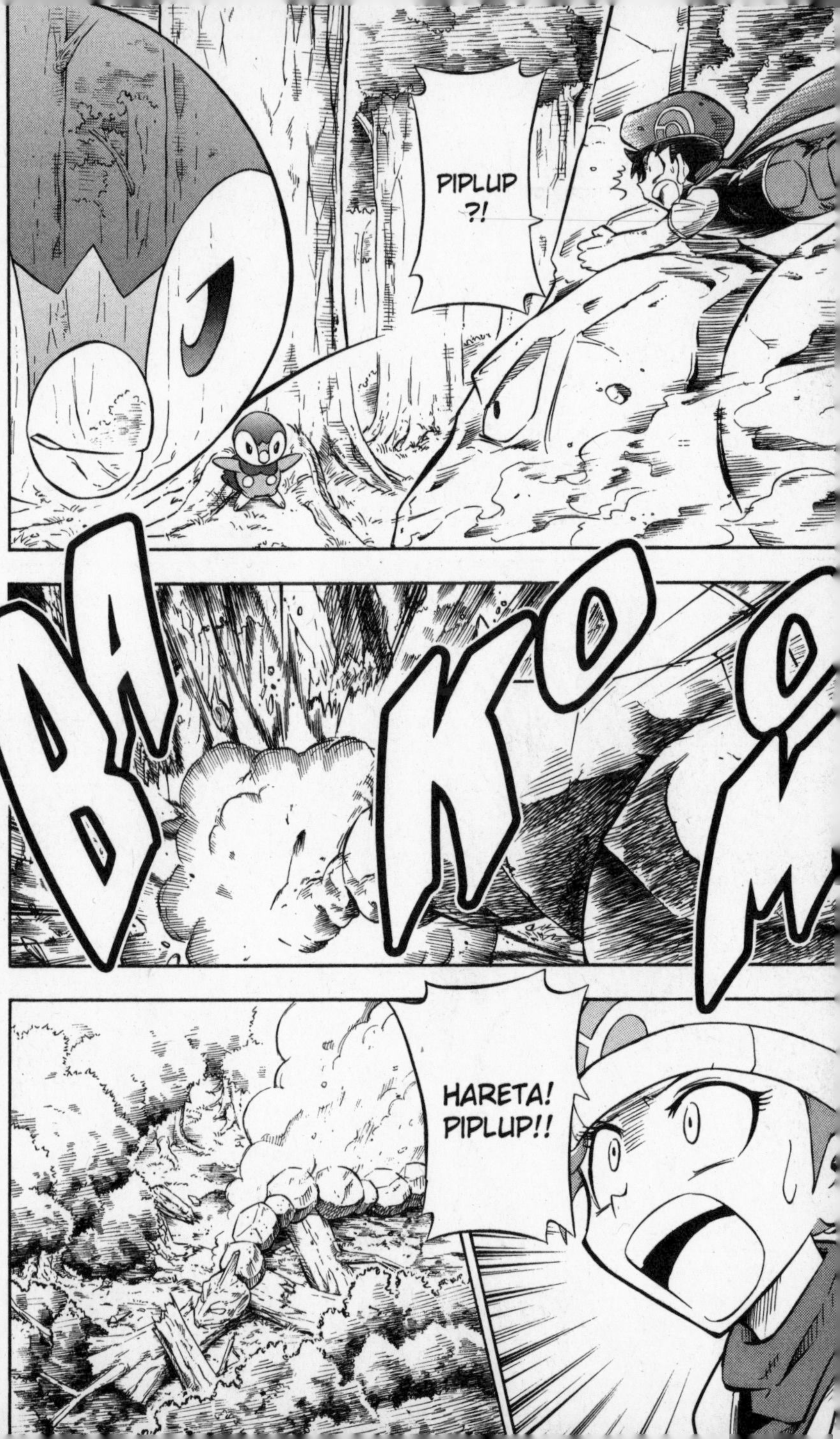
PIPLUP ?!
BA KOOM
HARETA! PIPLUP!!

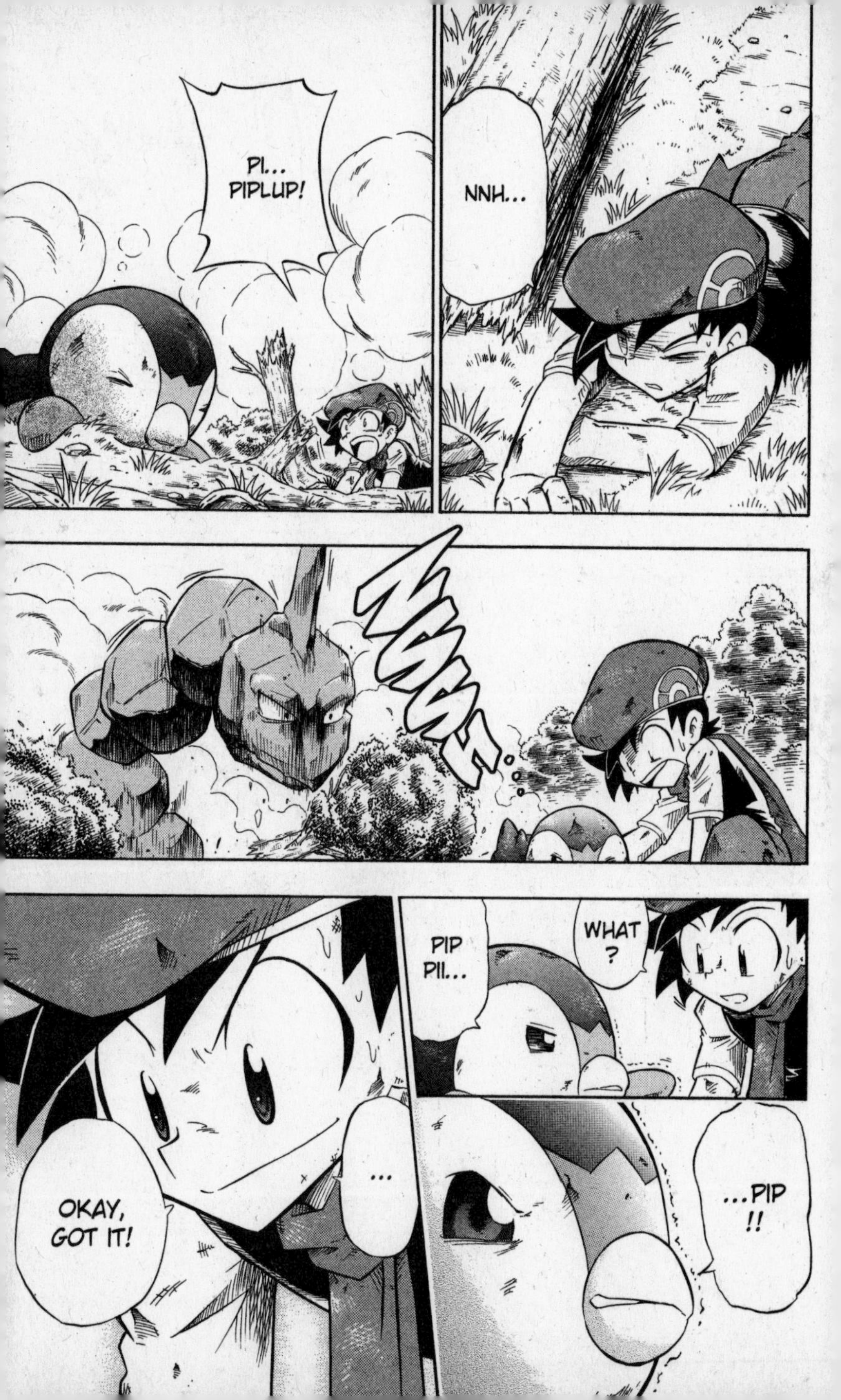
NNH...
PI... PIPLUP!
WHAT?
PIP PII...
...PIP !!
...
OKAY, GOT IT!

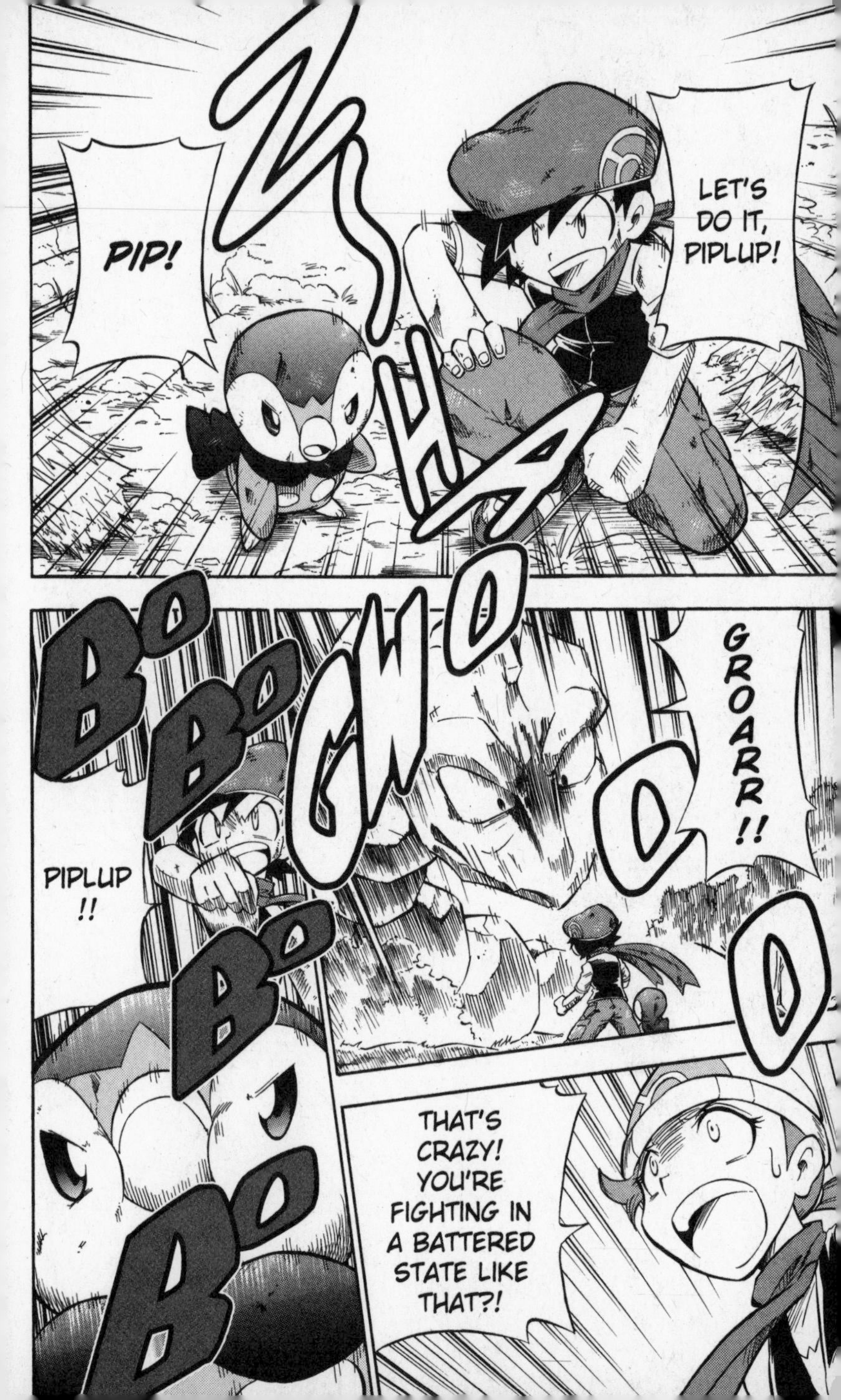
LET'S DO IT, PIPLUP!
PIP!
GROARR!!
GWOOOO
BOBOBOBO
PIPLUP!!
THAT'S CRAZY! YOU'RE FIGHTING IN A BATTERED STATE LIKE THAT?!

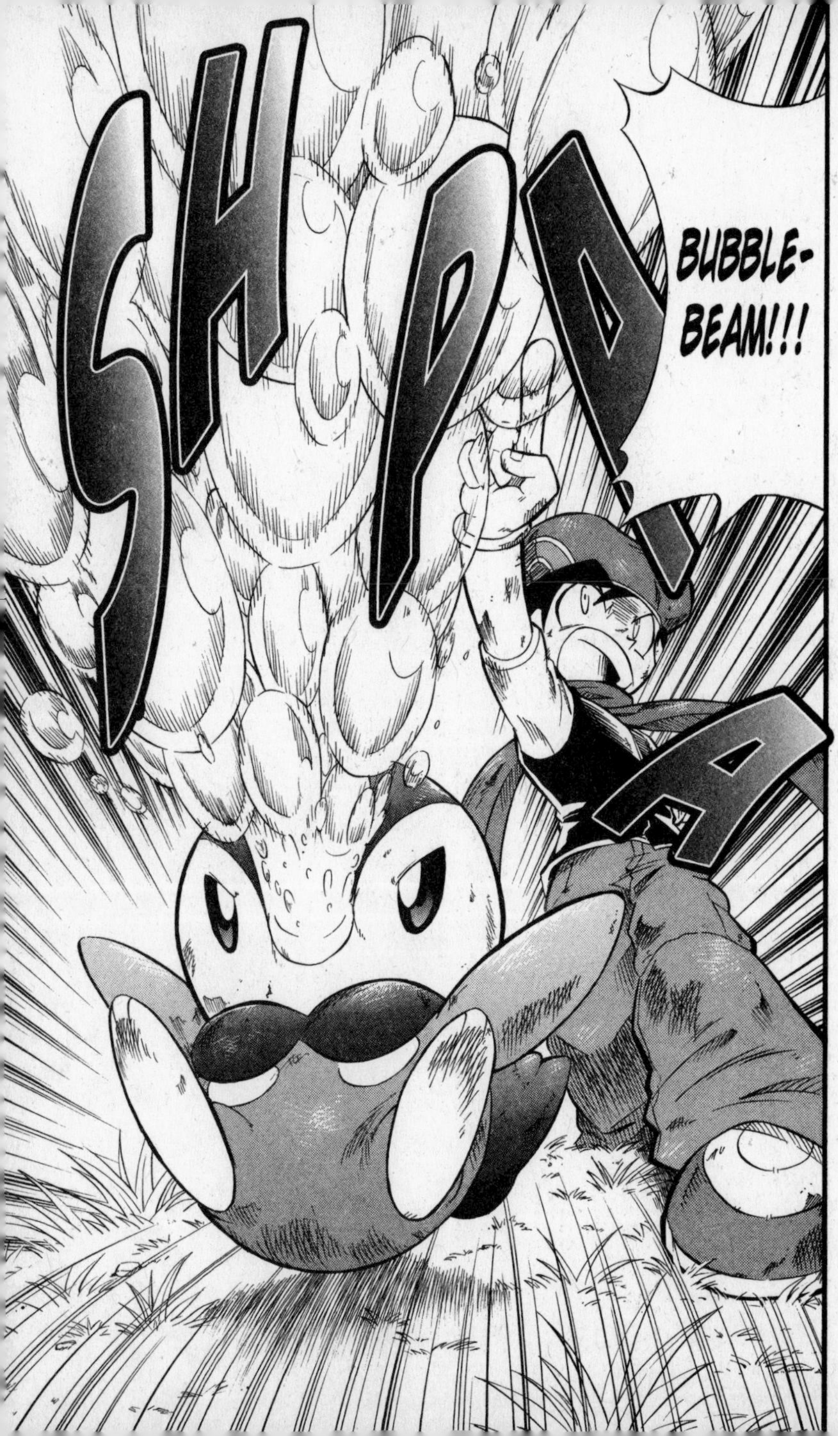
BUBBLE-
BEAM!!!
SHPA

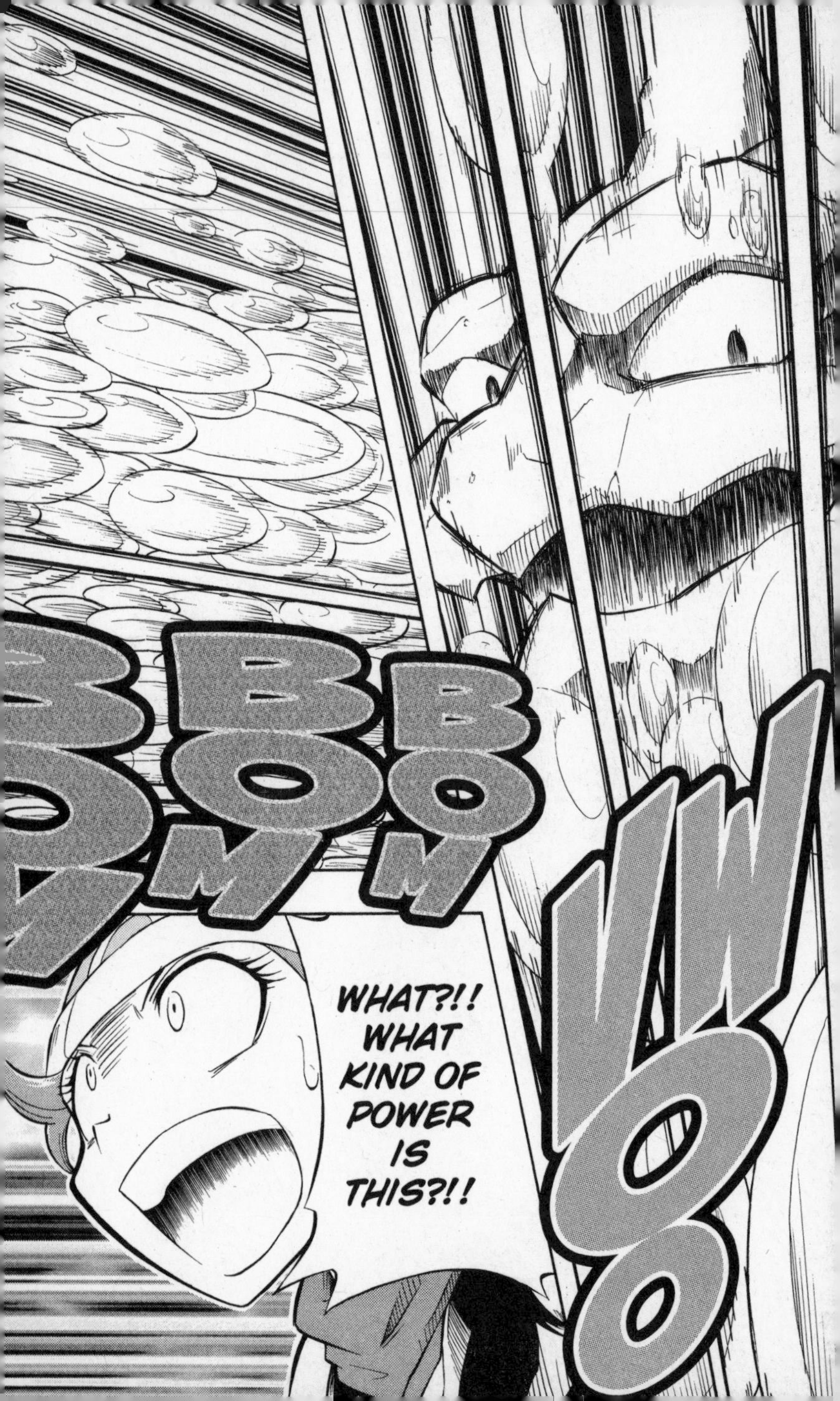
BOOM
BOOM
WHAT?!! WHAT KIND OF POWER IS THIS?!!

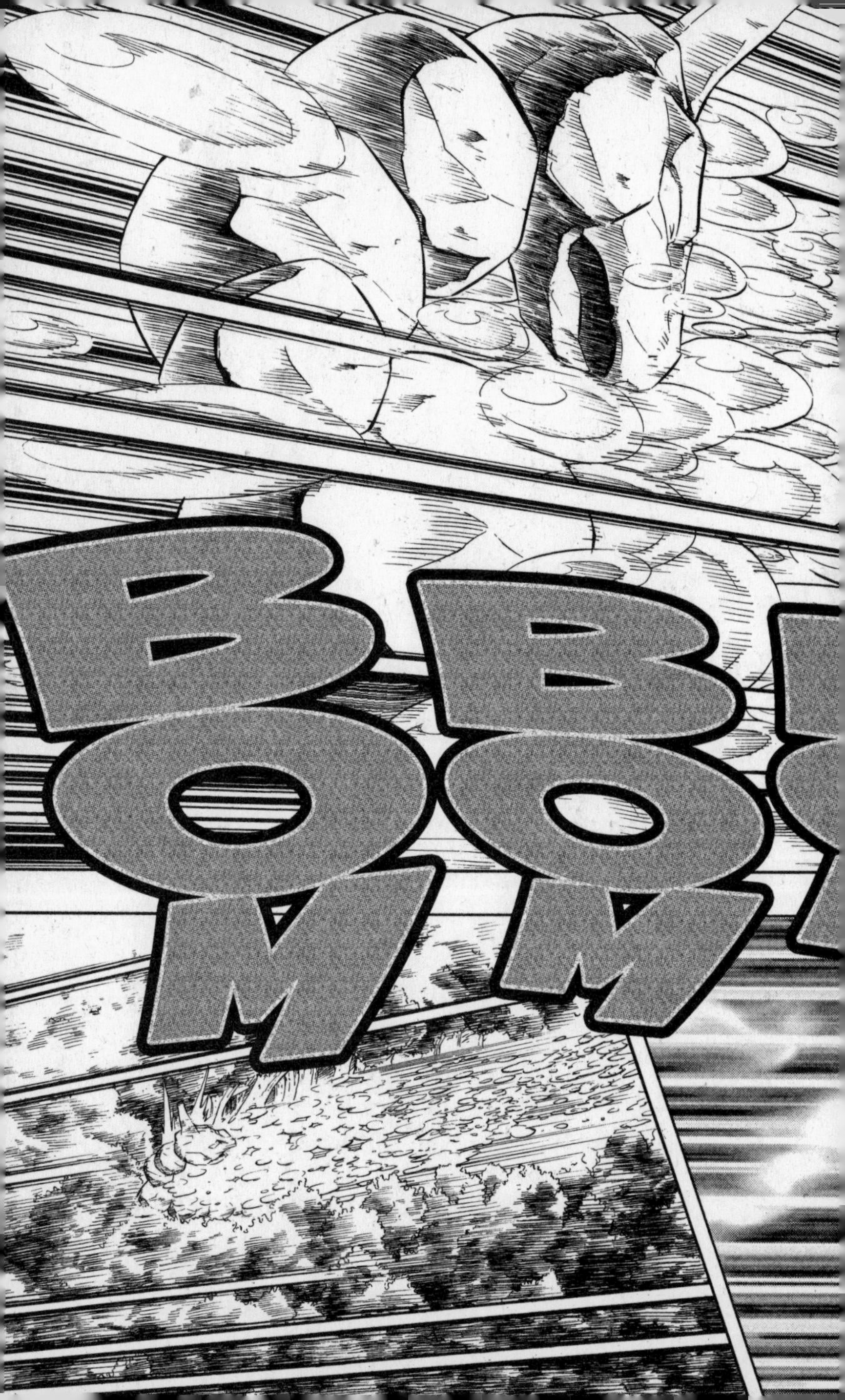
BOOM
BOOM

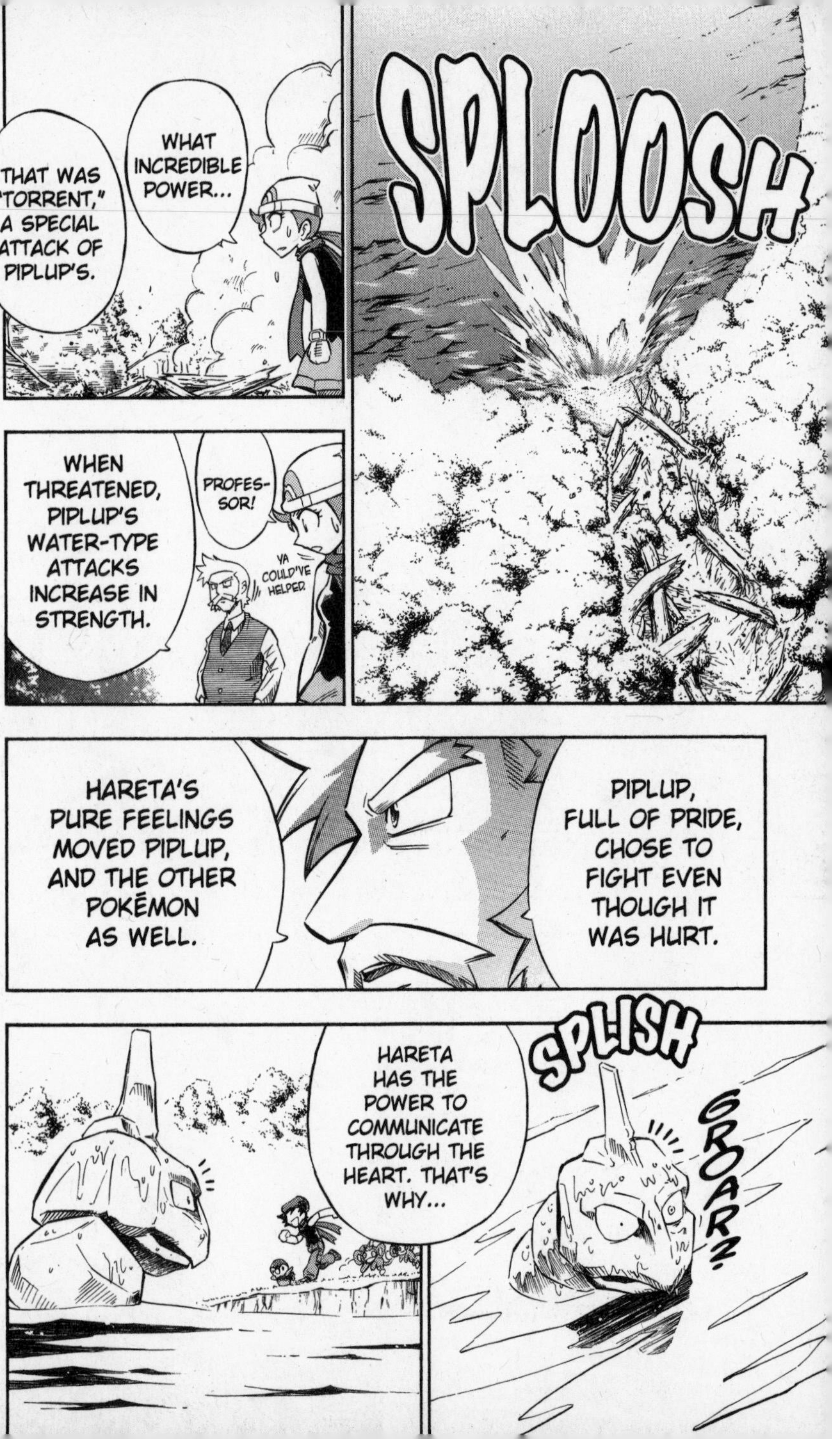
SPLOOSH
WHAT INCREDIBLE POWER...
THAT WAS "TORRENT," A SPECIAL ATTACK OF PIPLUP'S.
PROFES-SOR!
YA COULD'VE HELPED.
WHEN THREATENED, PIPLUP'S WATER-TYPE ATTACKS INCREASE IN STRENGTH.
PIPLUP, FULL OF PRIDE, CHOSE TO FIGHT EVEN THOUGH IT WAS HURT.
HARETA'S PURE FEELINGS MOVED PIPLUP, AND THE OTHER POKéMON AS WELL.
SPLISH
GROAR?
HARETA HAS THE POWER TO COMMUNICATE THROUGH THE HEART. THAT'S WHY...

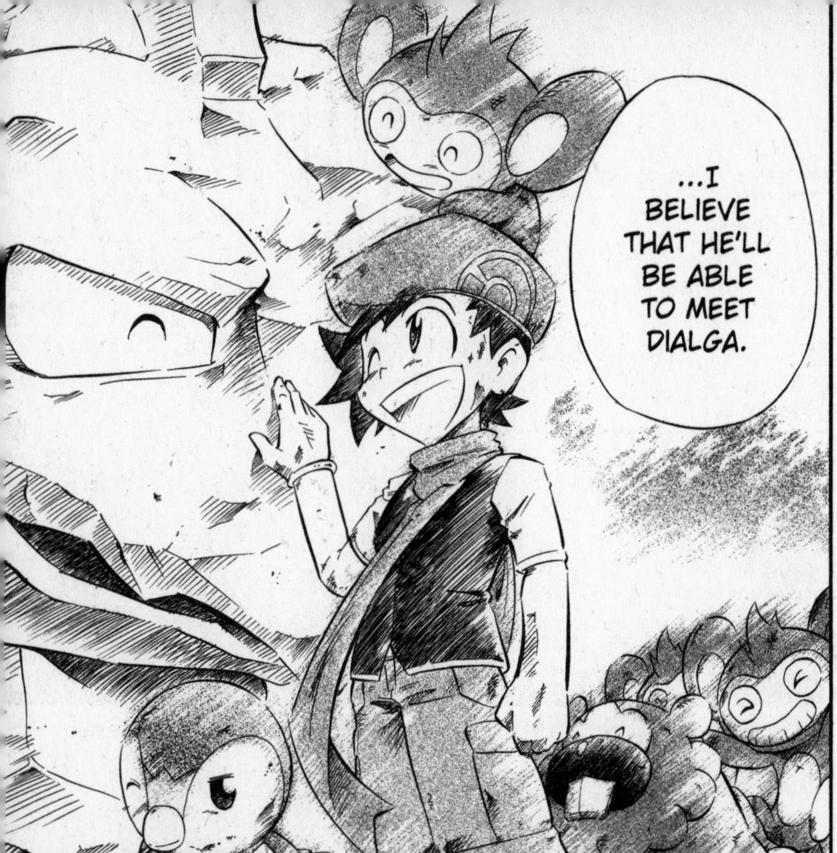
...I BELIEVE THAT HE'LL BE ABLE TO MEET DIALGA.

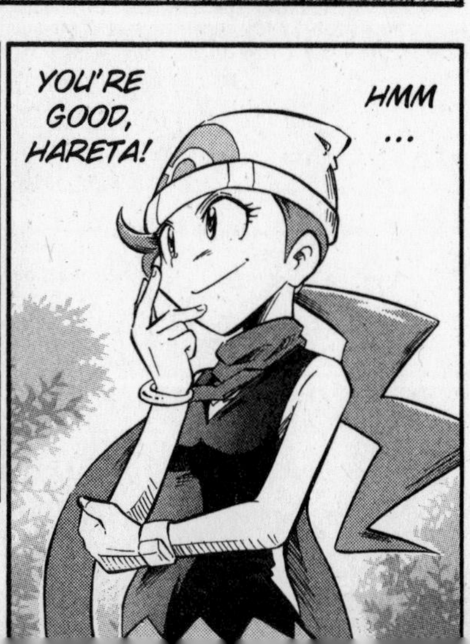
HMM ...
YOU'RE GOOD, HARETA!

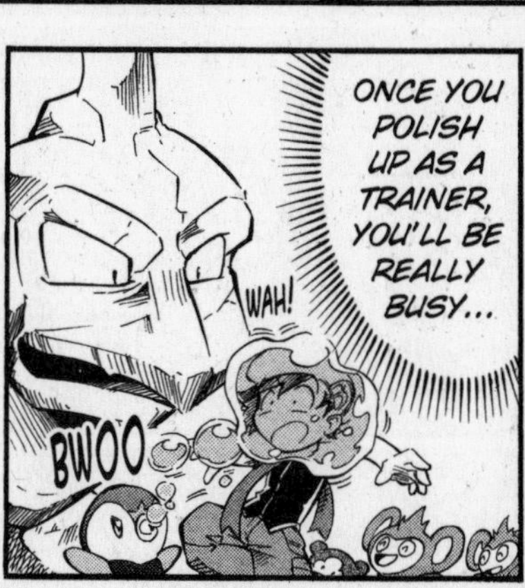
ONCE YOU POLISH UP AS A TRAINER, YOU'LL BE REALLY BUSY...
WAH!
BWOO

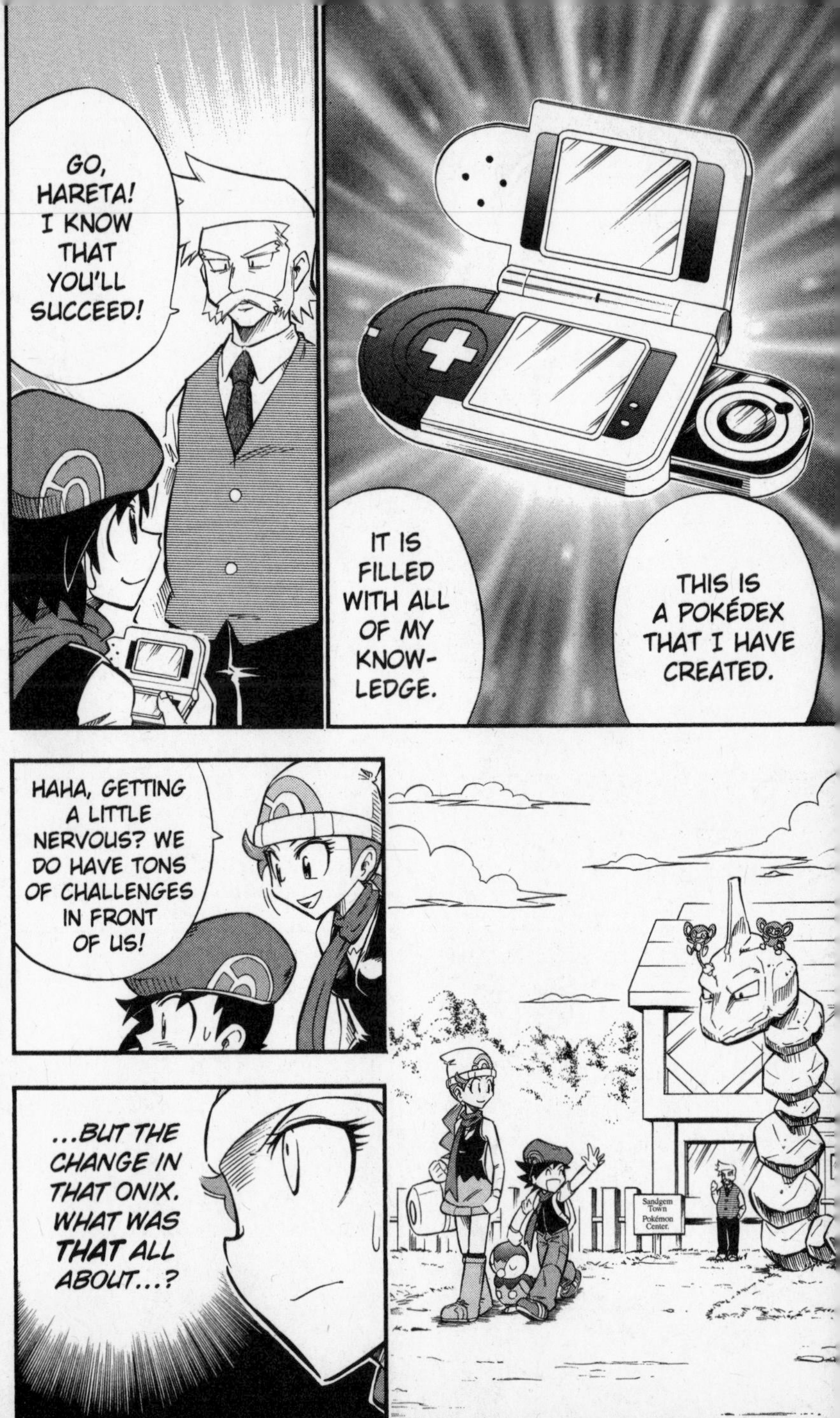
THIS IS A POKÉDEX THAT I HAVE CREATED.
IT IS FILLED WITH ALL OF MY KNOW-LEDGE.
GO, HARETA! I KNOW THAT YOU'LL SUCCEED!
Sandgem Town Pokémon Center.
HAHA, GETTING A LITTLE NERVOUS? WE DO HAVE TONS OF CHALLENGES IN FRONT OF US!
...BUT THE CHANGE IN THAT ONIX. WHAT WAS THAT ALL ABOUT...?

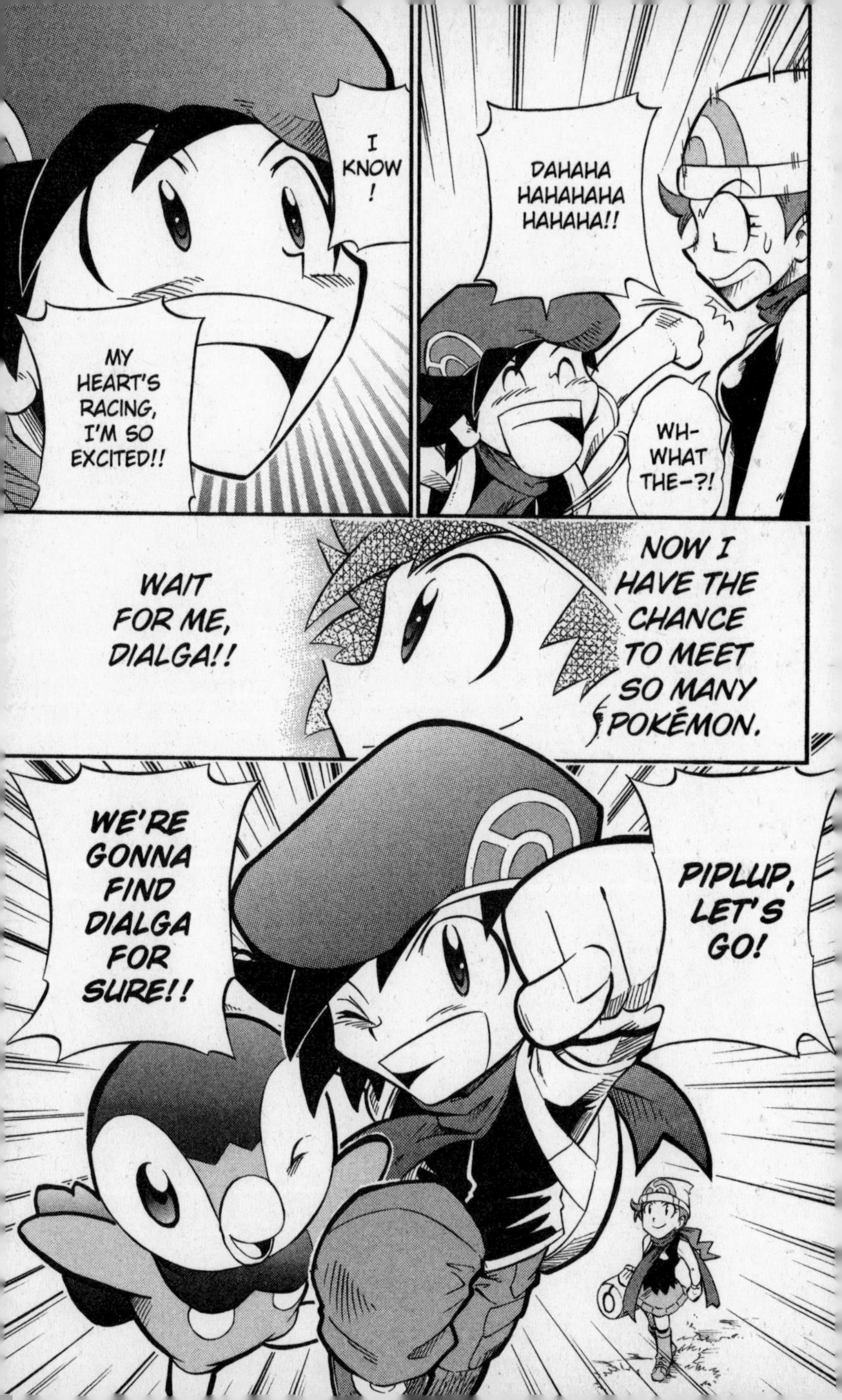
DAHAHA HAHAHAHA HAHAHA!!
WH- WHAT THE-?!
I KNOW!
MY HEART'S RACING, I'M SO EXCITED!!
NOW I HAVE THE CHANCE TO MEET SO MANY POKÉMON.
WAIT FOR ME, DIALGA!!
PIPLUP, LET'S GO!
WE'RE GONNA FIND DIALGA FOR SURE!!

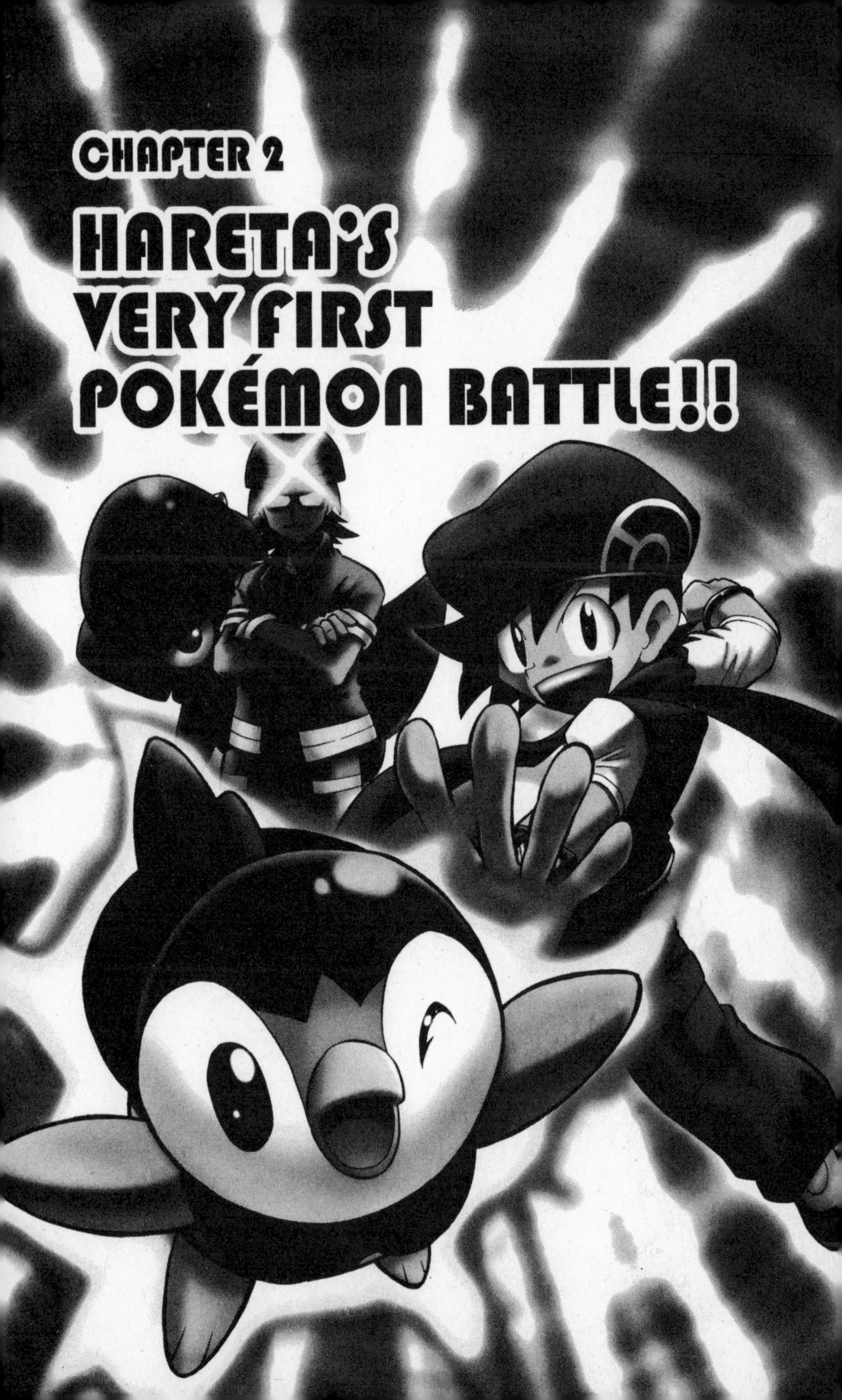
CHAPTER 2
HARETA'S VERY FIRST POKÉMON BATTLE!!

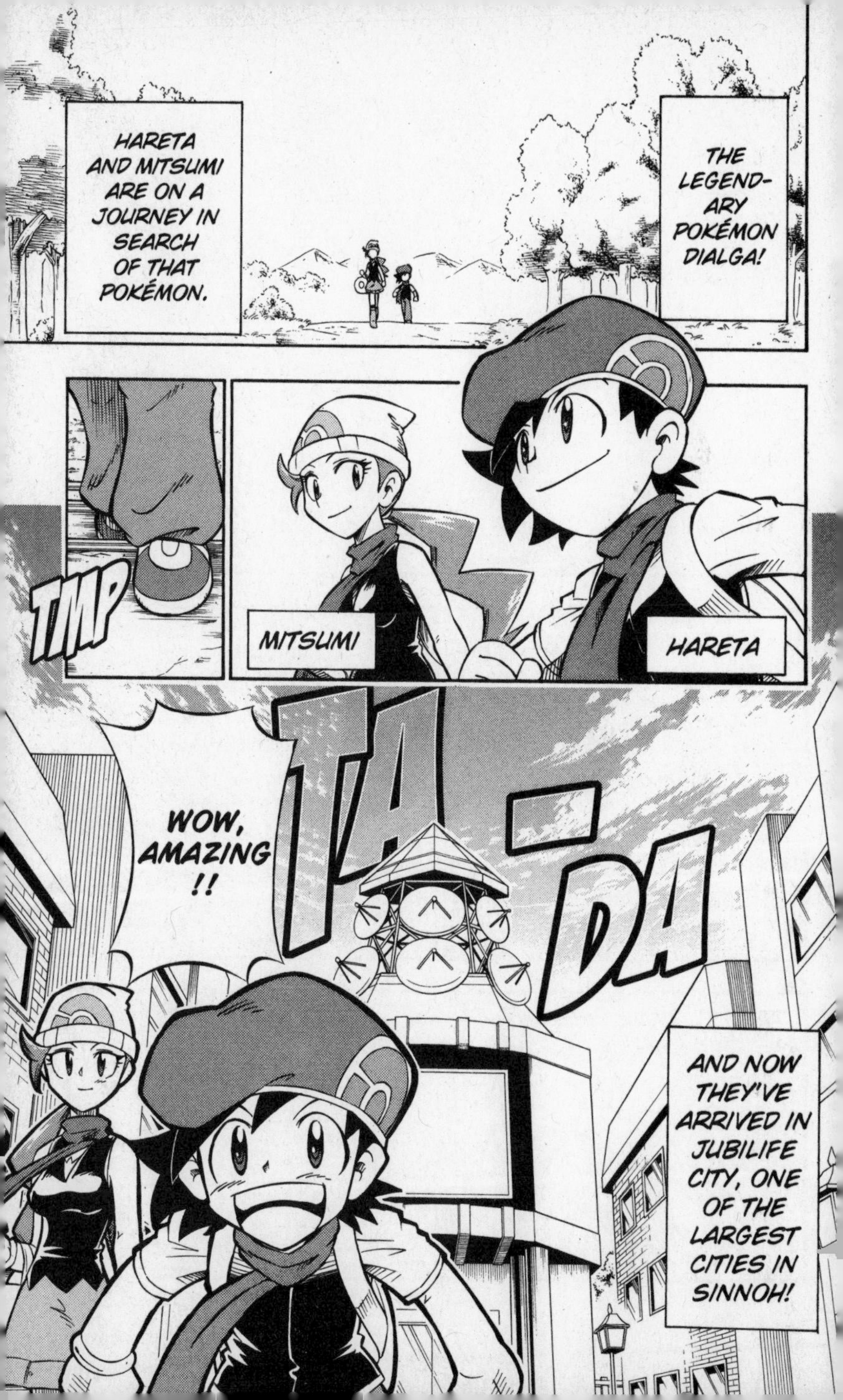
THE LEGENDARY POKÉMON DIALGA!
HARETA AND MITSUMI ARE ON A JOURNEY IN SEARCH OF THAT POKÉMON.
HARETA
MITSUMI
TMP
TA-DA
WOW, AMAZING!!
AND NOW THEY'VE ARRIVED IN JUBILIFE CITY, ONE OF THE LARGEST CITIES IN SINNOH!

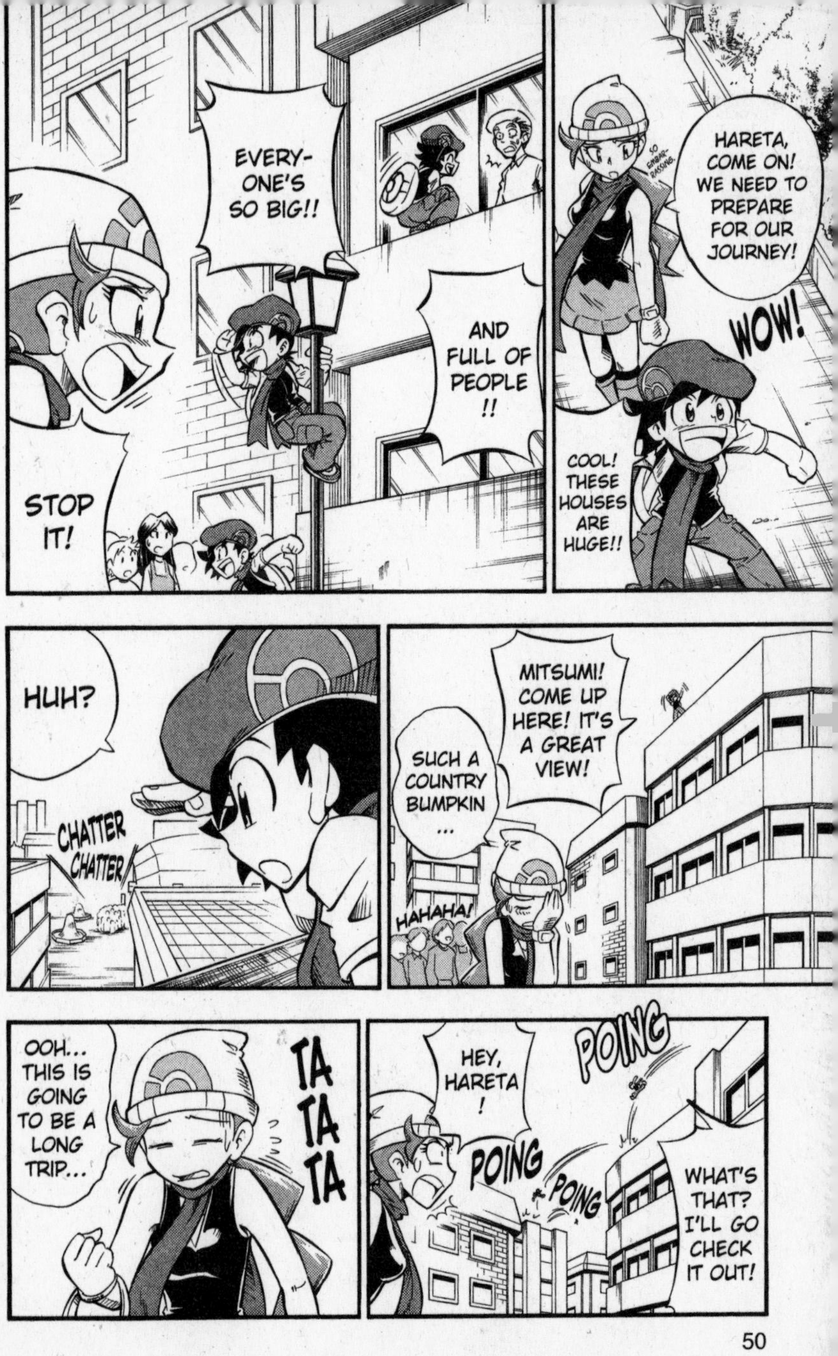
HARETA, COME ON! WE NEED TO PREPARE FOR OUR JOURNEY!
SO EMBARRASSING.
WOW!
COOL! THESE HOUSES ARE HUGE!!
EVERY-ONE'S SO BIG!!
AND FULL OF PEOPLE !!
STOP IT!
MITSUMI! COME UP HERE! IT'S A GREAT VIEW!
SUCH A COUNTRY BUMPKIN ...
HAHAHA!
HUH?
CHATTER CHATTER
HEY, HARETA !
POING
POING
POING
WHAT'S THAT? I'LL GO CHECK IT OUT!
OOH... THIS IS GOING TO BE A LONG TRIP...
TA TA TA

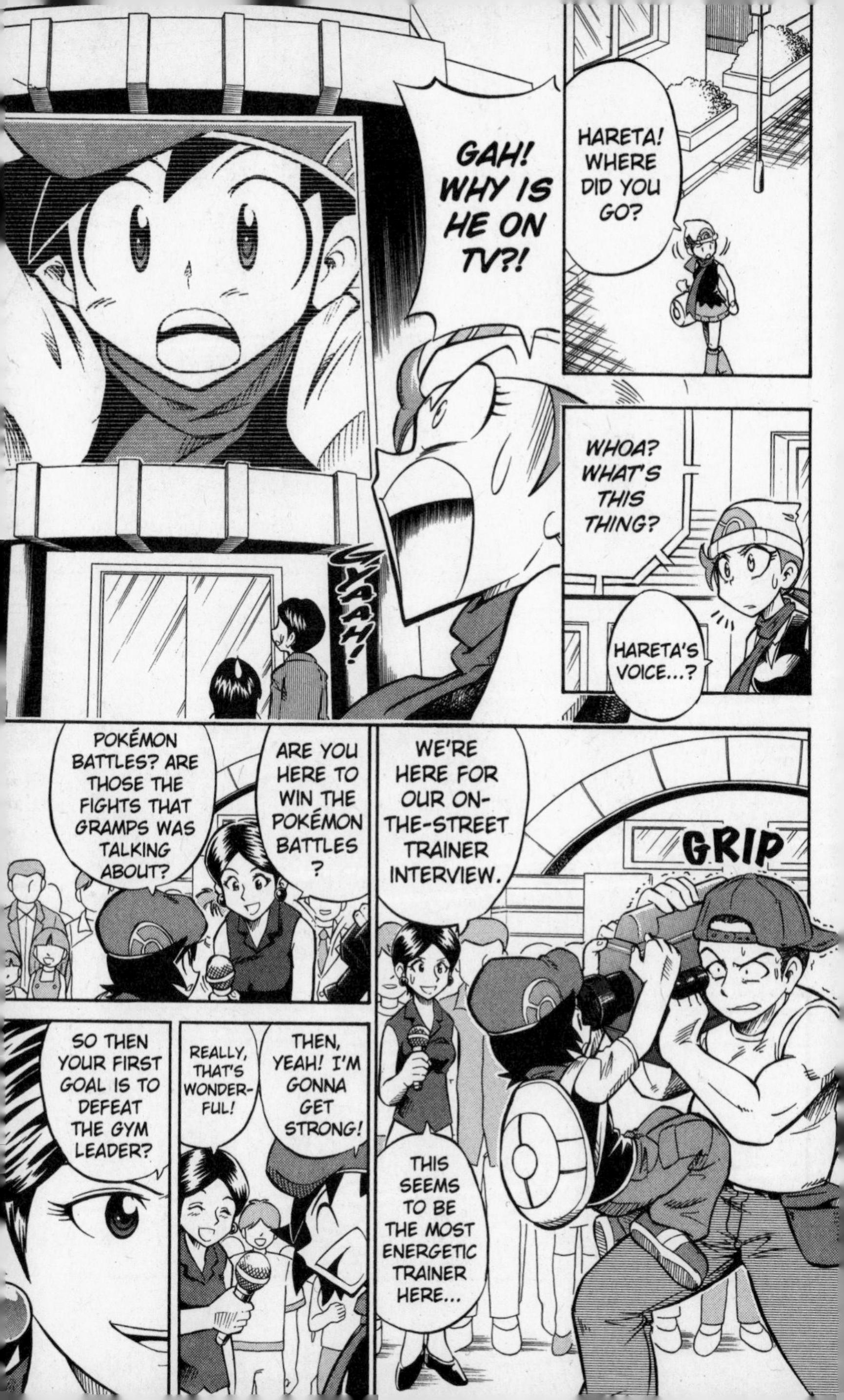
HARETA! WHERE DID YOU GO?
WHOA? WHAT'S THIS THING?
HARETA'S VOICE...?
GAH! WHY IS HE ON TV?!
GYAAH!
WE'RE HERE FOR OUR ON-THE-STREET TRAINER INTERVIEW.
GRIP
THIS SEEMS TO BE THE MOST ENERGETIC TRAINER HERE...
ARE YOU HERE TO WIN THE POKÉMON BATTLES?
POKÉMON BATTLES? ARE THOSE THE FIGHTS THAT GRAMPS WAS TALKING ABOUT?
THEN, YEAH! I'M GONNA GET STRONG!
REALLY, THAT'S WONDERFUL!
SO THEN YOUR FIRST GOAL IS TO DEFEAT THE GYM LEADER?

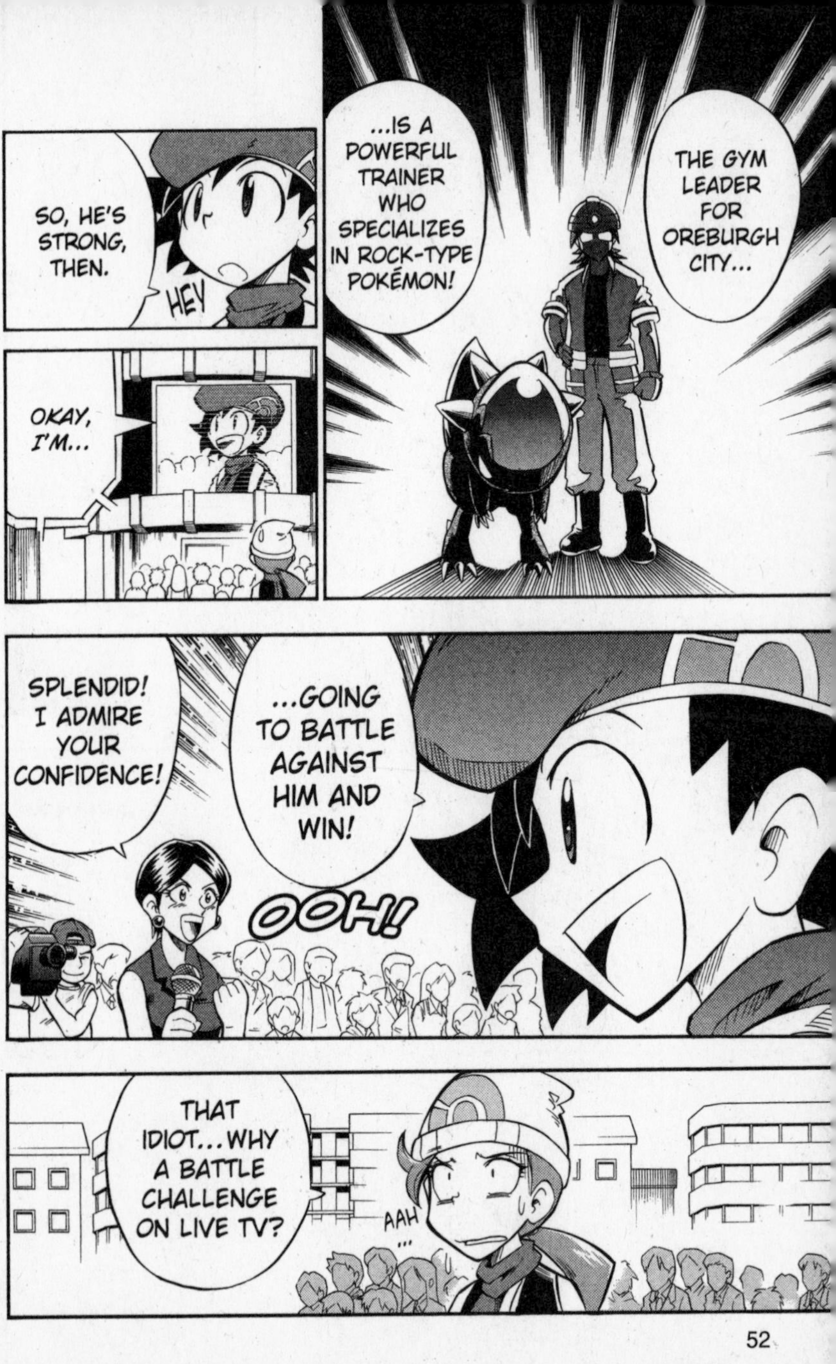
THE GYM LEADER FOR OREBURGH CITY...
...IS A POWERFUL TRAINER WHO SPECIALIZES IN ROCK-TYPE POKÉMON!
SO, HE'S STRONG, THEN.
HEY
OKAY, I'M...
...GOING TO BATTLE AGAINST HIM AND WIN!
SPLENDID! I ADMIRE YOUR CONFIDENCE!
OOH!
THAT IDIOT...WHY A BATTLE CHALLENGE ON LIVE TV?
AAH...

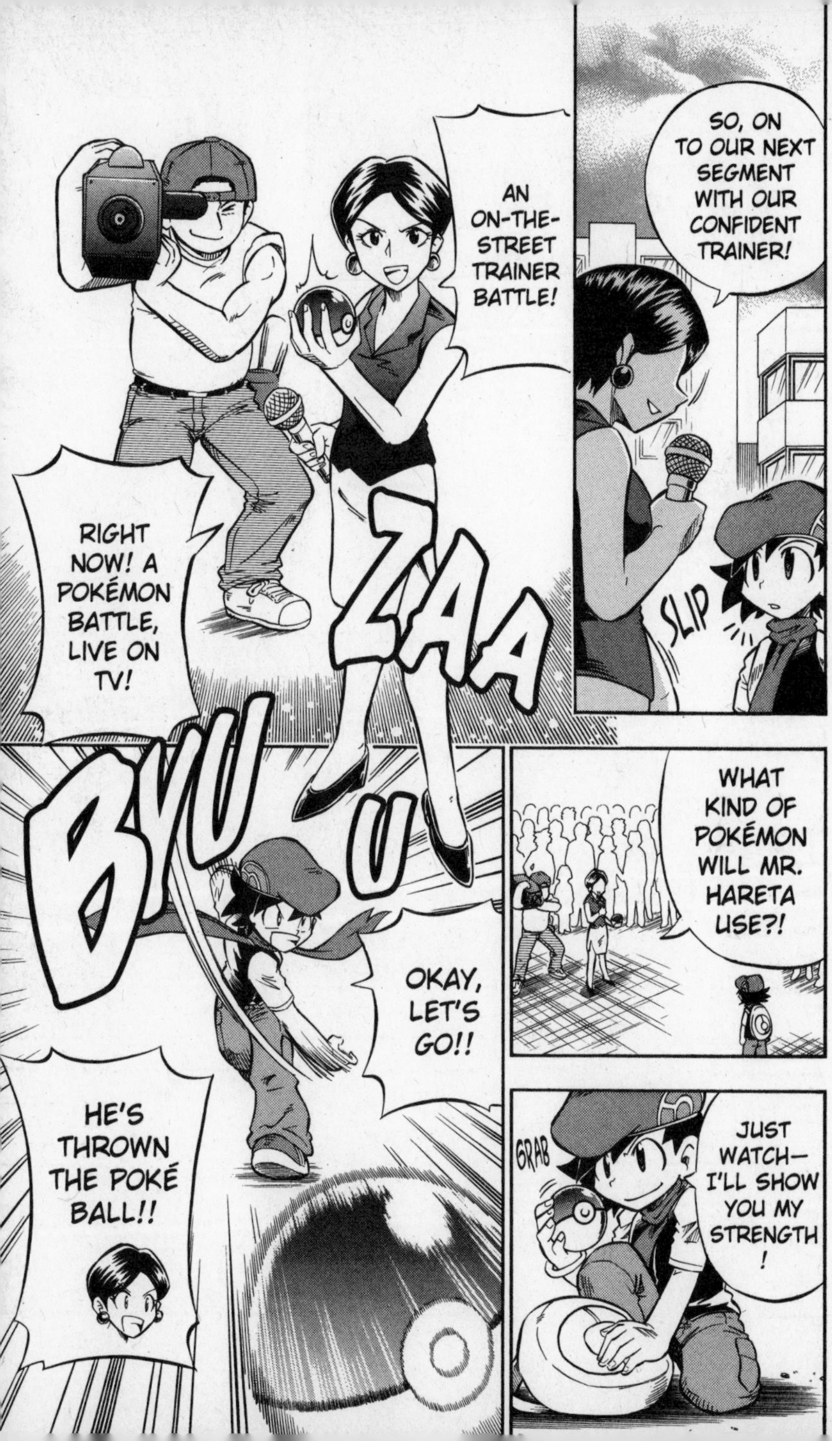
SO, ON TO OUR NEXT SEGMENT WITH OUR CONFIDENT TRAINER!
SLIP
AN ON-THE-STREET TRAINER BATTLE!
RIGHT NOW! A POKÉMON BATTLE, LIVE ON TV!
ZAA
WHAT KIND OF POKÉMON WILL MR. HARETA USE?!
JUST WATCH— I'LL SHOW YOU MY STRENGTH!
GRAB
BYUU
OKAY, LET'S GO!!
HE'S THROWN THE POKÉ BALL!!

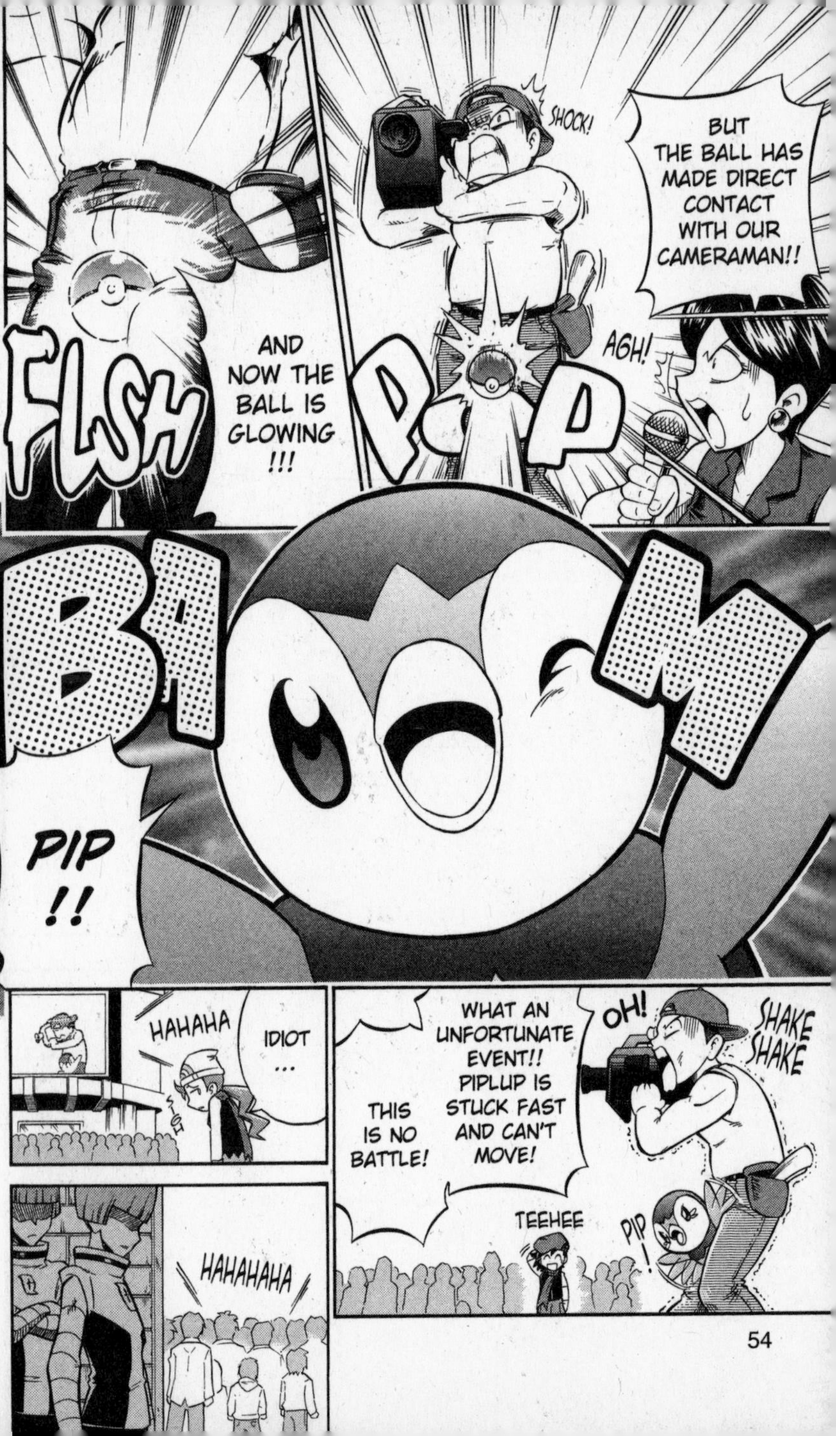
BUT THE BALL HAS MADE DIRECT CONTACT WITH OUR CAMERAMAN!!
AGH!
SHOCK!
P P
AND NOW THE BALL IS GLOWING!!!
FLSH
BA M
PIP!!
OH!
SHAKE SHAKE
WHAT AN UNFORTUNATE EVENT!! PIPLUP IS STUCK FAST AND CAN'T MOVE!
THIS IS NO BATTLE!
PIP!
TEEHEE
IDIOT...
HAHAHA
SIGH
HAHAHAHA

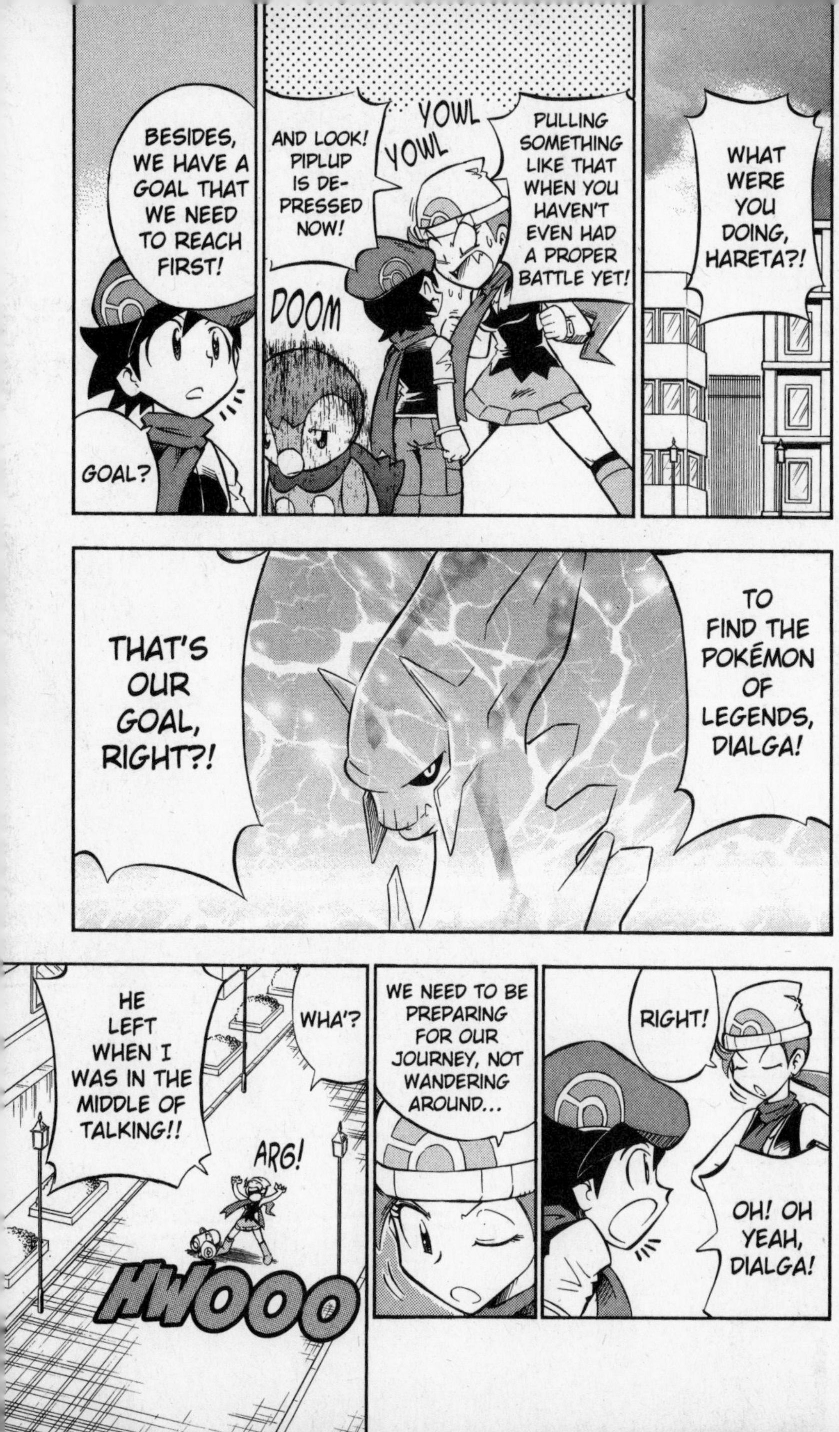
WHAT WERE YOU DOING, HARETA?!
PULLING SOMETHING LIKE THAT WHEN YOU HAVEN'T EVEN HAD A PROPER BATTLE YET!
YOWL
YOWL
AND LOOK! PIPLUP IS DE-PRESSED NOW!
DOOM
BESIDES, WE HAVE A GOAL THAT WE NEED TO REACH FIRST!
GOAL?
TO FIND THE POKÉMON OF LEGENDS, DIALGA!
THAT'S OUR GOAL, RIGHT?!
RIGHT!
OH! OH YEAH, DIALGA!
WE NEED TO BE PREPARING FOR OUR JOURNEY, NOT WANDERING AROUND...
WHA'?
HE LEFT WHEN I WAS IN THE MIDDLE OF TALKING!!
ARG!
HWOOO

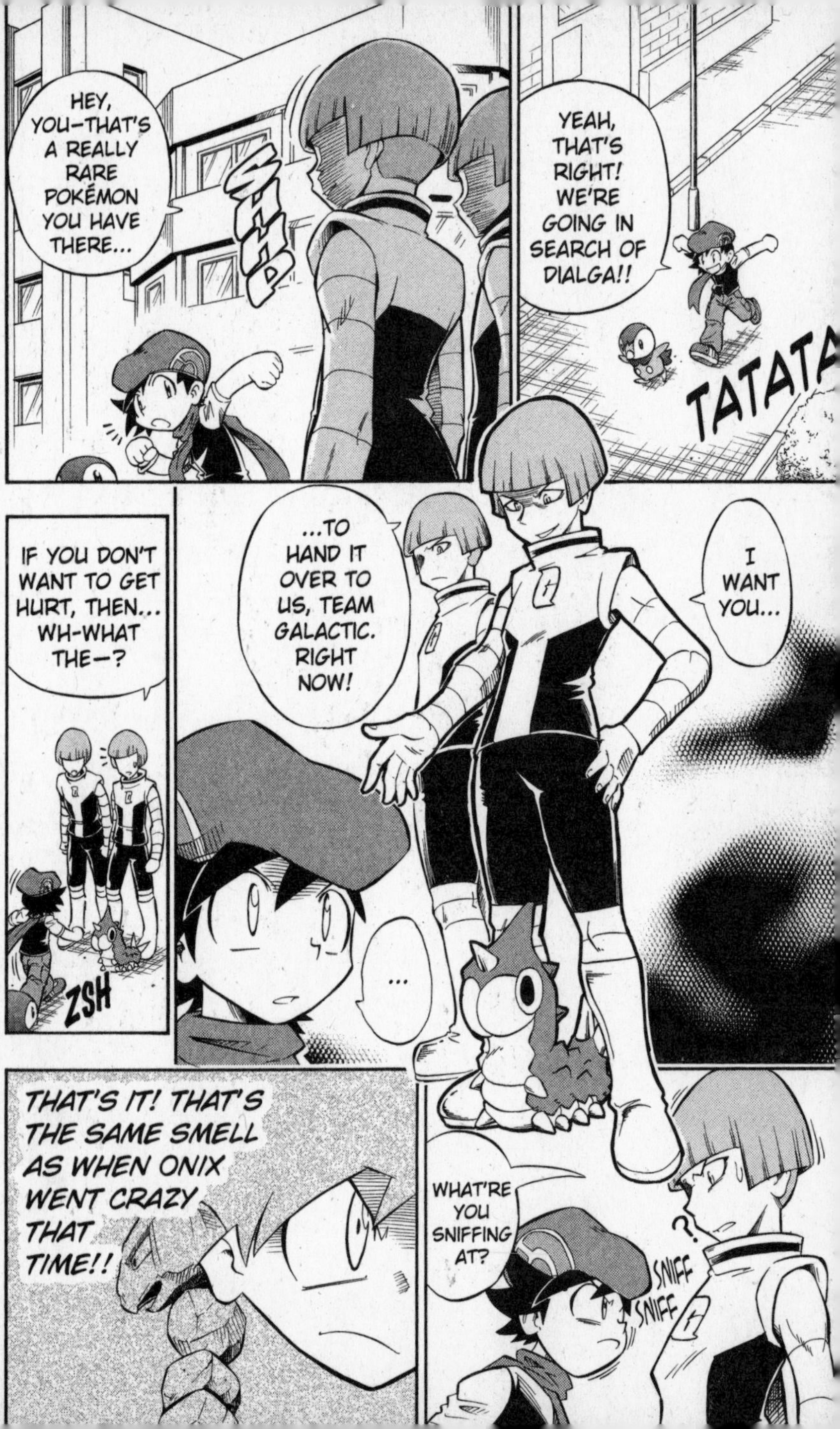
YEAH, THAT'S RIGHT! WE'RE GOING IN SEARCH OF DIALGA!!
TATATA
SHHP
HEY, YOU—THAT'S A REALLY RARE POKÉMON YOU HAVE THERE...
I WANT YOU...
...TO HAND IT OVER TO US, TEAM GALACTIC. RIGHT NOW!
...
IF YOU DON'T WANT TO GET HURT, THEN... WH-WHAT THE—?
ZSH
WHAT'RE YOU SNIFFING AT?
SNIFF SNIFF
THAT'S IT! THAT'S THE SAME SMELL AS WHEN ONIX WENT CRAZY THAT TIME!!

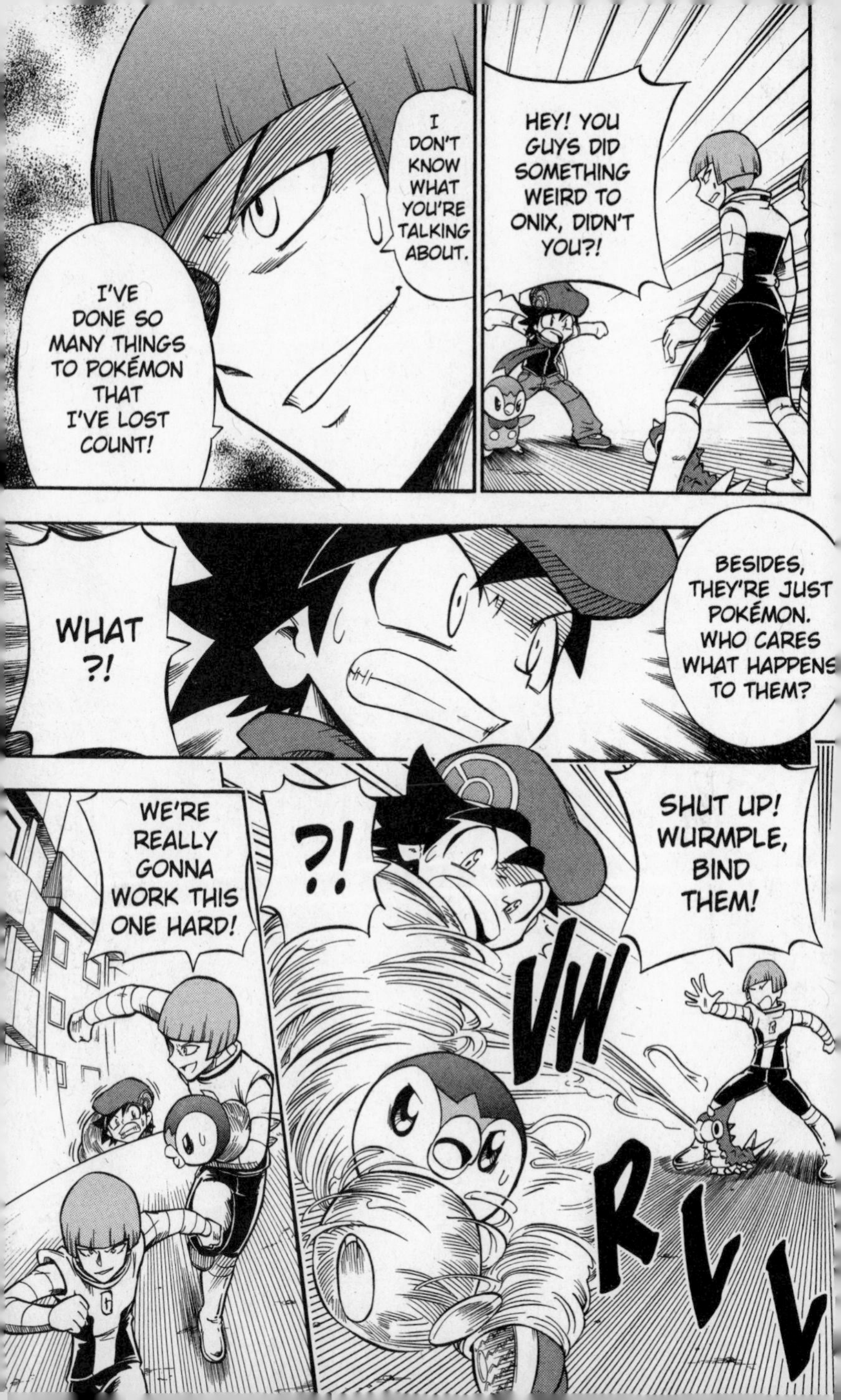
HEY! YOU GUYS DID SOMETHING WEIRD TO ONIX, DIDN'T YOU?!
I DON'T KNOW WHAT YOU'RE TALKING ABOUT.
I'VE DONE SO MANY THINGS TO POKÉMON THAT I'VE LOST COUNT!
BESIDES, THEY'RE JUST POKÉMON. WHO CARES WHAT HAPPENS TO THEM?
WHAT ?!
SHUT UP! WURMPLE, BIND THEM!
VWRLL
?!
WE'RE REALLY GONNA WORK THIS ONE HARD!

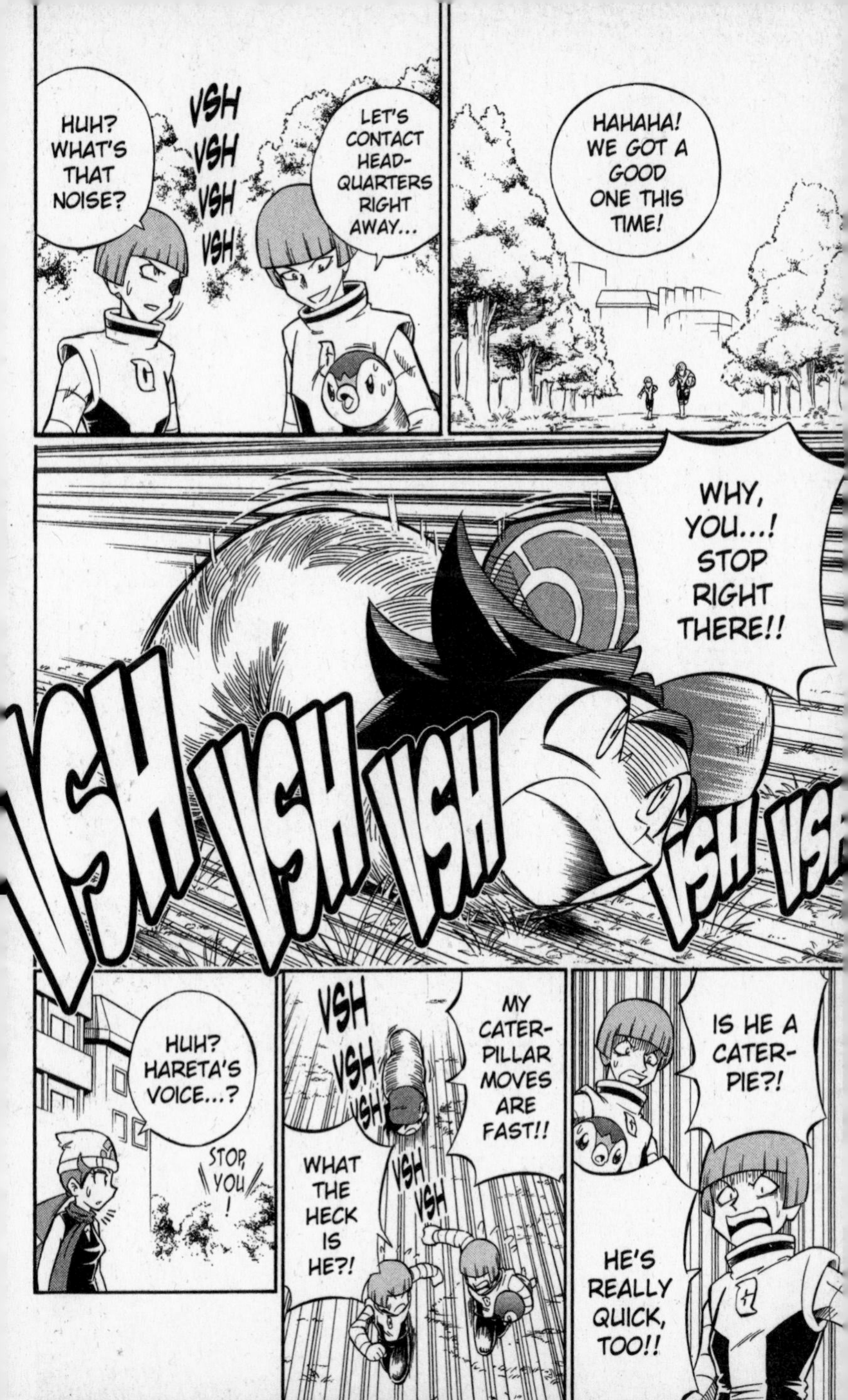
HAHAHA! WE GOT A GOOD ONE THIS TIME!
LET'S CONTACT HEAD-QUARTERS RIGHT AWAY...
VSH VSH VSH VSH
HUH? WHAT'S THAT NOISE?
WHY, YOU...! STOP RIGHT THERE!!
VSH VSH VSH VSH VSH
IS HE A CATER-PIE?!
HE'S REALLY QUICK, TOO!!
MY CATER-PILLAR MOVES ARE FAST!!
VSH VSH VSH
WHAT THE HECK IS HE?!
VSH VSH
HUH? HARETA'S VOICE...?
STOP, YOU!

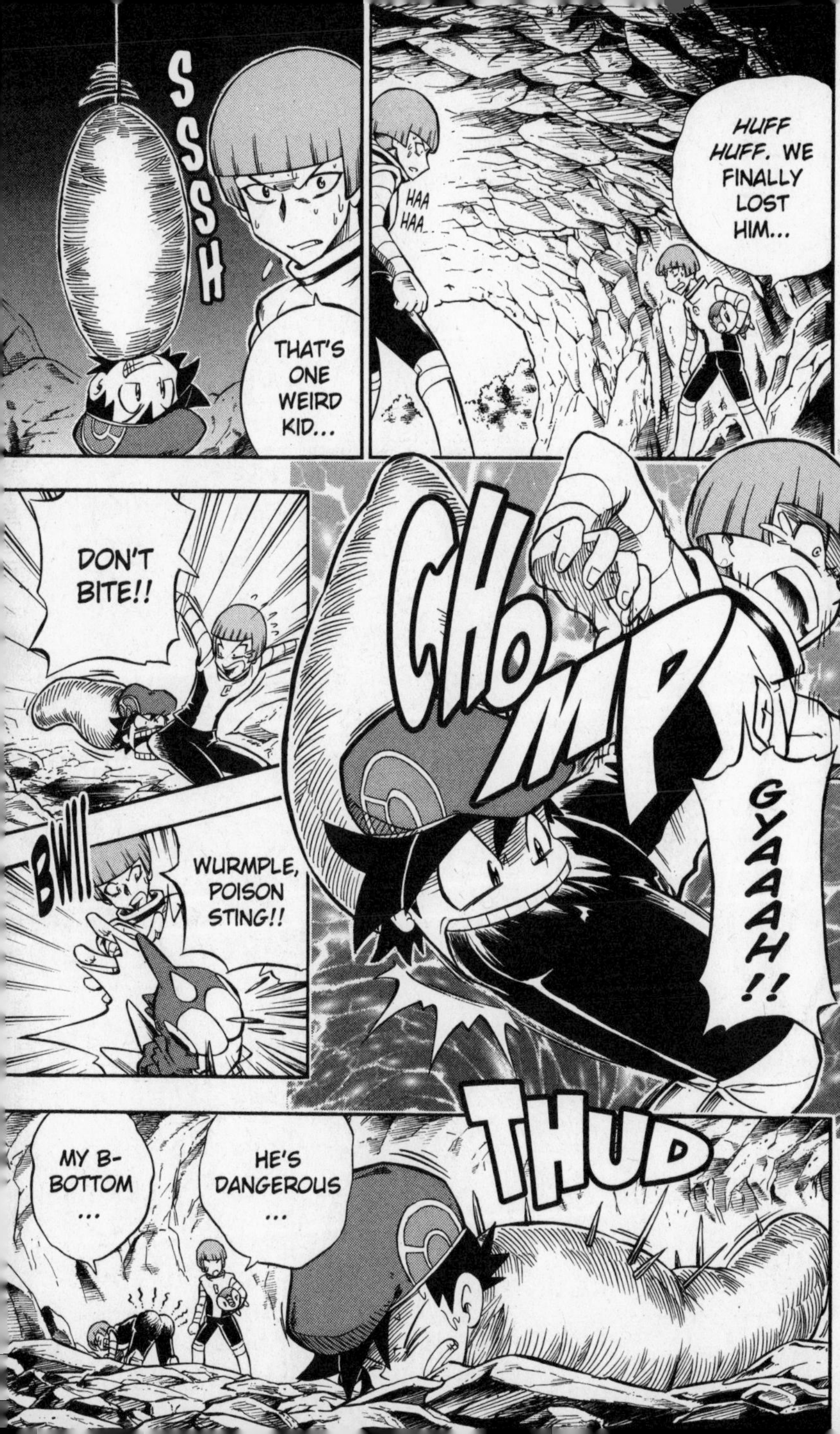
HUFF HUFF. WE FINALLY LOST HIM...
HAA HAA
SSSH
THAT'S ONE WEIRD KID...
CHOMP
GYAAAH!!
DON'T BITE!!
BWII
WURMPLE, POISON STING!!
THUD
HE'S DANGEROUS ...
MY B-BOTTOM ...

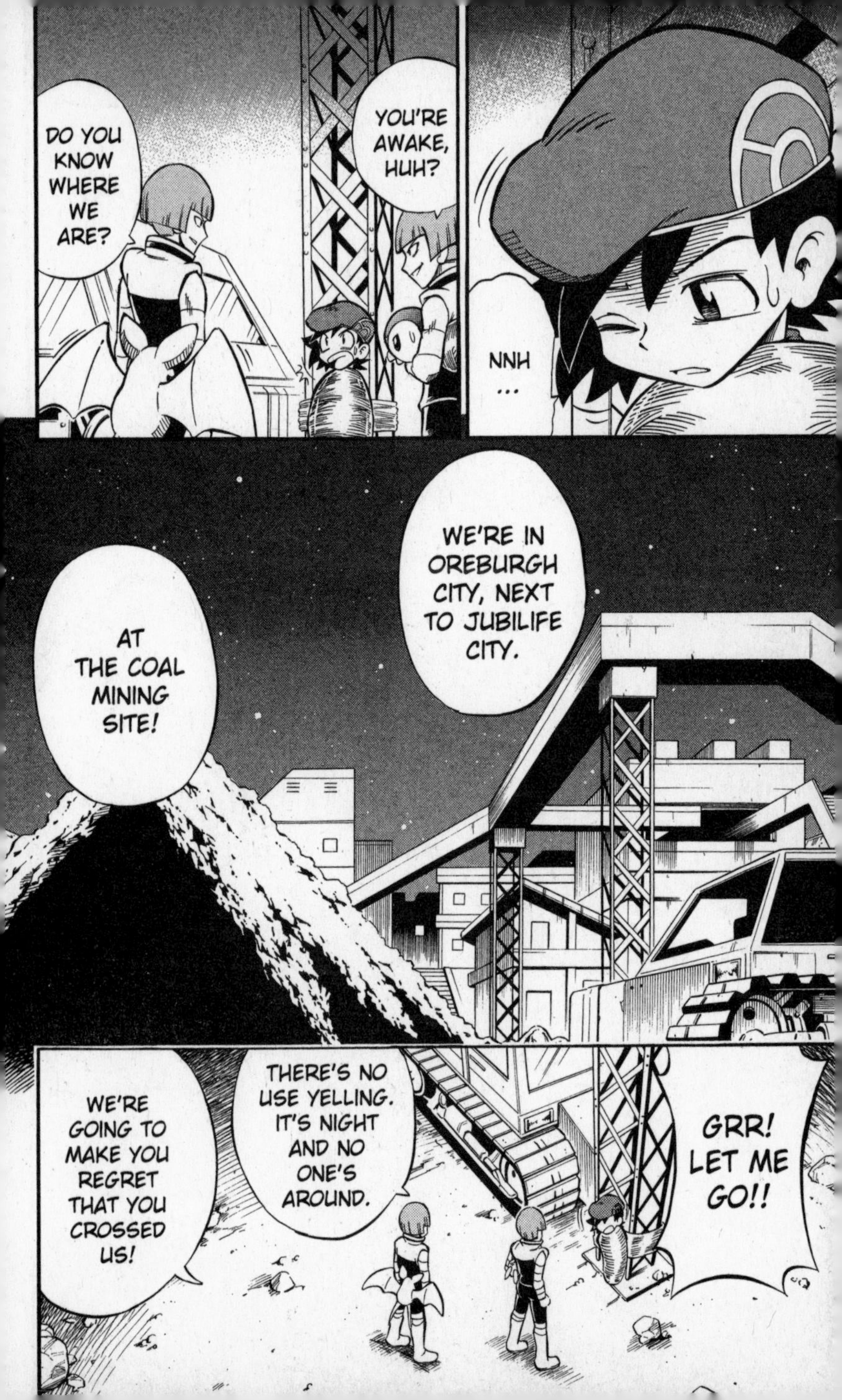
NNH ...
YOU'RE AWAKE, HUH?
DO YOU KNOW WHERE WE ARE?
WE'RE IN OREBURGH CITY, NEXT TO JUBILIFE CITY.
AT THE COAL MINING SITE!
GRR! LET ME GO!!
THERE'S NO USE YELLING. IT'S NIGHT AND NO ONE'S AROUND.
WE'RE GOING TO MAKE YOU REGRET THAT YOU CROSSED US!

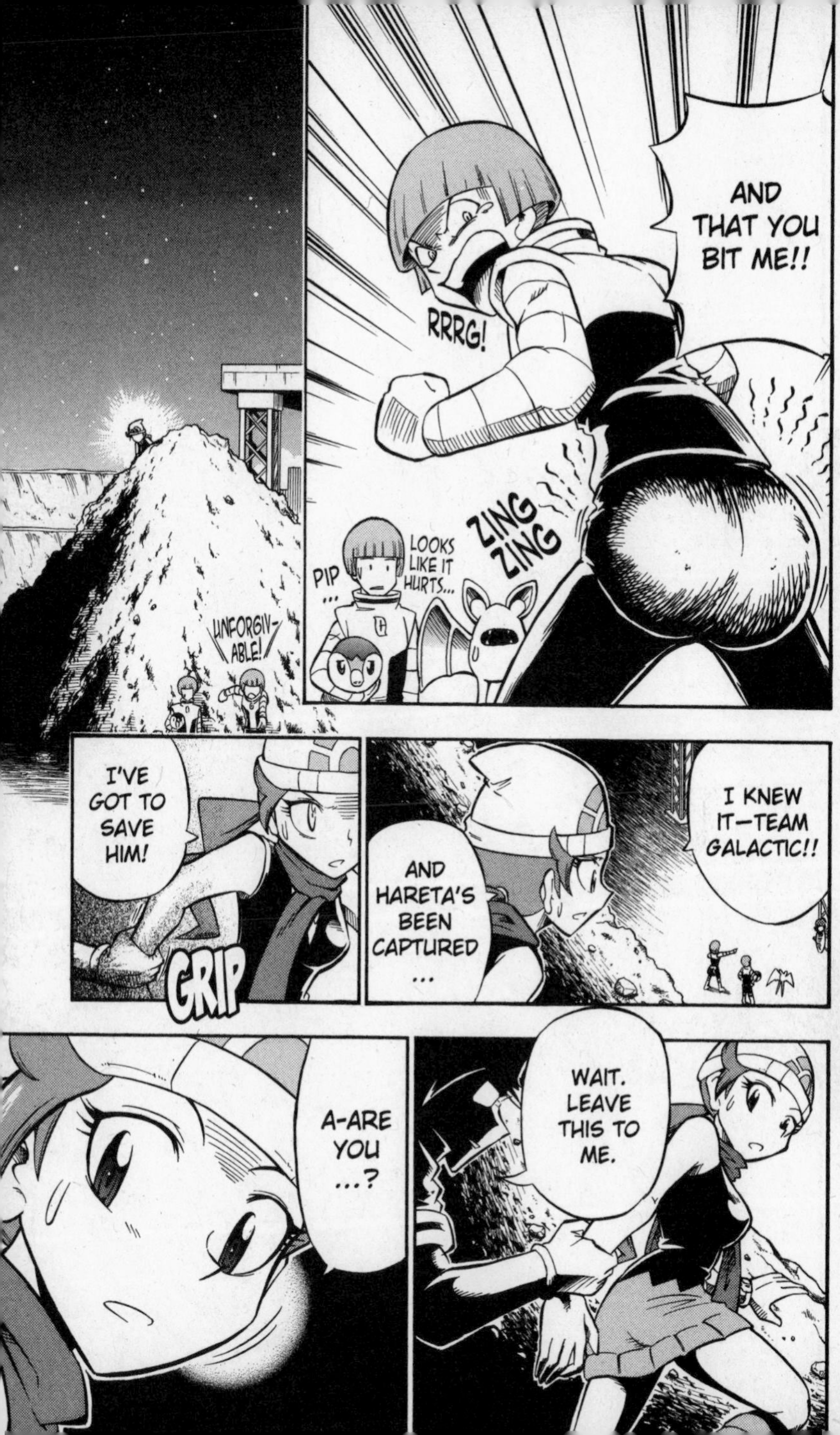
AND THAT YOU BIT ME!!
RRRG!
ZING ZING
LOOKS LIKE IT HURTS...
PIP ...
UNFORGIVABLE!
I KNEW IT—TEAM GALACTIC!!
AND HARETA'S BEEN CAPTURED ...
I'VE GOT TO SAVE HIM!
GRIP
WAIT. LEAVE THIS TO ME.
A-ARE YOU ...?

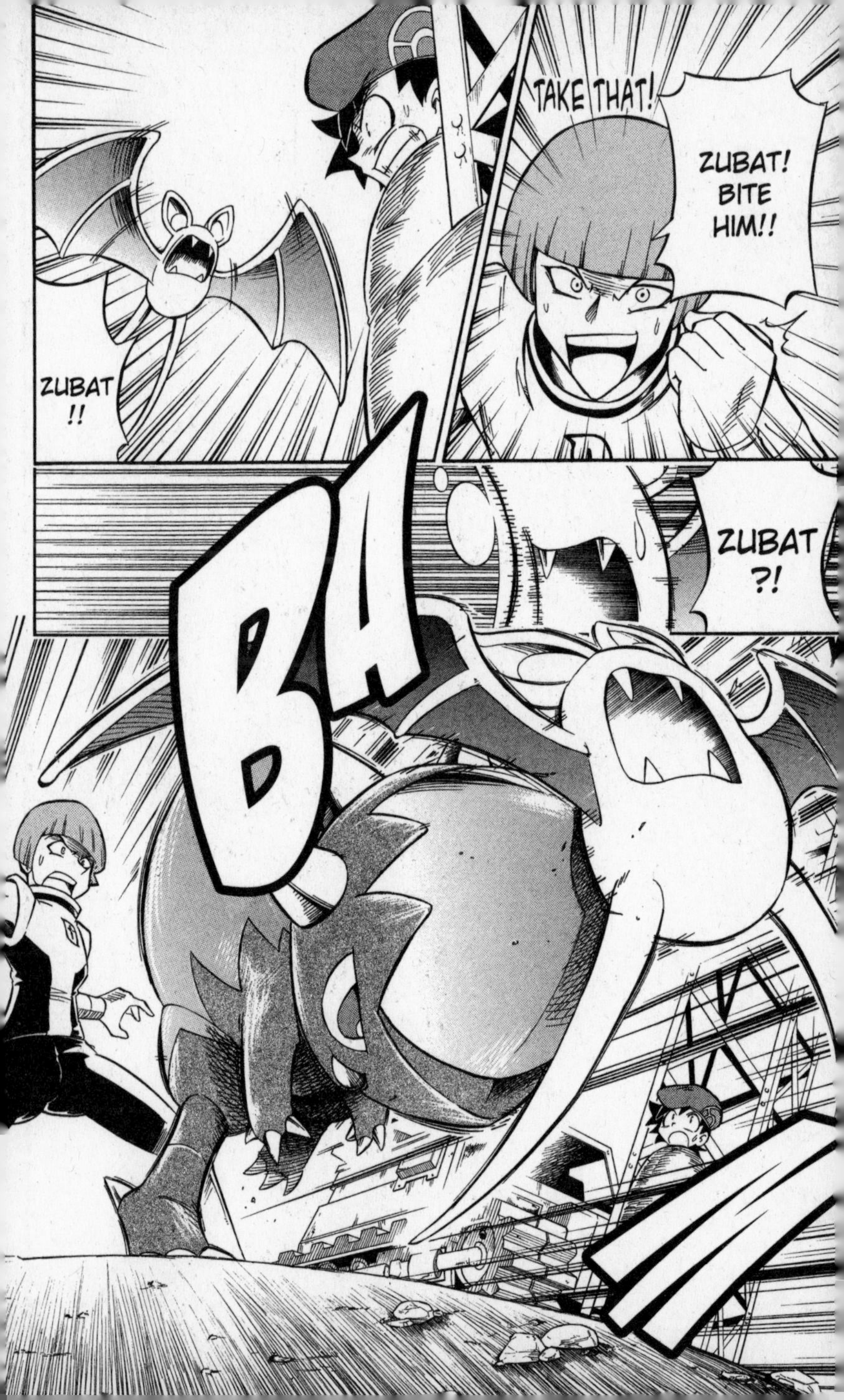
ZUBAT! BITE HIM!!
TAKE THAT!
ZUBAT !!
ZUBAT ?!
BA

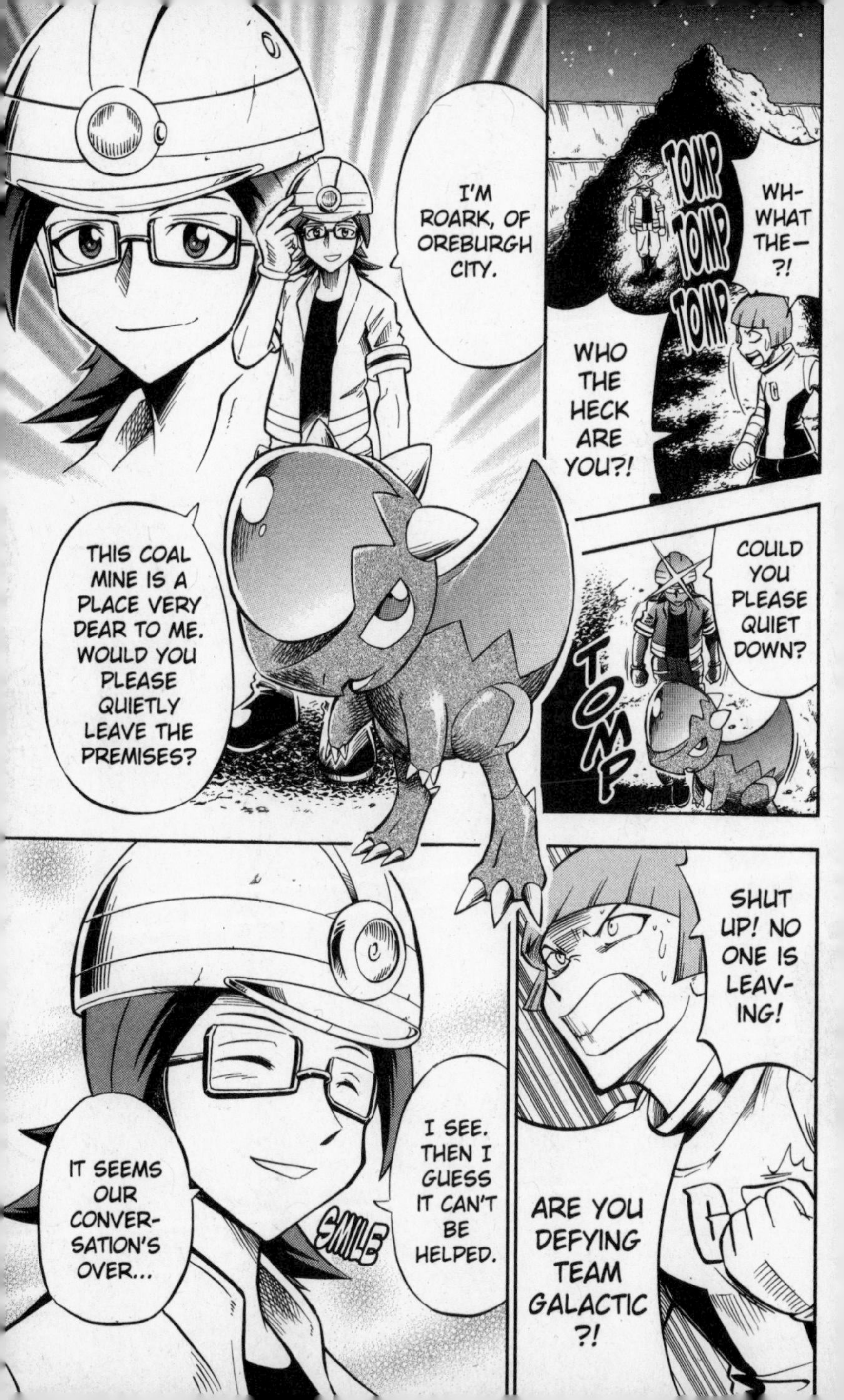
TOMP TOMP TOMP
WH-WHAT THE—?!
WHO THE HECK ARE YOU?!
COULD YOU PLEASE QUIET DOWN?
TOMP
I'M ROARK, OF OREBURGH CITY.
THIS COAL MINE IS A PLACE VERY DEAR TO ME. WOULD YOU PLEASE QUIETLY LEAVE THE PREMISES?
SHUT UP! NO ONE IS LEAV-ING!
ARE YOU DEFYING TEAM GALACTIC?!
I SEE. THEN I GUESS IT CAN'T BE HELPED.
SMILE
IT SEEMS OUR CONVER-SATION'S OVER...

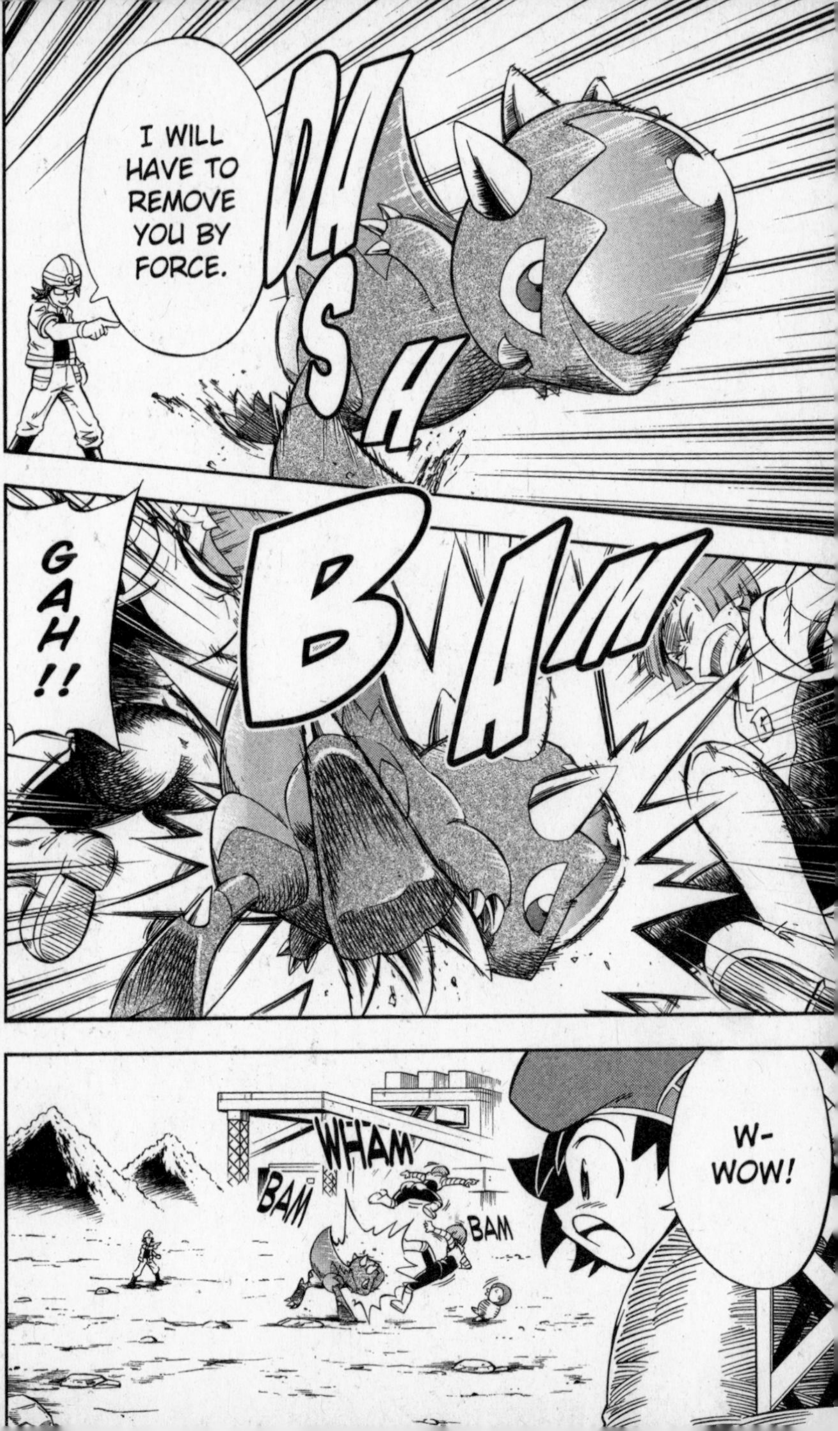
I WILL HAVE TO REMOVE YOU BY FORCE.
DASH
BAM
GAH!!
W-WOW!
WHAM
BAM
BAM

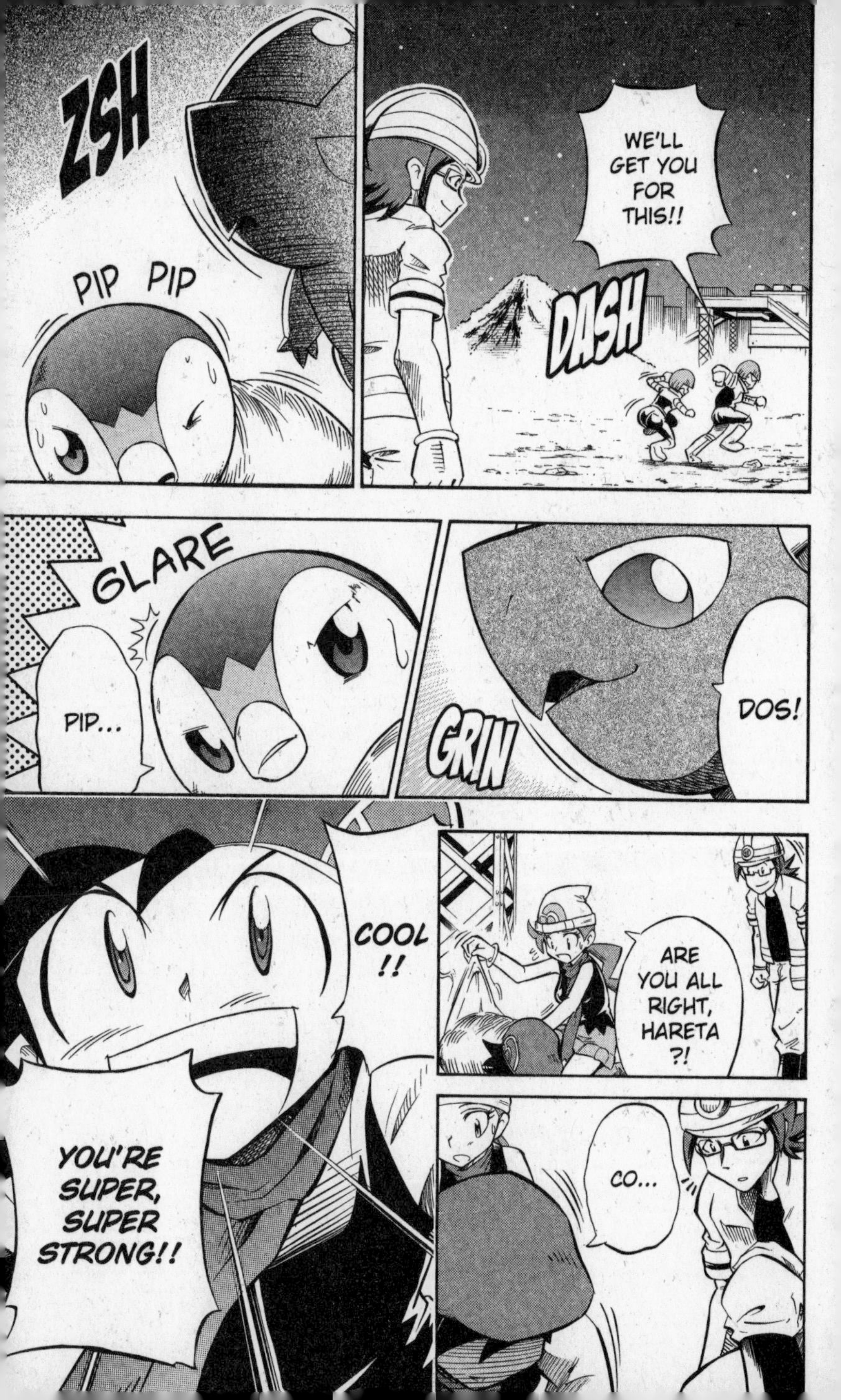
WE'LL GET YOU FOR THIS!!
DASH
ZSH
PIP PIP
DOS!
GRIN
GLARE
PIP...
ARE YOU ALL RIGHT, HARETA?!
CO...
COOL!!
YOU'RE SUPER, SUPER STRONG!!

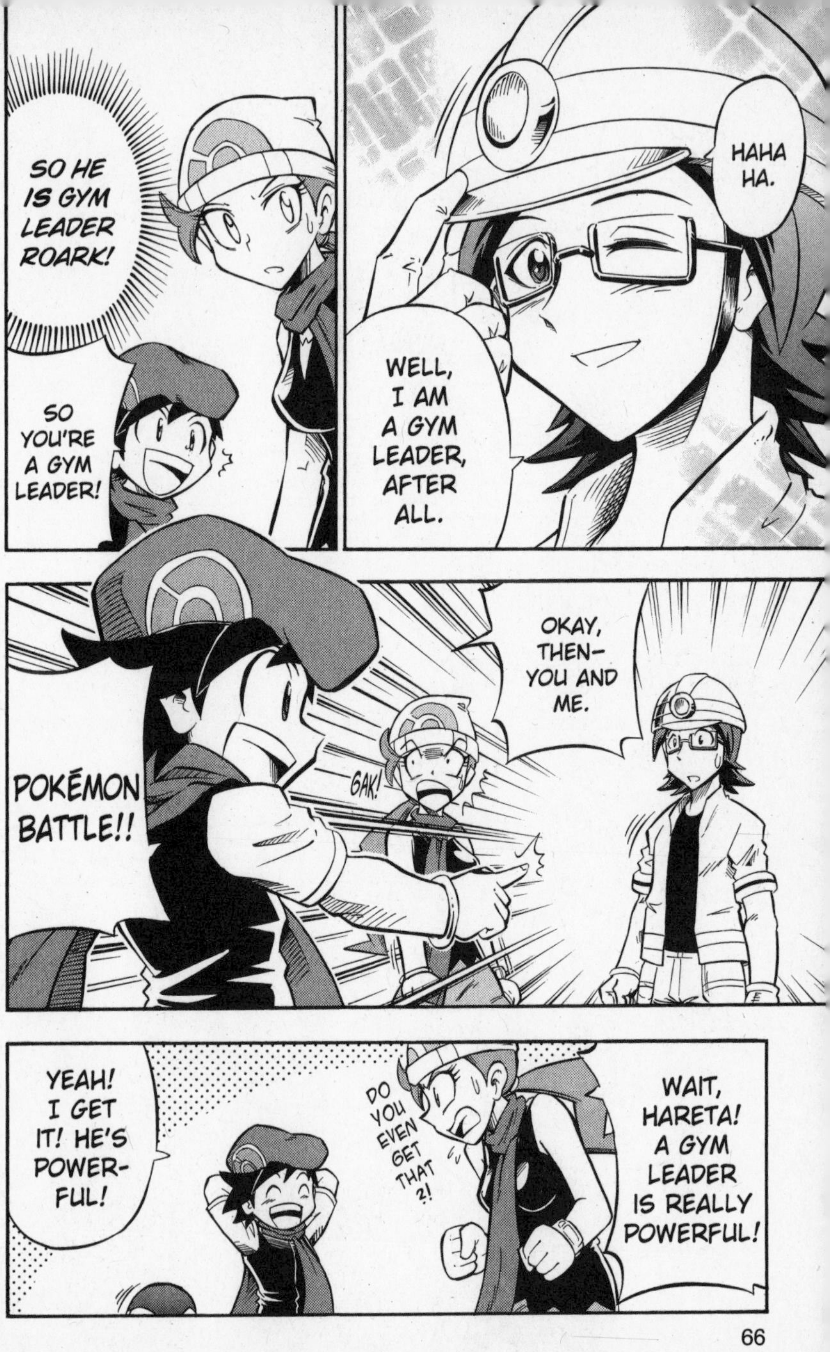
HAHA HA.
WELL, I AM A GYM LEADER, AFTER ALL.
SO HE IS GYM LEADER ROARK!
SO YOU'RE A GYM LEADER!
OKAY, THEN— YOU AND ME.
GAK!
POKÉMON BATTLE!!
WAIT, HARETA! A GYM LEADER IS REALLY POWERFUL!
DO YOU EVEN GET THAT?!
YEAH! I GET IT! HE'S POWERFUL!

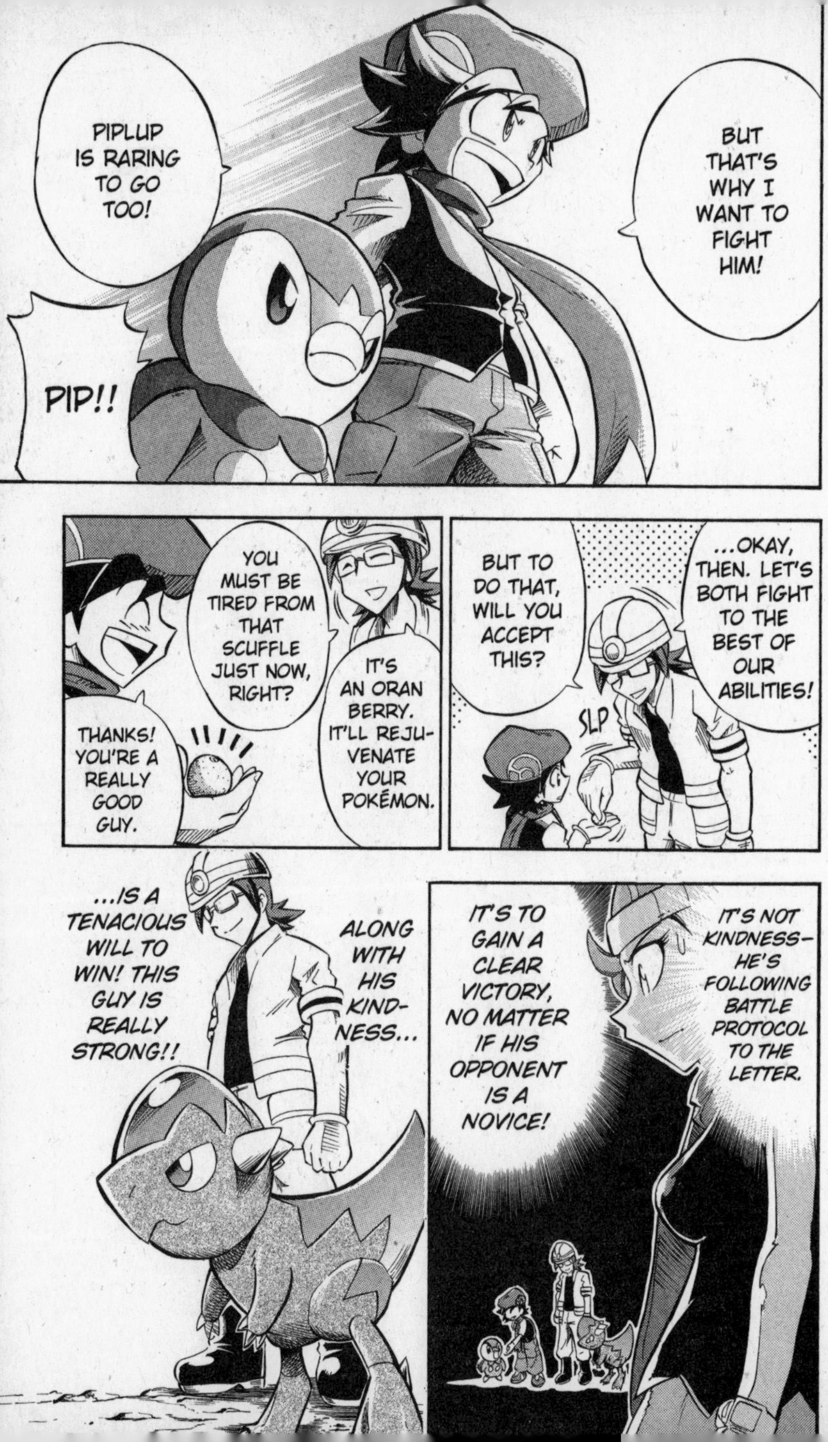
BUT THAT'S WHY I WANT TO FIGHT HIM!
PIPLUP IS RARING TO GO TOO!
PIP!!
...OKAY, THEN. LET'S BOTH FIGHT TO THE BEST OF OUR ABILITIES!
BUT TO DO THAT, WILL YOU ACCEPT THIS?
SLP
YOU MUST BE TIRED FROM THAT SCUFFLE JUST NOW, RIGHT?
IT'S AN ORAN BERRY. IT'LL REJUVENATE YOUR POKÉMON.
THANKS! YOU'RE A REALLY GOOD GUY.
IT'S NOT KINDNESS—HE'S FOLLOWING BATTLE PROTOCOL TO THE LETTER.
IT'S TO GAIN A CLEAR VICTORY, NO MATTER IF HIS OPPONENT IS A NOVICE!
ALONG WITH HIS KINDNESS...
...IS A TENACIOUS WILL TO WIN! THIS GUY IS REALLY STRONG!!

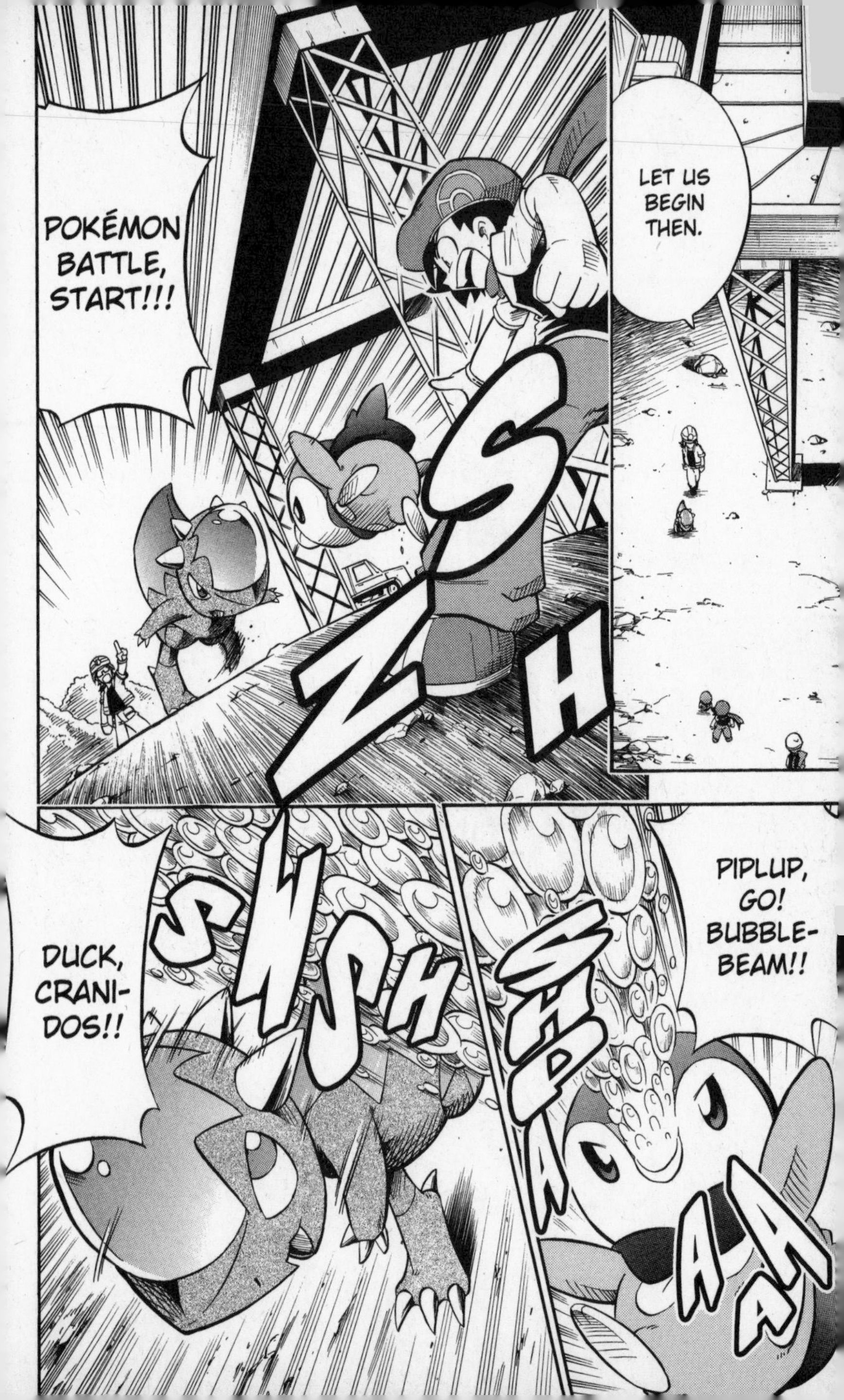
LET US BEGIN THEN.
POKÉMON BATTLE, START!!!
PIPLUP, GO! BUBBLE-BEAM!!
DUCK, CRANI-DOS!!

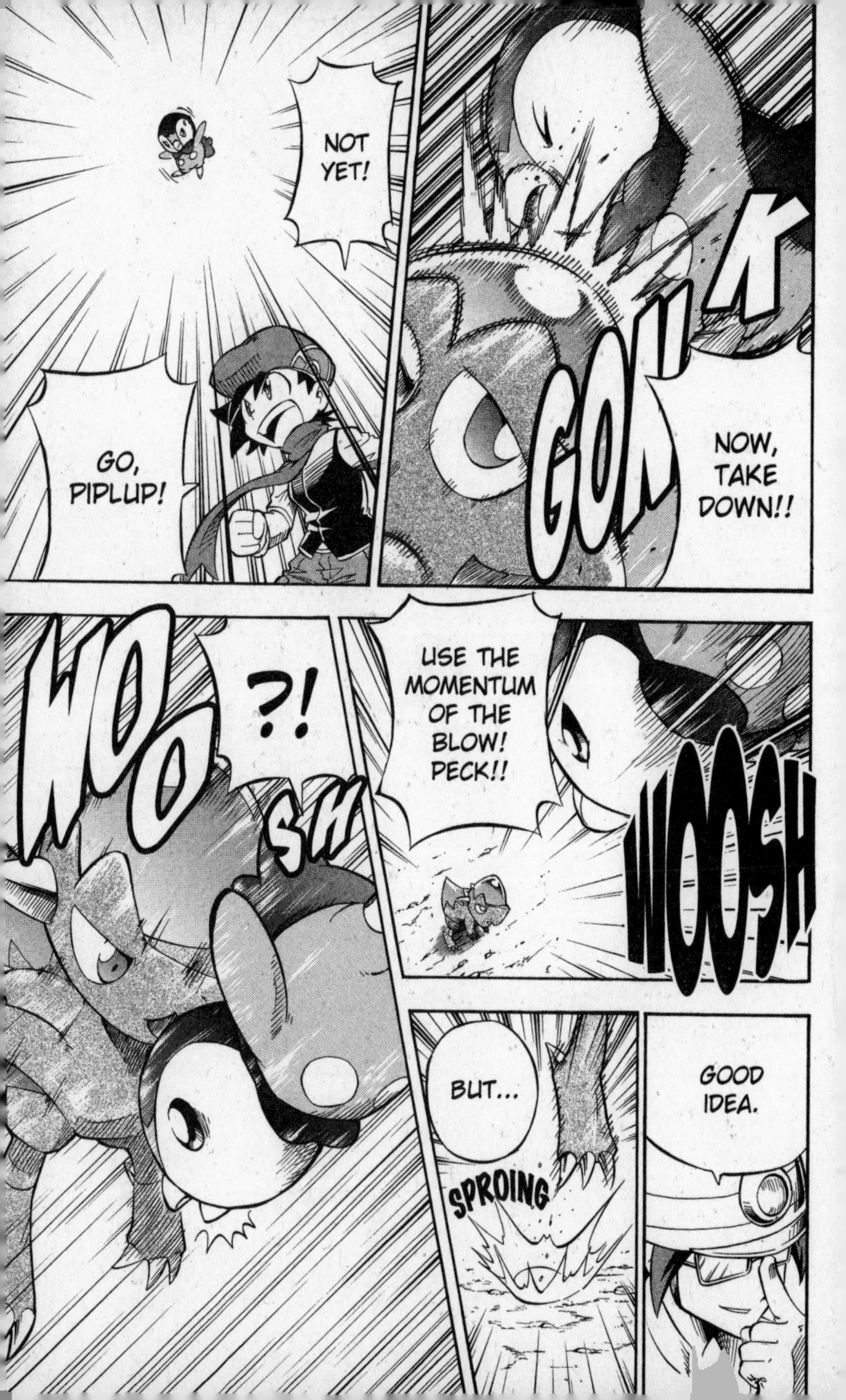
GONK
NOW, TAKE DOWN!!
NOT YET!
GO, PIPLUP!
USE THE MOMENTUM OF THE BLOW! PECK!!
WOOSH
GOOD IDEA.
BUT...
SPROING
WHOOSH
?!

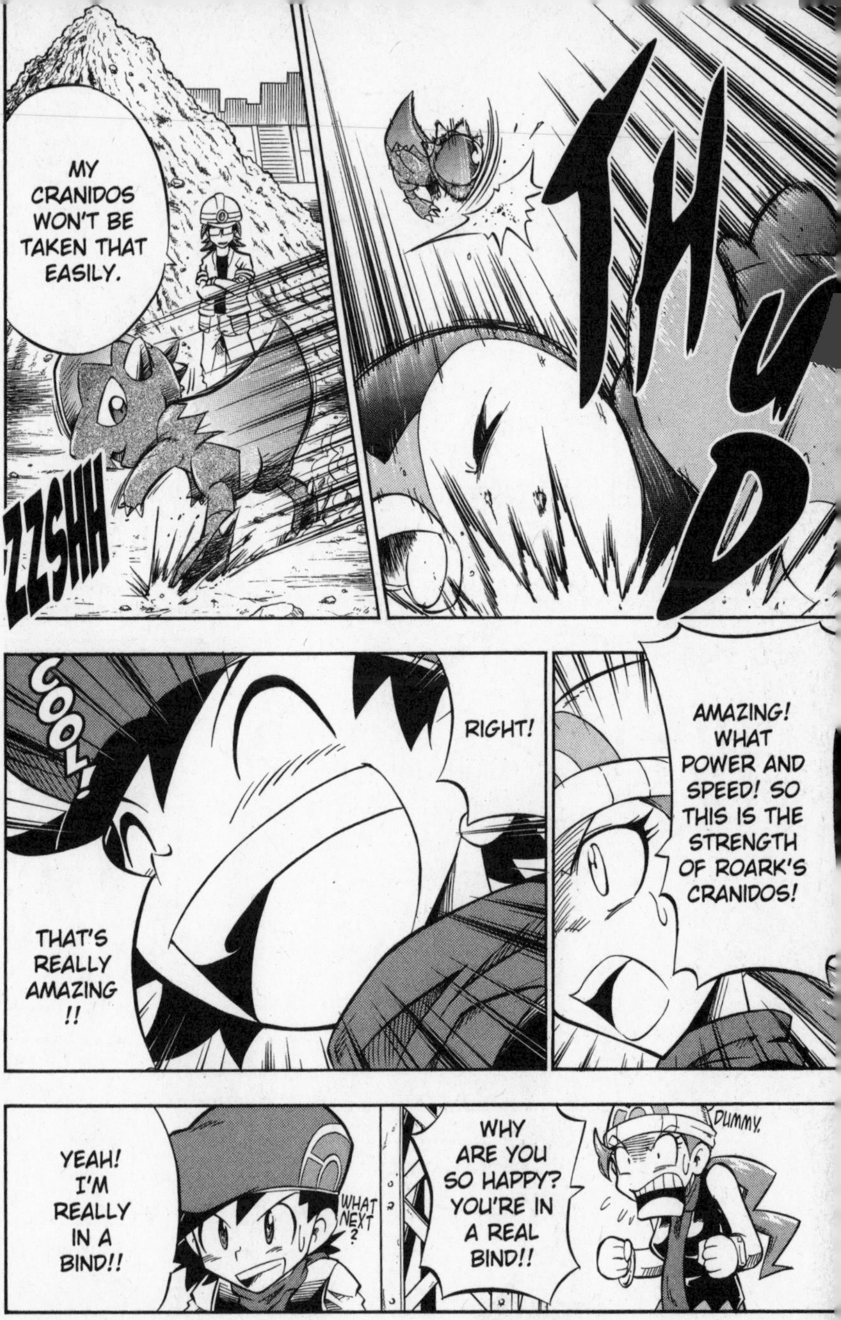
THUD
MY CRANIDOS WON'T BE TAKEN THAT EASILY.
ZZSHH
AMAZING! WHAT POWER AND SPEED! SO THIS IS THE STRENGTH OF ROARK'S CRANIDOS!
RIGHT!
COOL!
THAT'S REALLY AMAZING!!
DUMMY.
WHY ARE YOU SO HAPPY? YOU'RE IN A REAL BIND!!
WHAT NEXT?
YEAH! I'M REALLY IN A BIND!!

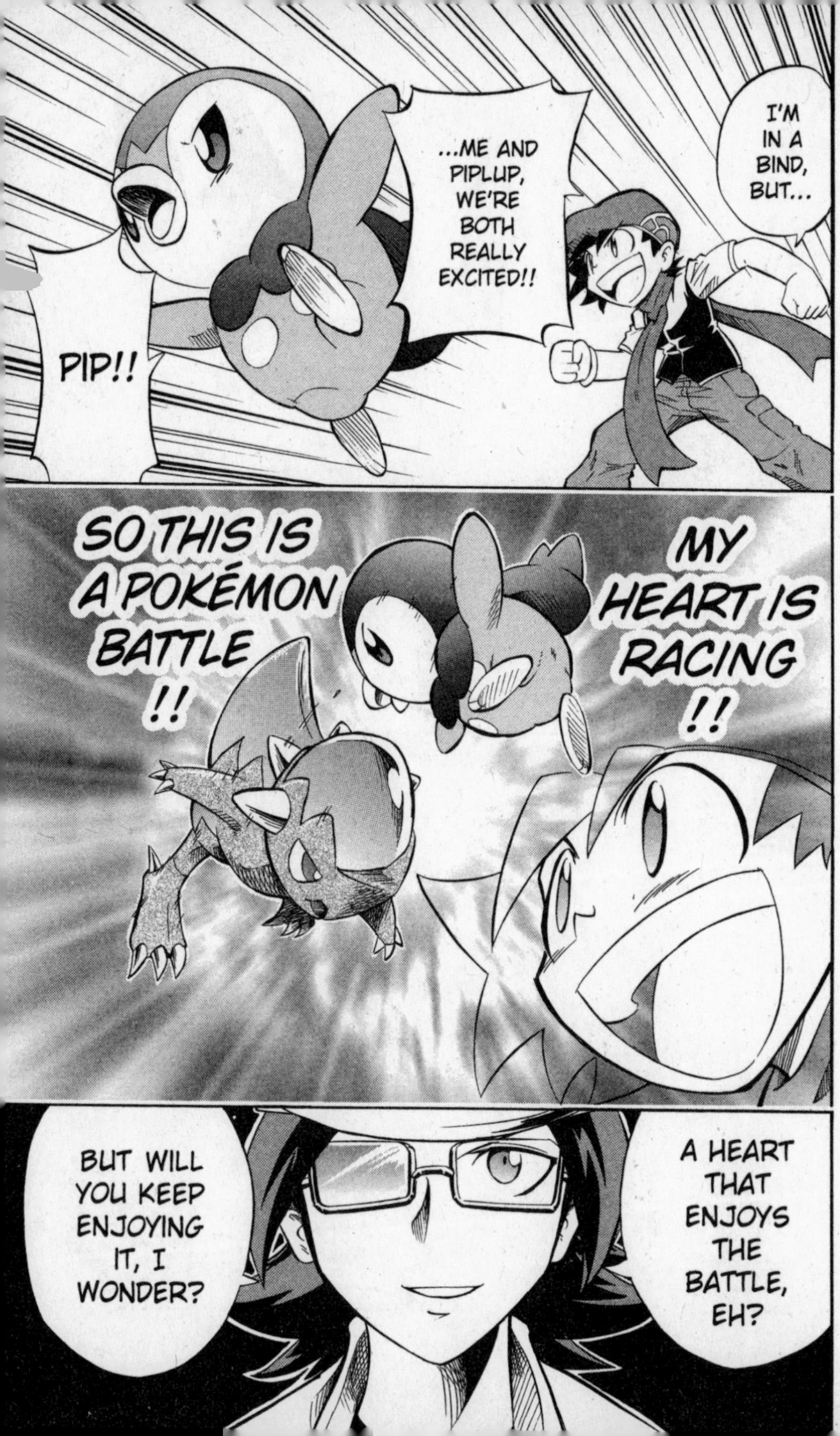
I'M IN A BIND, BUT...
...ME AND PIPLUP, WE'RE BOTH REALLY EXCITED!!
PIP!!
MY HEART IS RACING !!
SO THIS IS A POKÉMON BATTLE !!
A HEART THAT ENJOYS THE BATTLE, EH?
BUT WILL YOU KEEP ENJOYING IT, I WONDER?

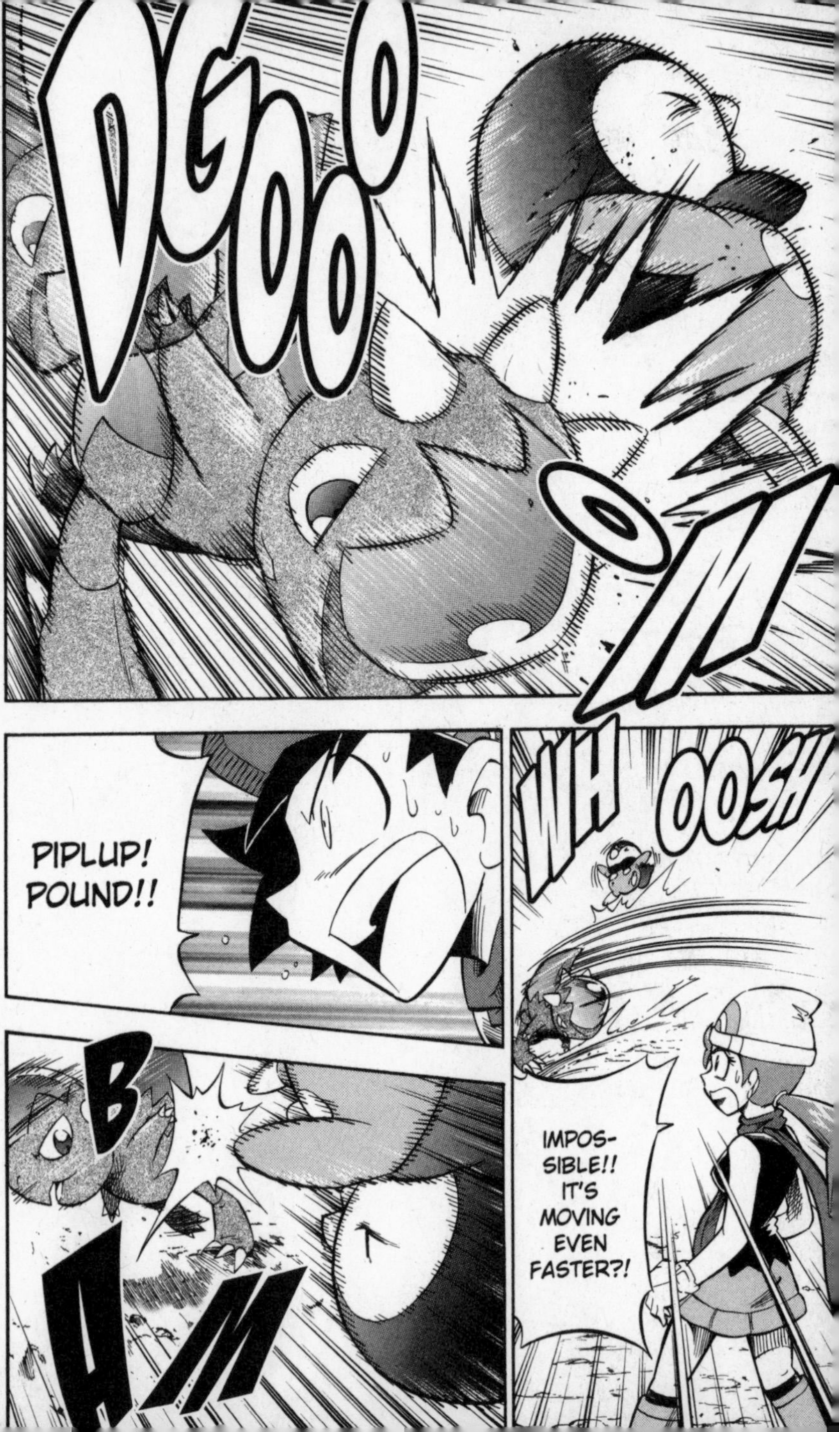
DGOOOOOOM
WHOOSH
IMPOS-SIBLE!! IT'S MOVING EVEN FASTER?!
PIPLUP! POUND!!
BAM

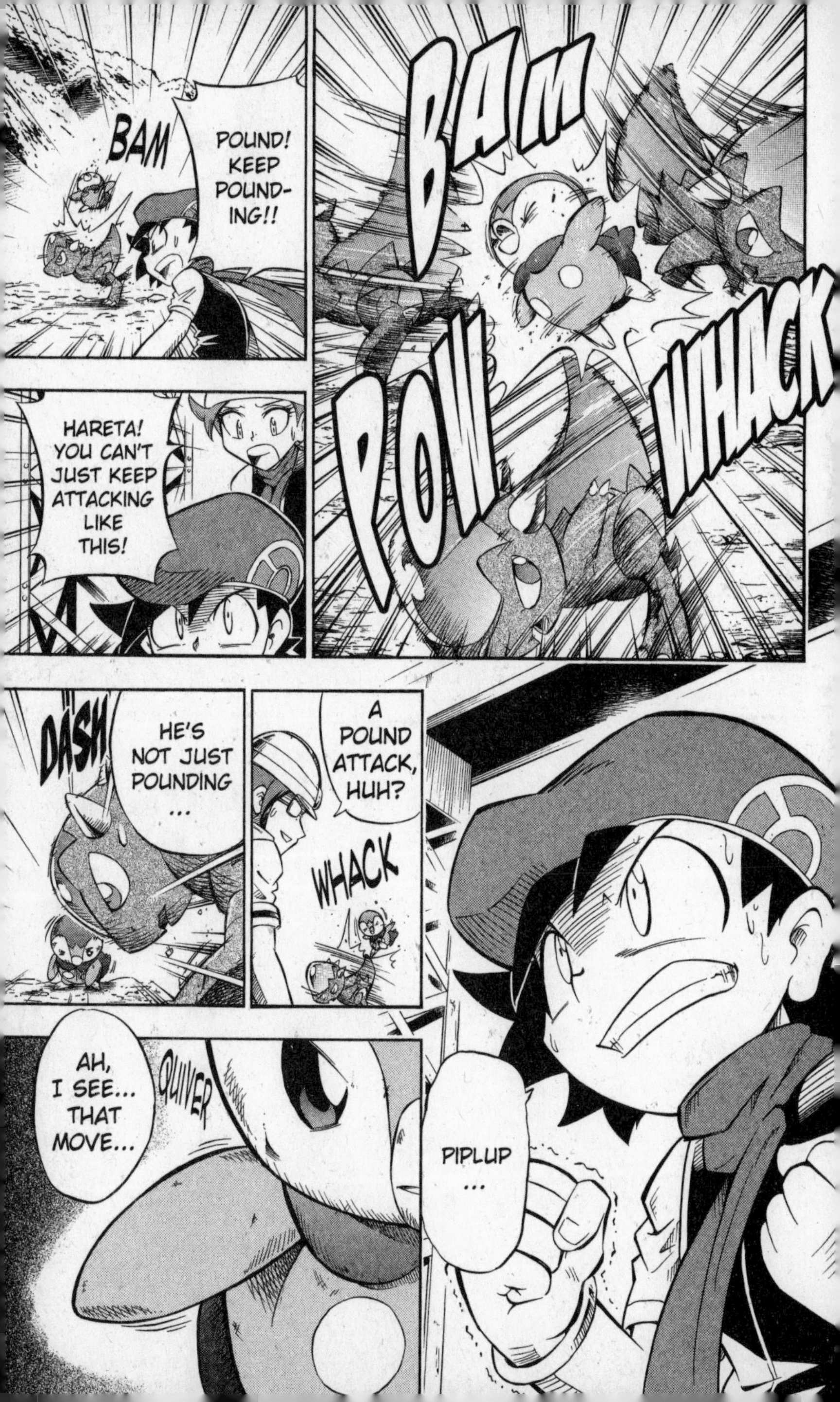
BAM
WHACK
POW
BAM
POUND! KEEP POUND-ING!!
HARETA! YOU CAN'T JUST KEEP ATTACKING LIKE THIS!
PIPLUP ...
A POUND ATTACK, HUH?
WHACK
HE'S NOT JUST POUNDING ...
DASH
AH, I SEE... THAT MOVE...
QUIVER

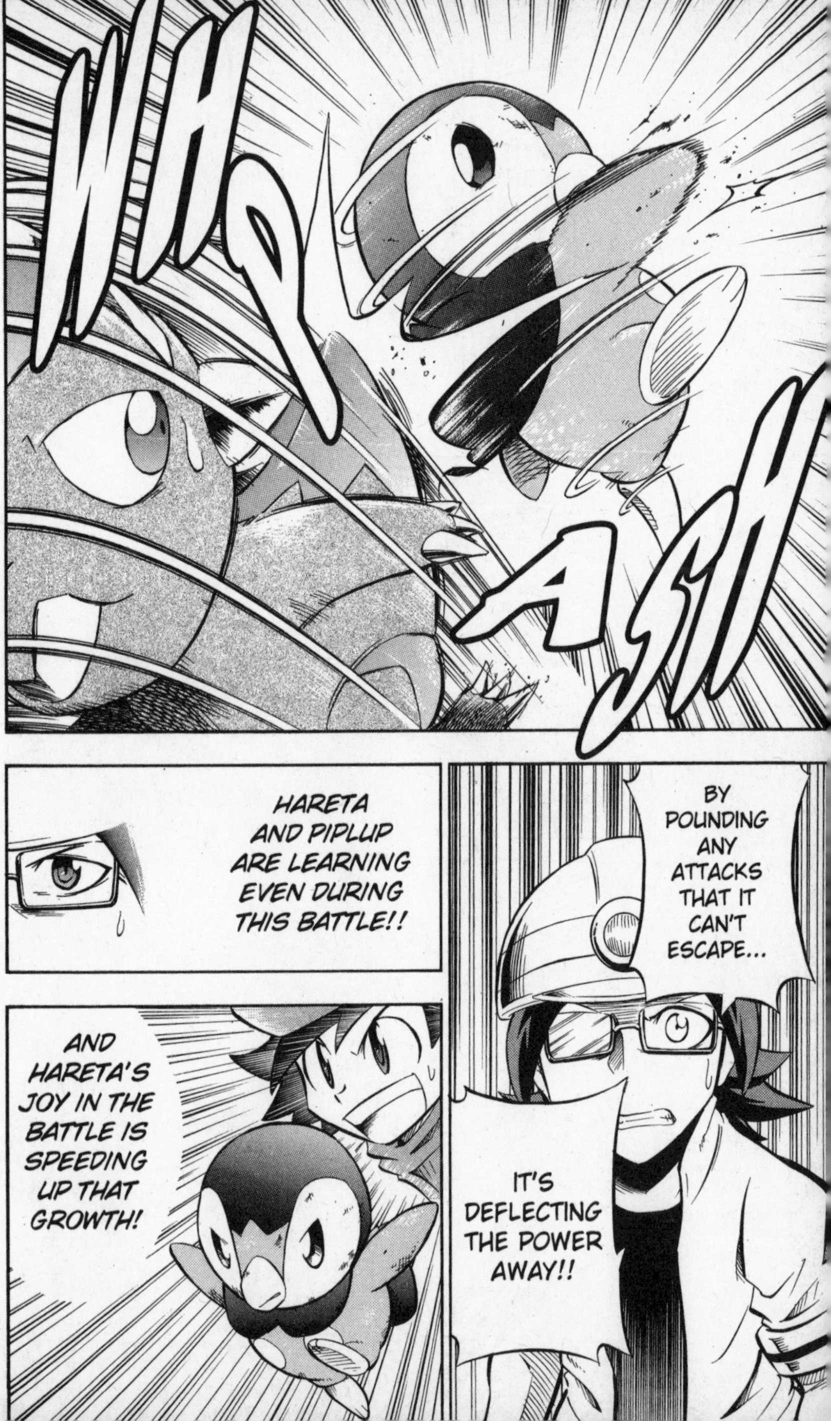
WHAP
ASH
BY POUNDING ANY ATTACKS THAT IT CAN'T ESCAPE...
IT'S DEFLECTING THE POWER AWAY!!
HARETA AND PIPLUP ARE LEARNING EVEN DURING THIS BATTLE!!
AND HARETA'S JOY IN THE BATTLE IS SPEEDING UP THAT GROWTH!

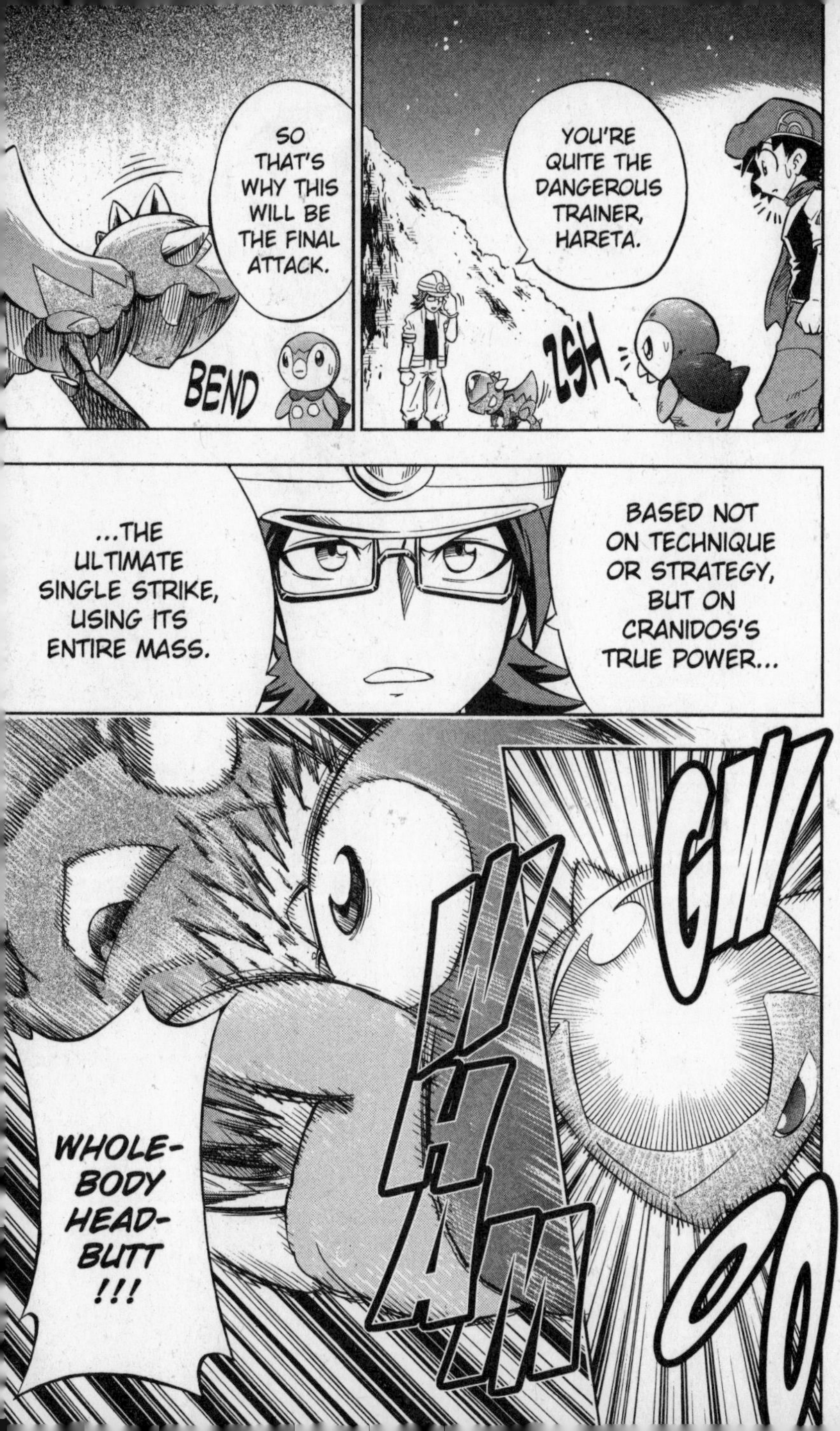
YOU'RE QUITE THE DANGEROUS TRAINER, HARETA.
ZSH
SO THAT'S WHY THIS WILL BE THE FINAL ATTACK.
BEND
BASED NOT ON TECHNIQUE OR STRATEGY, BUT ON CRANIDOS'S TRUE POWER...
...THE ULTIMATE SINGLE STRIKE, USING ITS ENTIRE MASS.
WHAM
WHOLE-BODY HEAD-BUTT!!!

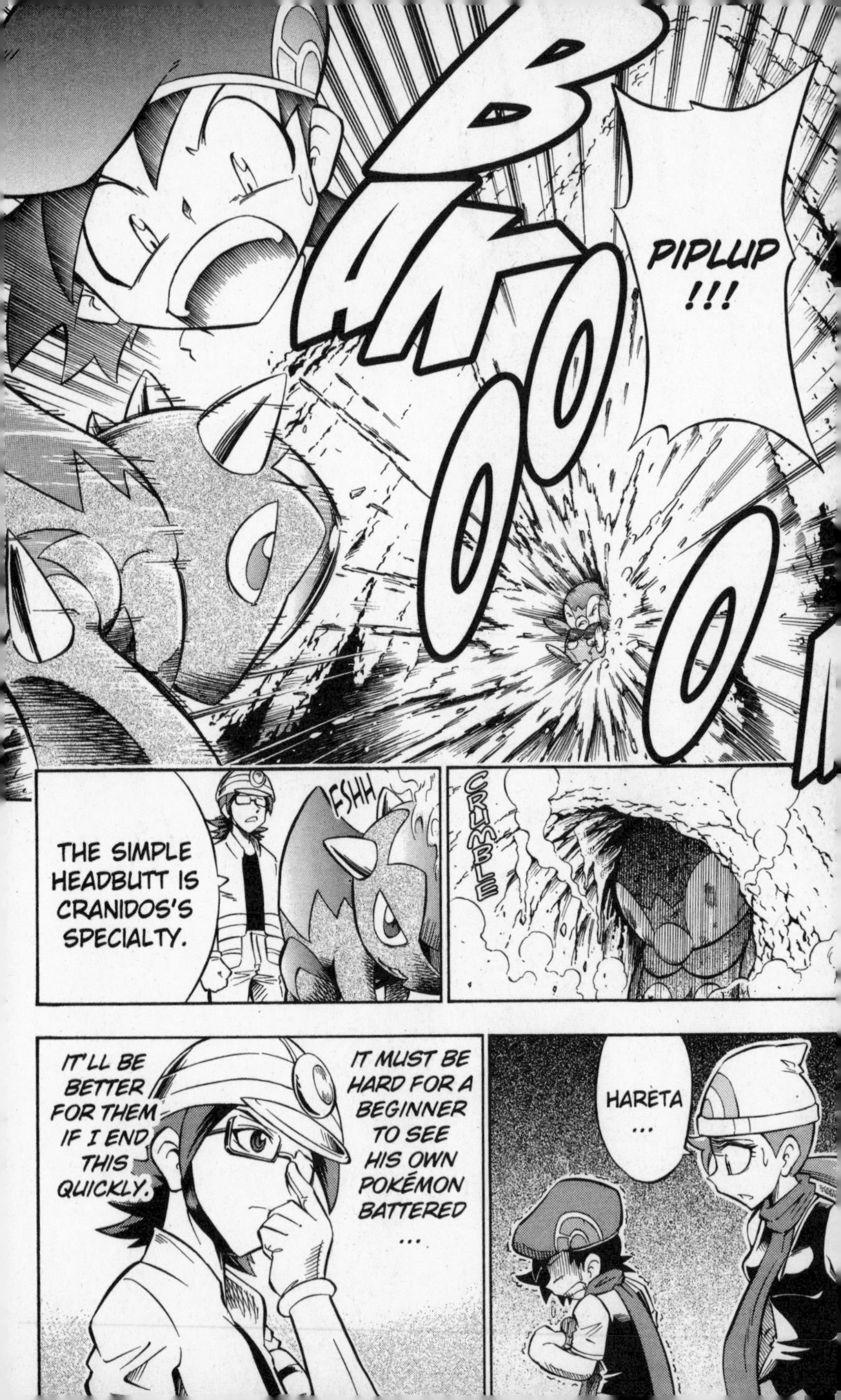
PIPLUP !!!
CRUMBLE
FSHH
THE SIMPLE HEADBUTT IS CRANIDOS'S SPECIALTY.
HARETA ...
IT MUST BE HARD FOR A BEGINNER TO SEE HIS OWN POKÉMON BATTERED ...
IT'LL BE BETTER FOR THEM IF I END THIS QUICKLY.

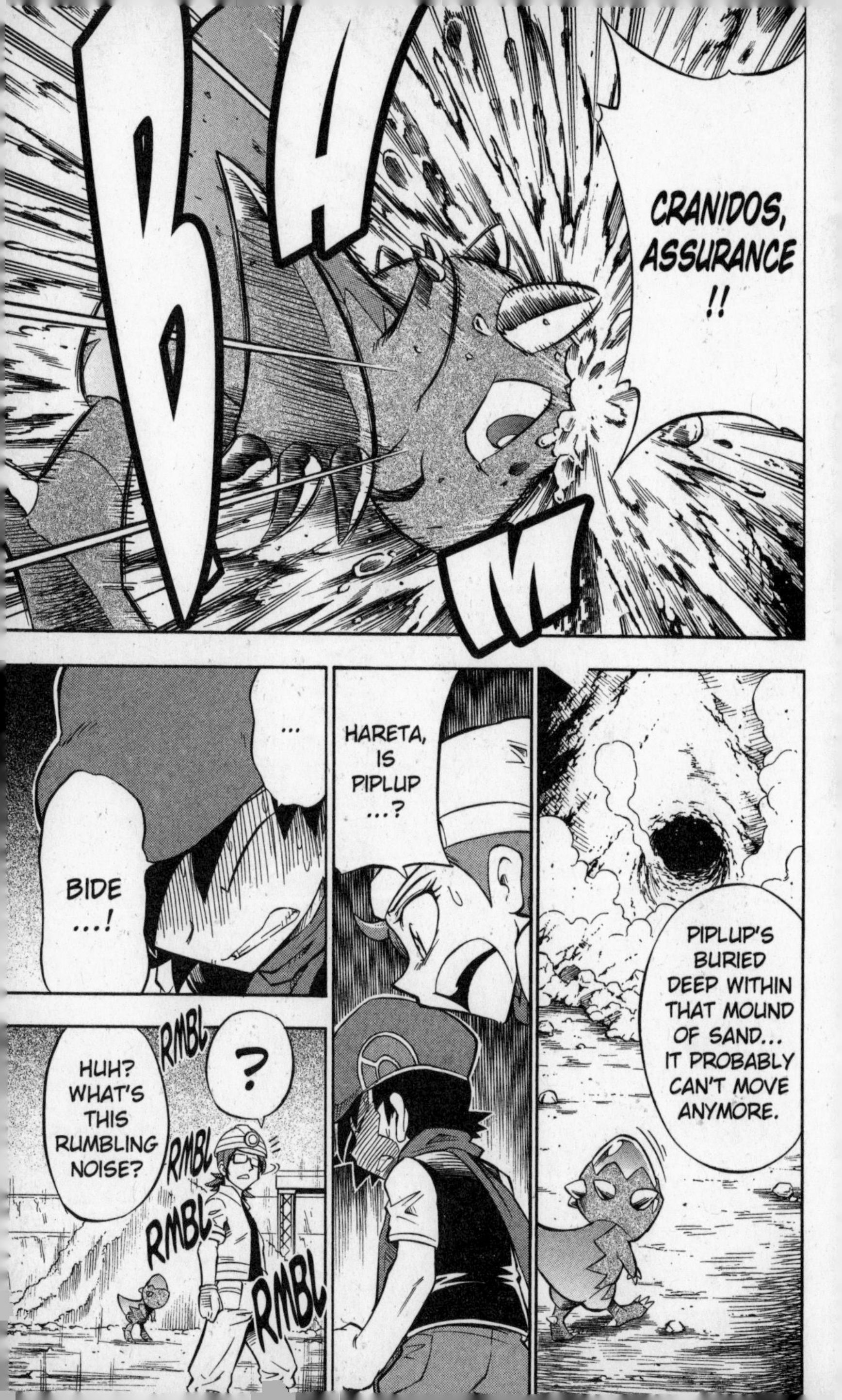
CRANIDOS, ASSURANCE !!
BAM
PIPLUP'S BURIED DEEP WITHIN THAT MOUND OF SAND... IT PROBABLY CAN'T MOVE ANYMORE.
HARETA, IS PIPLUP ...?
...
BIDE ...!
?
HUH? WHAT'S THIS RUMBLING NOISE?
RMBL
RMBL
RMBL
RMBL

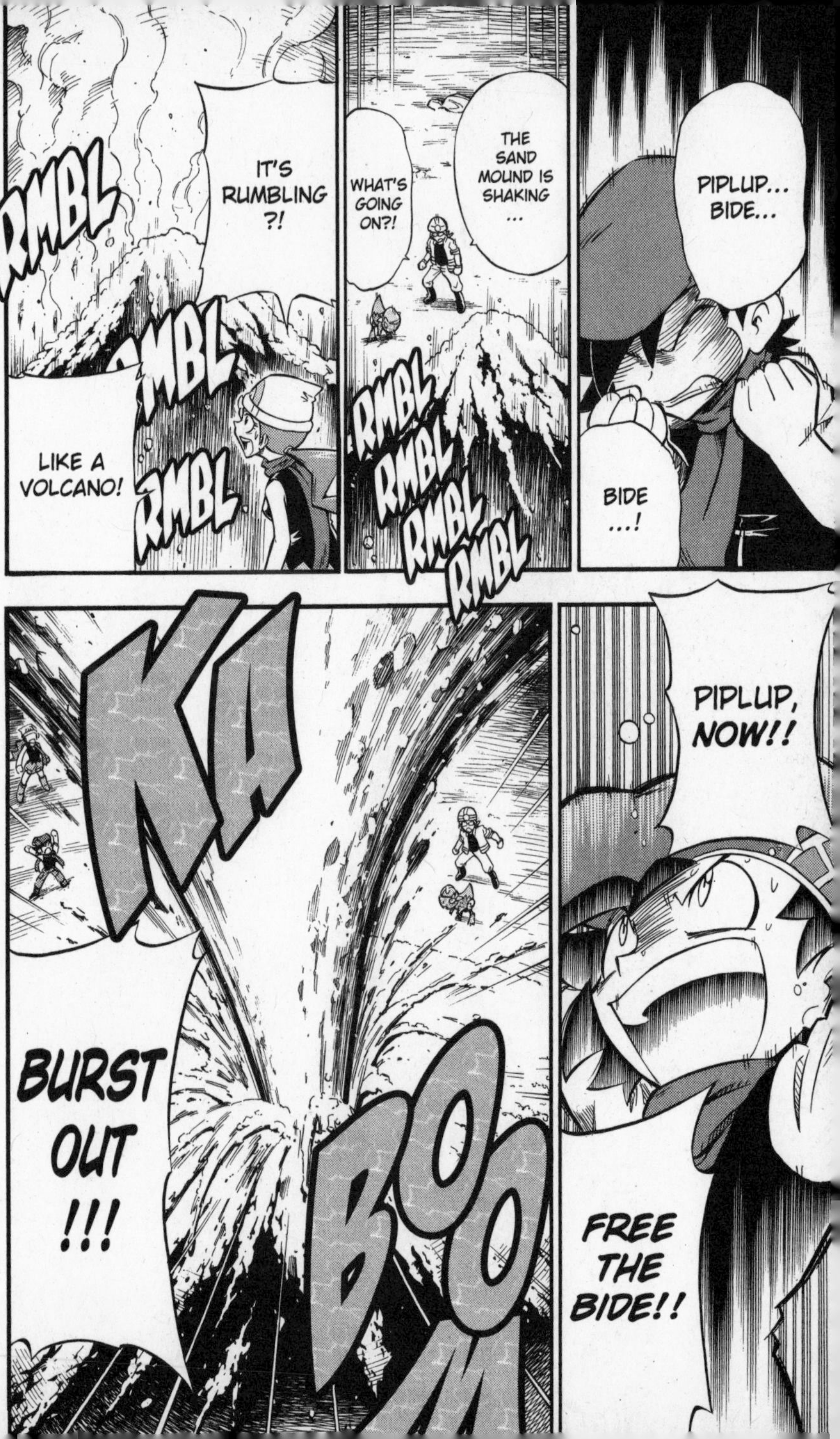
PIPLUP... BIDE...
BIDE ...!
THE SAND MOUND IS SHAKING ...
WHAT'S GOING ON?!
RMBL
RMBL
RMBL
RMBL
RMBL
IT'S RUMBLING ?!
MBL
RMBL
LIKE A VOLCANO!
PIPLUP, NOW!!
FREE THE BIDE!!
KA
BOOM
BURST OUT !!!

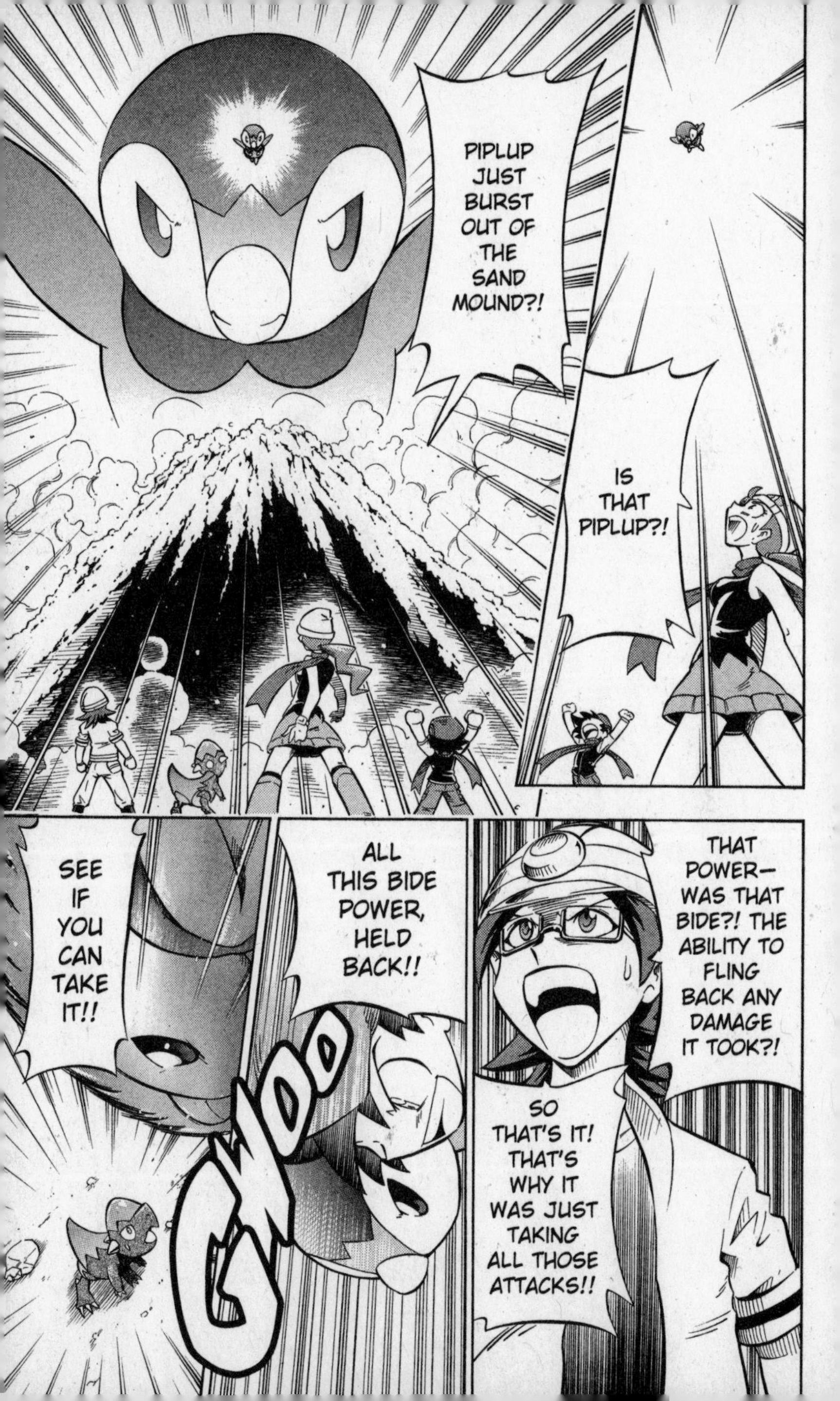
IS THAT PIPLUP?!
PIPLUP JUST BURST OUT OF THE SAND MOUND?!
THAT POWER— WAS THAT BIDE?! THE ABILITY TO FLING BACK ANY DAMAGE IT TOOK?!
SO THAT'S IT! THAT'S WHY IT WAS JUST TAKING ALL THOSE ATTACKS!!
ALL THIS BIDE POWER, HELD BACK!!
SEE IF YOU CAN TAKE IT!!
GWOOO

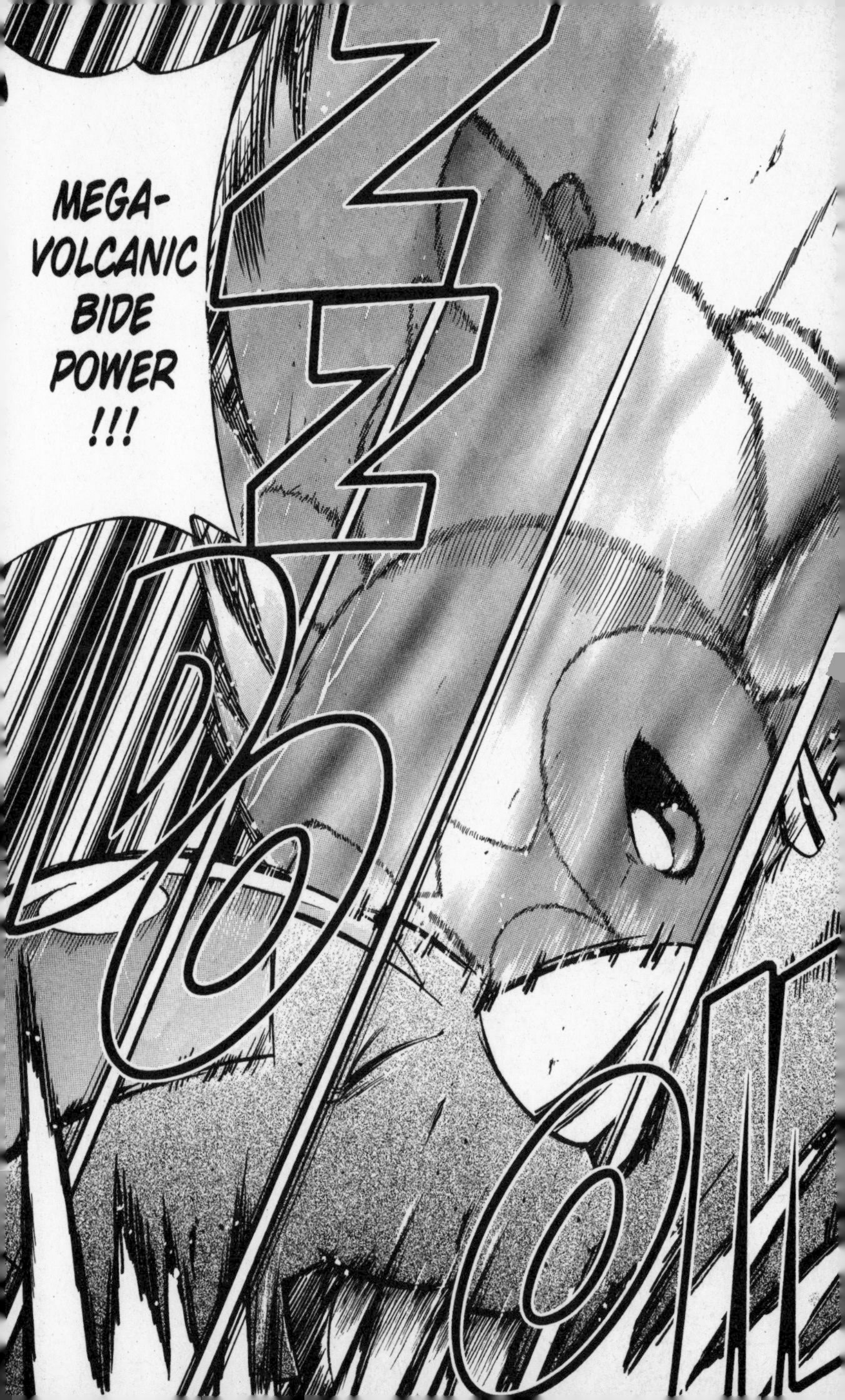
MEGA-VOLCANIC BIDE POWER !!!

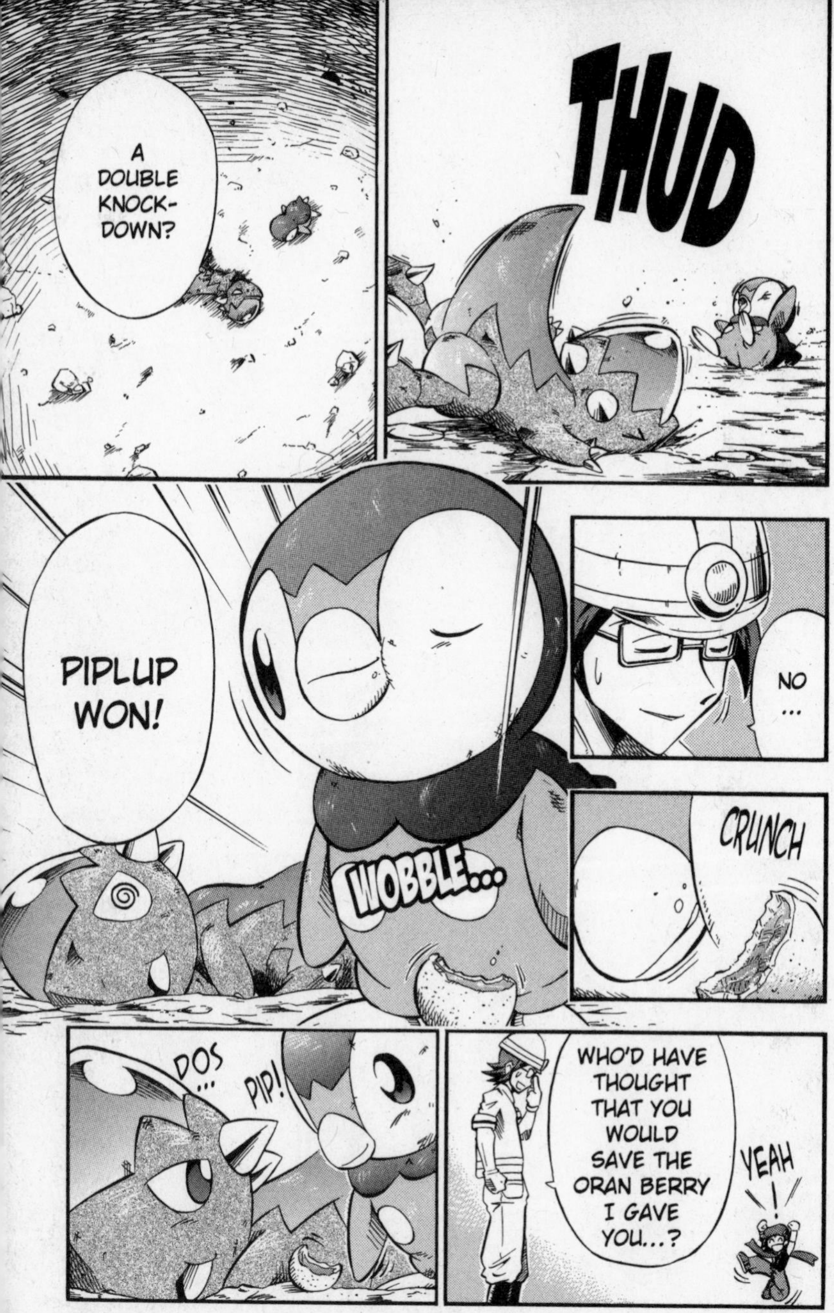
THUD
A DOUBLE KNOCK-DOWN?
NO...
CRUNCH
PIPLUP WON!
WOBBLE...
WHO'D HAVE THOUGHT THAT YOU WOULD SAVE THE ORAN BERRY I GAVE YOU...?
YEAH!
DOS...
PIP!

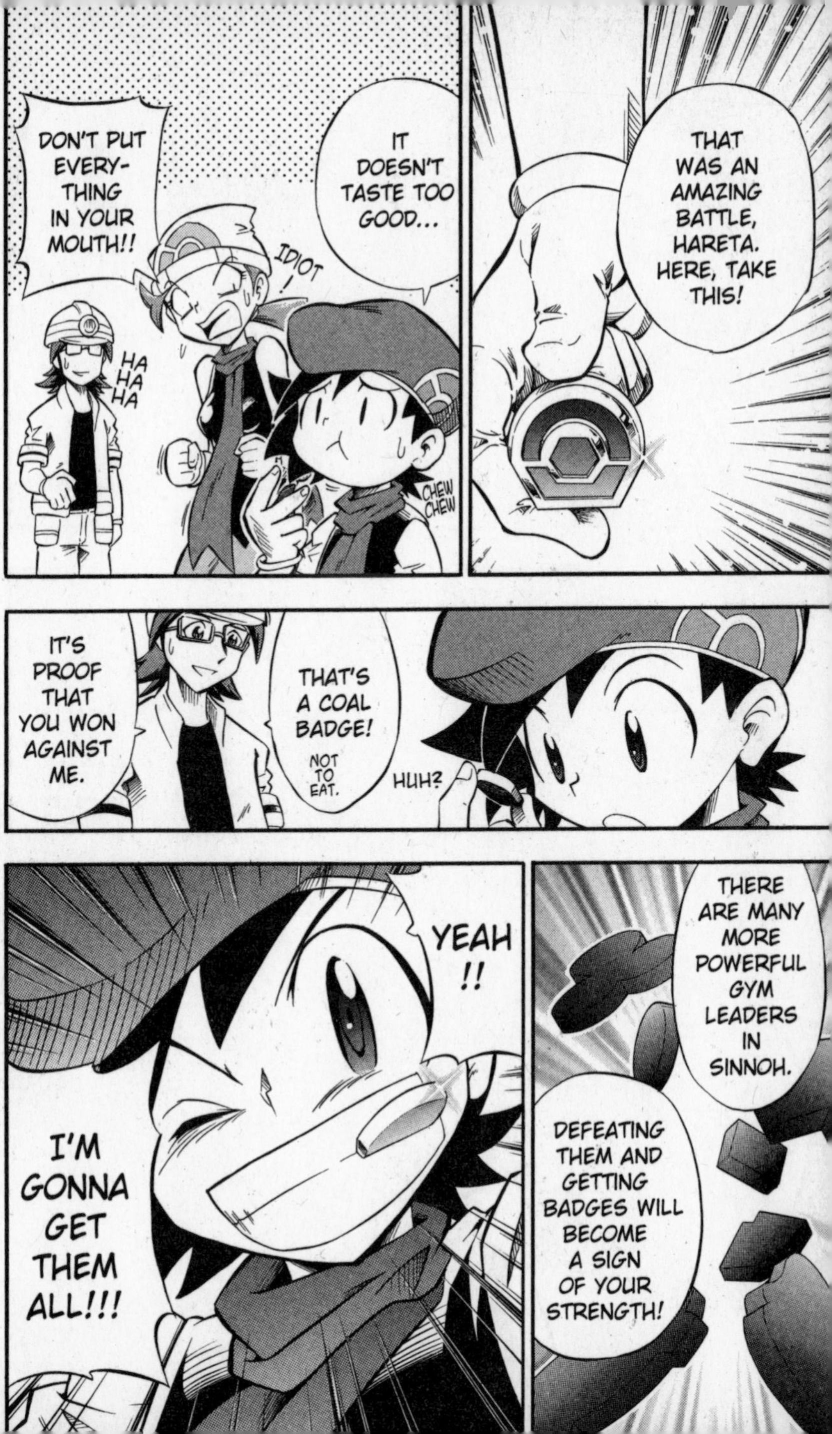
THAT WAS AN AMAZING BATTLE, HARETA. HERE, TAKE THIS!
IT DOESN'T TASTE TOO GOOD...
DON'T PUT EVERY-THING IN YOUR MOUTH!!
IDIOT!
HA HA HA
CHEW CHEW
HUH?
THAT'S A COAL BADGE!
NOT TO EAT.
IT'S PROOF THAT YOU WON AGAINST ME.
THERE ARE MANY MORE POWERFUL GYM LEADERS IN SINNOH.
DEFEATING THEM AND GETTING BADGES WILL BECOME A SIGN OF YOUR STRENGTH!
YEAH!!
I'M GONNA GET THEM ALL!!!

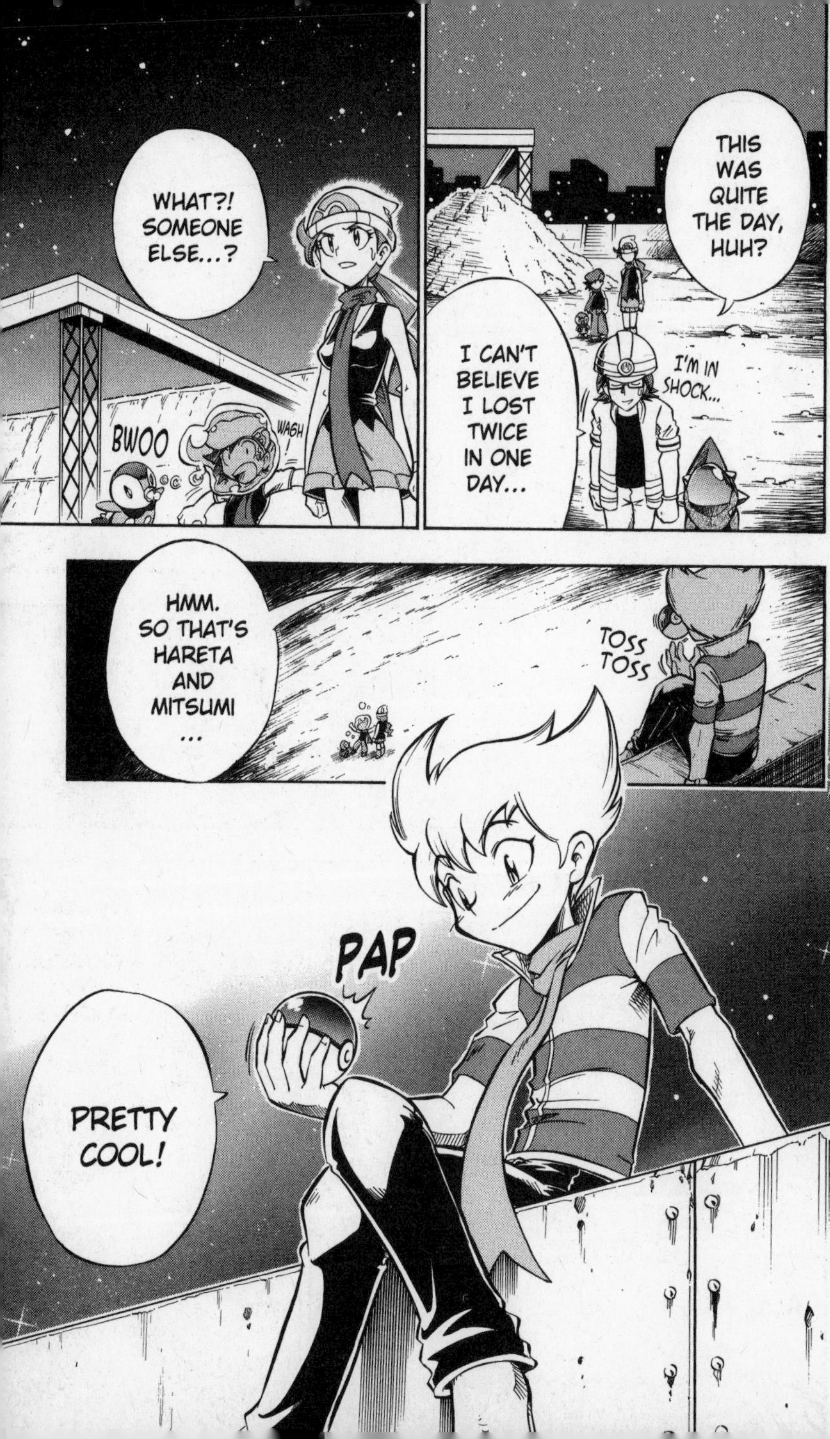

THIS WAS QUITE THE DAY, HUH?
I CAN'T BELIEVE I LOST TWICE IN ONE DAY...
I'M IN SHOCK...
WHAT?! SOMEONE ELSE...?
WAGH!
BWOO
TOSS TOSS
HMM. SO THAT'S HARETA AND MITSUMI...
PAP
PRETTY COOL!

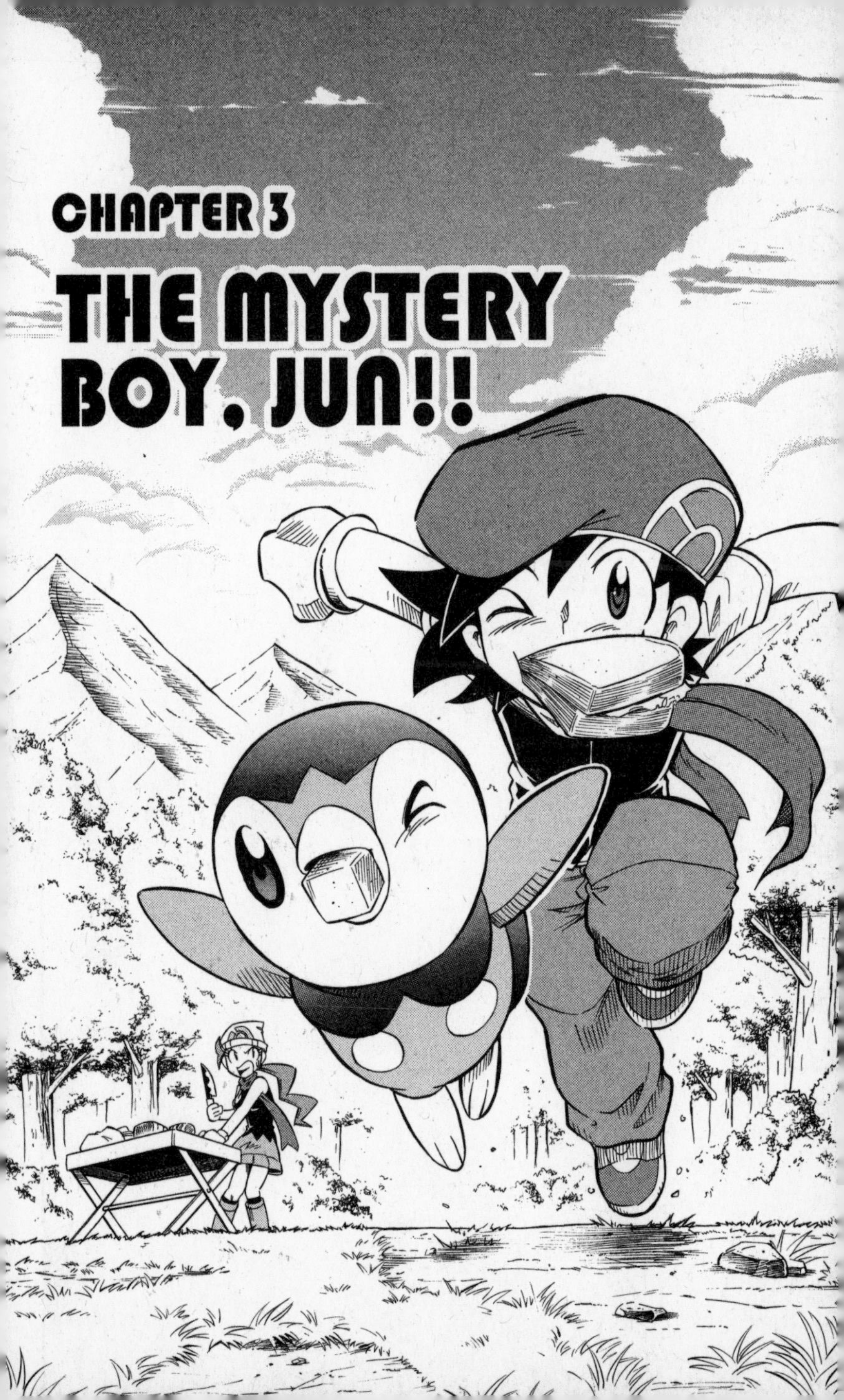
CHAPTER 3
THE MYSTERY BOY, JUN!!

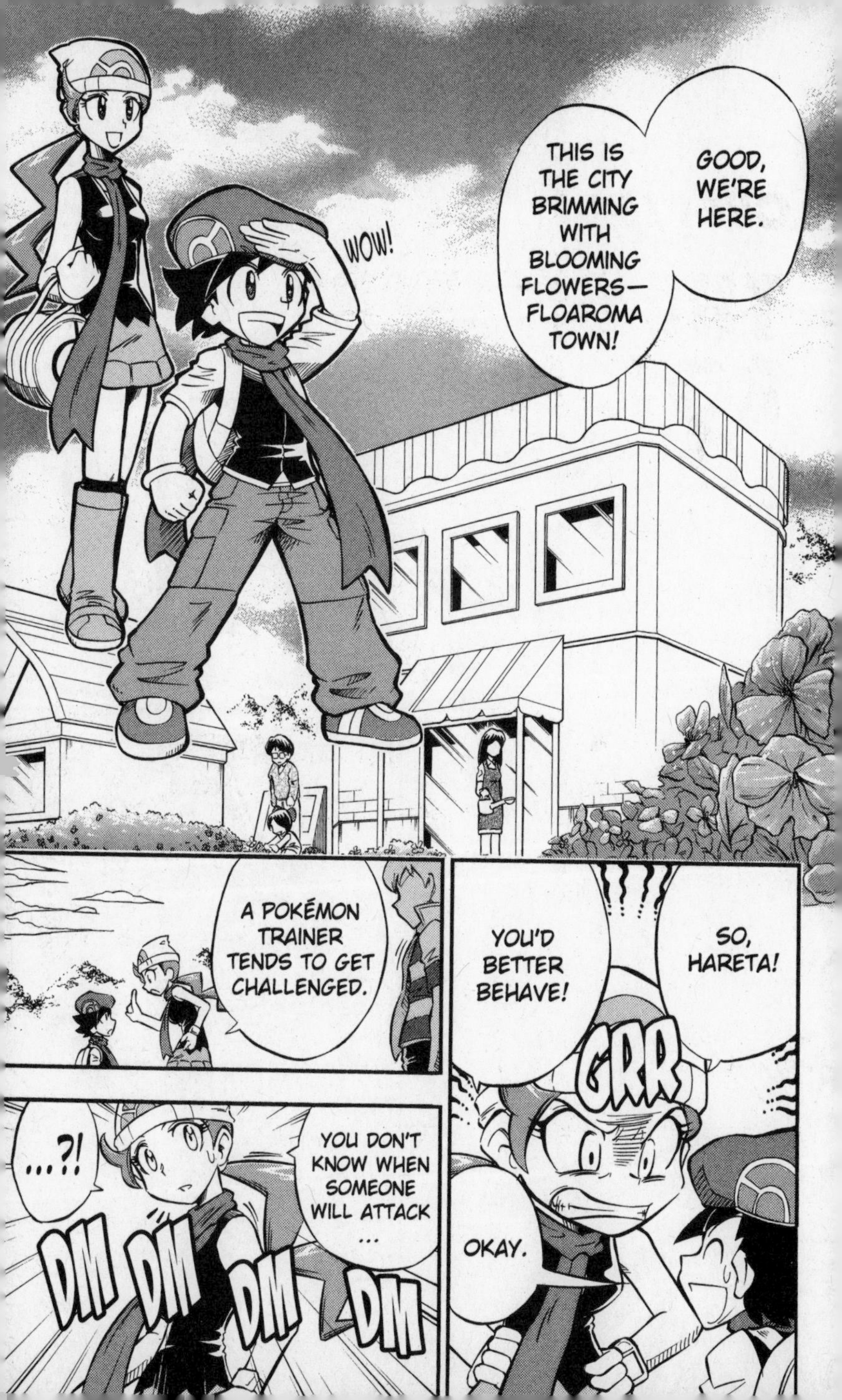
GOOD, WE'RE HERE.
THIS IS THE CITY BRIMMING WITH BLOOMING FLOWERS— FLOAROMA TOWN!
WOW!
SO, HARETA!
YOU'D BETTER BEHAVE!
GRR
OKAY.
A POKÉMON TRAINER TENDS TO GET CHALLENGED.
YOU DON'T KNOW WHEN SOMEONE WILL ATTACK ...
...?!
DM DM DM DM

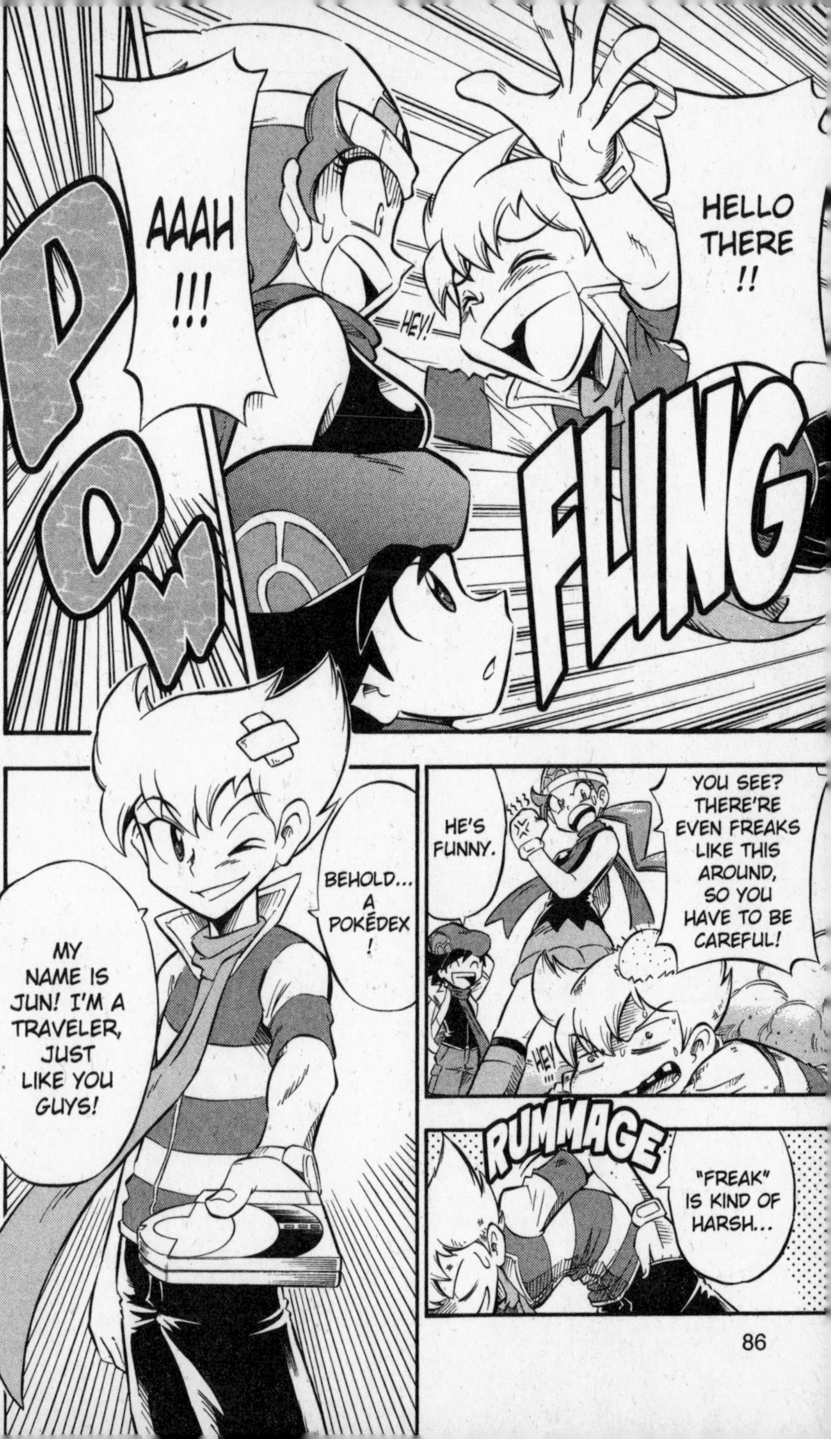
HELLO THERE !!
FLING
HEY!
AAAH !!!
POW
YOU SEE? THERE'RE EVEN FREAKS LIKE THIS AROUND, SO YOU HAVE TO BE CAREFUL!
HE'S FUNNY.
HEY!
RUMMAGE
"FREAK" IS KIND OF HARSH...
BEHOLD... A POKÉDEX !
MY NAME IS JUN! I'M A TRAVELER, JUST LIKE YOU GUYS!

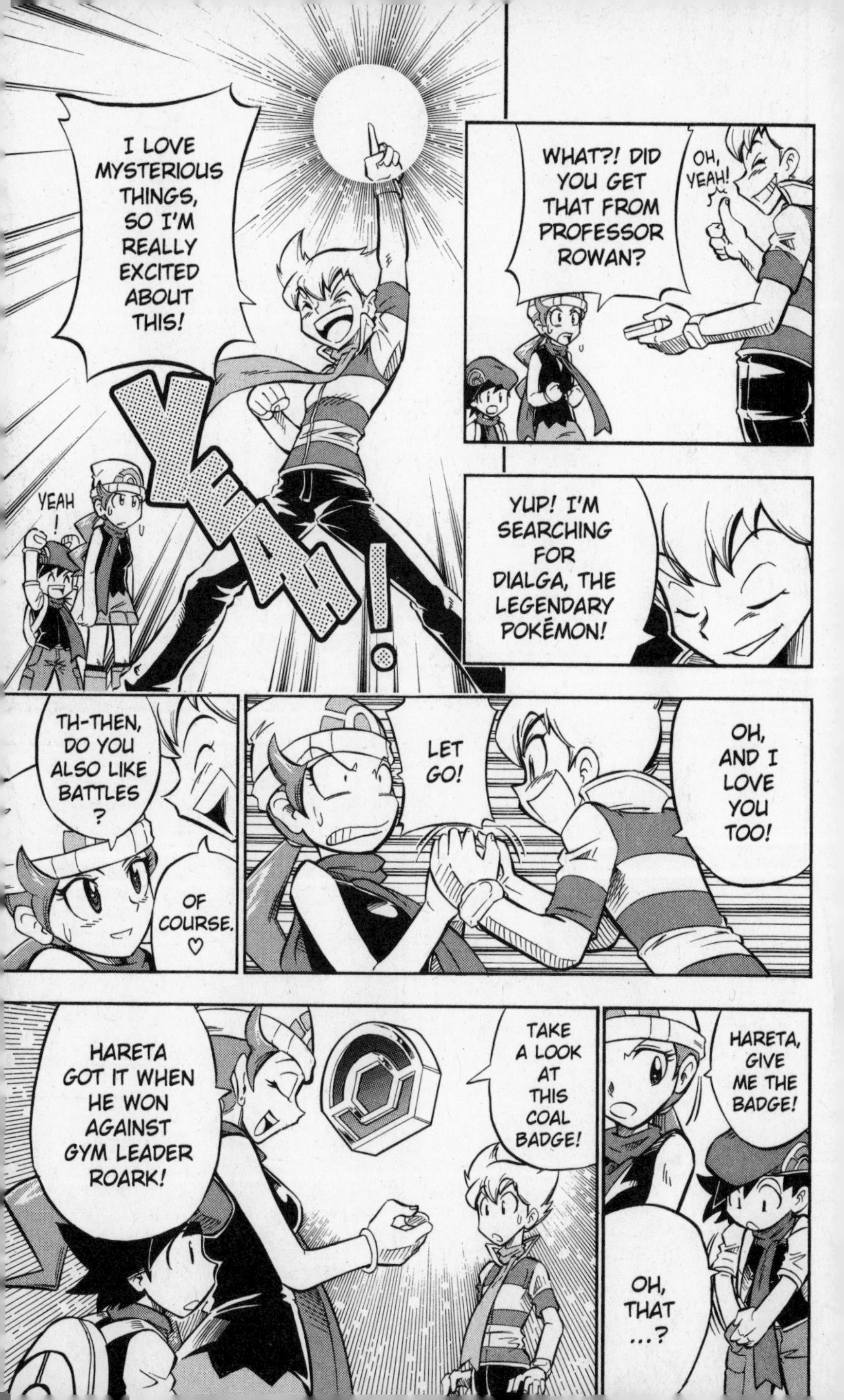
WHAT?! DID YOU GET THAT FROM PROFESSOR ROWAN?
OH, YEAH!
YUP! I'M SEARCHING FOR DIALGA, THE LEGENDARY POKÉMON!
I LOVE MYSTERIOUS THINGS, SO I'M REALLY EXCITED ABOUT THIS!
YEAH!
YEAH !
OH, AND I LOVE YOU TOO!
LET GO!
TH-THEN, DO YOU ALSO LIKE BATTLES ?
OF COURSE. ♡
HARETA, GIVE ME THE BADGE!
OH, THAT ...?
TAKE A LOOK AT THIS COAL BADGE!
HARETA GOT IT WHEN HE WON AGAINST GYM LEADER ROARK!

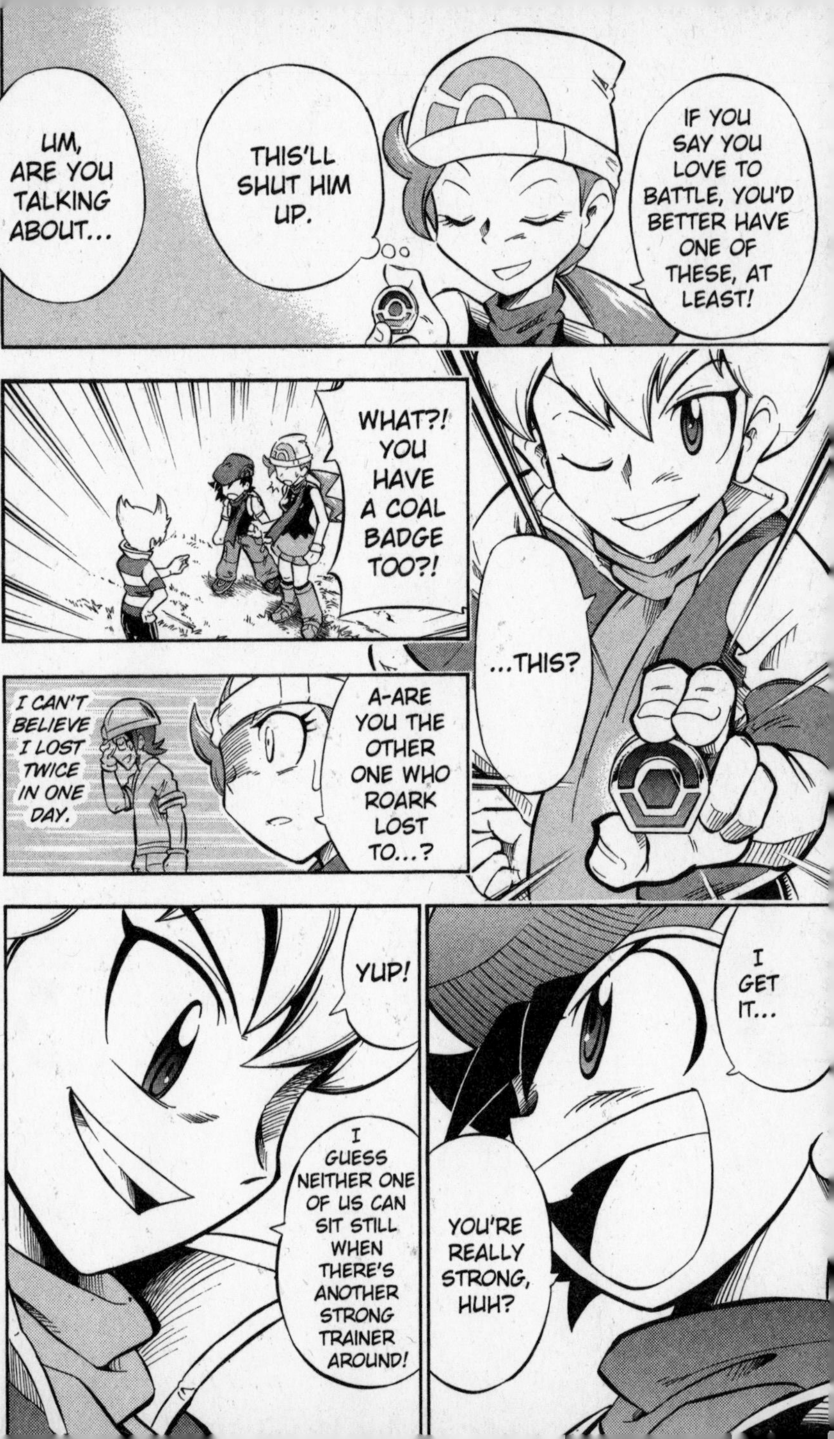
IF YOU SAY YOU LOVE TO BATTLE, YOU'D BETTER HAVE ONE OF THESE, AT LEAST!
THIS'LL SHUT HIM UP.
UM, ARE YOU TALKING ABOUT...
...THIS?
WHAT?! YOU HAVE A COAL BADGE TOO?!
A-ARE YOU THE OTHER ONE WHO ROARK LOST TO...?
I CAN'T BELIEVE I LOST TWICE IN ONE DAY.
I GET IT...
YOU'RE REALLY STRONG, HUH?
YUP!
I GUESS NEITHER ONE OF US CAN SIT STILL WHEN THERE'S ANOTHER STRONG TRAINER AROUND!

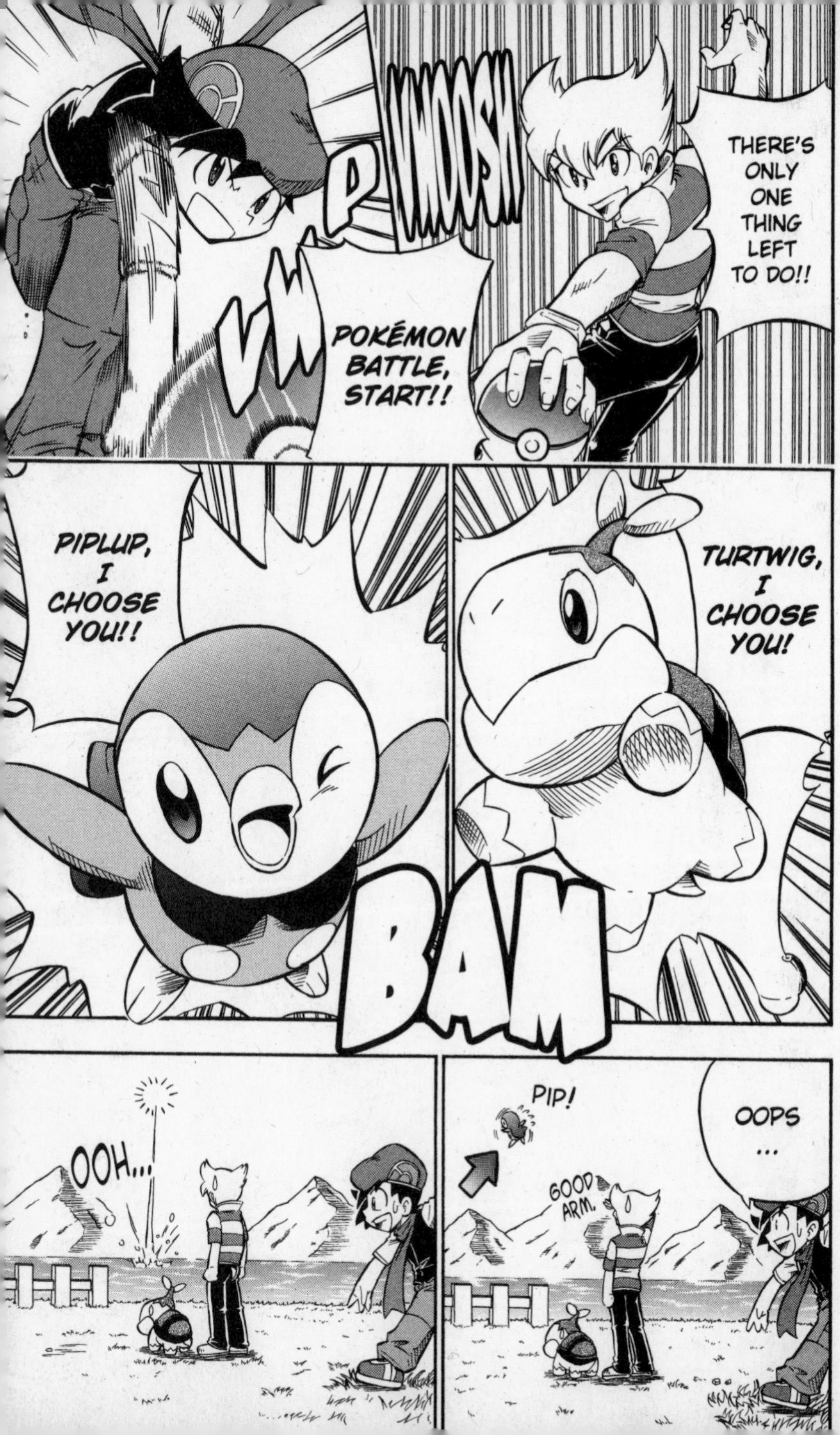
THERE'S ONLY ONE THING LEFT TO DO!!
WHOOSH
VWP
POKÉMON BATTLE, START!!
TURTWIG, I CHOOSE YOU!
PIPLUP, I CHOOSE YOU!!
BAM
OOPS ...
PIP!
GOOD ARM.
OOH...

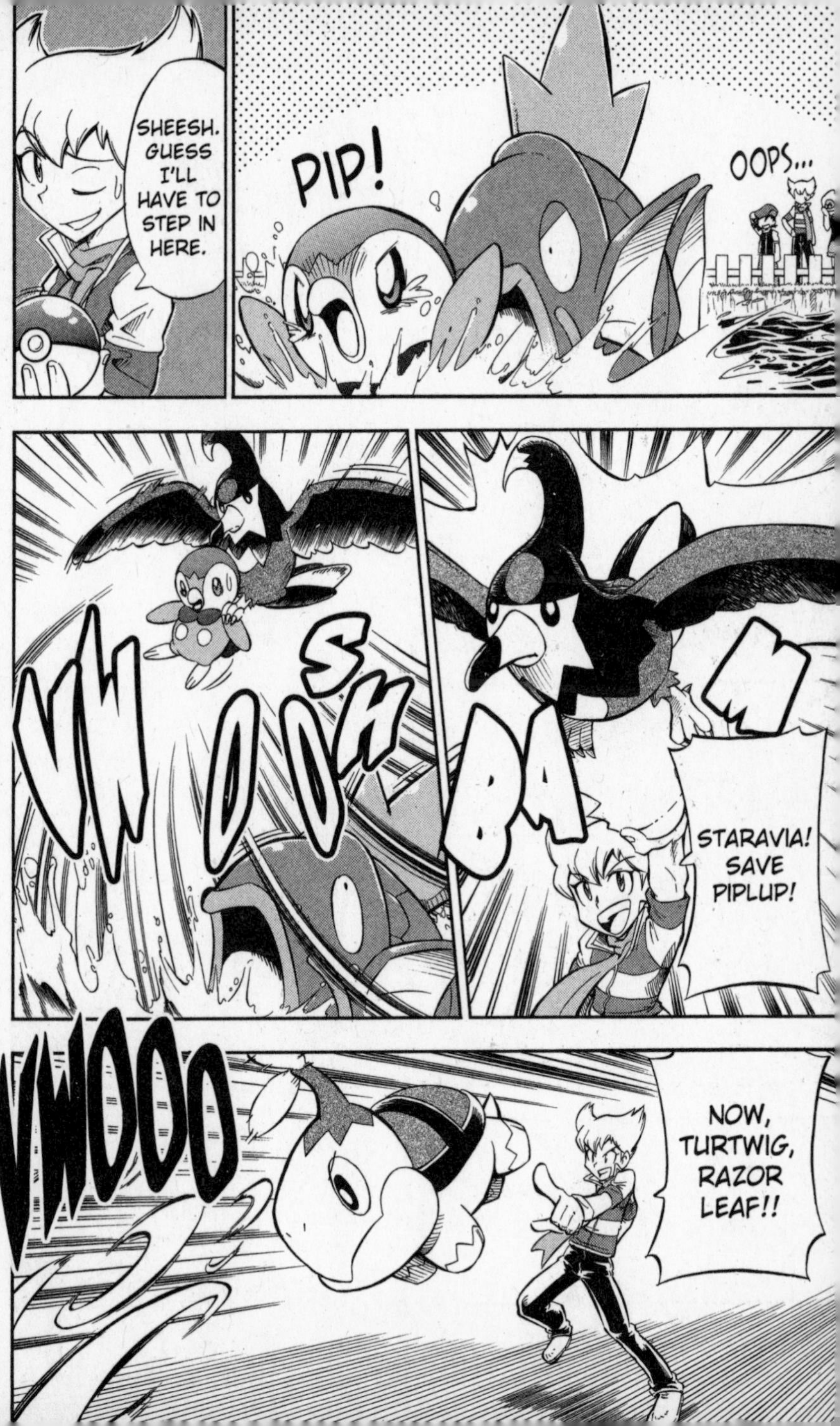
OOPS...
PIP!
SHEESH. GUESS I'LL HAVE TO STEP IN HERE.
BAM
STARAVIA! SAVE PIPLUP!
VWOOSH
VWOOO
NOW, TURTWIG, RAZOR LEAF!!

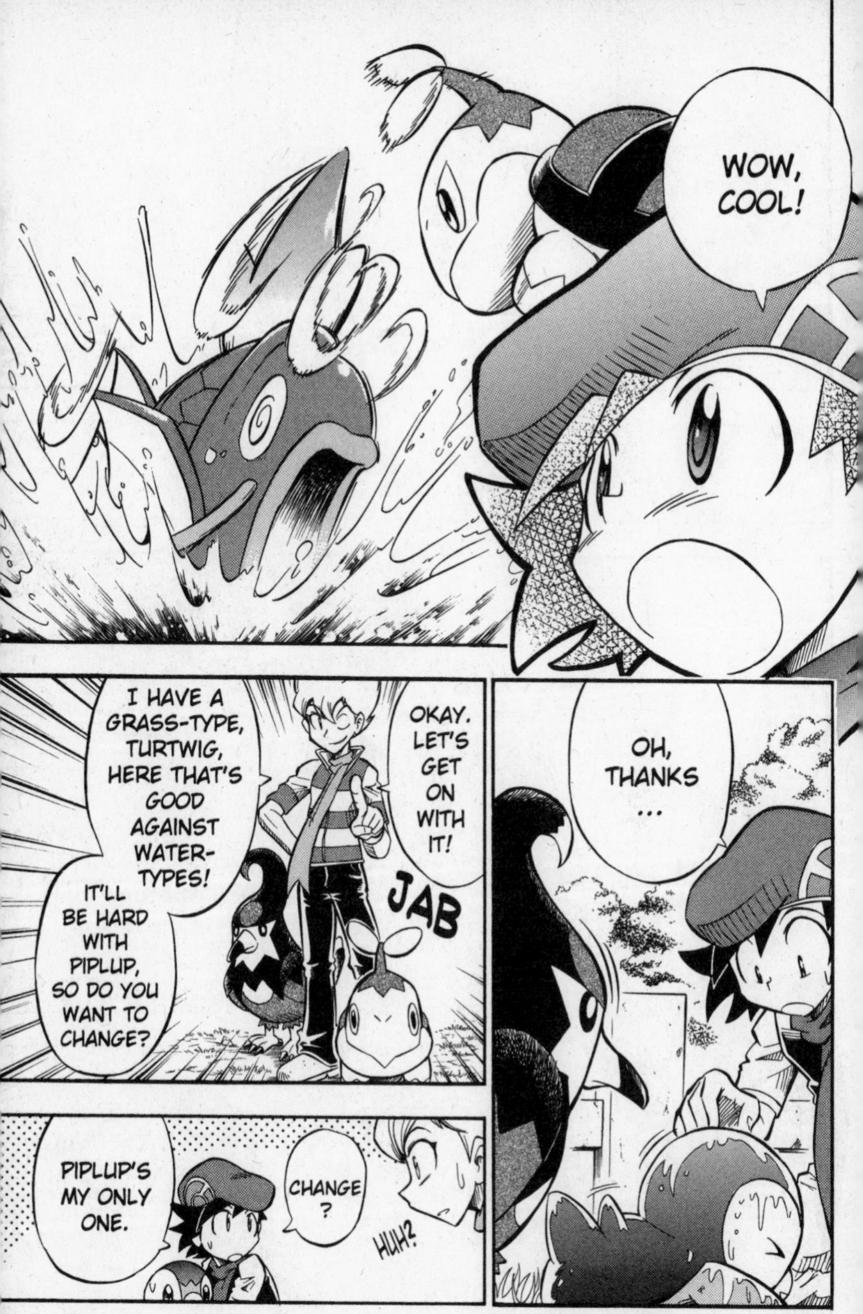
WOW, COOL!
OH, THANKS ...
OKAY. LET'S GET ON WITH IT!
JAB
I HAVE A GRASS-TYPE, TURTWIG, HERE THAT'S GOOD AGAINST WATER-TYPES!
IT'LL BE HARD WITH PIPLUP, SO DO YOU WANT TO CHANGE?
CHANGE?
HUH?
PIPLUP'S MY ONLY ONE.

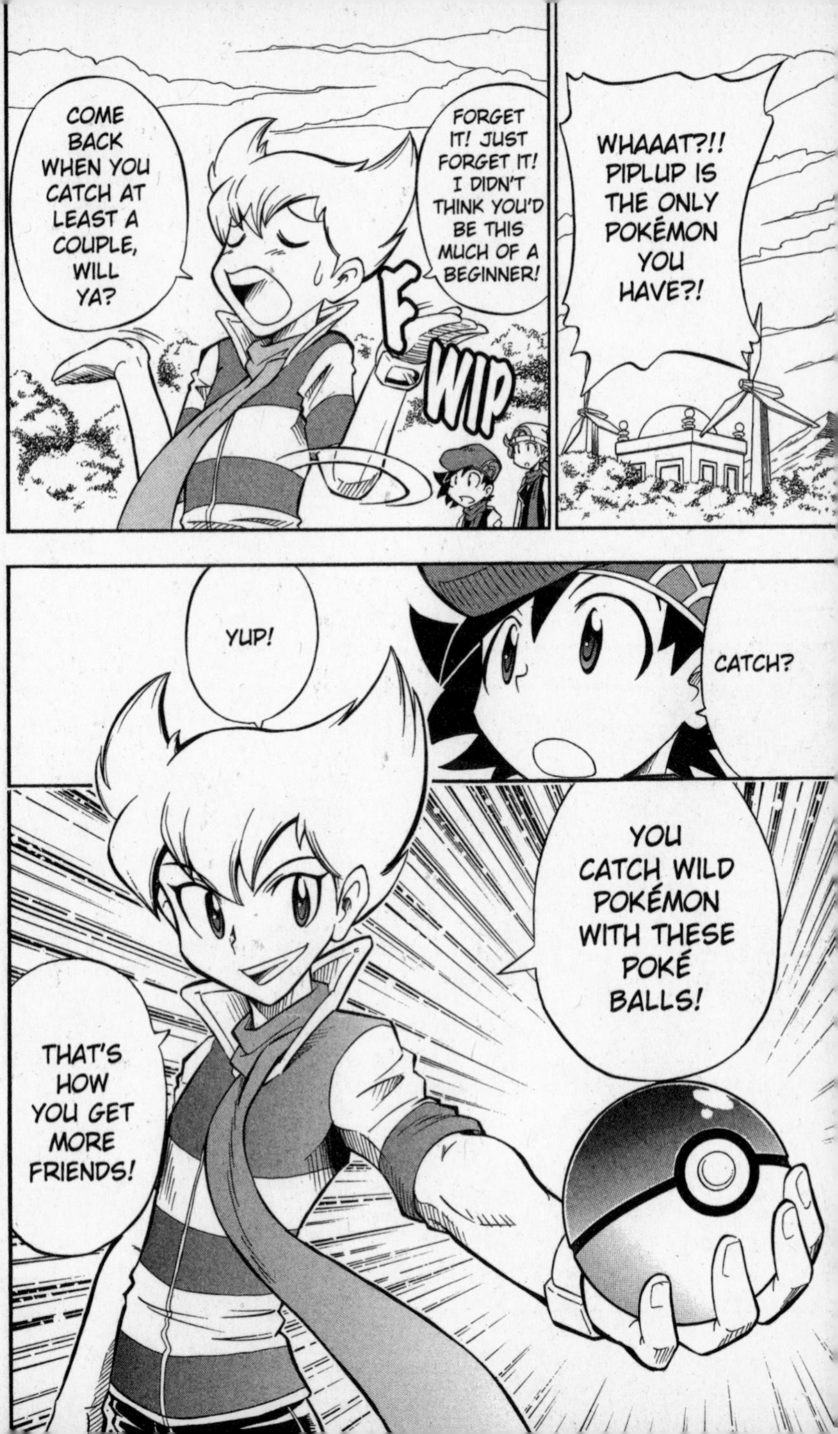
WHAAAT?!! PIPLUP IS THE ONLY POKÉMON YOU HAVE?!
FORGET IT! JUST FORGET IT! I DIDN'T THINK YOU'D BE THIS MUCH OF A BEGINNER!
FWIP
COME BACK WHEN YOU CATCH AT LEAST A COUPLE, WILL YA?
CATCH?
YUP!
YOU CATCH WILD POKÉMON WITH THESE POKÉ BALLS!
THAT'S HOW YOU GET MORE FRIENDS!

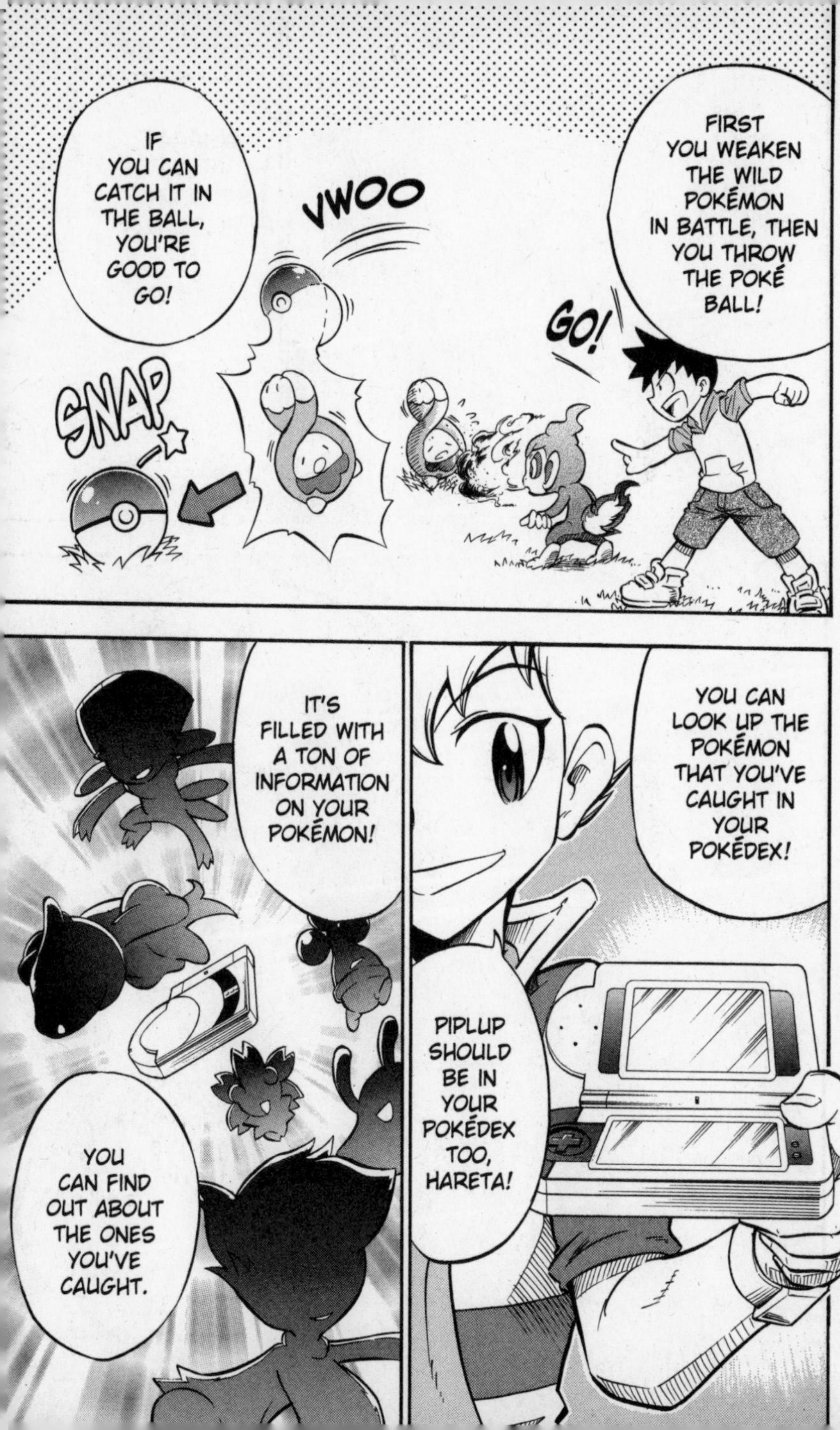
FIRST YOU WEAKEN THE WILD POKÉMON IN BATTLE, THEN YOU THROW THE POKÉ BALL!
GO!
VWOO
IF YOU CAN CATCH IT IN THE BALL, YOU'RE GOOD TO GO!
SNAP
YOU CAN LOOK UP THE POKÉMON THAT YOU'VE CAUGHT IN YOUR POKÉDEX!
PIPLUP SHOULD BE IN YOUR POKÉDEX TOO, HARETA!
IT'S FILLED WITH A TON OF INFORMATION ON YOUR POKÉMON!
YOU CAN FIND OUT ABOUT THE ONES YOU'VE CAUGHT.

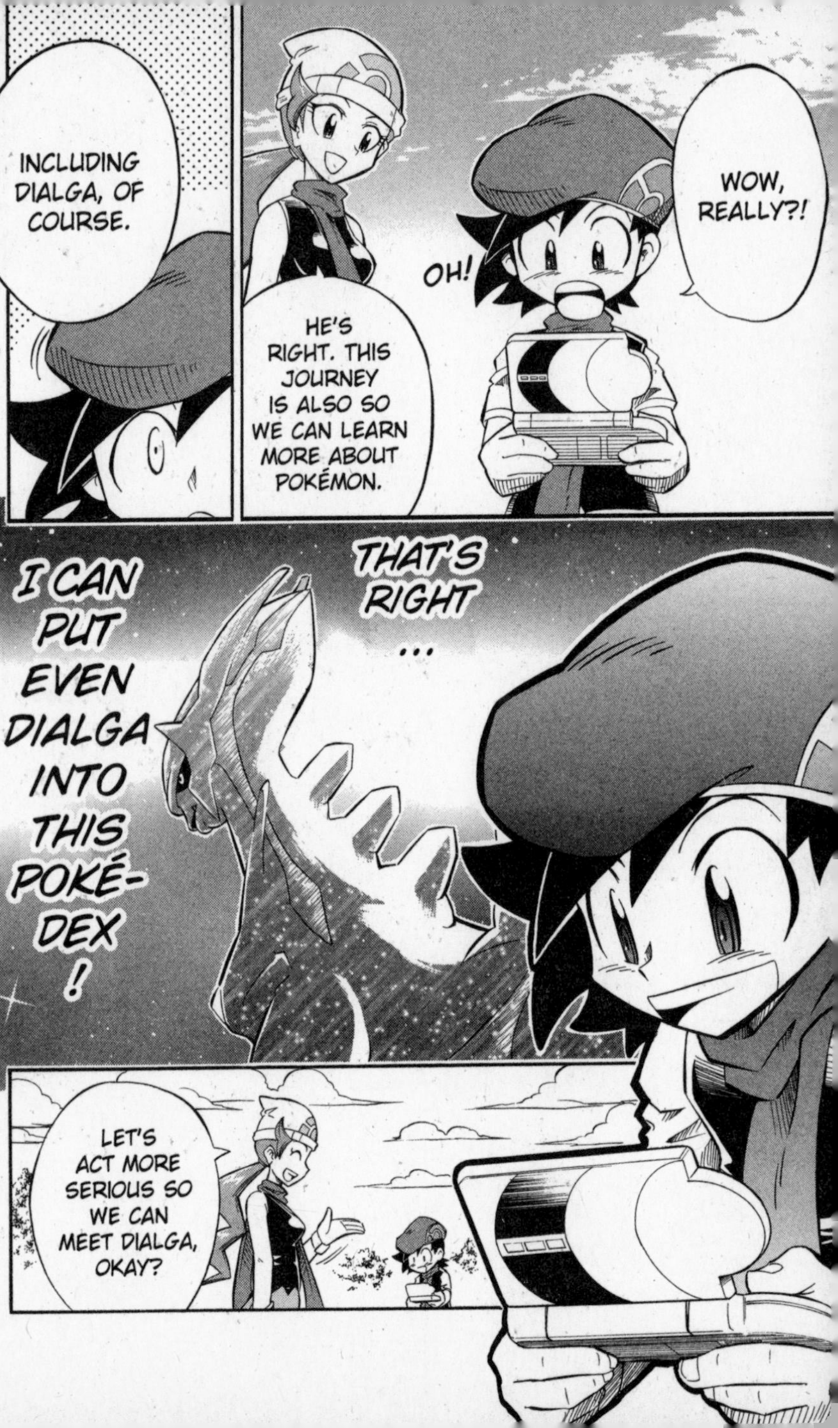
WOW, REALLY?!
OH!
HE'S RIGHT. THIS JOURNEY IS ALSO SO WE CAN LEARN MORE ABOUT POKÉMON.
INCLUDING DIALGA, OF COURSE.
THAT'S RIGHT ...
I CAN PUT EVEN DIALGA INTO THIS POKÉ-DEX!
LET'S ACT MORE SERIOUS SO WE CAN MEET DIALGA, OKAY?

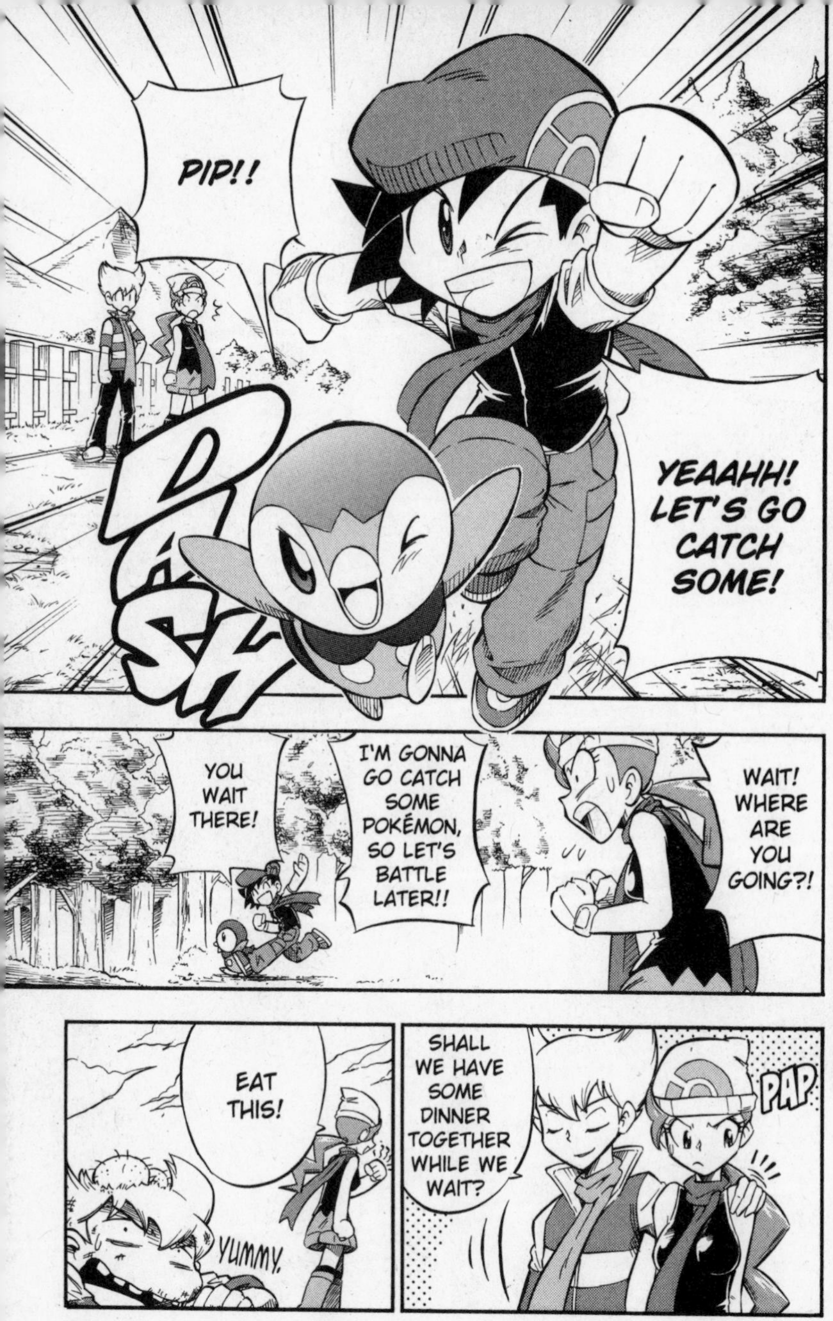
PIP!!
YEAAHH! LET'S GO CATCH SOME!
DASH
WAIT! WHERE ARE YOU GOING?!
I'M GONNA GO CATCH SOME POKÉMON, SO LET'S BATTLE LATER!!
YOU WAIT THERE!
PAP
SHALL WE HAVE SOME DINNER TOGETHER WHILE WE WAIT?
EAT THIS!
YUMMY

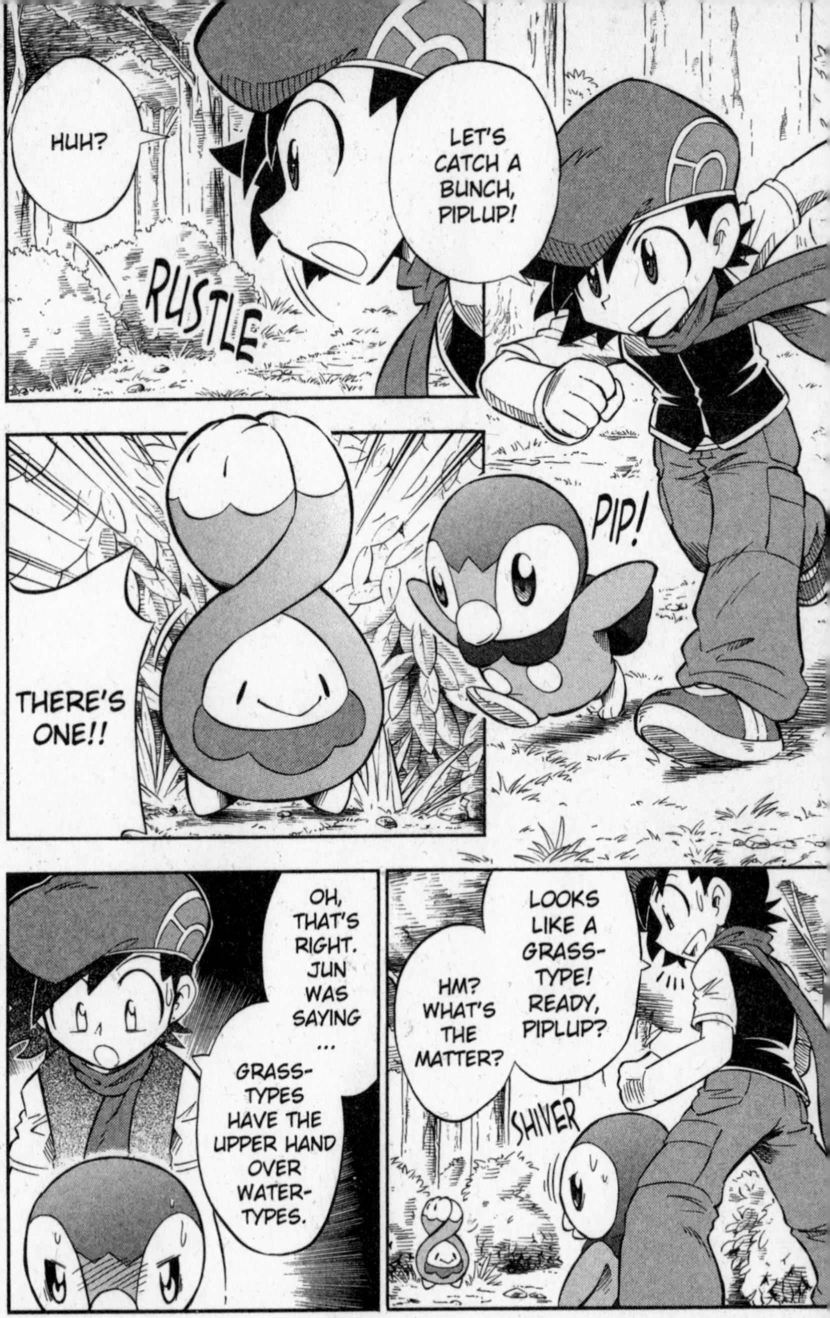
LET'S CATCH A BUNCH, PIPLUP!
PIP!
HUH?
RUSTLE
THERE'S ONE!!
LOOKS LIKE A GRASS-TYPE! READY, PIPLUP?
HM? WHAT'S THE MATTER?
SHIVER
OH, THAT'S RIGHT. JUN WAS SAYING...
GRASS-TYPES HAVE THE UPPER HAND OVER WATER-TYPES.

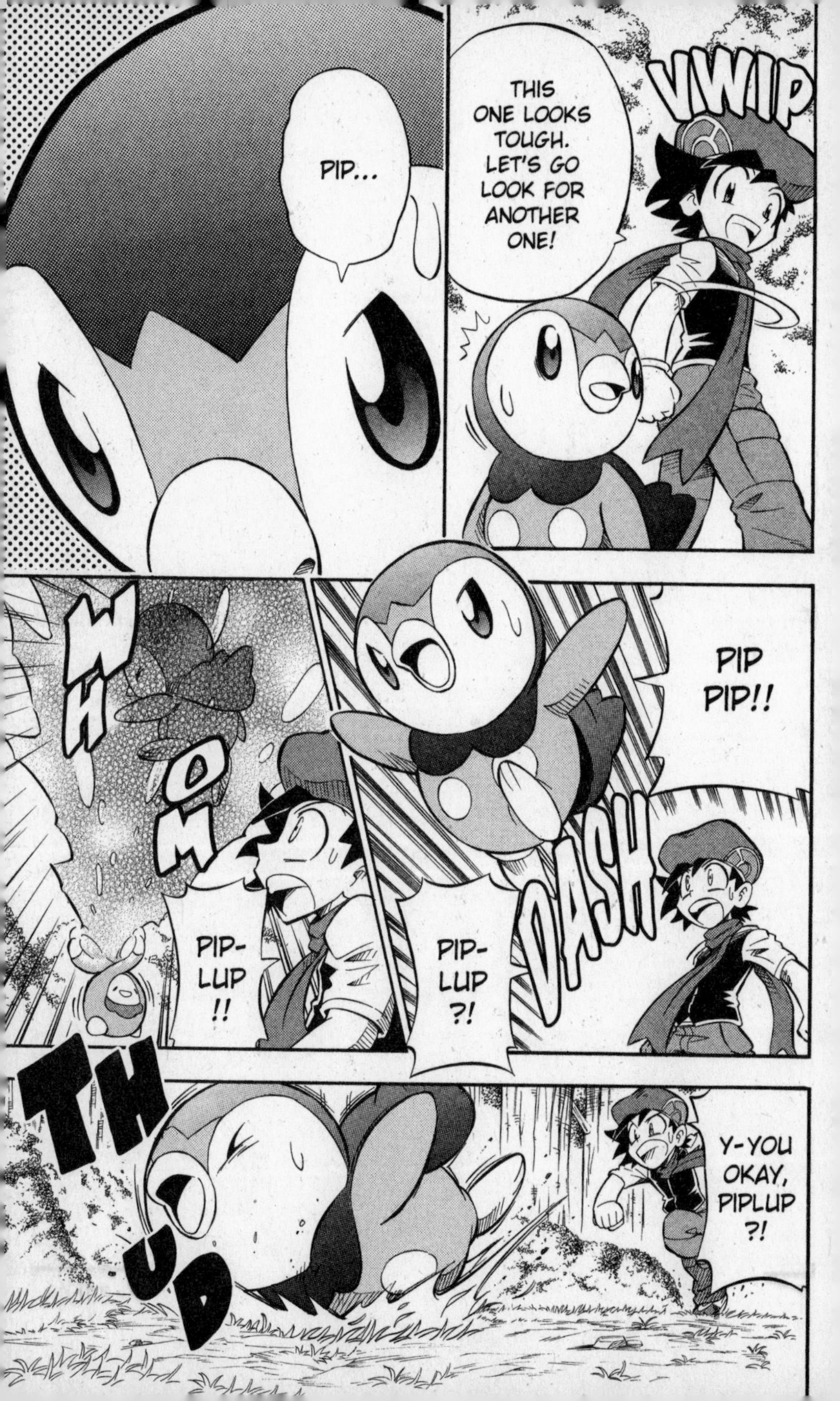
VWIP
THIS ONE LOOKS TOUGH. LET'S GO LOOK FOR ANOTHER ONE!
PIP...
PIP PIP!!
DASH
PIP-LUP ?!
WHOM
PIP-LUP !!
Y-YOU OKAY, PIPLUP ?!
THUD

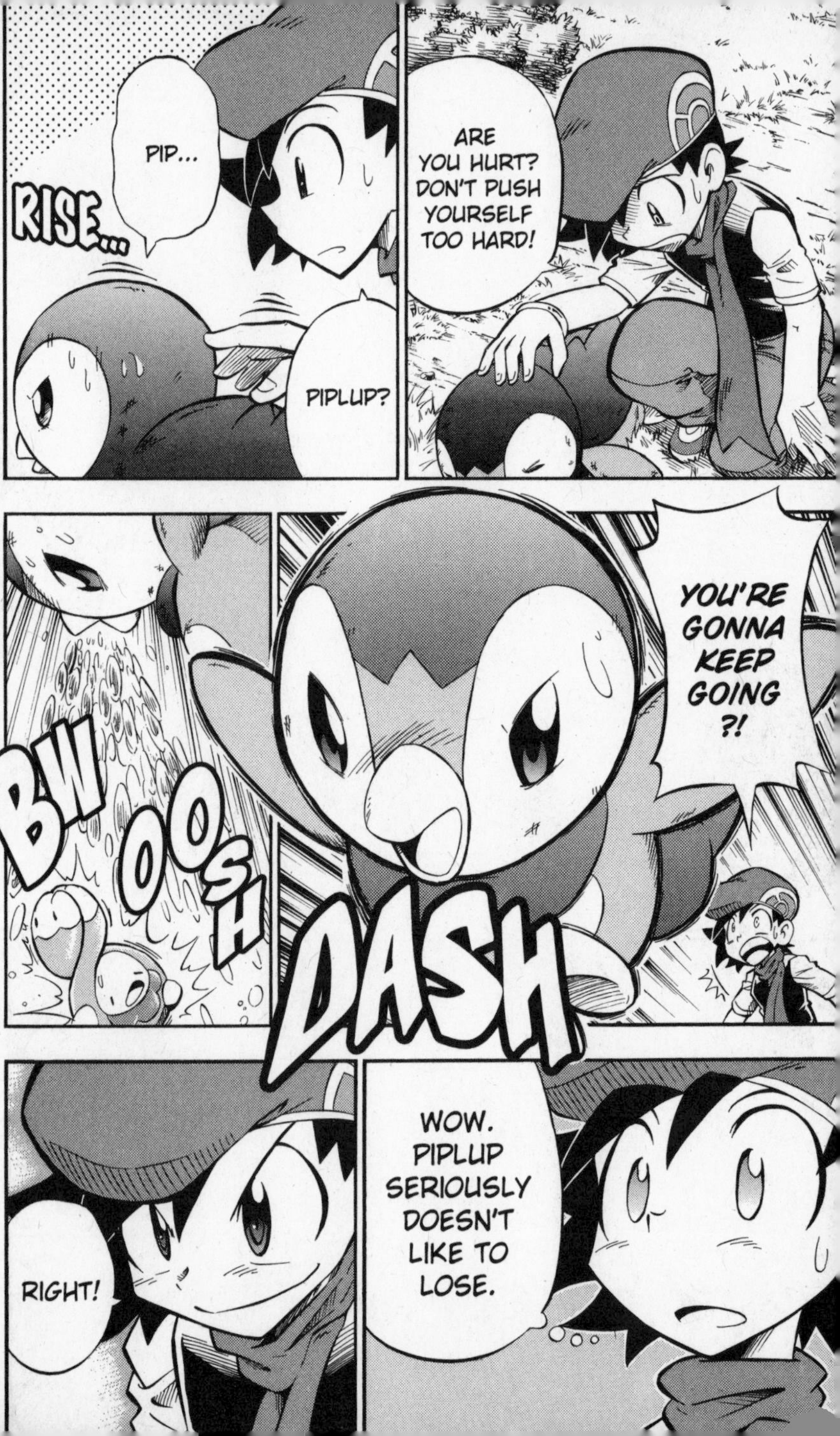

ARE YOU HURT? DON'T PUSH YOURSELF TOO HARD!
PIP...
RISE...
PIPLUP?
YOU'RE GONNA KEEP GOING?!
DASH
BWOOSH
WOW. PIPLUP SERIOUSLY DOESN'T LIKE TO LOSE.
RIGHT!

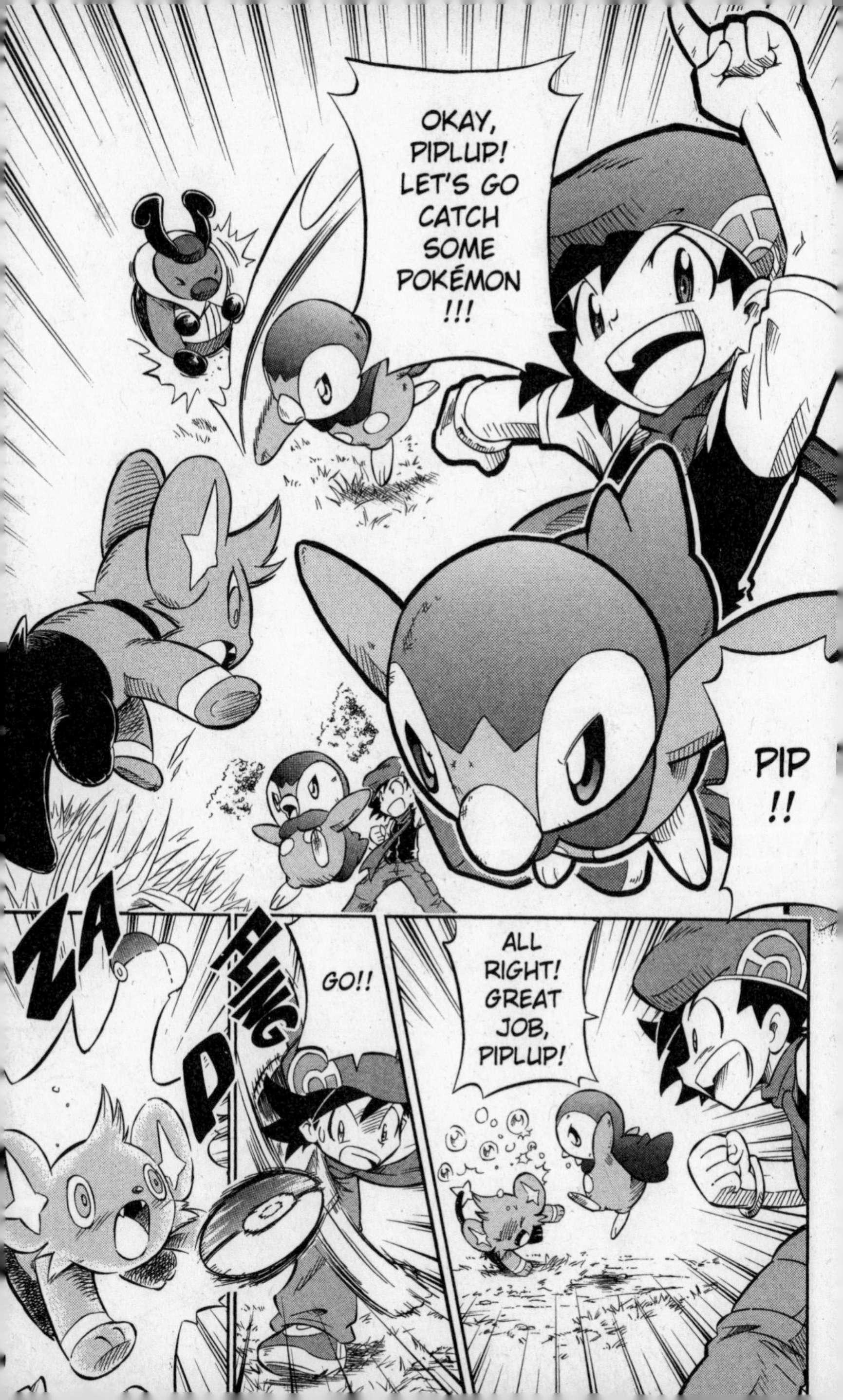
OKAY, PIPLUP! LET'S GO CATCH SOME POKÉMON!!!
PIP!!
ALL RIGHT! GREAT JOB, PIPLUP!
GO!!
FLING
ZAP

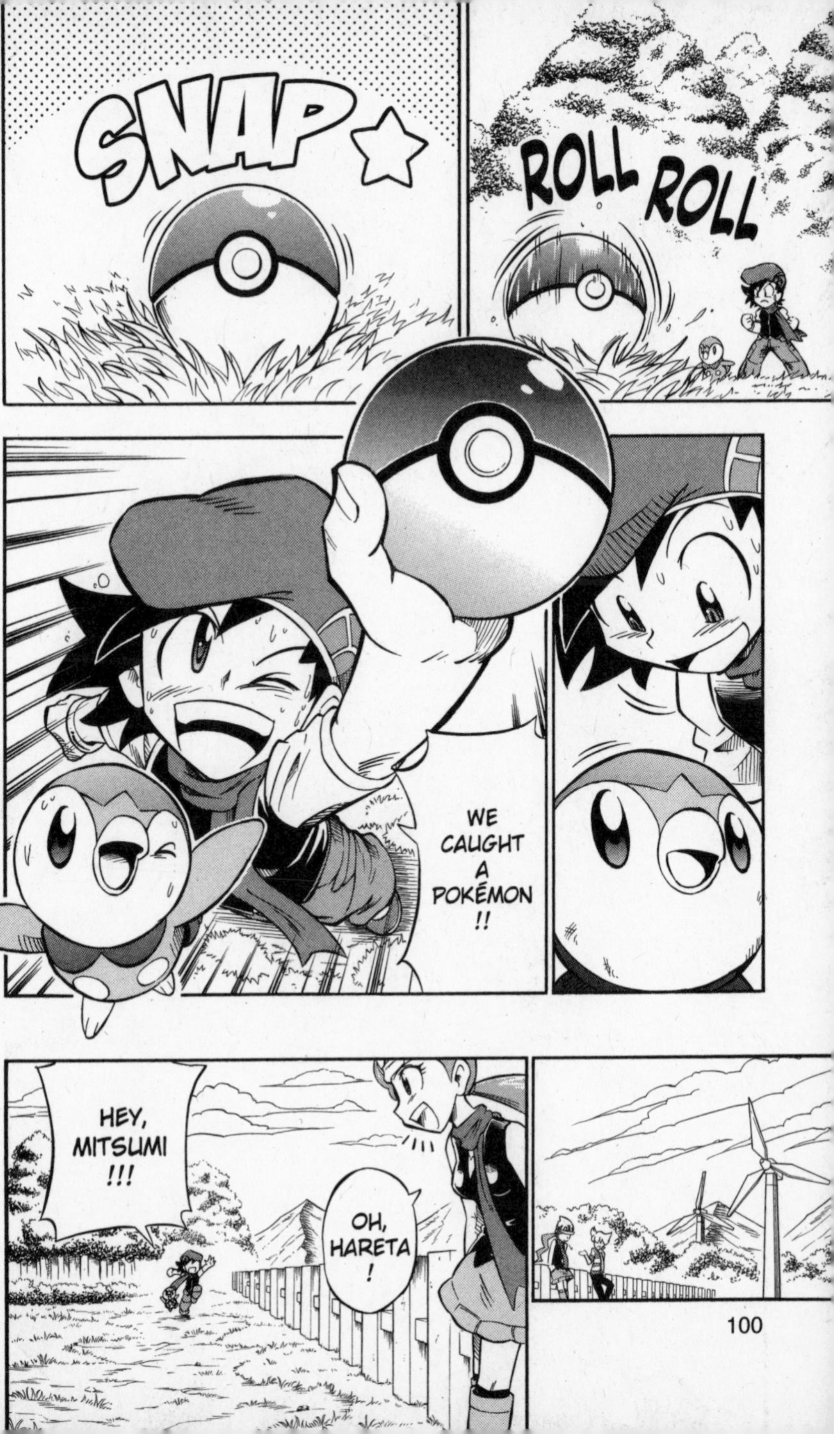
ROLL ROLL
SNAP ☆
WE CAUGHT A POKÉMON !!
HEY, MITSUMI !!!
OH, HARETA !

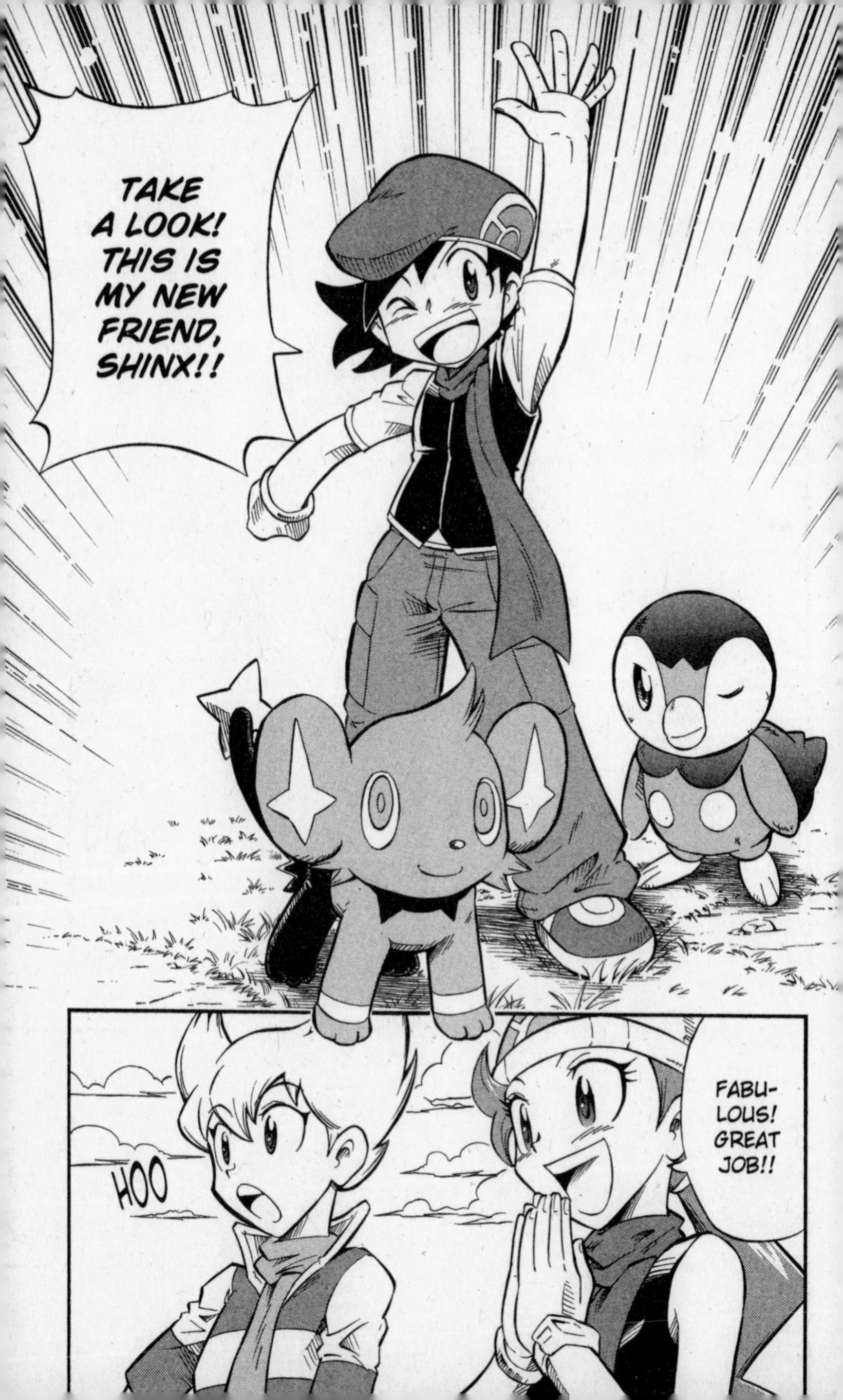
TAKE A LOOK! THIS IS MY NEW FRIEND, SHINX!!
FABU-LOUS! GREAT JOB!!
HOO

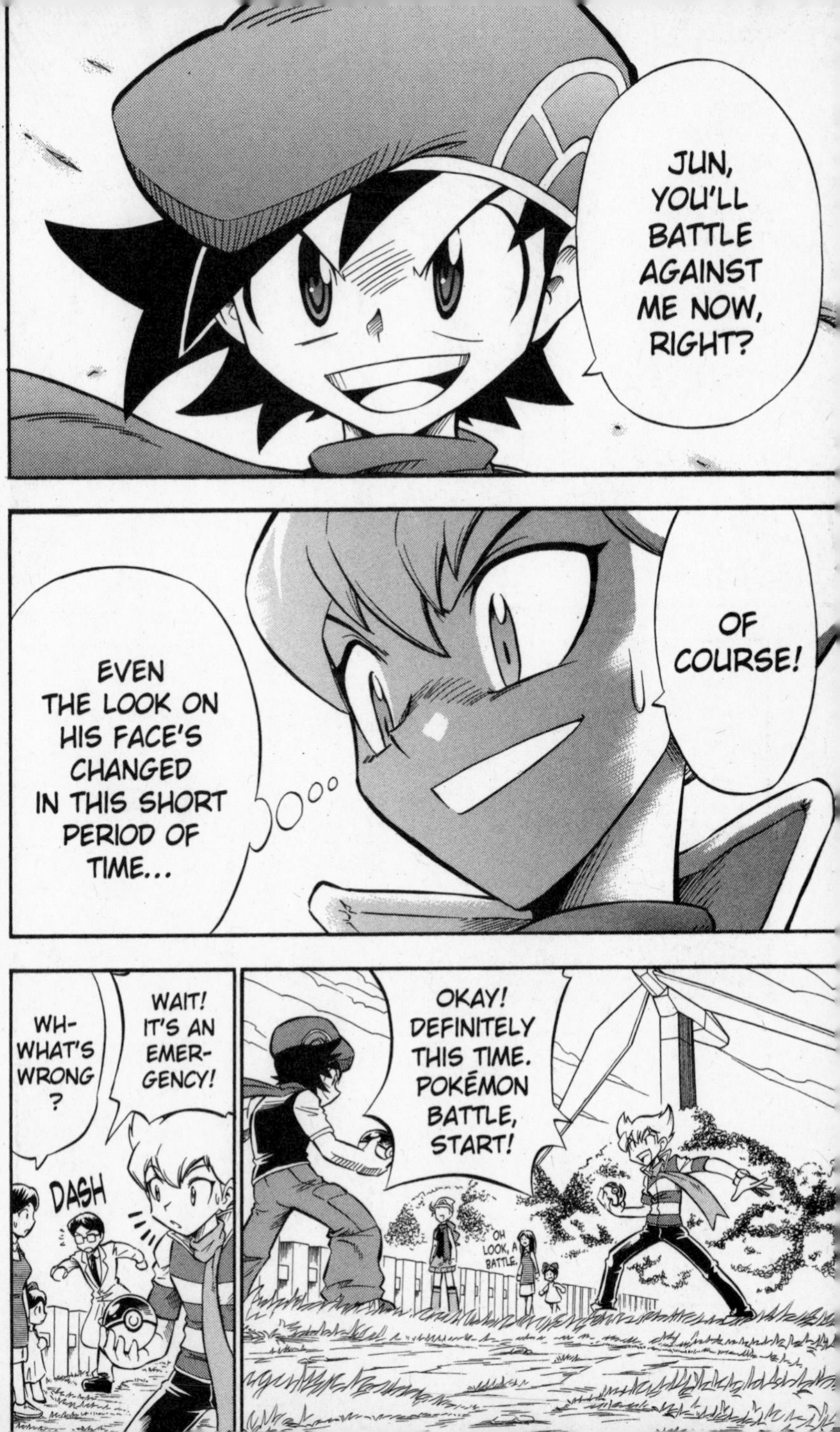

JUN, YOU'LL BATTLE AGAINST ME NOW, RIGHT?
OF COURSE!
EVEN THE LOOK ON HIS FACE'S CHANGED IN THIS SHORT PERIOD OF TIME...
OKAY! DEFINITELY THIS TIME. POKÉMON BATTLE, START!
OH LOOK, A BATTLE.
WAIT! IT'S AN EMER-GENCY!
WH-WHAT'S WRONG?
DASH

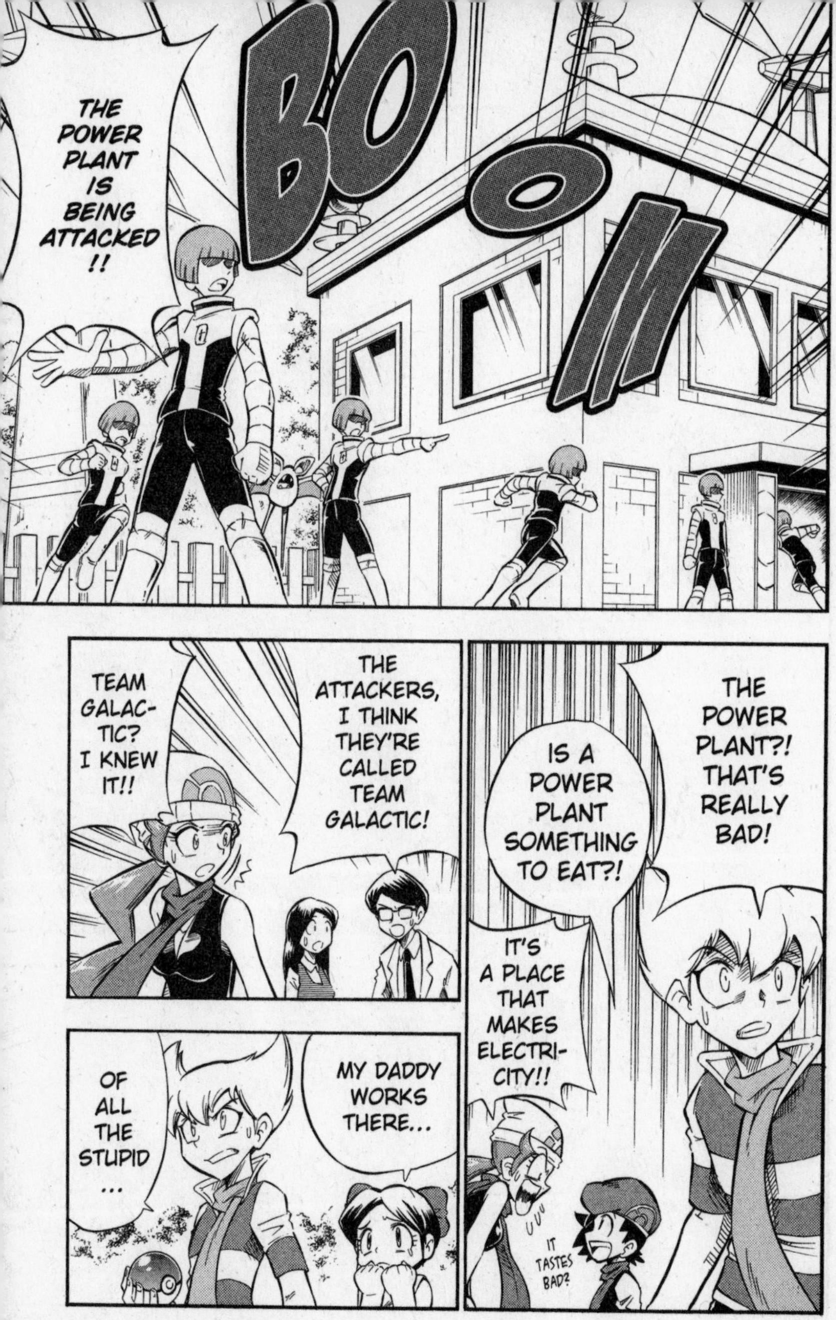
BOOM
THE POWER PLANT IS BEING ATTACKED!!
THE POWER PLANT?! THAT'S REALLY BAD!
IS A POWER PLANT SOMETHING TO EAT?!
IT'S A PLACE THAT MAKES ELECTRICITY!!
IT TASTES BAD?
THE ATTACKERS, I THINK THEY'RE CALLED TEAM GALACTIC!
TEAM GALACTIC? I KNEW IT!!
MY DADDY WORKS THERE...
OF ALL THE STUPID...

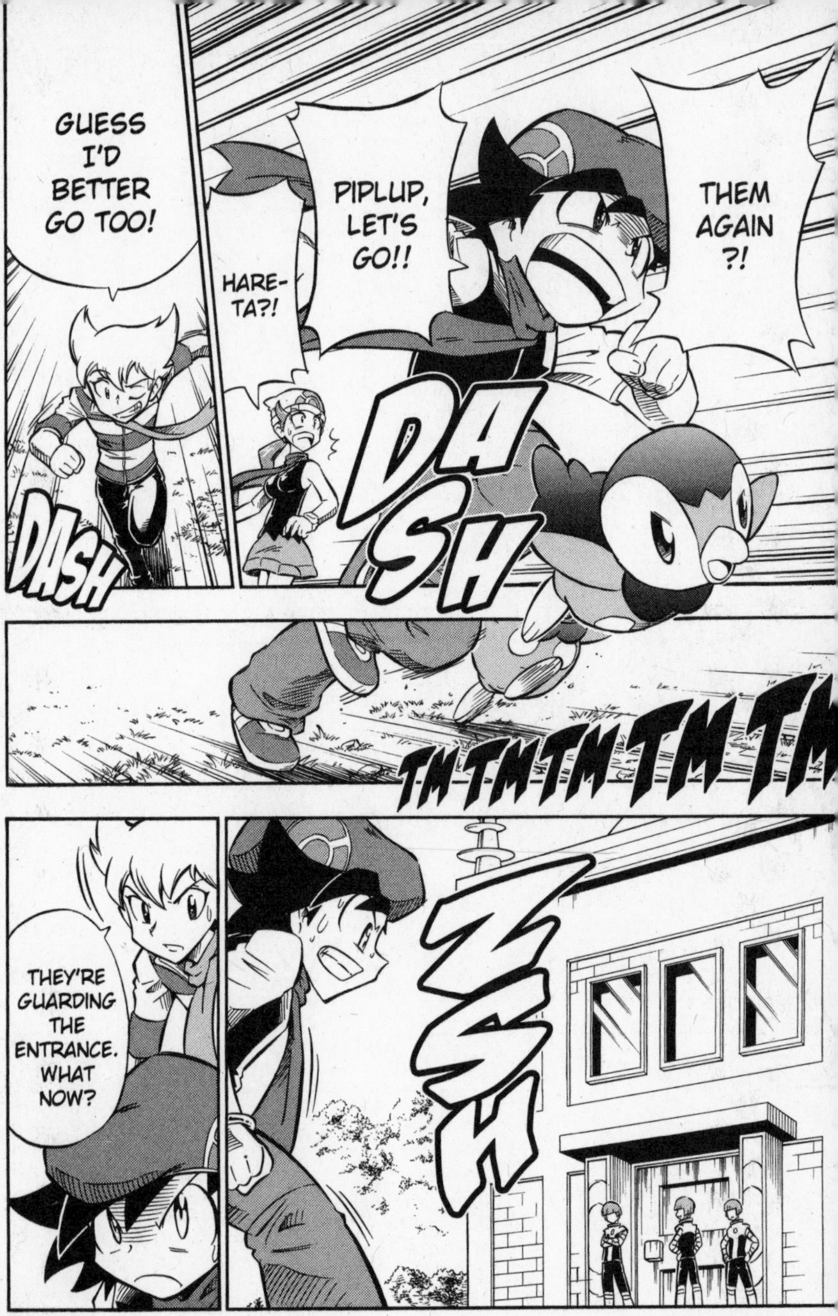
THEM AGAIN?!
PIPLUP, LET'S GO!!
DASH
HARE-TA?!
GUESS I'D BETTER GO TOO!
DASH
TMTMTMTMTM
ZSH
THEY'RE GUARDING THE ENTRANCE. WHAT NOW?

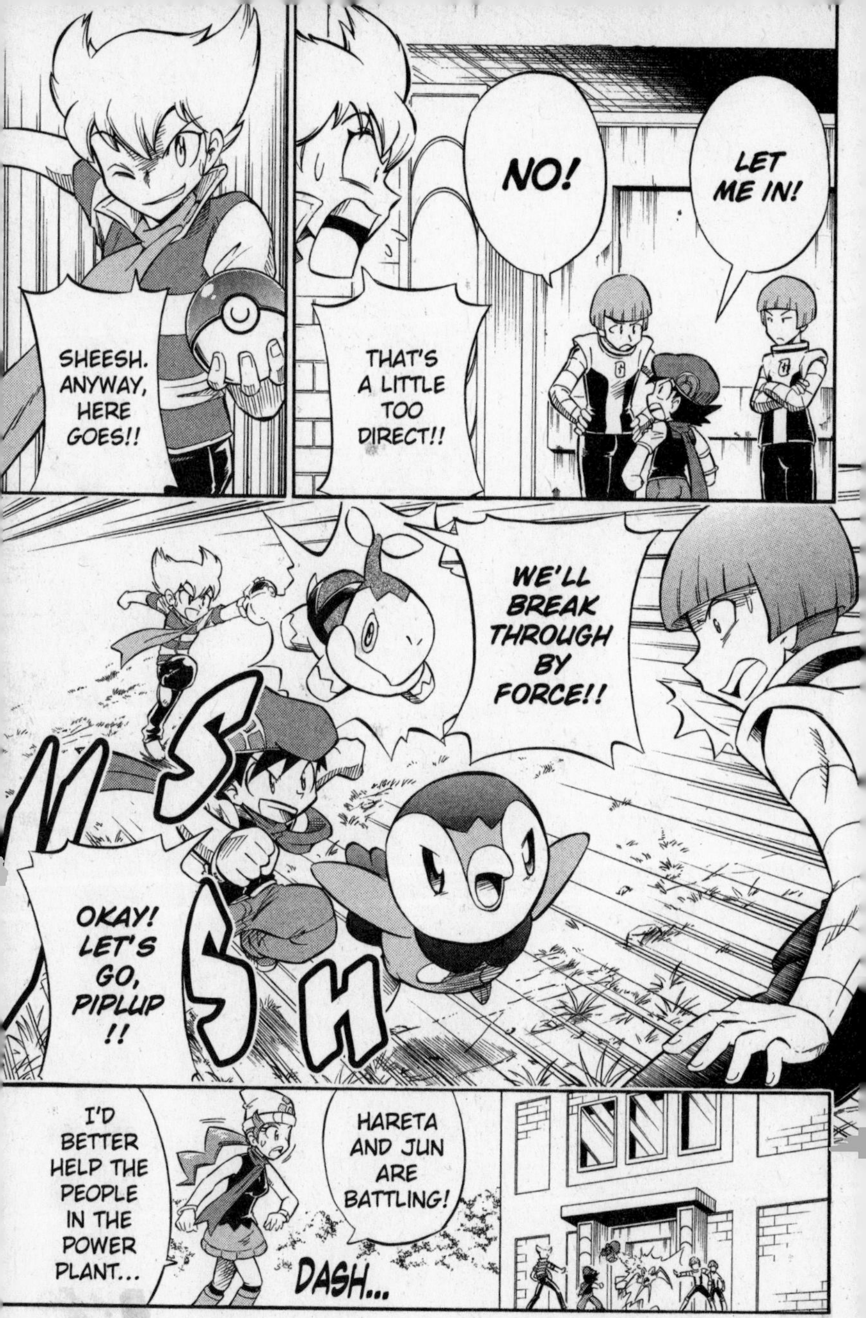
LET ME IN!
NO!
THAT'S A LITTLE TOO DIRECT!!
SHEESH. ANYWAY, HERE GOES!!
WE'LL BREAK THROUGH BY FORCE!!
OKAY! LET'S GO, PIPLUP!!
HARETA AND JUN ARE BATTLING!
I'D BETTER HELP THE PEOPLE IN THE POWER PLANT...
DASH...

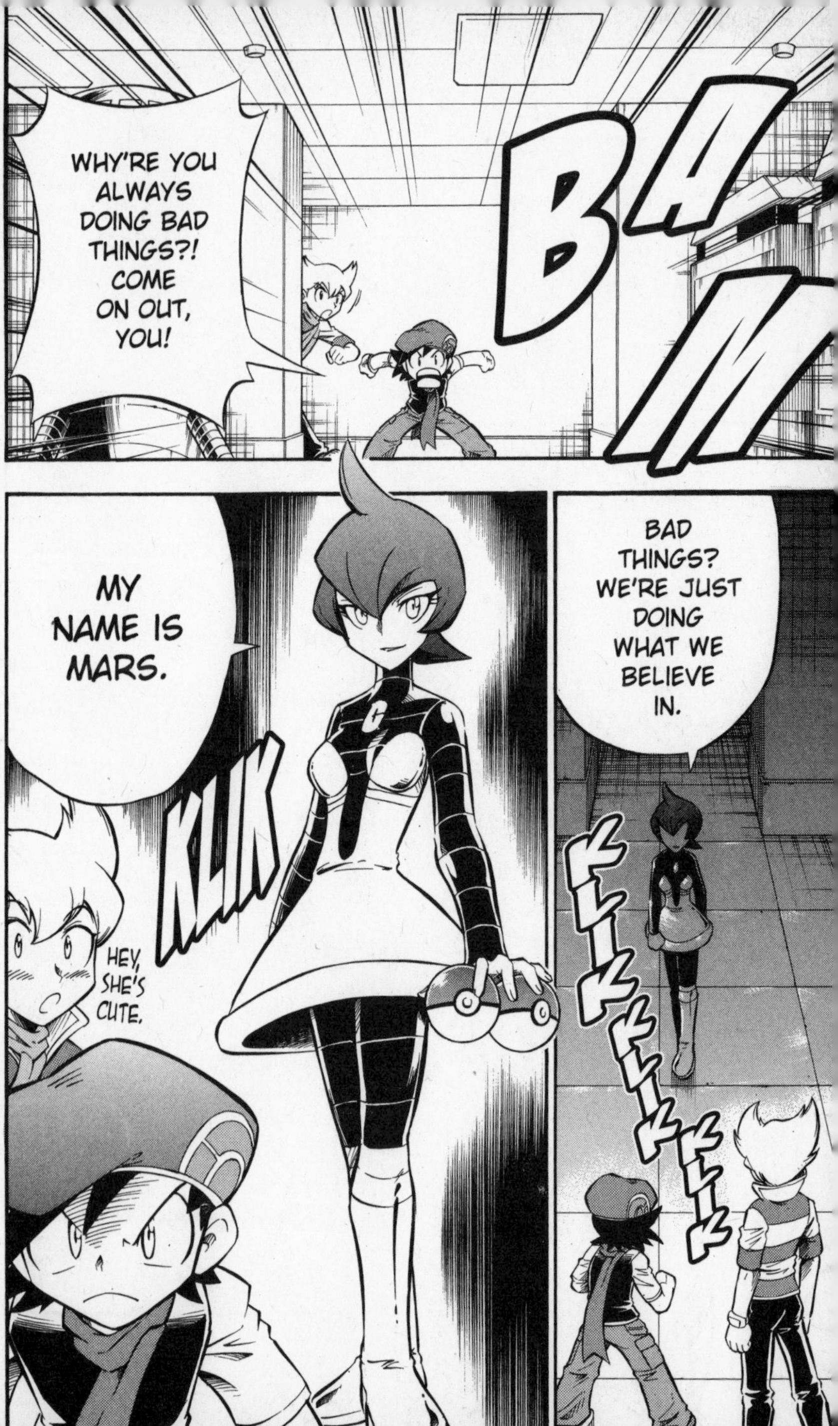
BAM
WHY'RE YOU ALWAYS DOING BAD THINGS?! COME ON OUT, YOU!
BAD THINGS? WE'RE JUST DOING WHAT WE BELIEVE IN.
KLIK KLIK KLIK
MY NAME IS MARS.
KLIK
HEY, SHE'S CUTE.

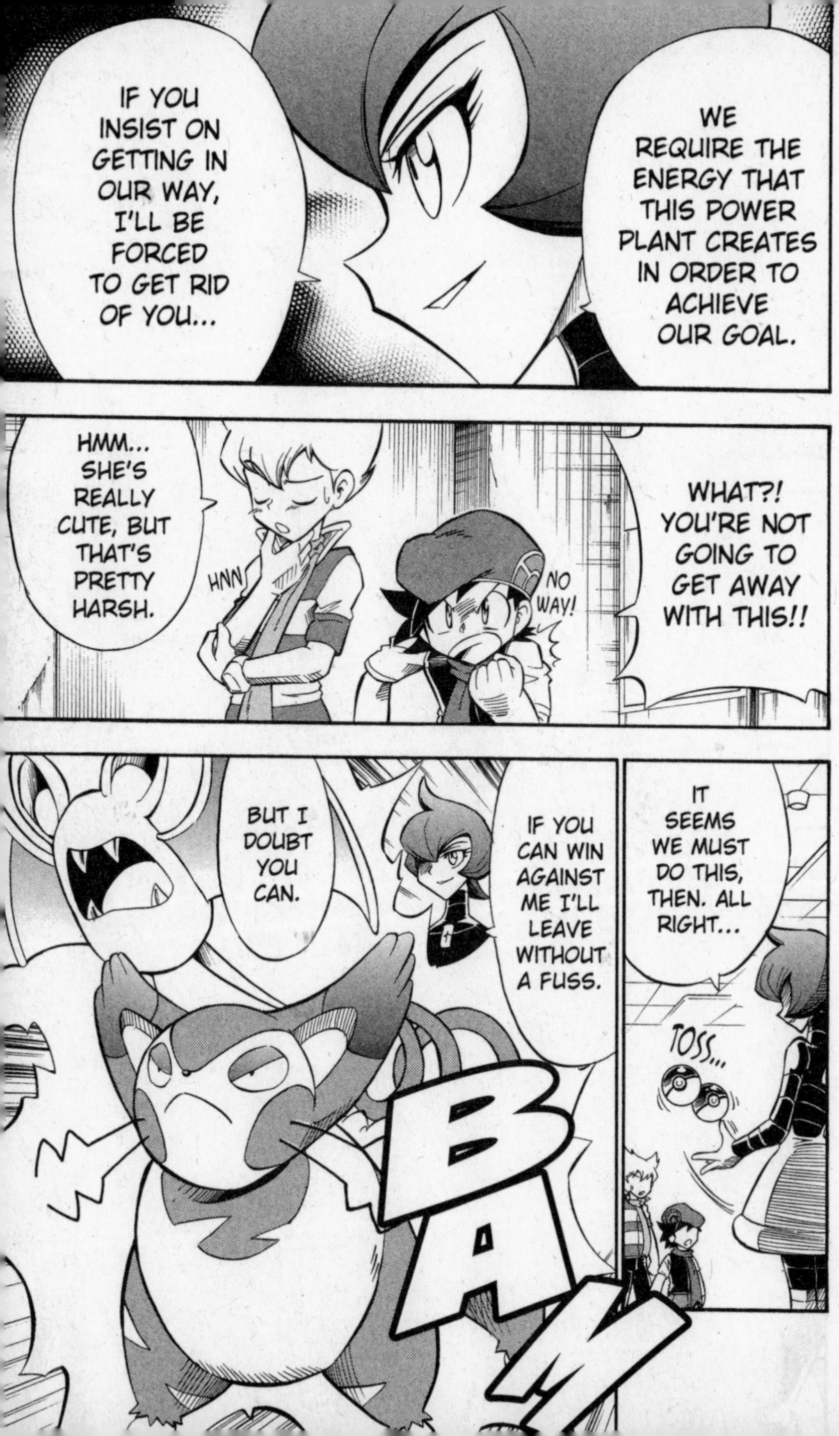
WE REQUIRE THE ENERGY THAT THIS POWER PLANT CREATES IN ORDER TO ACHIEVE OUR GOAL.
IF YOU INSIST ON GETTING IN OUR WAY, I'LL BE FORCED TO GET RID OF YOU...
WHAT?! YOU'RE NOT GOING TO GET AWAY WITH THIS!!
NO WAY!
HNN
HMM... SHE'S REALLY CUTE, BUT THAT'S PRETTY HARSH.
IT SEEMS WE MUST DO THIS, THEN. ALL RIGHT...
TOSS...
IF YOU CAN WIN AGAINST ME I'LL LEAVE WITHOUT A FUSS.
BUT I DOUBT YOU CAN.
BAM

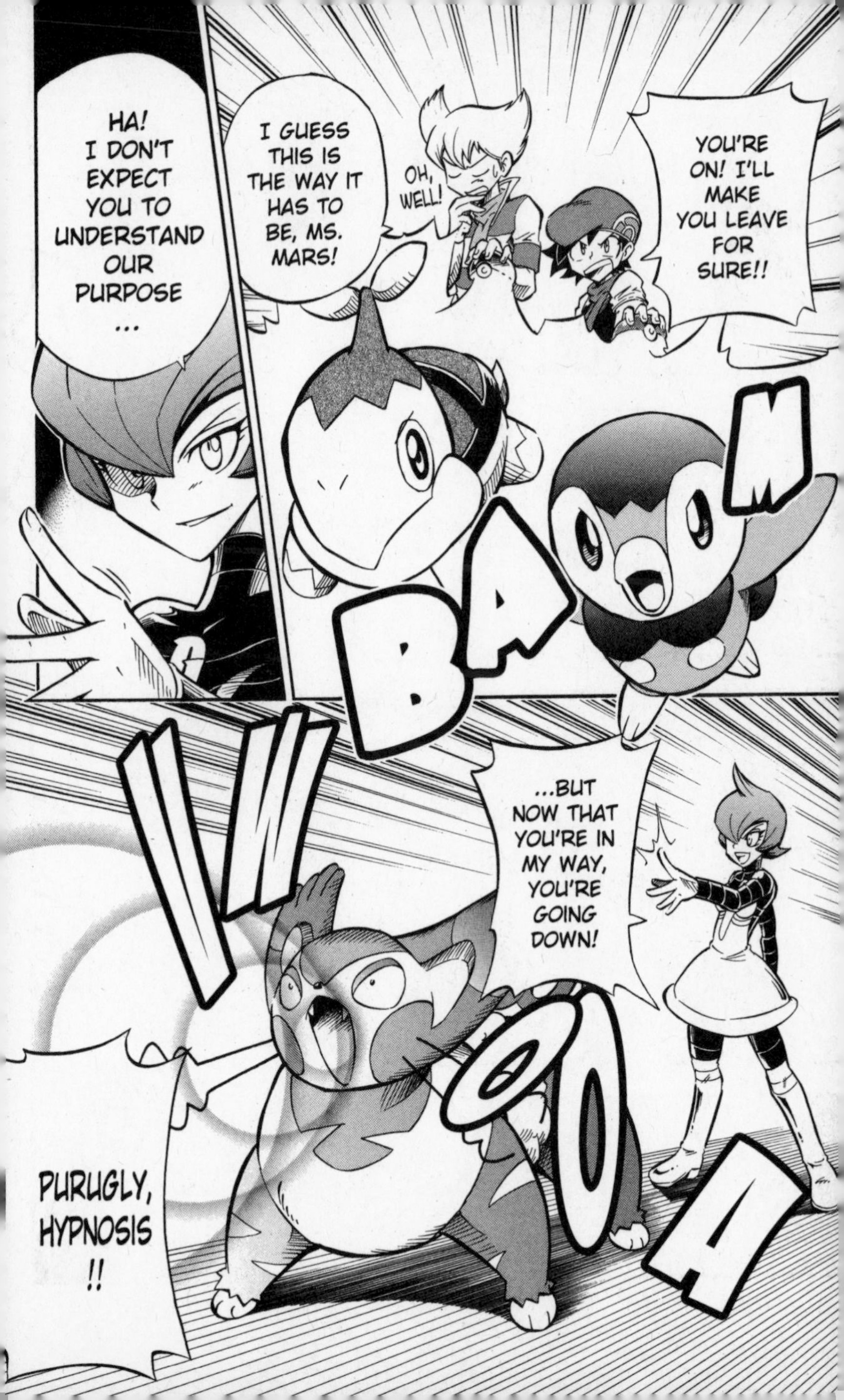
YOU'RE ON! I'LL MAKE YOU LEAVE FOR SURE!!
OH, WELL!
I GUESS THIS IS THE WAY IT HAS TO BE, MS. MARS!
HA! I DON'T EXPECT YOU TO UNDERSTAND OUR PURPOSE ...
BAOOM
...BUT NOW THAT YOU'RE IN MY WAY, YOU'RE GOING DOWN!
PURUGLY, HYPNOSIS !!

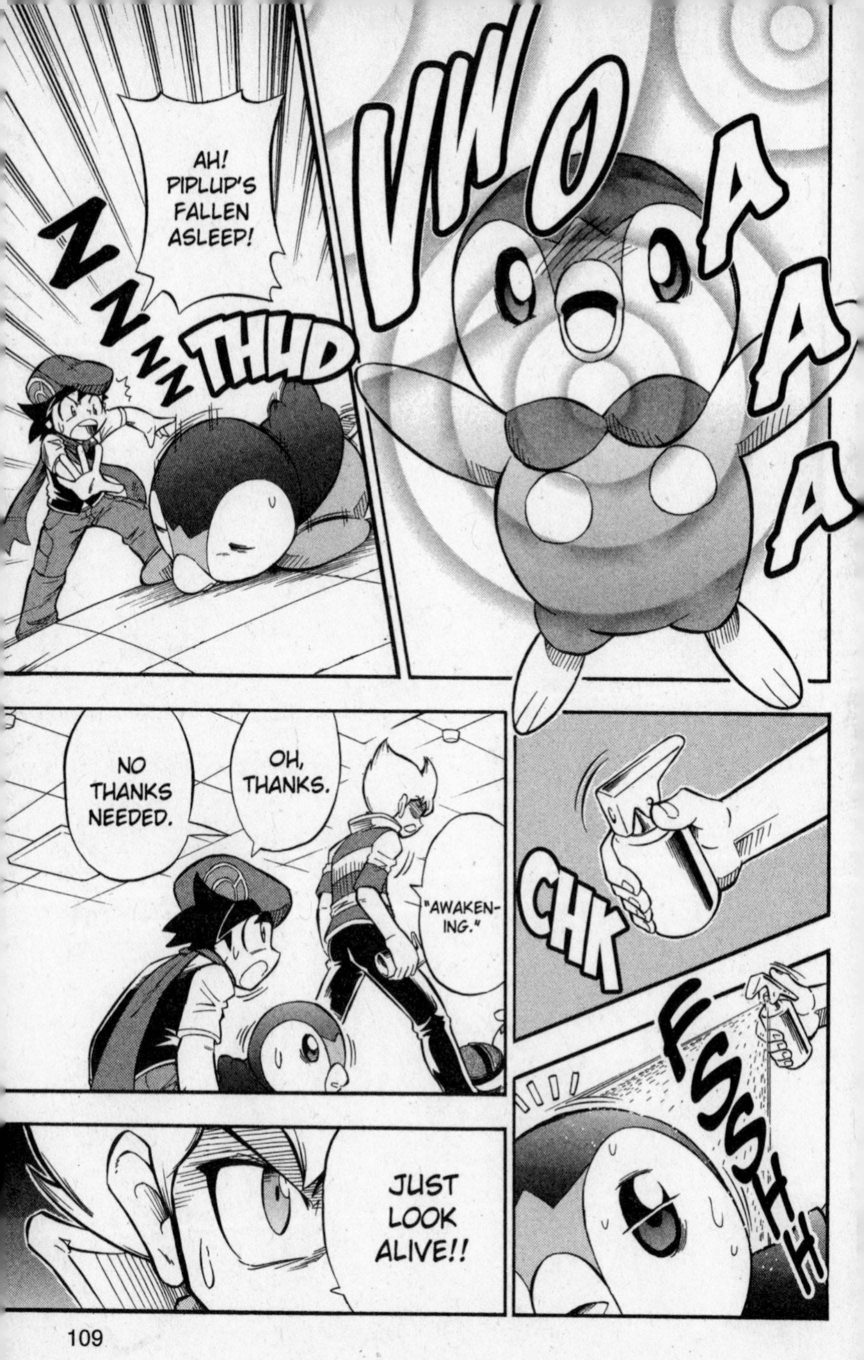
VWOOAAA
AH! PIPLUP'S FALLEN ASLEEP!
ZZZZ
THUD
CHK
FSSSHH
OH, THANKS.
NO THANKS NEEDED.
"AWAKEN-ING."
JUST LOOK ALIVE!!

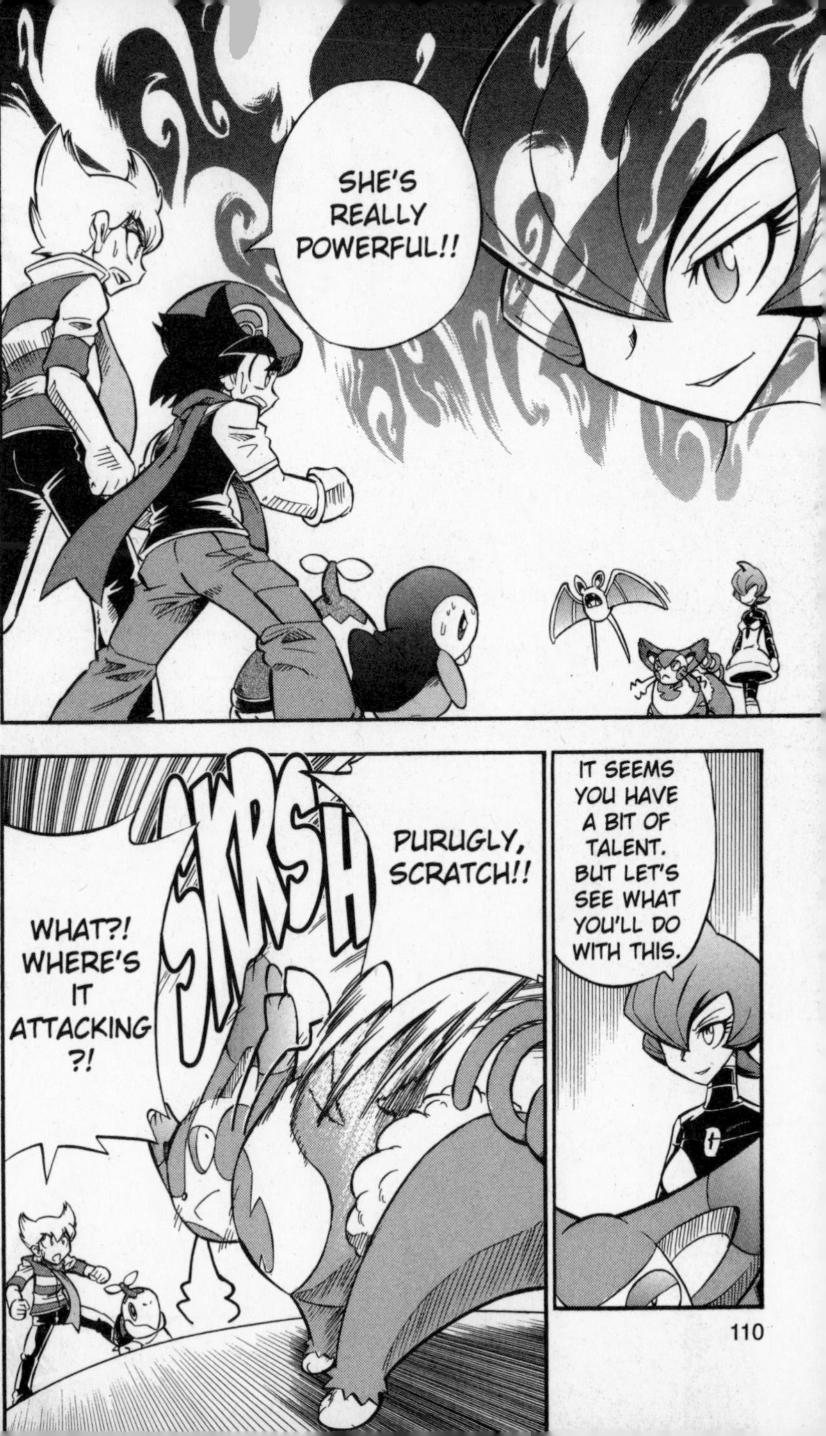
SHE'S REALLY POWERFUL!!
IT SEEMS YOU HAVE A BIT OF TALENT. BUT LET'S SEE WHAT YOU'LL DO WITH THIS.
PURUGLY, SCRATCH!!
SKRSH
WHAT?! WHERE'S IT ATTACKING?!

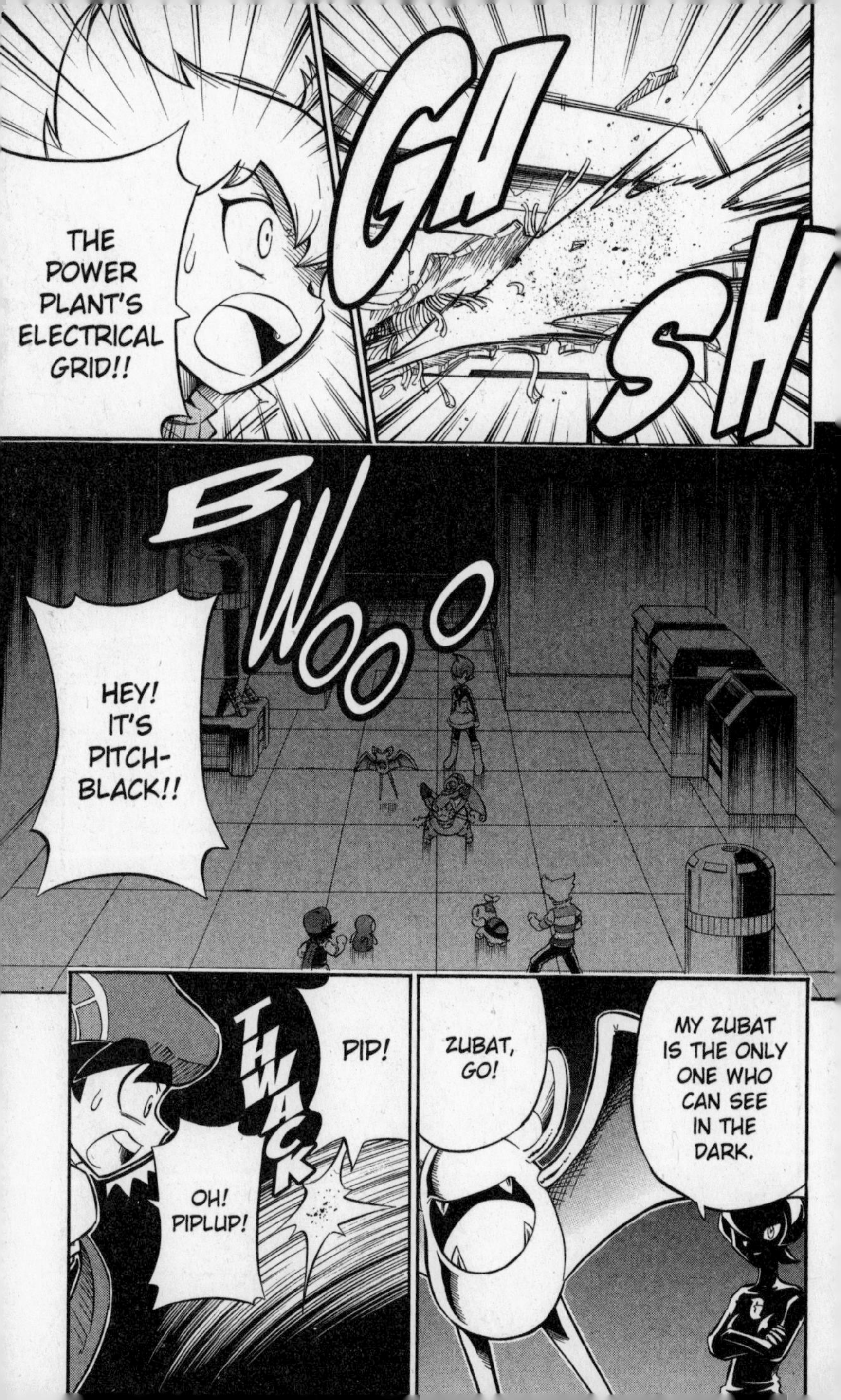
GASH
THE POWER PLANT'S ELECTRICAL GRID!!
BWOOO
HEY! IT'S PITCH-BLACK!!
MY ZUBAT IS THE ONLY ONE WHO CAN SEE IN THE DARK.
ZUBAT, GO!
THWACK
PIP!
OH! PIPLUP!

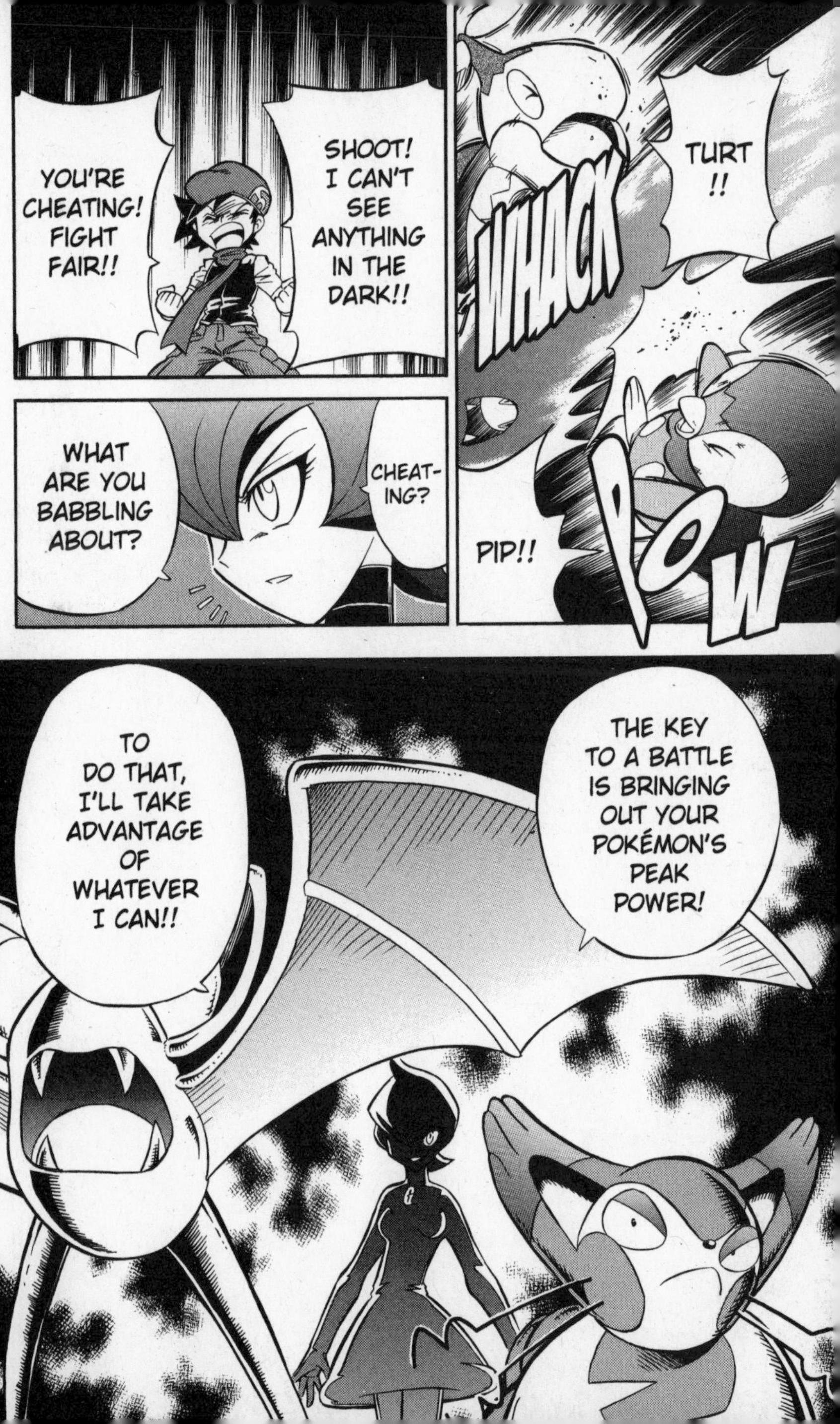
TURT !!
WHACK
PIP!!
POW
SHOOT! I CAN'T SEE ANYTHING IN THE DARK!!
YOU'RE CHEATING! FIGHT FAIR!!
CHEAT-ING?
WHAT ARE YOU BABBLING ABOUT?
THE KEY TO A BATTLE IS BRINGING OUT YOUR POKÉMON'S PEAK POWER!
TO DO THAT, I'LL TAKE ADVANTAGE OF WHATEVER I CAN!!

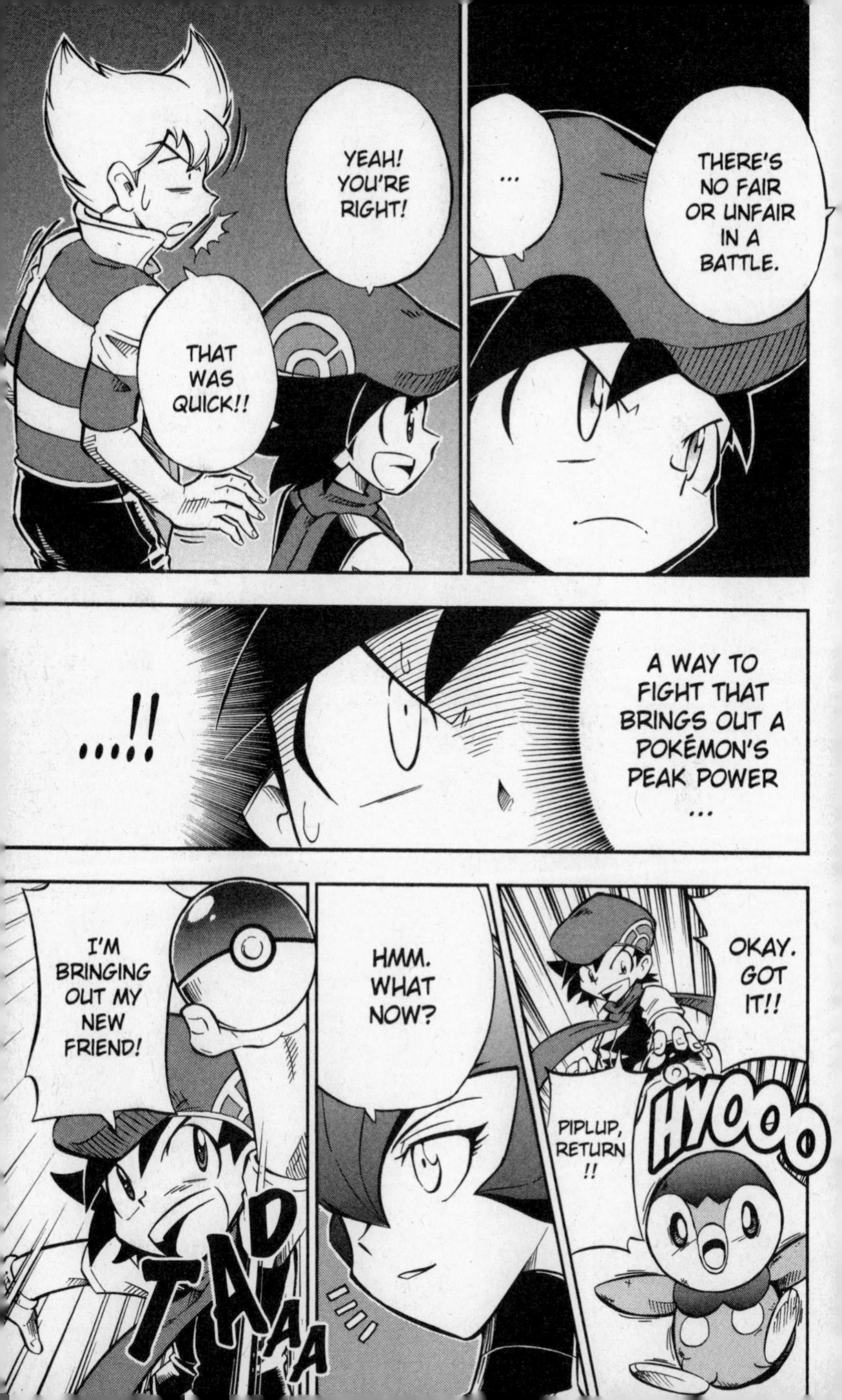
THERE'S NO FAIR OR UNFAIR IN A BATTLE.
...
YEAH! YOU'RE RIGHT!
THAT WAS QUICK!!
A WAY TO FIGHT THAT BRINGS OUT A POKÉMON'S PEAK POWER ...
....!!
OKAY. GOT IT!!
PIPLUP, RETURN !!
HYOOO
HMM. WHAT NOW?
I'M BRINGING OUT MY NEW FRIEND!
TADAAA

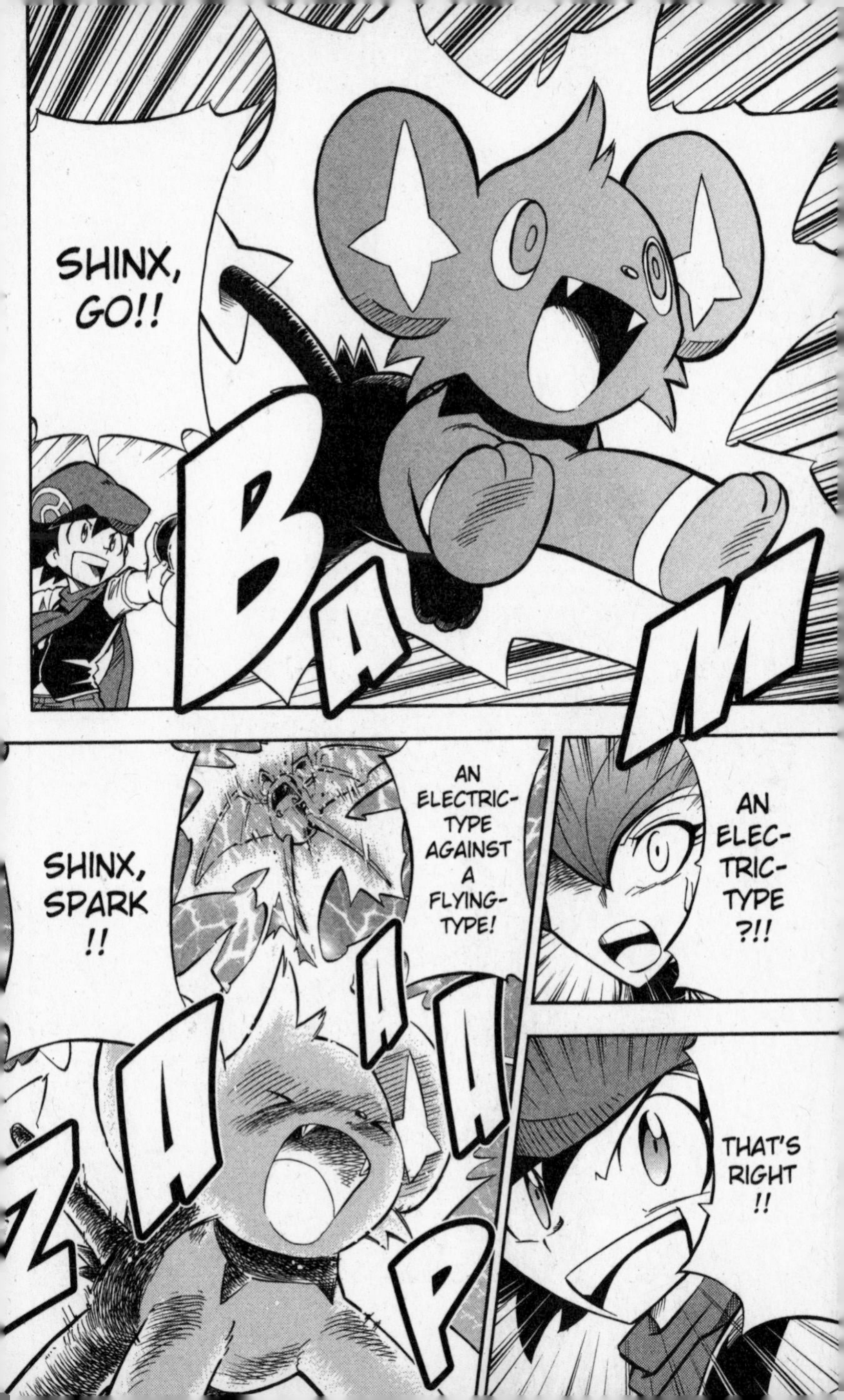
SHINX, GO!!
BAM
AN ELEC-TRIC-TYPE?!!
THAT'S RIGHT!!
AN ELECTRIC-TYPE AGAINST A FLYING-TYPE!
SHINX, SPARK!!
ZAAAP

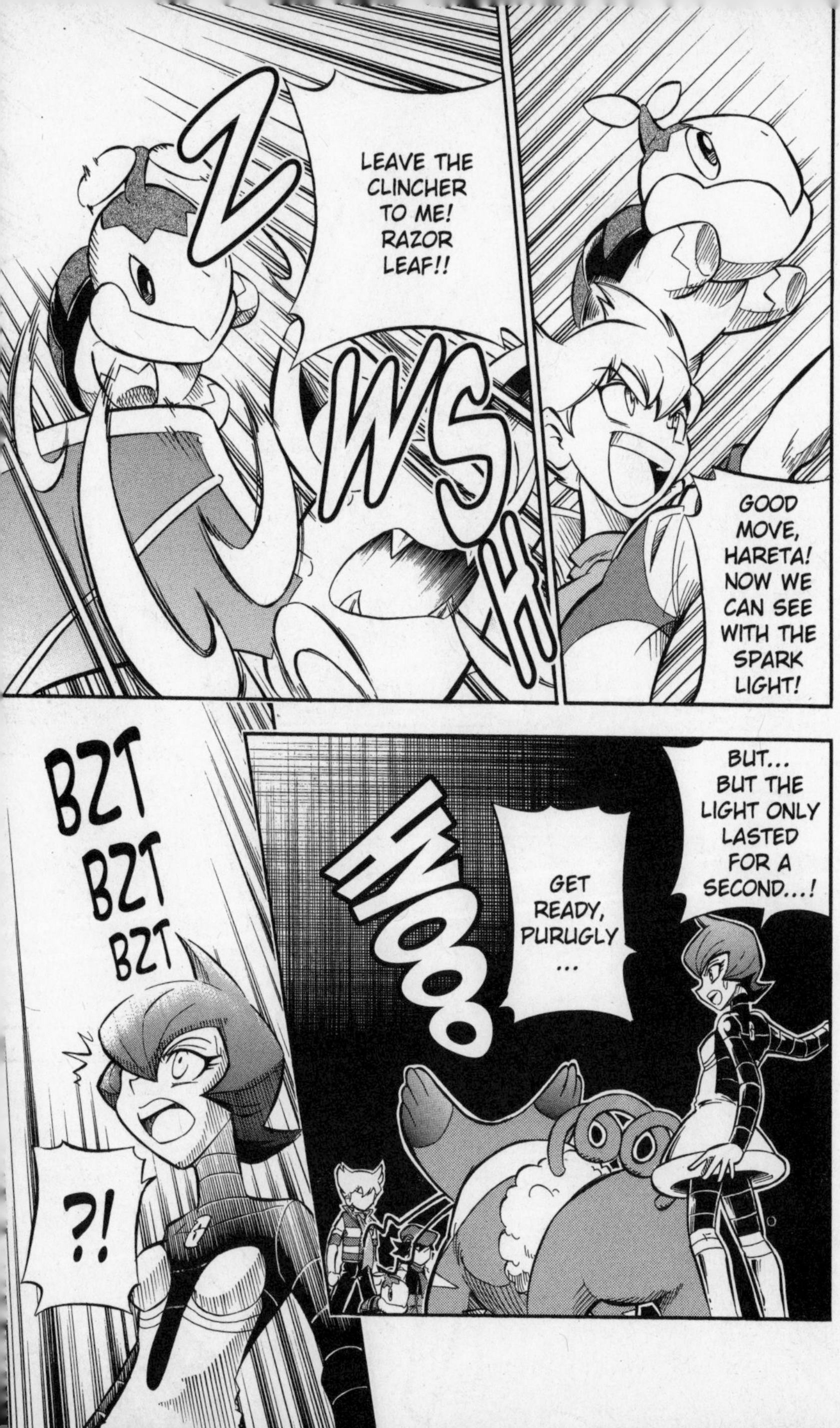
GOOD MOVE, HARETA! NOW WE CAN SEE WITH THE SPARK LIGHT!
LEAVE THE CLINCHER TO ME! RAZOR LEAF!!
ZWSH
BUT... BUT THE LIGHT ONLY LASTED FOR A SECOND...!
GET READY, PURUGLY ...
WHOOO
BZT BZT BZT
?!

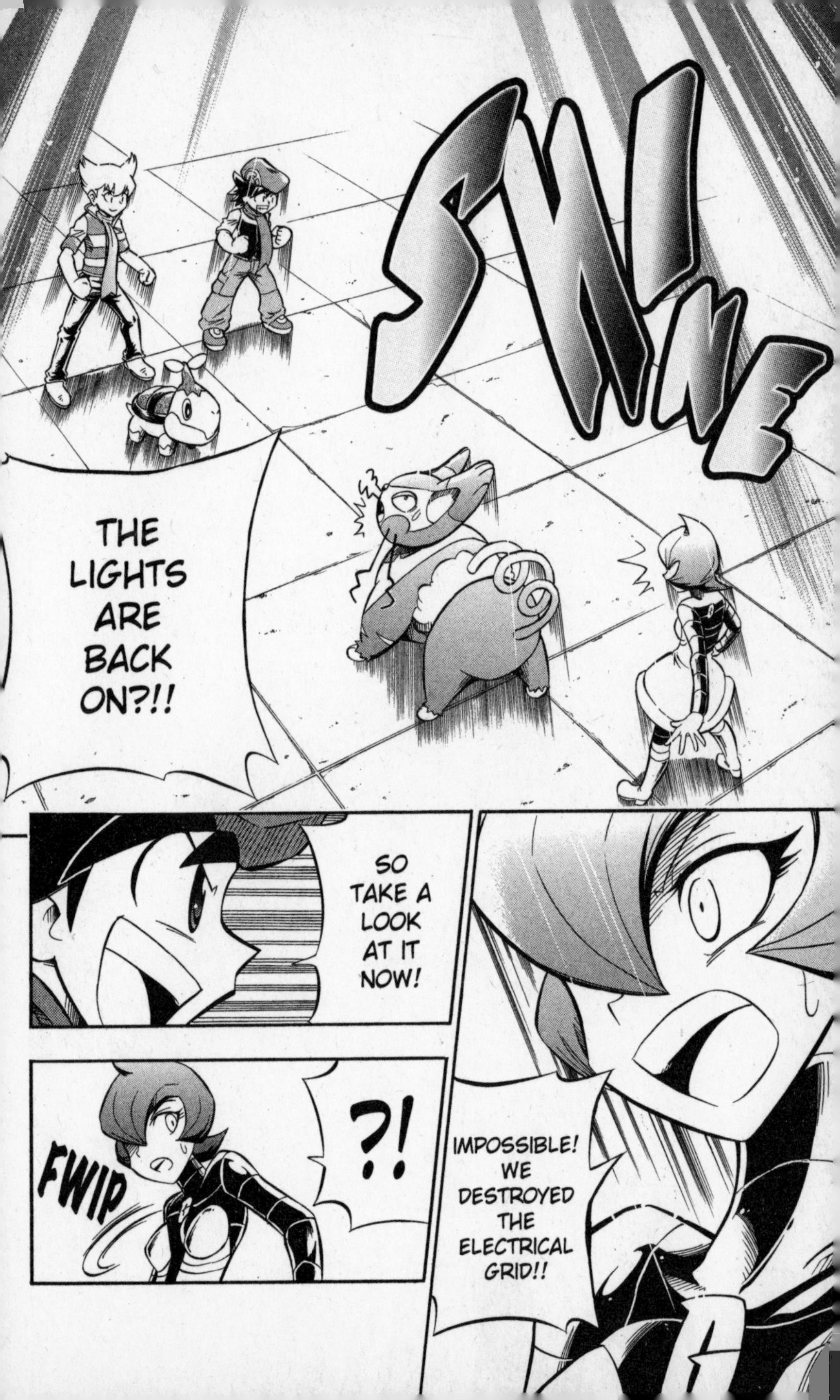
SHINE
THE LIGHTS ARE BACK ON?!!
IMPOSSIBLE! WE DESTROYED THE ELECTRICAL GRID!!
SO TAKE A LOOK AT IT NOW!
?!
FWIP

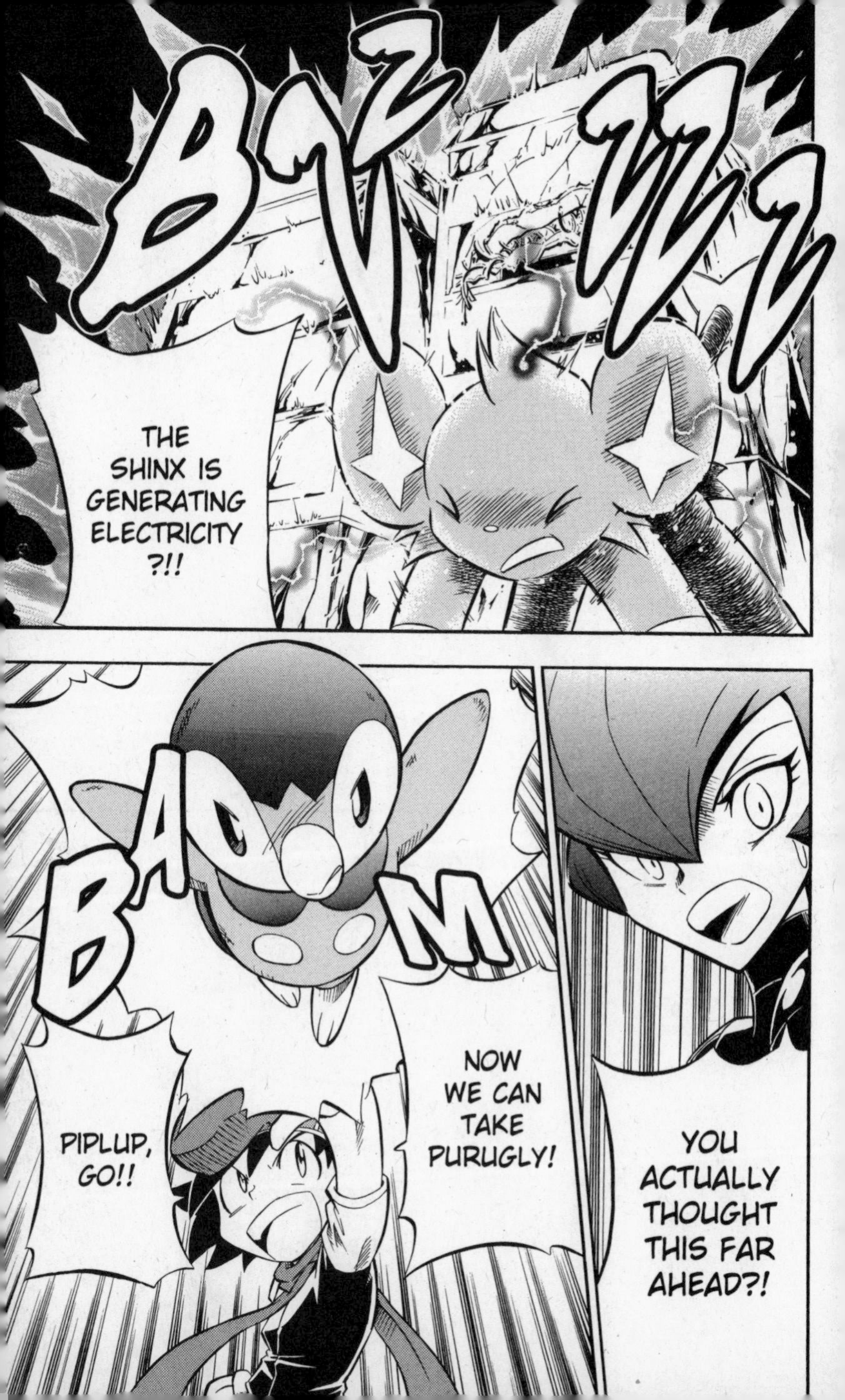
THE SHINX IS GENERATING ELECTRICITY ?!!
YOU ACTUALLY THOUGHT THIS FAR AHEAD?!
NOW WE CAN TAKE PURUGLY!
PIPLUP, GO!!

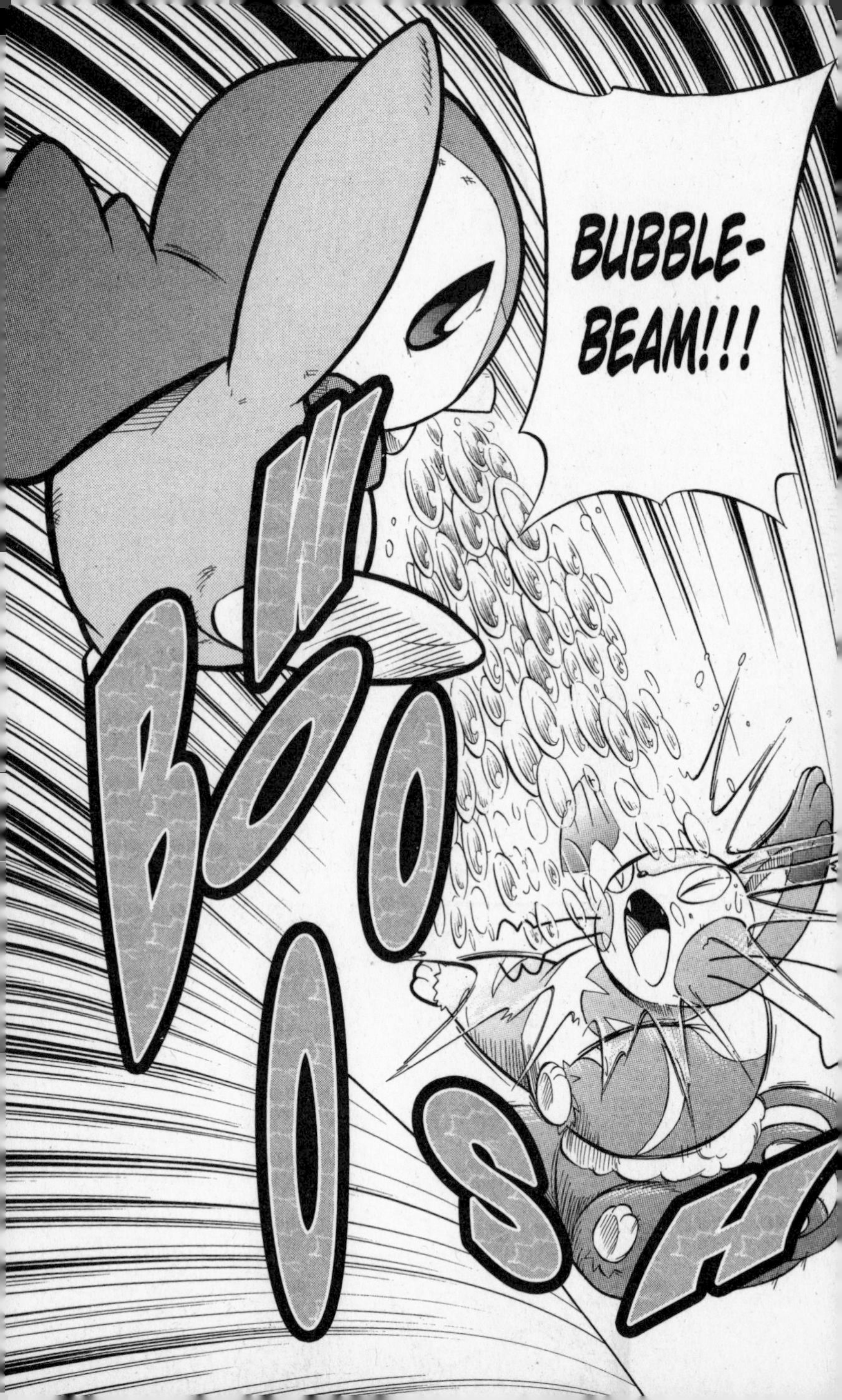
BUBBLE-
BEAM!!!
BWOOOOSH

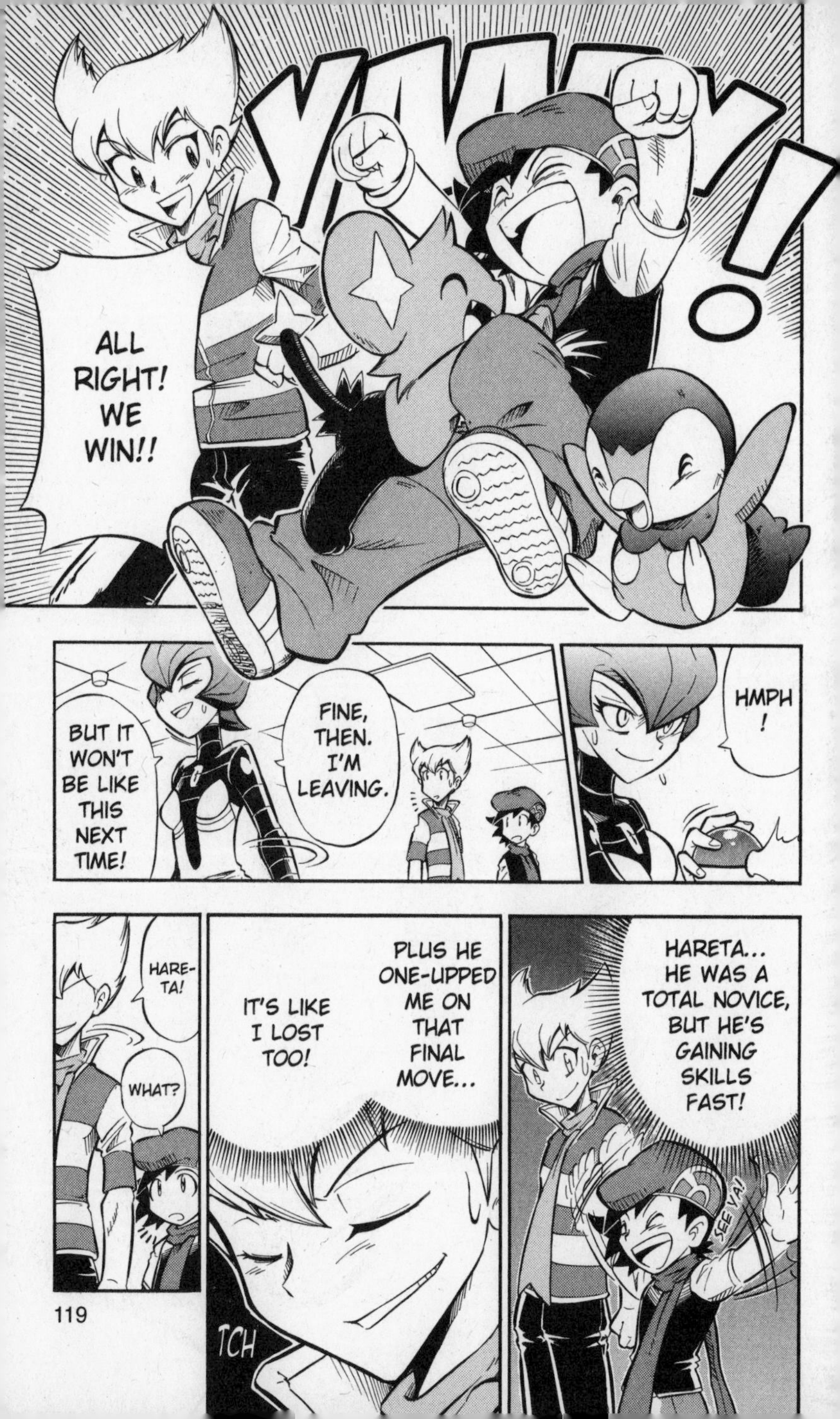
ALL RIGHT! WE WIN!!
HMPH!
FINE, THEN. I'M LEAVING.
BUT IT WON'T BE LIKE THIS NEXT TIME!
HARETA... HE WAS A TOTAL NOVICE, BUT HE'S GAINING SKILLS FAST!
SEE YA!
PLUS HE ONE-UPPED ME ON THAT FINAL MOVE...
IT'S LIKE I LOST TOO!
TCH
HARE-TA!
WHAT?

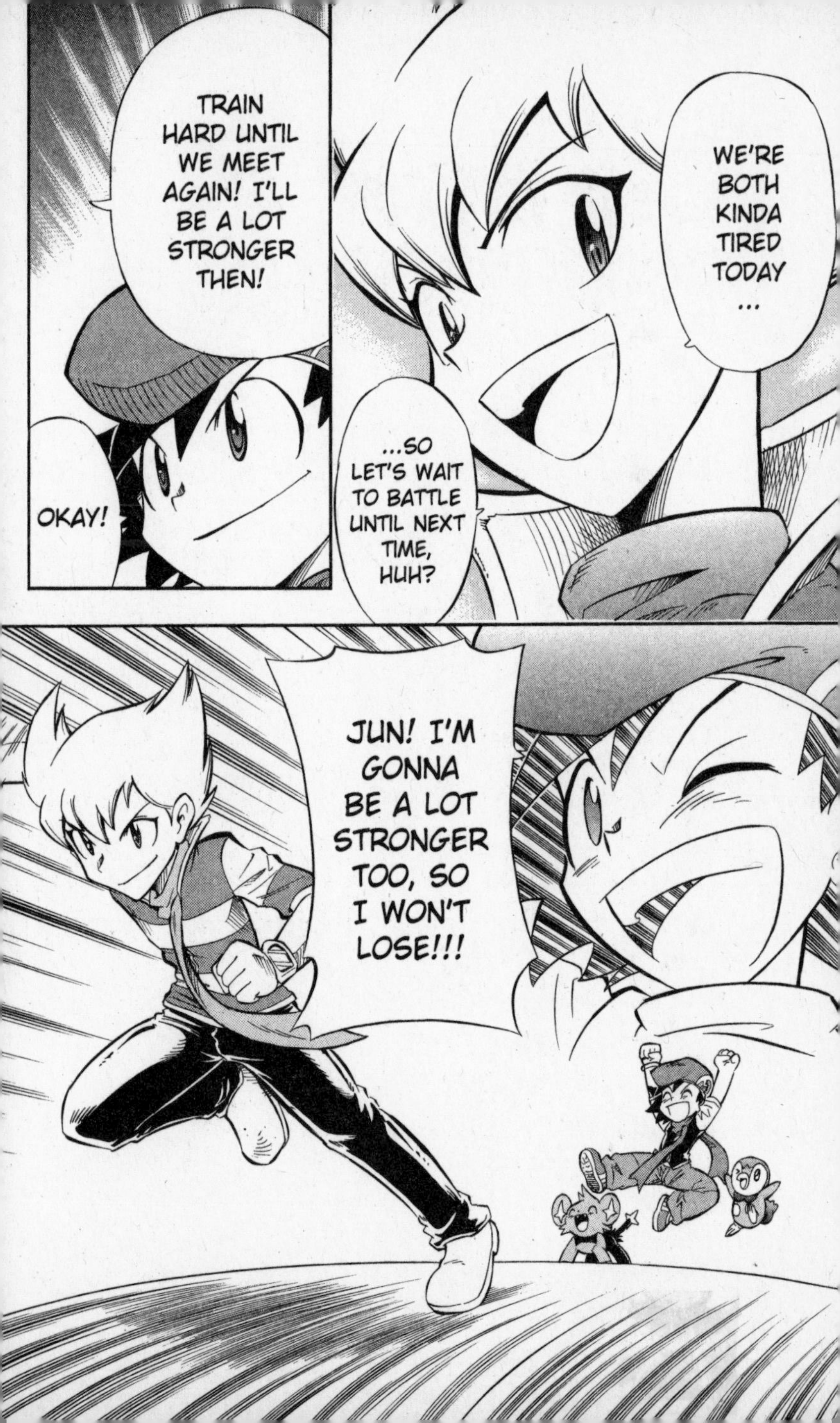
WE'RE BOTH KINDA TIRED TODAY ...
...SO LET'S WAIT TO BATTLE UNTIL NEXT TIME, HUH?
TRAIN HARD UNTIL WE MEET AGAIN! I'LL BE A LOT STRONGER THEN!
OKAY!
JUN! I'M GONNA BE A LOT STRONGER TOO, SO I WON'T LOSE!!!

CHAPTER 4
WIN WITH TEAMWORK!!

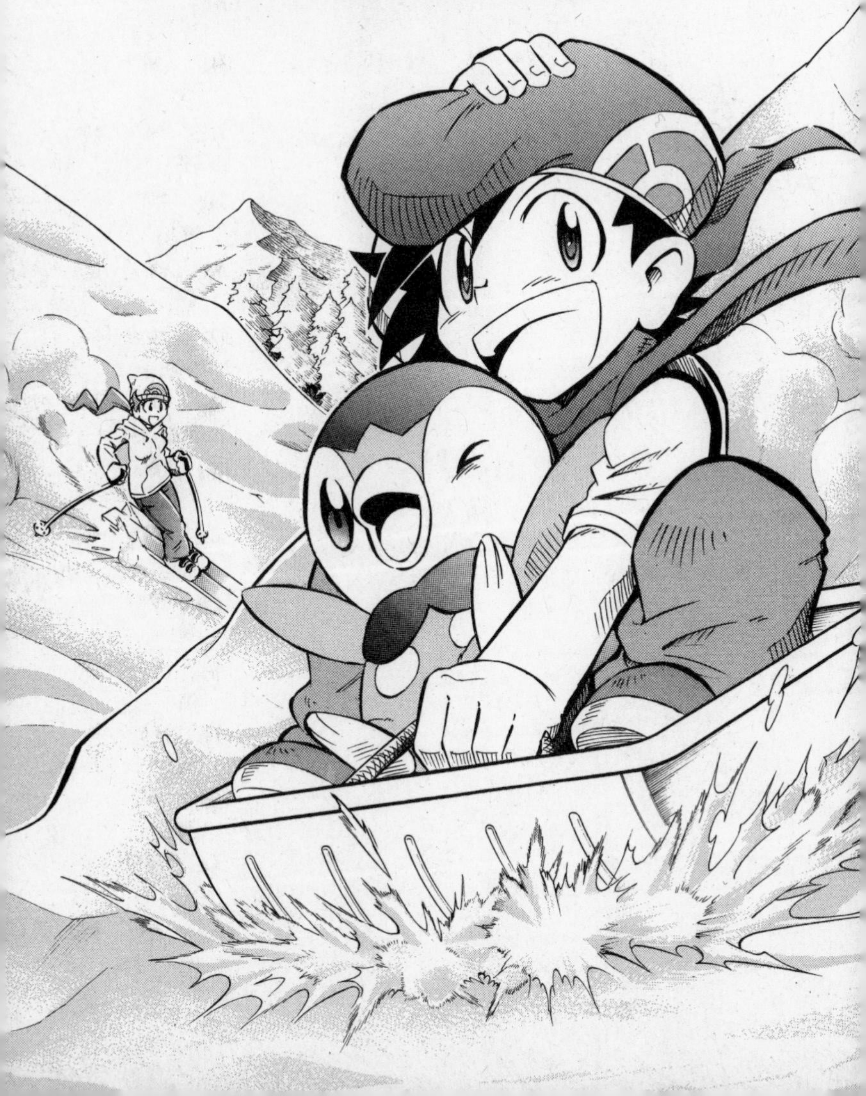

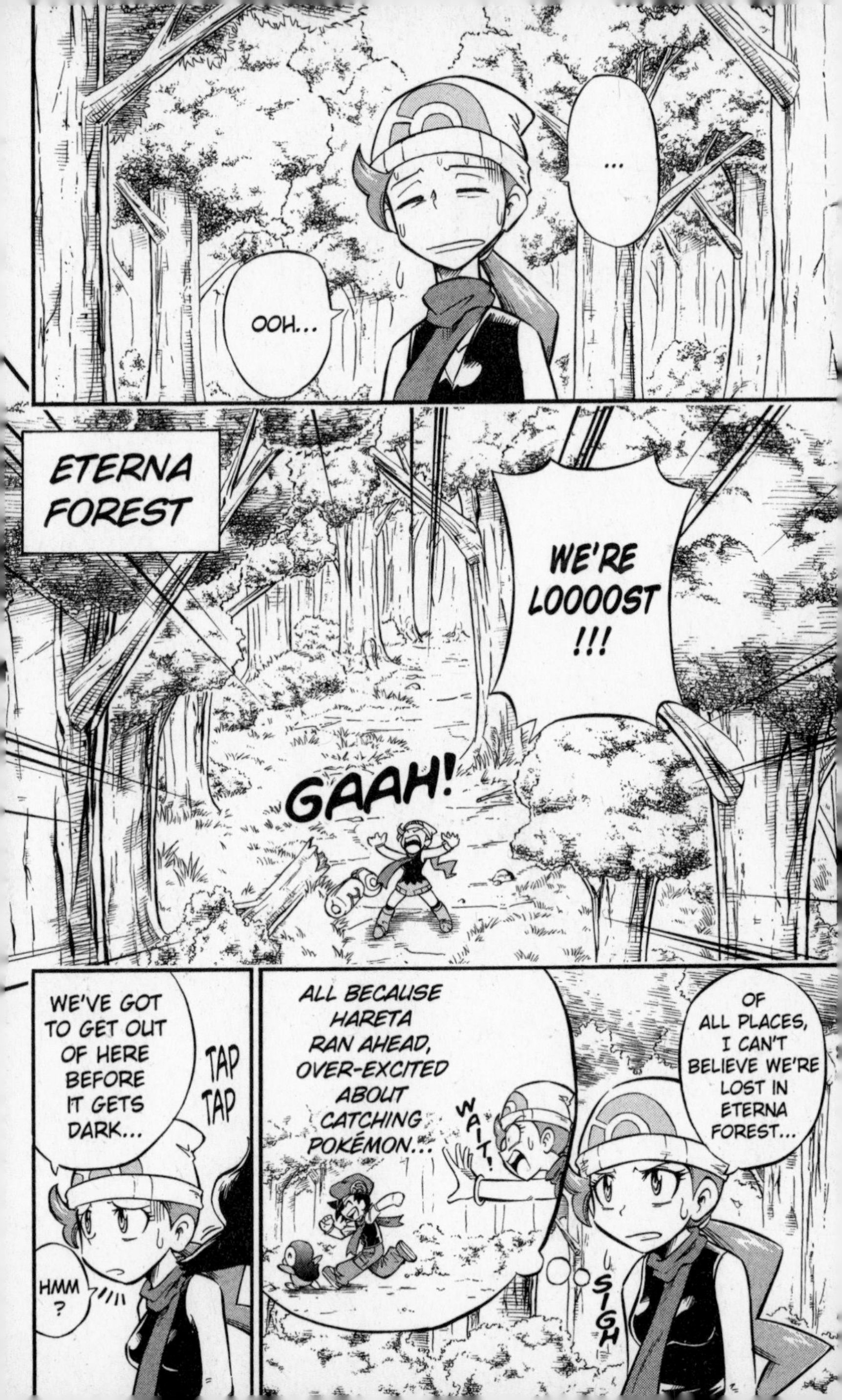
...
OOH...
ETERNA FOREST
WE'RE LOOOOST !!!
GAAH!
OF ALL PLACES, I CAN'T BELIEVE WE'RE LOST IN ETERNA FOREST...
ALL BECAUSE HARETA RAN AHEAD, OVER-EXCITED ABOUT CATCHING POKÉMON...
WAIT!
SIGH
WE'VE GOT TO GET OUT OF HERE BEFORE IT GETS DARK...
TAP TAP
HMM ?

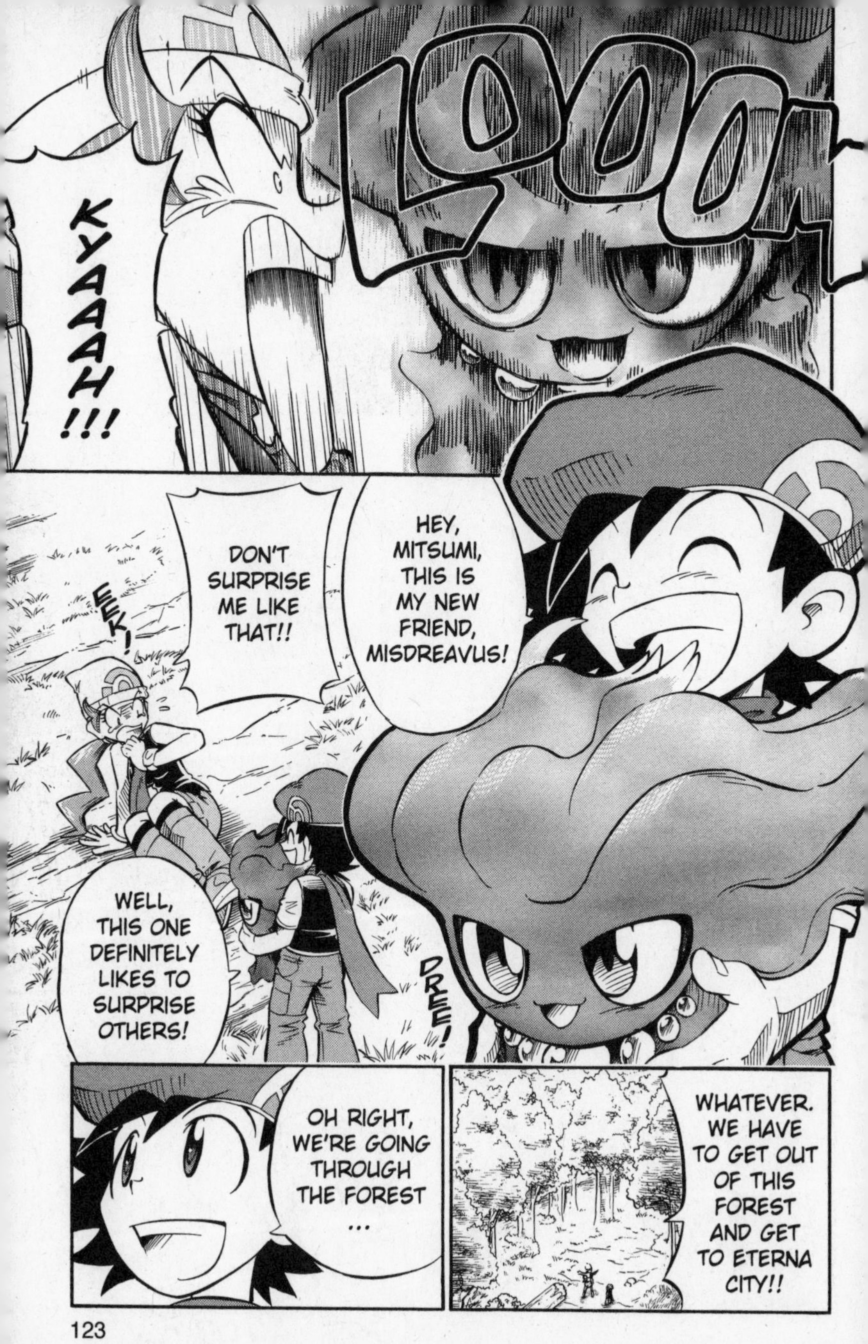
LOOOM
KYAAAAH!!!
HEY, MITSUMI, THIS IS MY NEW FRIEND, MISDREAVUS!
DON'T SURPRISE ME LIKE THAT!!
EEK!
DREE!
WELL, THIS ONE DEFINITELY LIKES TO SURPRISE OTHERS!
WHATEVER. WE HAVE TO GET OUT OF THIS FOREST AND GET TO ETERNA CITY!!
OH RIGHT, WE'RE GOING THROUGH THE FOREST ...

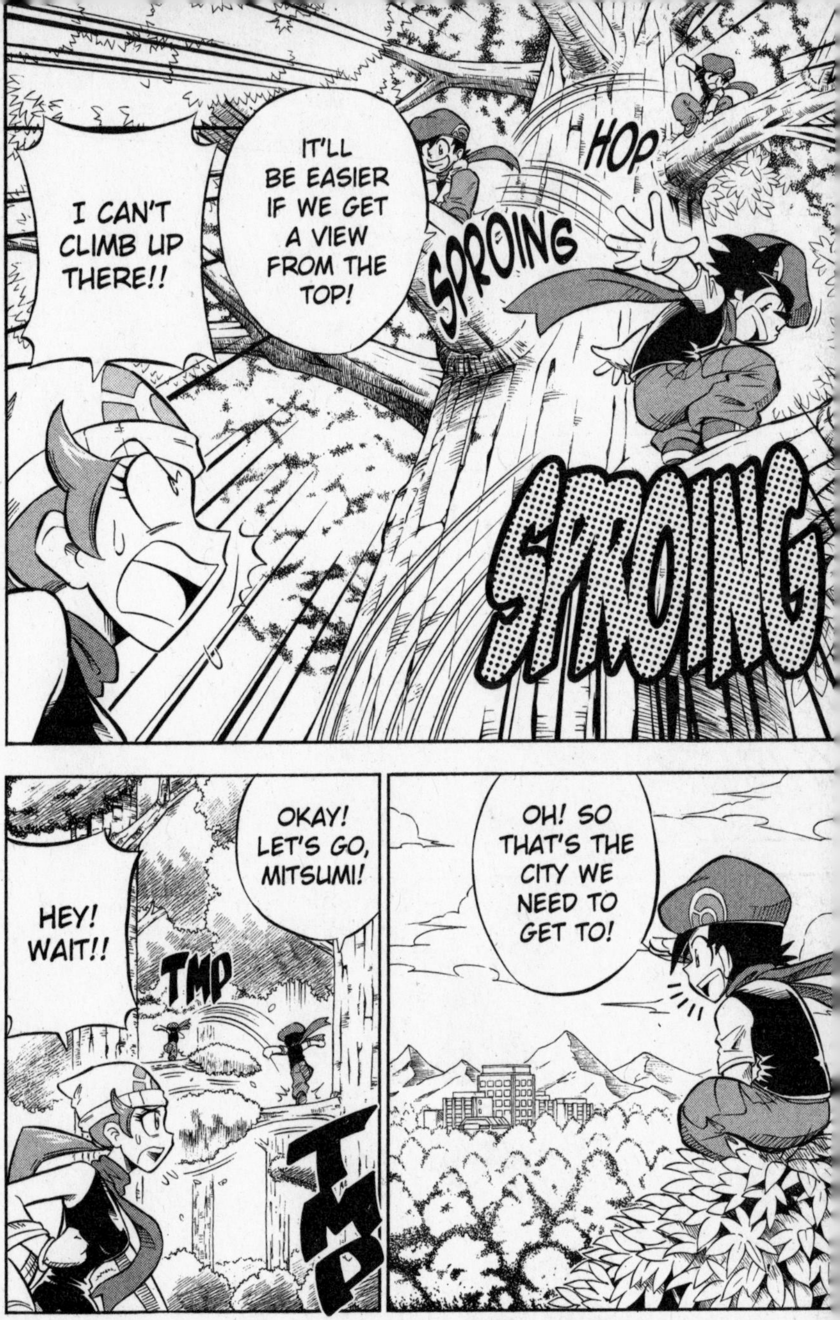
HOP
SPROING
IT'LL BE EASIER IF WE GET A VIEW FROM THE TOP!
I CAN'T CLIMB UP THERE!!
SPROING
OH! SO THAT'S THE CITY WE NEED TO GET TO!
OKAY! LET'S GO, MITSUMI!
TMP
TMP
HEY! WAIT!!

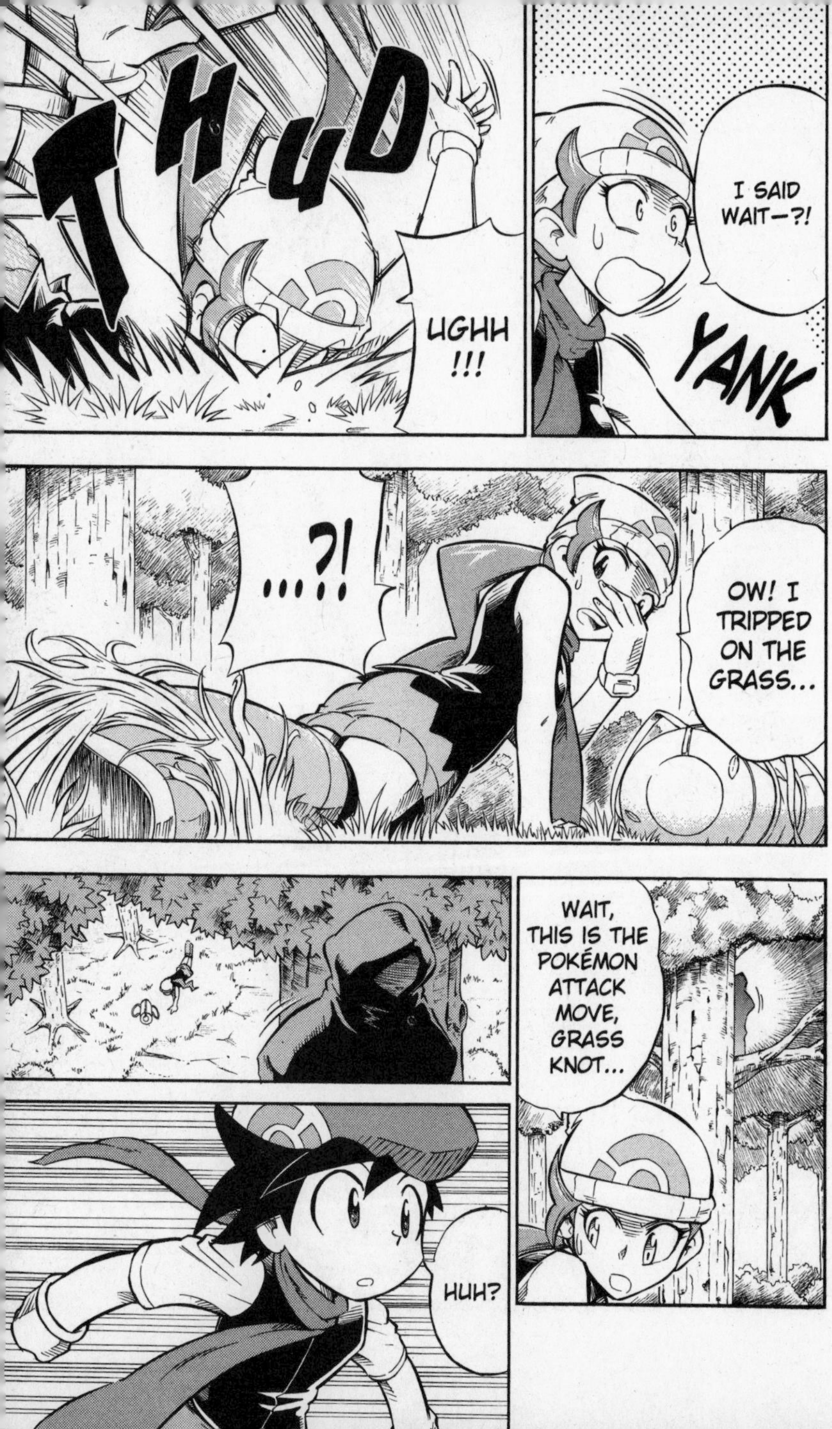
I SAID WAIT—?!
YANK
THUD
UGHH !!!
OW! I TRIPPED ON THE GRASS...
...?!
WAIT, THIS IS THE POKÉMON ATTACK MOVE, GRASS KNOT...
HUH?

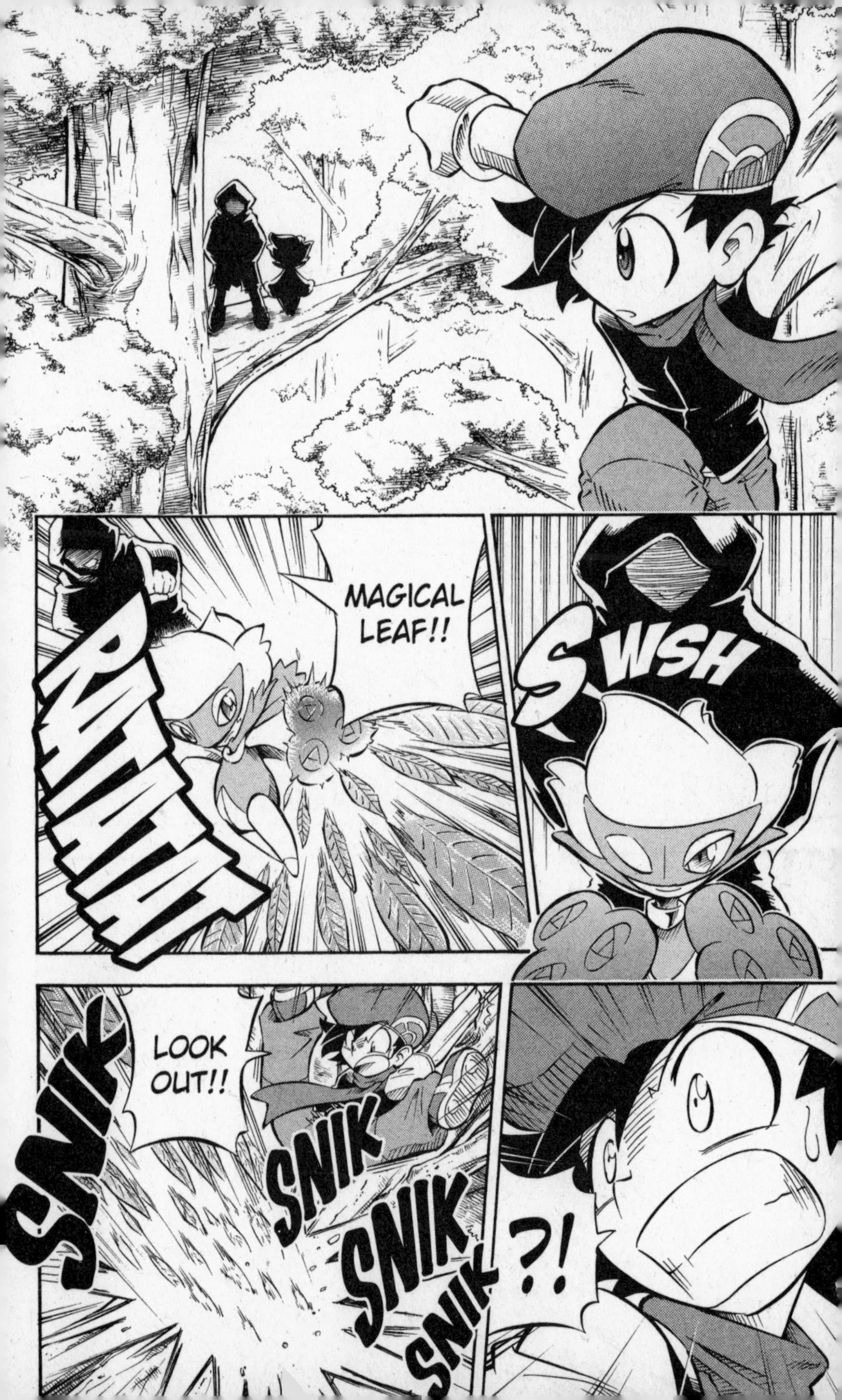
SWSH
MAGICAL LEAF!!
RATATAT
?!
LOOK OUT!!
SNIK
SNIK
SNIK
SNIK

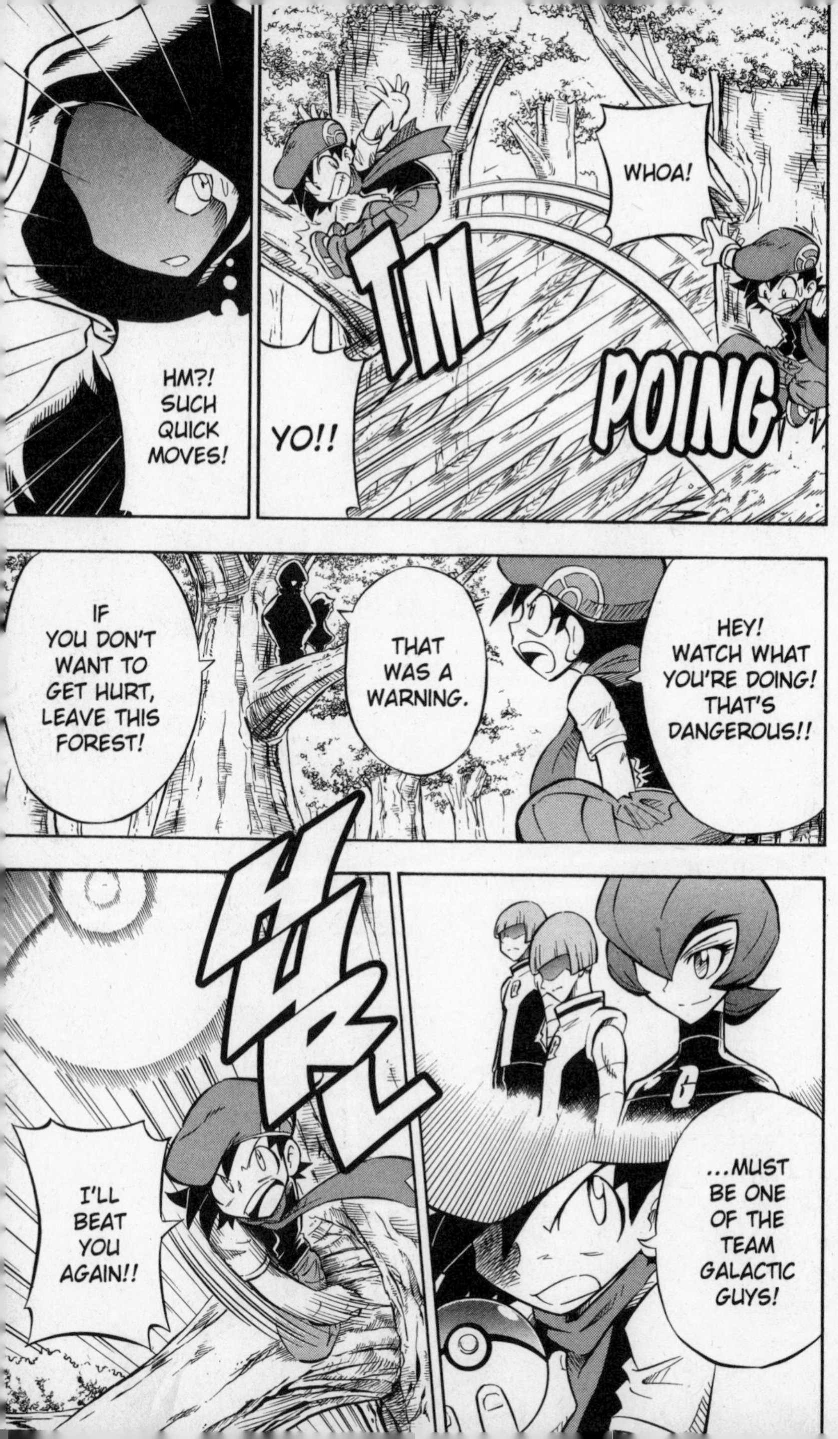
WHOA!
POING
TM
YO!!
HM?! SUCH QUICK MOVES!
HEY! WATCH WHAT YOU'RE DOING! THAT'S DANGEROUS!!
THAT WAS A WARNING.
IF YOU DON'T WANT TO GET HURT, LEAVE THIS FOREST!
...MUST BE ONE OF THE TEAM GALACTIC GUYS!
HURL
I'LL BEAT YOU AGAIN!!

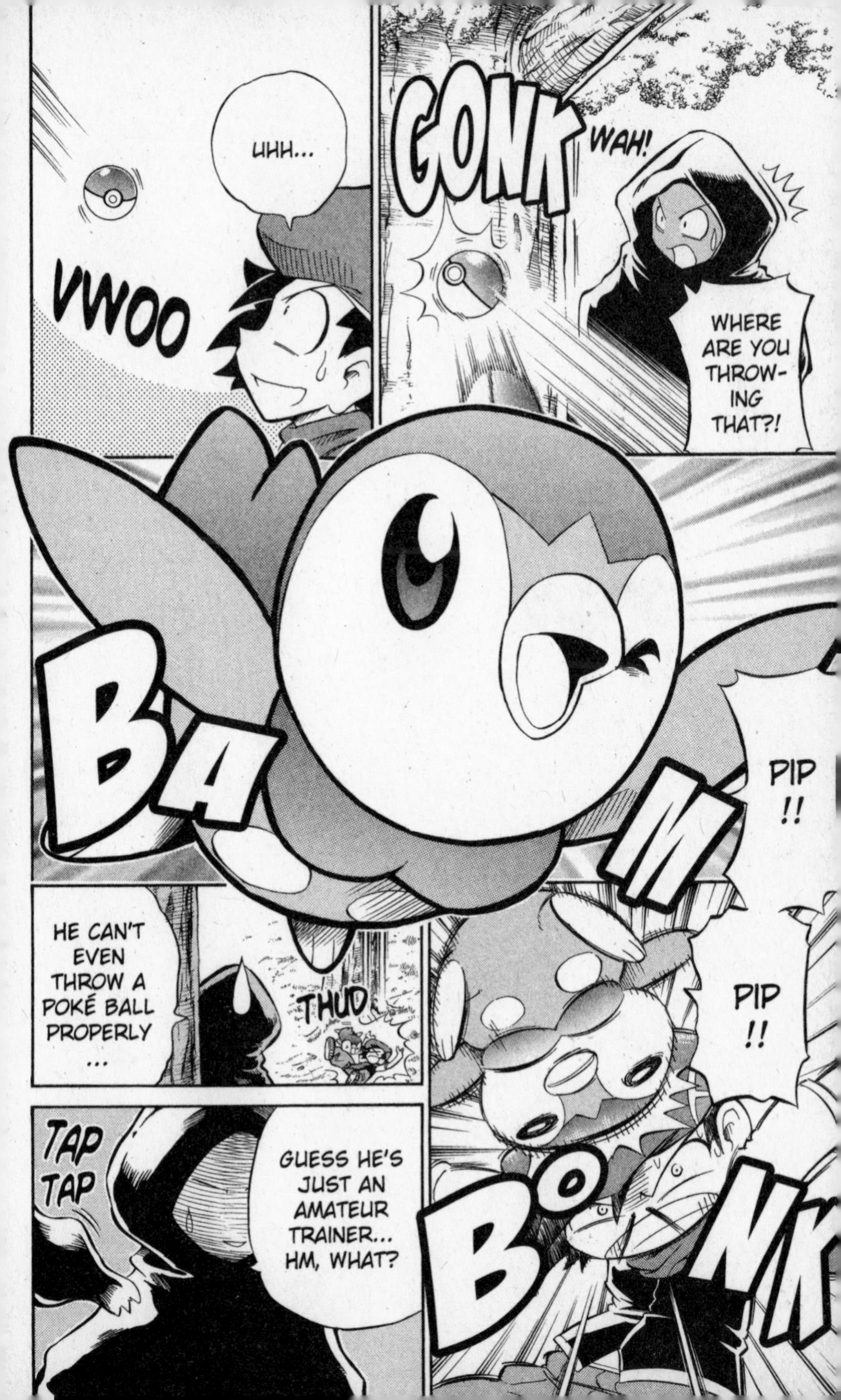
GONK
WAH!
WHERE ARE YOU THROWING THAT?!
UHH...
VWOO
BAM
PIP !!
PIP !!
BONK
HE CAN'T EVEN THROW A POKÉ BALL PROPERLY ...
THUD
GUESS HE'S JUST AN AMATEUR TRAINER... HM, WHAT?
TAP TAP

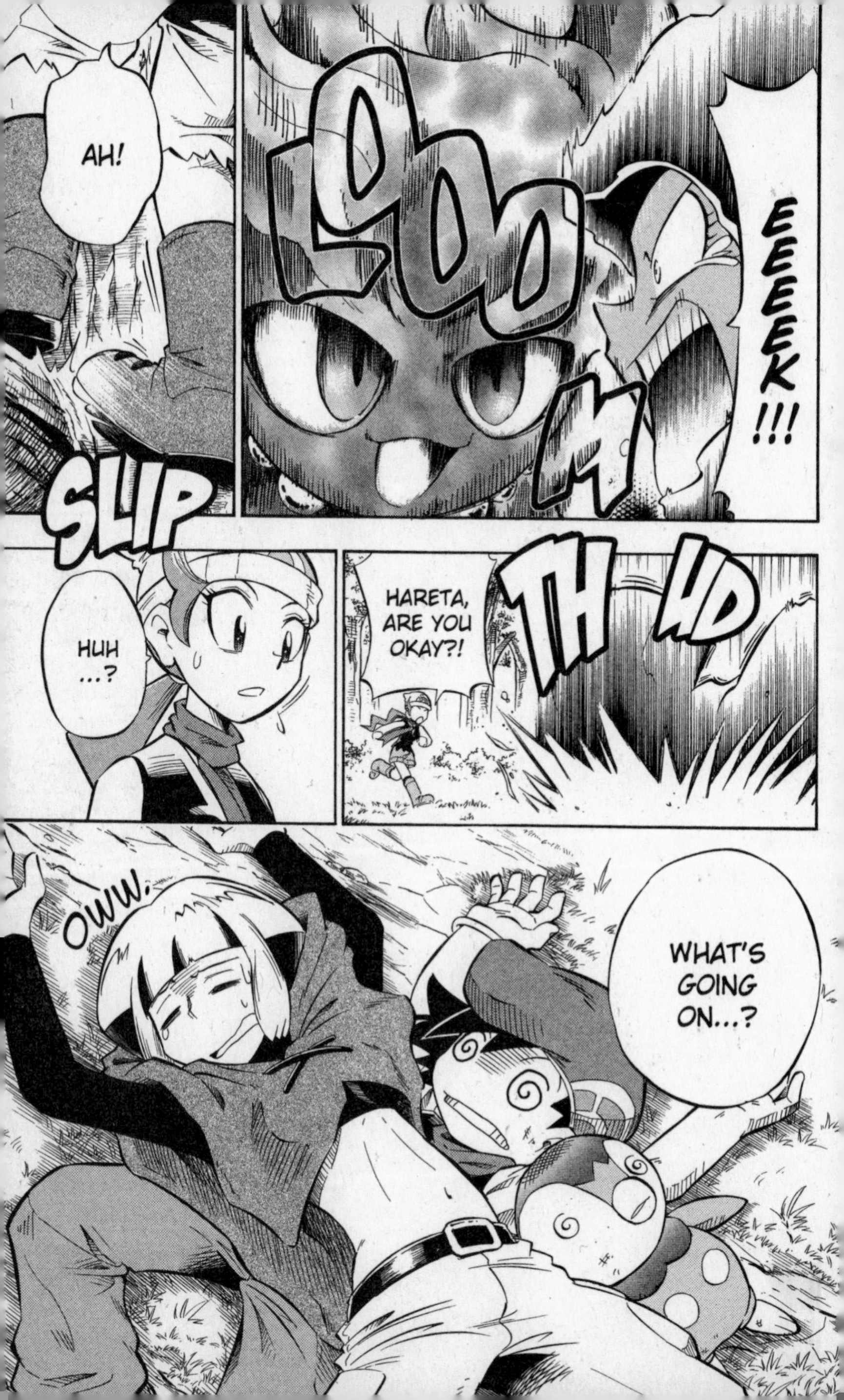
EEEEEK!!!
AH!
SLIP
THUD
HARETA, ARE YOU OKAY?!
HUH ...?
WHAT'S GOING ON...?
OWW.

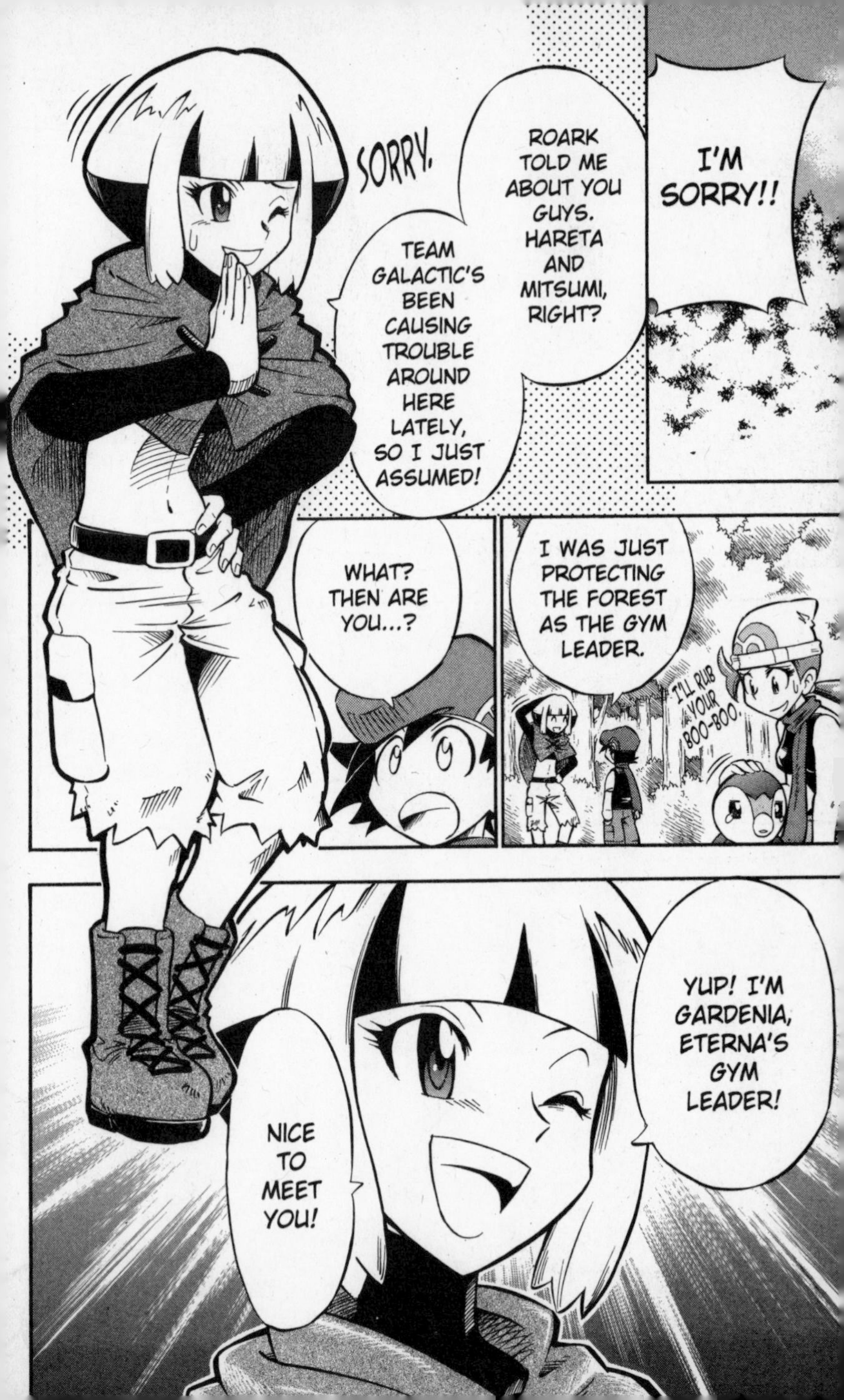
I'M SORRY!!
SORRY.
ROARK TOLD ME ABOUT YOU GUYS. HARETA AND MITSUMI, RIGHT?
TEAM GALACTIC'S BEEN CAUSING TROUBLE AROUND HERE LATELY, SO I JUST ASSUMED!
WHAT? THEN ARE YOU...?
I WAS JUST PROTECTING THE FOREST AS THE GYM LEADER.
I'LL RUB YOUR BOO-BOO.
YUP! I'M GARDENIA, ETERNA'S GYM LEADER!
NICE TO MEET YOU!

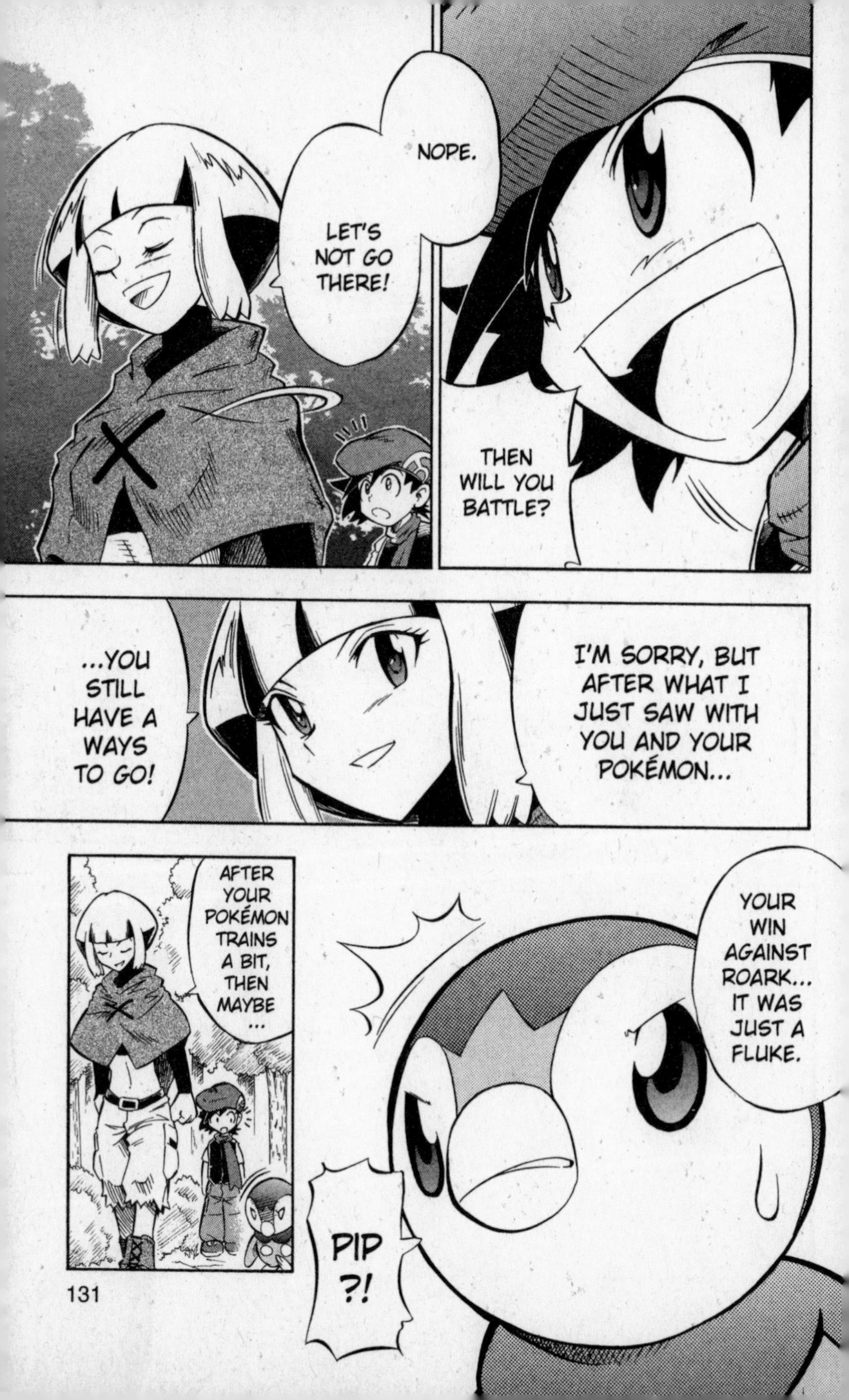
THEN WILL YOU BATTLE?
NOPE.
LET'S NOT GO THERE!
I'M SORRY, BUT AFTER WHAT I JUST SAW WITH YOU AND YOUR POKÉMON...
...YOU STILL HAVE A WAYS TO GO!
YOUR WIN AGAINST ROARK... IT WAS JUST A FLUKE.
PIP ?!
AFTER YOUR POKÉMON TRAINS A BIT, THEN MAYBE ...

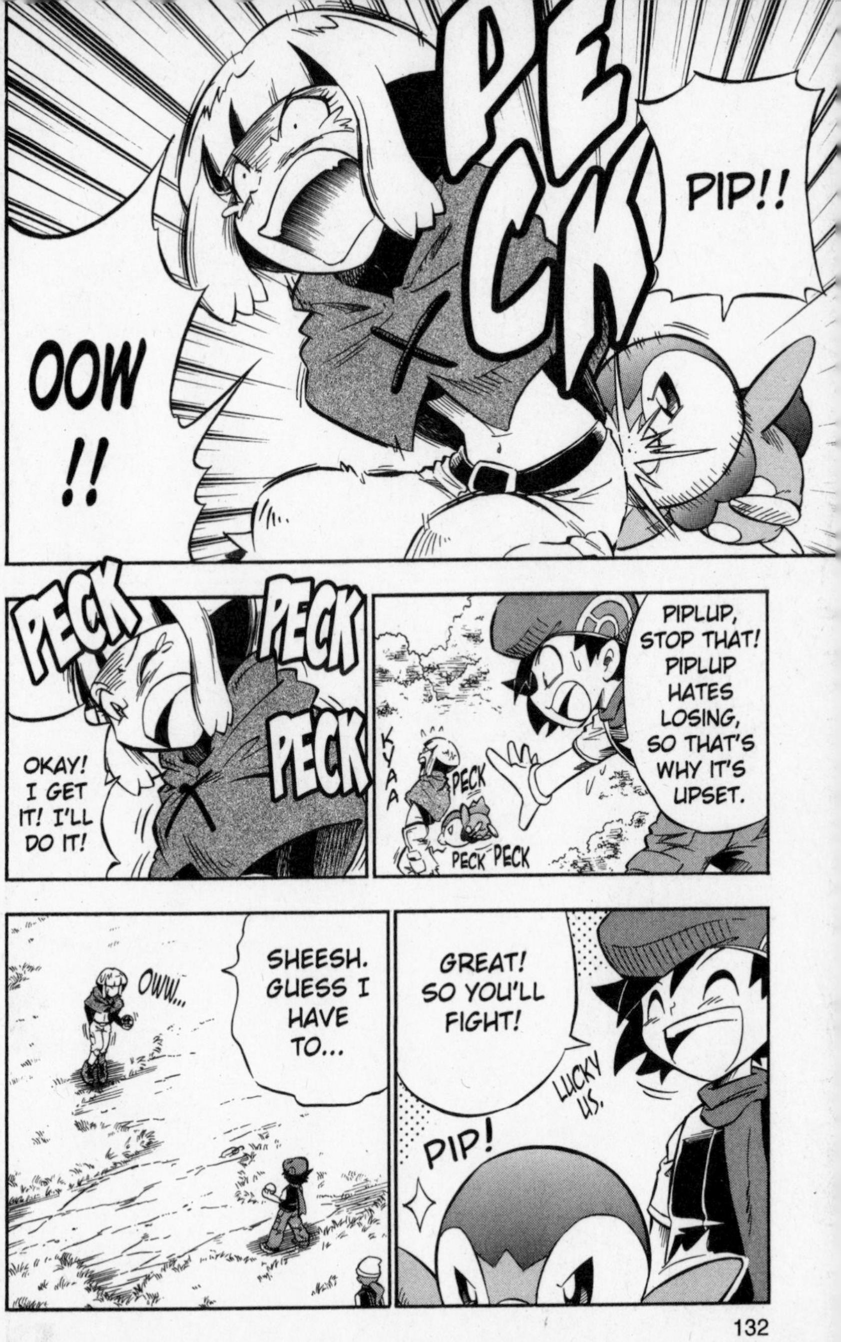
PIP!!
PECK
OOW!!
PIPLUP, STOP THAT! PIPLUP HATES LOSING, SO THAT'S WHY IT'S UPSET.
KYAA
PECK
PECK PECK
PECK
PECK
PECK
OKAY! I GET IT! I'LL DO IT!
GREAT! SO YOU'LL FIGHT!
LUCKY US.
PIP!
SHEESH. GUESS I HAVE TO...
OWW...

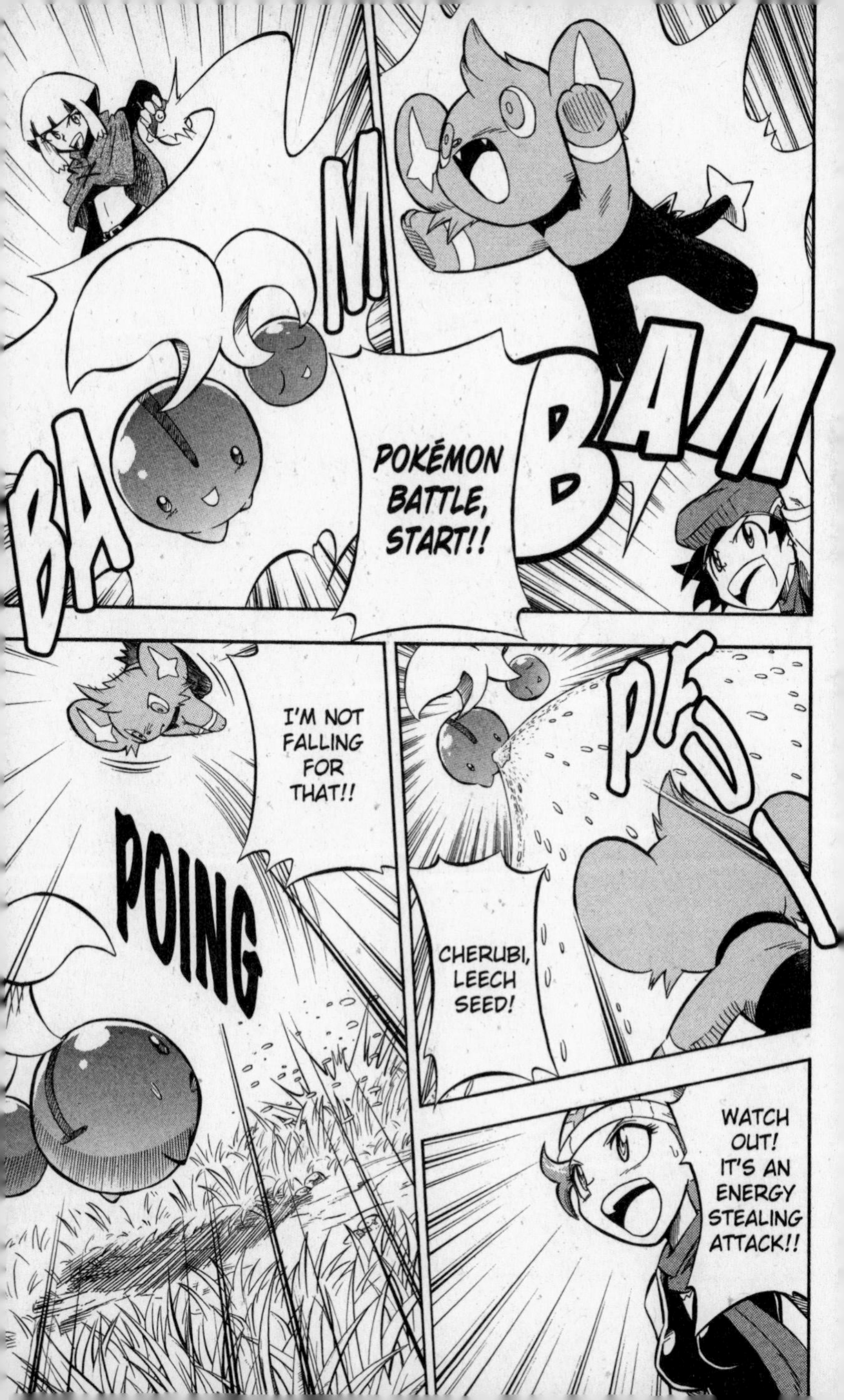
BAM
BAM
POKÉMON BATTLE, START!!
CHERUBI, LEECH SEED!
I'M NOT FALLING FOR THAT!!
POING
WATCH OUT! IT'S AN ENERGY STEALING ATTACK!!

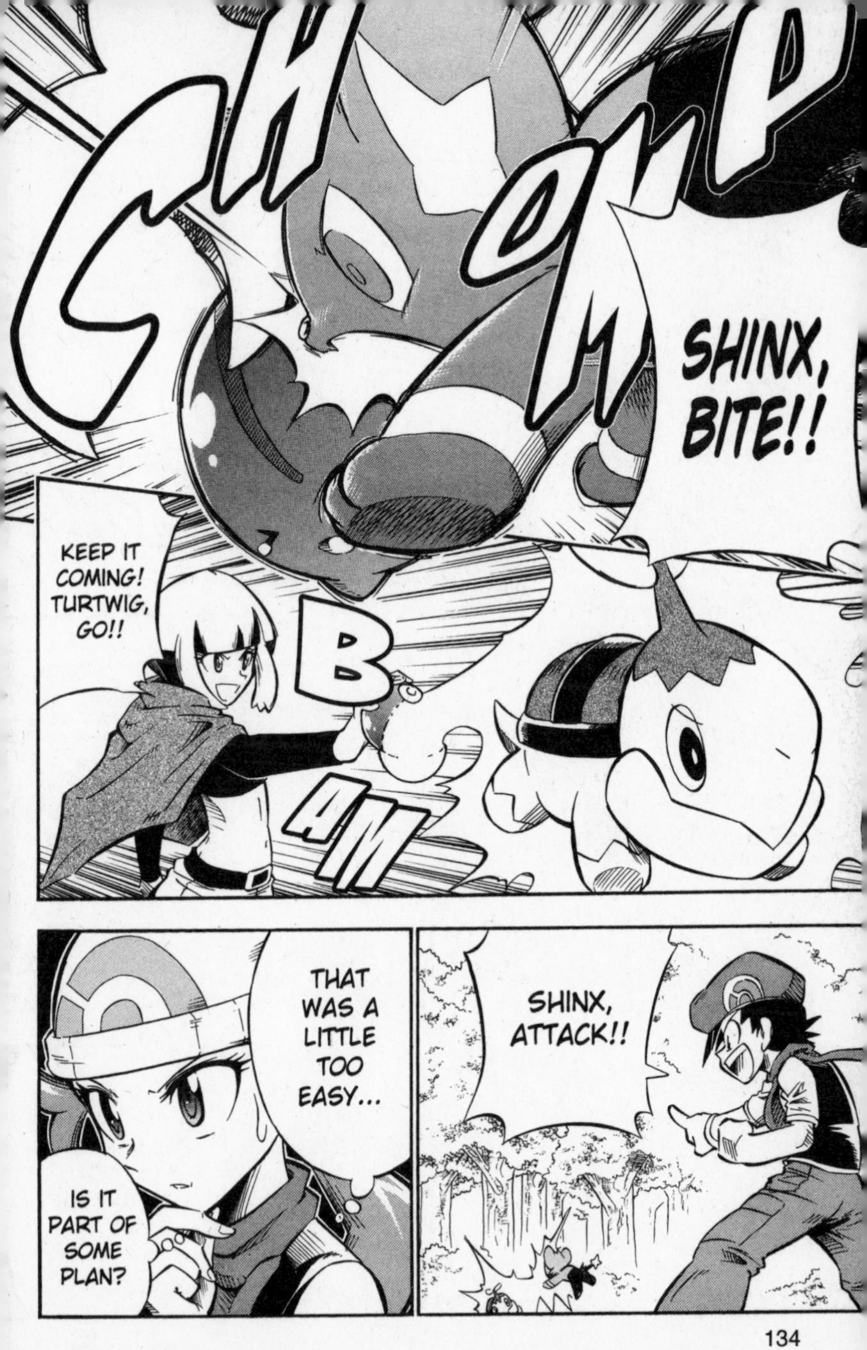
SHOMP
SHINX, BITE!!
KEEP IT COMING! TURTWIG, GO!!
BAM
SHINX, ATTACK!!
THAT WAS A LITTLE TOO EASY...
IS IT PART OF SOME PLAN?

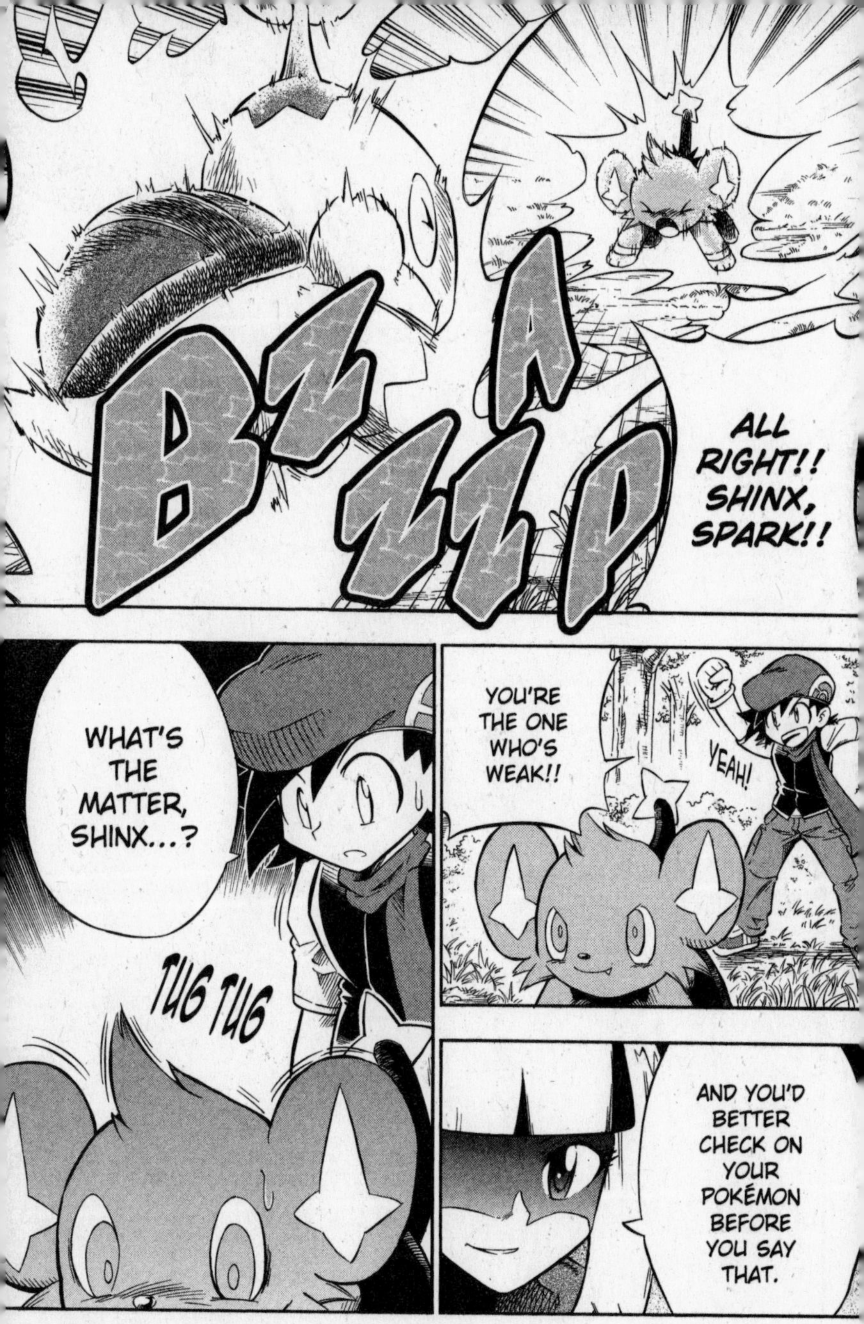
ALL RIGHT!! SHINX, SPARK!!
BZZZAP
YEAH!
YOU'RE THE ONE WHO'S WEAK!!
AND YOU'D BETTER CHECK ON YOUR POKÉMON BEFORE YOU SAY THAT.
WHAT'S THE MATTER, SHINX...?
TUG TUG

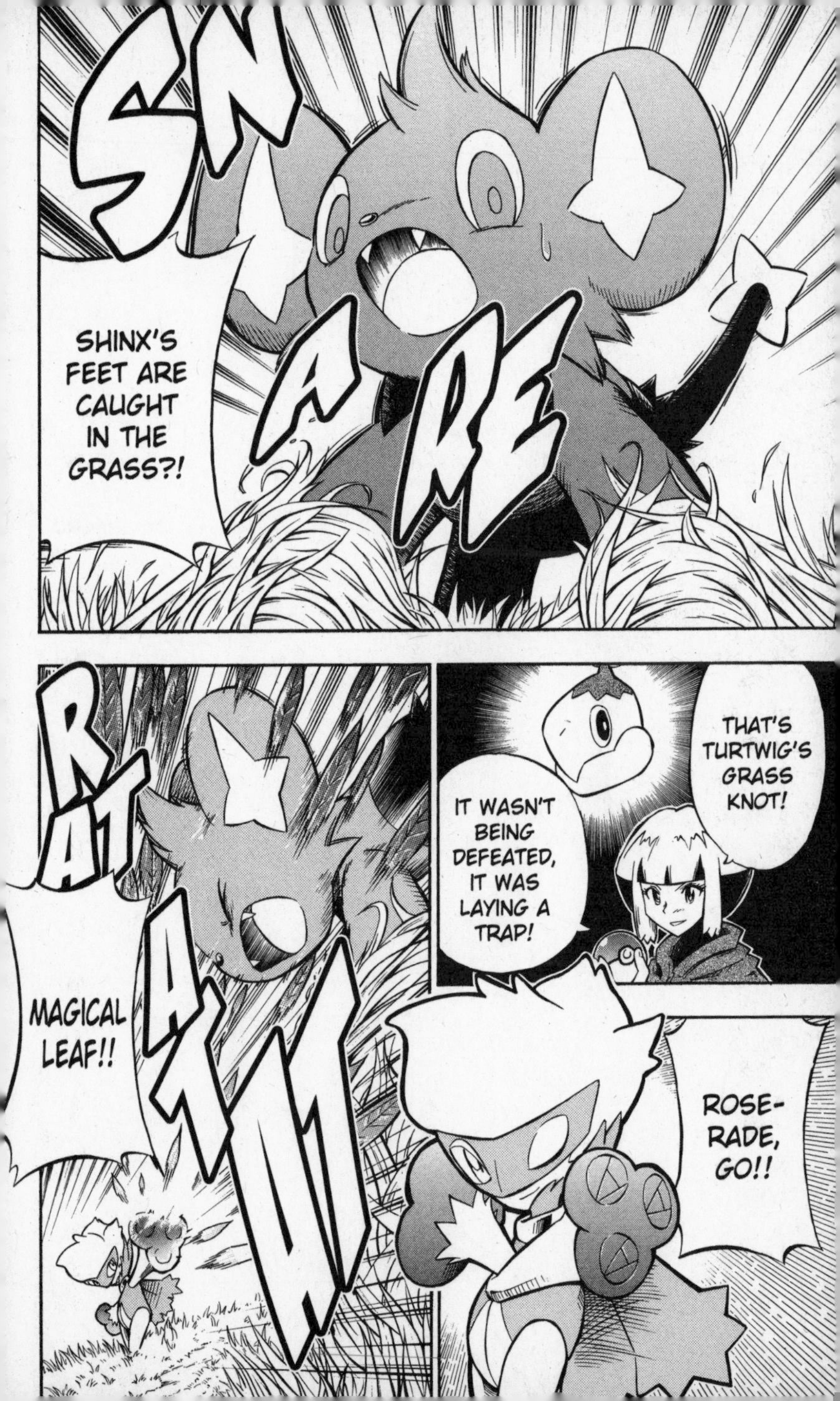
SNARE
SHINX'S FEET ARE CAUGHT IN THE GRASS?!
THAT'S TURTWIG'S GRASS KNOT!
IT WASN'T BEING DEFEATED, IT WAS LAYING A TRAP!
ROSE-RADE, GO!!
MAGICAL LEAF!!

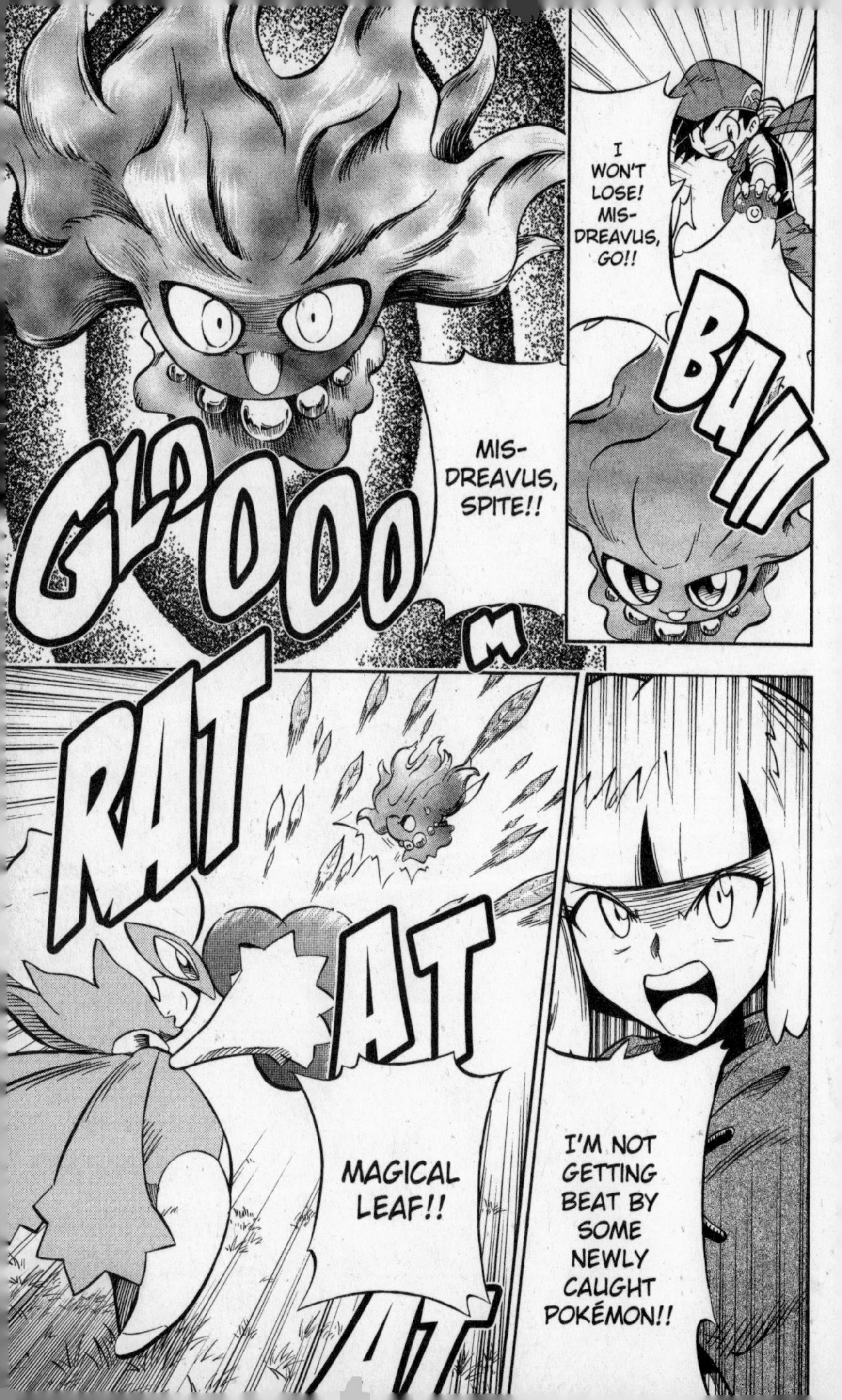

I WON'T LOSE! MIS-DREAVUS, GO!!
BAM
MIS-DREAVUS, SPITE!!
GLOOOOM
I'M NOT GETTING BEAT BY SOME NEWLY CAUGHT POKÉMON!!
RAT
AT
AT
MAGICAL LEAF!!

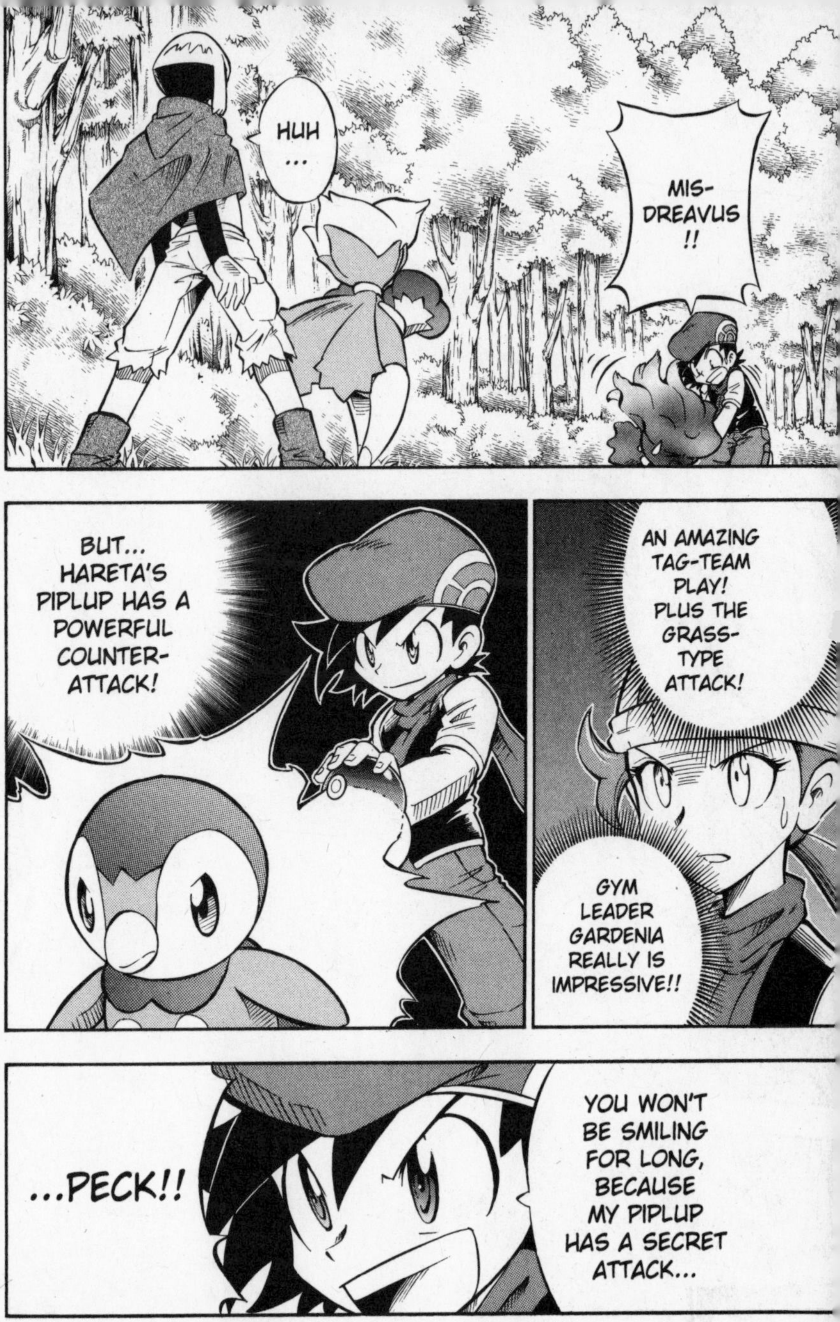
MIS-DREAVUS!!
HUH...
AN AMAZING TAG-TEAM PLAY! PLUS THE GRASS-TYPE ATTACK!
GYM LEADER GARDENIA REALLY IS IMPRESSIVE!!
BUT... HARETA'S PIPLUP HAS A POWERFUL COUNTER-ATTACK!
YOU WON'T BE SMILING FOR LONG, BECAUSE MY PIPLUP HAS A SECRET ATTACK...
...PECK!!

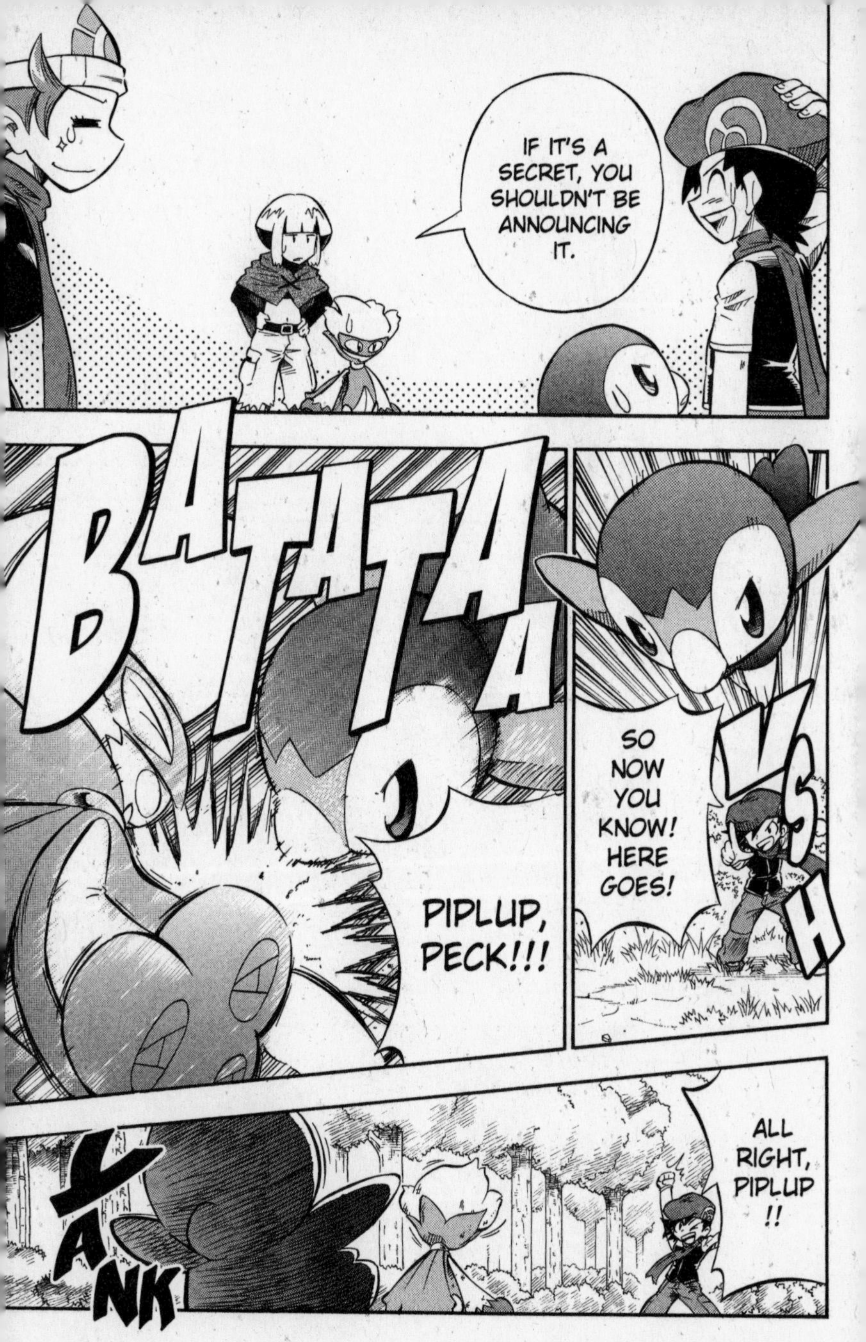
IF IT'S A SECRET, YOU SHOULDN'T BE ANNOUNCING IT.
SO NOW YOU KNOW! HERE GOES!
BATATAA
PIPLUP, PECK!!!
ALL RIGHT, PIPLUP!!
YANK

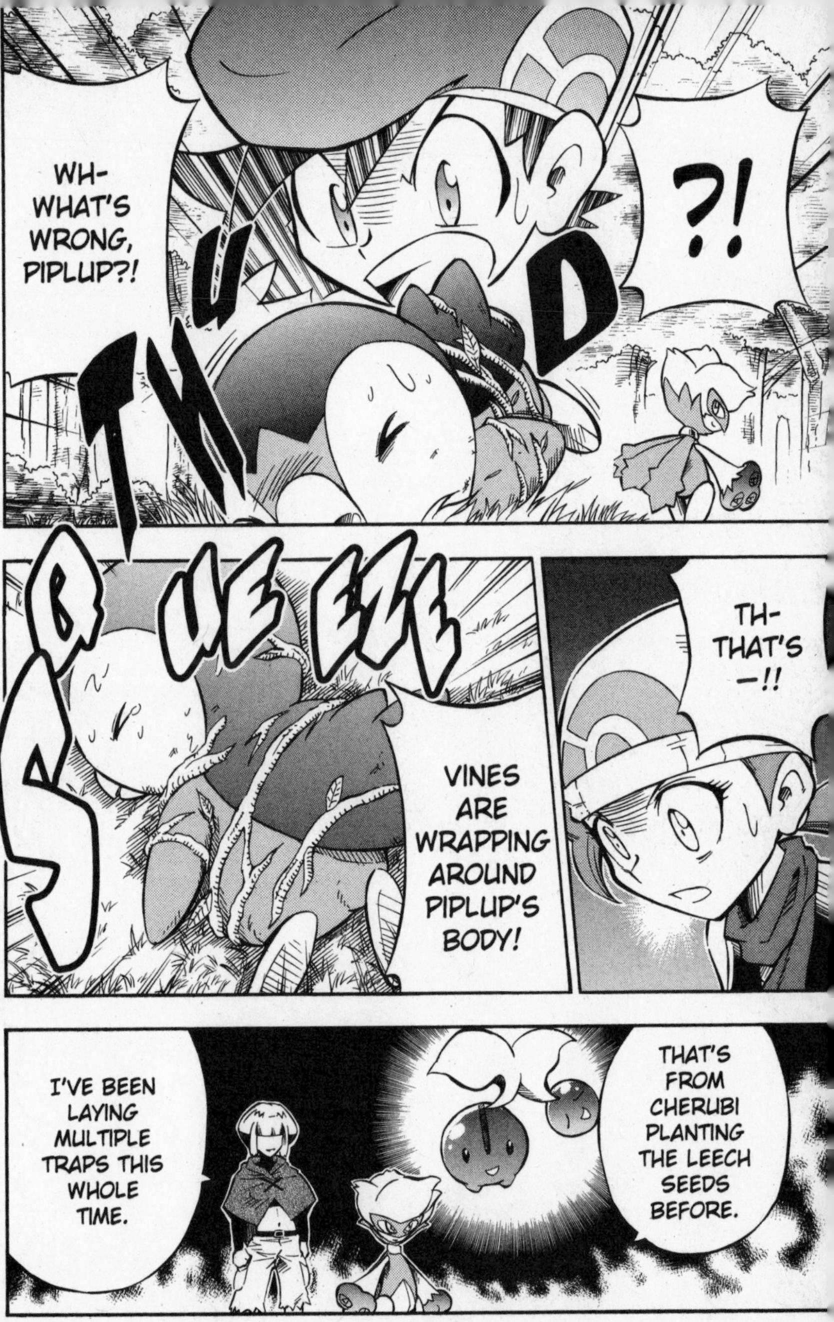
?!
WH- WHAT'S WRONG, PIPLUP?!
THUD
TH- THAT'S —!!
VINES ARE WRAPPING AROUND PIPLUP'S BODY!
SQUEEZE
THAT'S FROM CHERUBI PLANTING THE LEECH SEEDS BEFORE.
I'VE BEEN LAYING MULTIPLE TRAPS THIS WHOLE TIME.

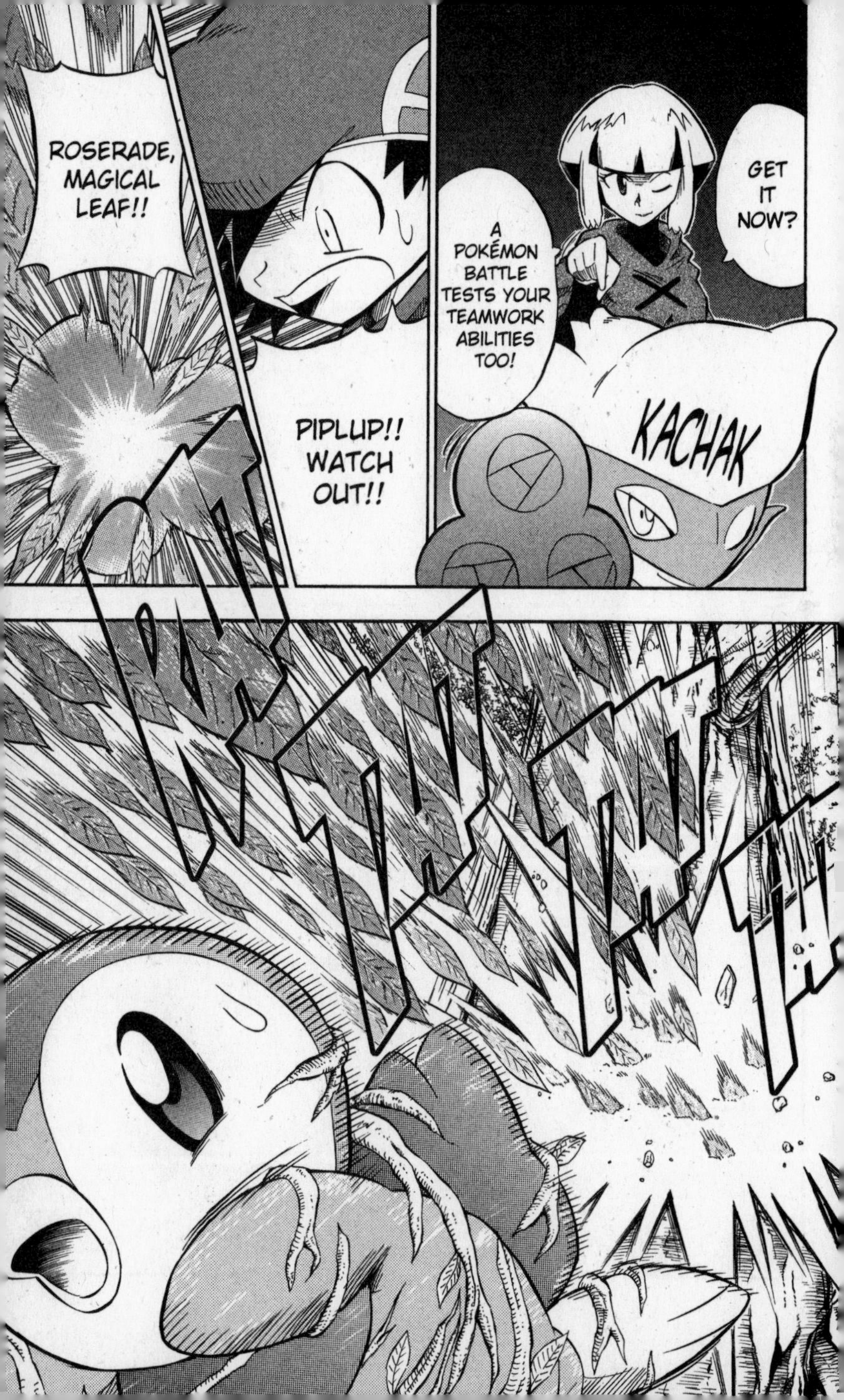
GET IT NOW?
A POKÉMON BATTLE TESTS YOUR TEAMWORK ABILITIES TOO!
KACHAK
ROSERADE, MAGICAL LEAF!!
PIPLUP!! WATCH OUT!!

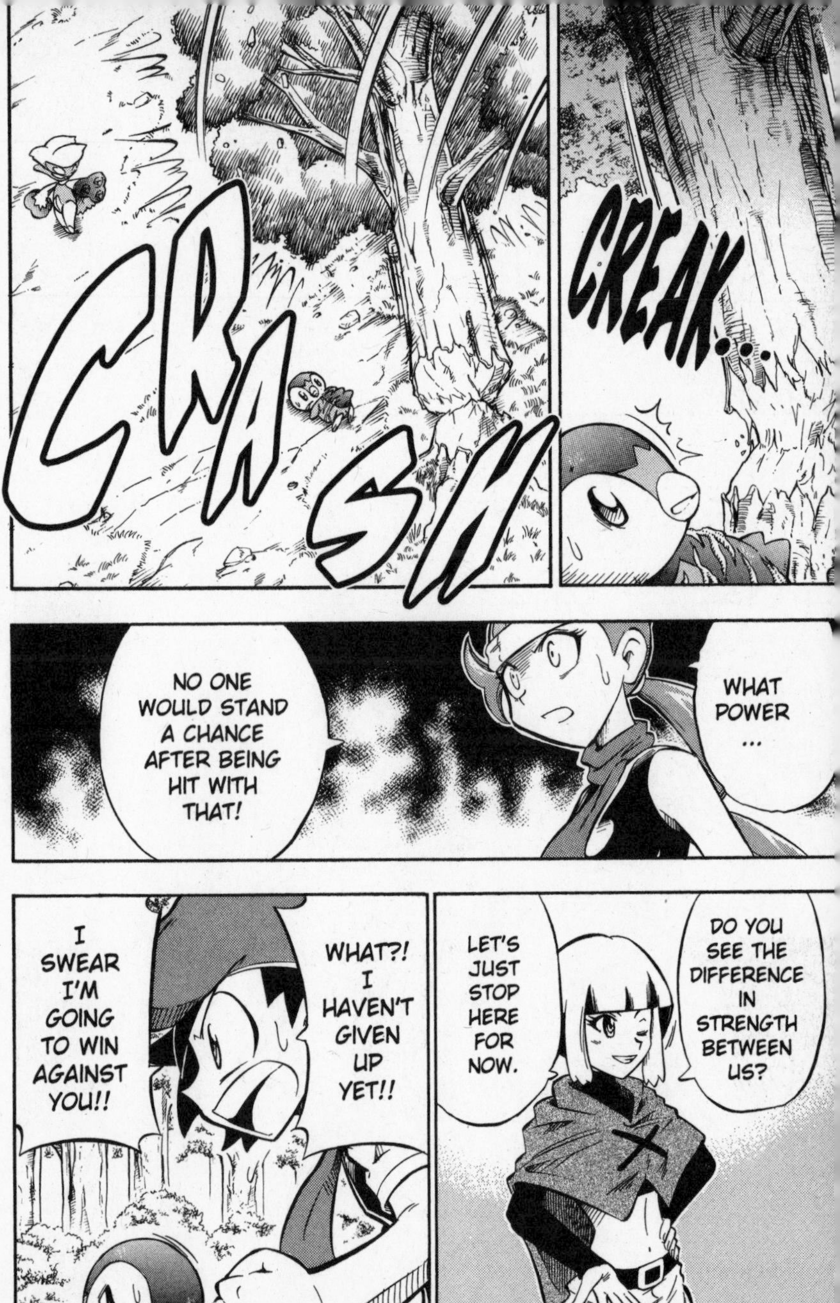
CREAK...
CRASH
WHAT POWER ...
NO ONE WOULD STAND A CHANCE AFTER BEING HIT WITH THAT!
DO YOU SEE THE DIFFERENCE IN STRENGTH BETWEEN US?
LET'S JUST STOP HERE FOR NOW.
WHAT?! I HAVEN'T GIVEN UP YET!!
I SWEAR I'M GOING TO WIN AGAINST YOU!!

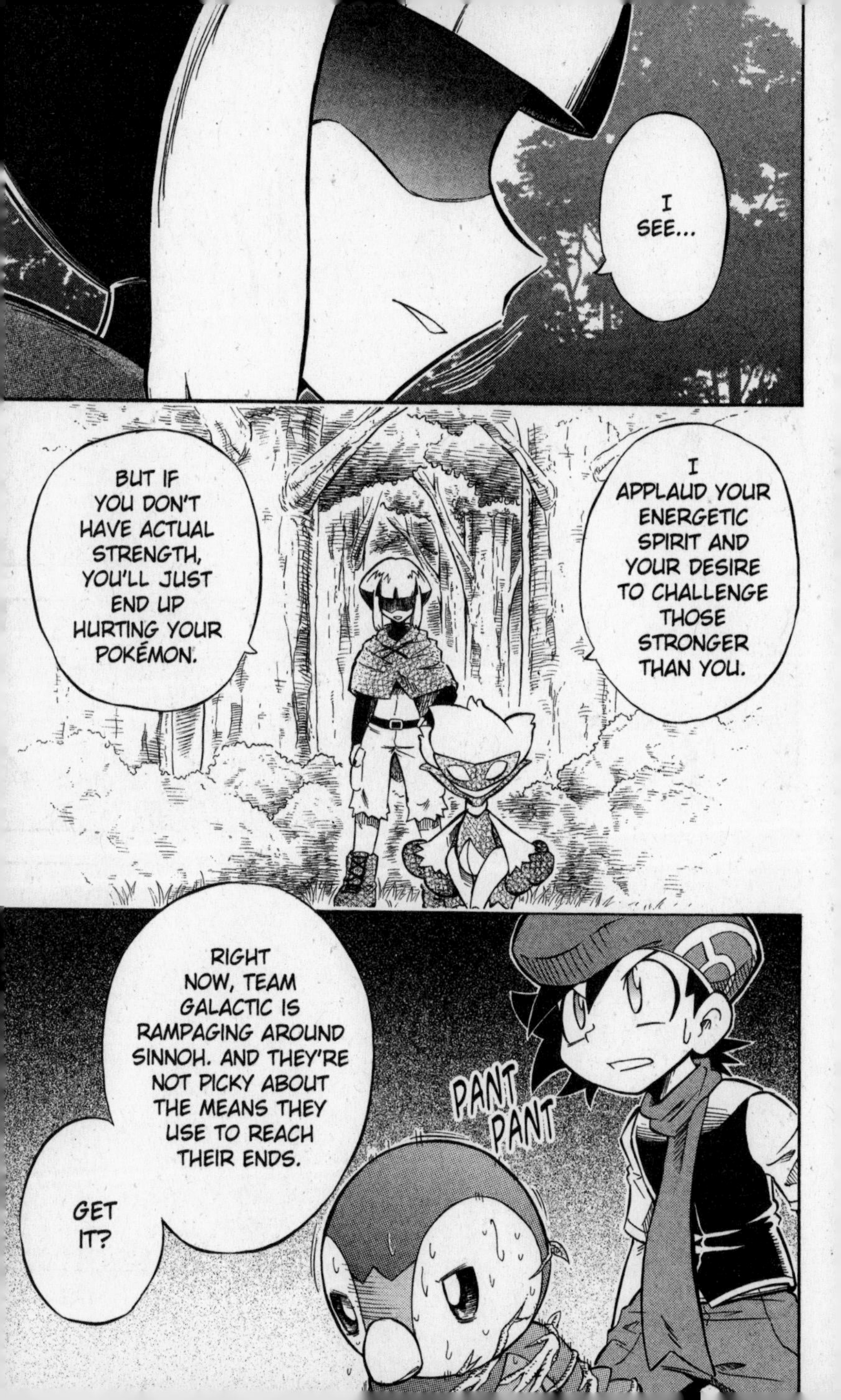
I SEE...
I APPLAUD YOUR ENERGETIC SPIRIT AND YOUR DESIRE TO CHALLENGE THOSE STRONGER THAN YOU.
BUT IF YOU DON'T HAVE ACTUAL STRENGTH, YOU'LL JUST END UP HURTING YOUR POKÉMON.
PANT PANT
RIGHT NOW, TEAM GALACTIC IS RAMPAGING AROUND SINNOH. AND THEY'RE NOT PICKY ABOUT THE MEANS THEY USE TO REACH THEIR ENDS.
GET IT?

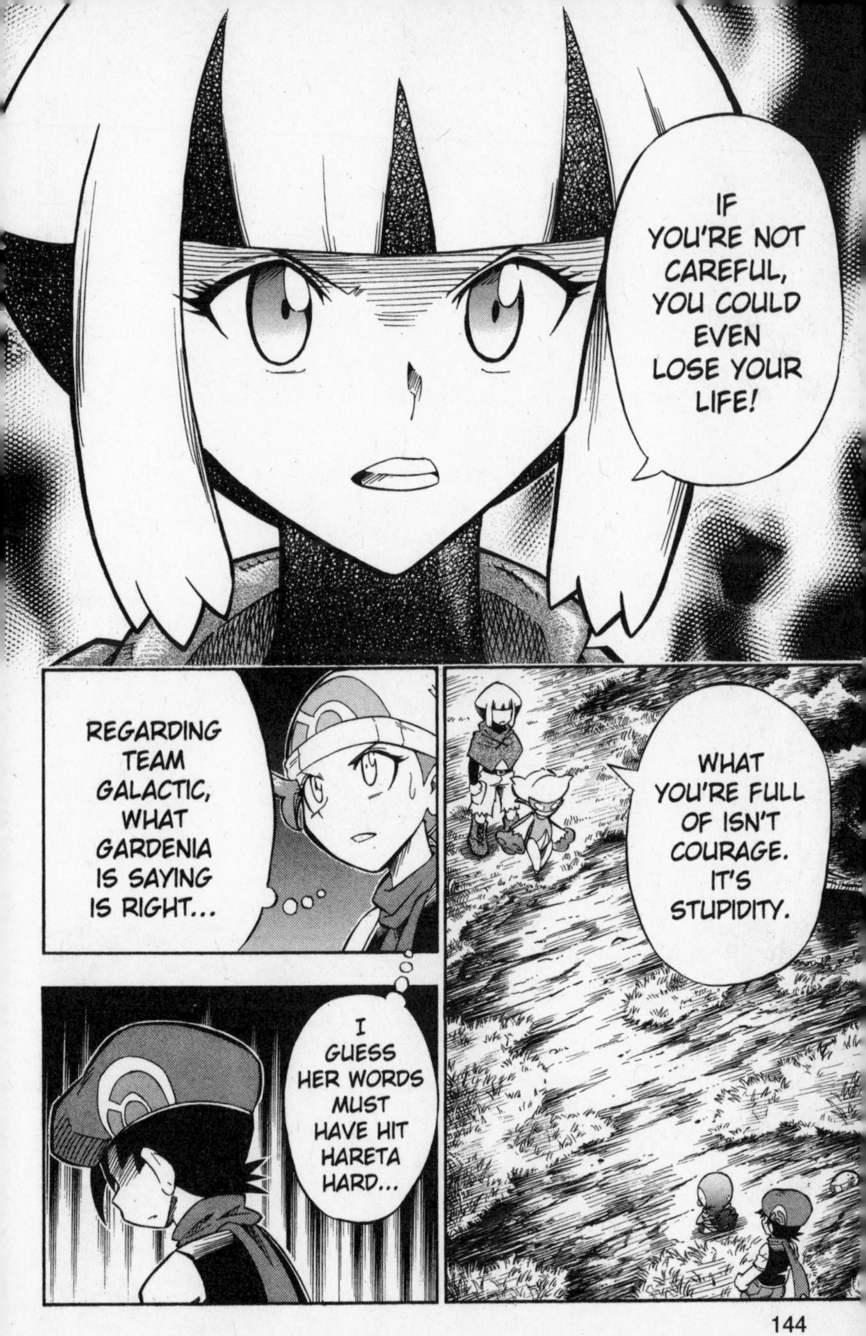
IF YOU'RE NOT CAREFUL, YOU COULD EVEN LOSE YOUR LIFE!
WHAT YOU'RE FULL OF ISN'T COURAGE. IT'S STUPIDITY.
REGARDING TEAM GALACTIC, WHAT GARDENIA IS SAYING IS RIGHT...
I GUESS HER WORDS MUST HAVE HIT HARETA HARD...

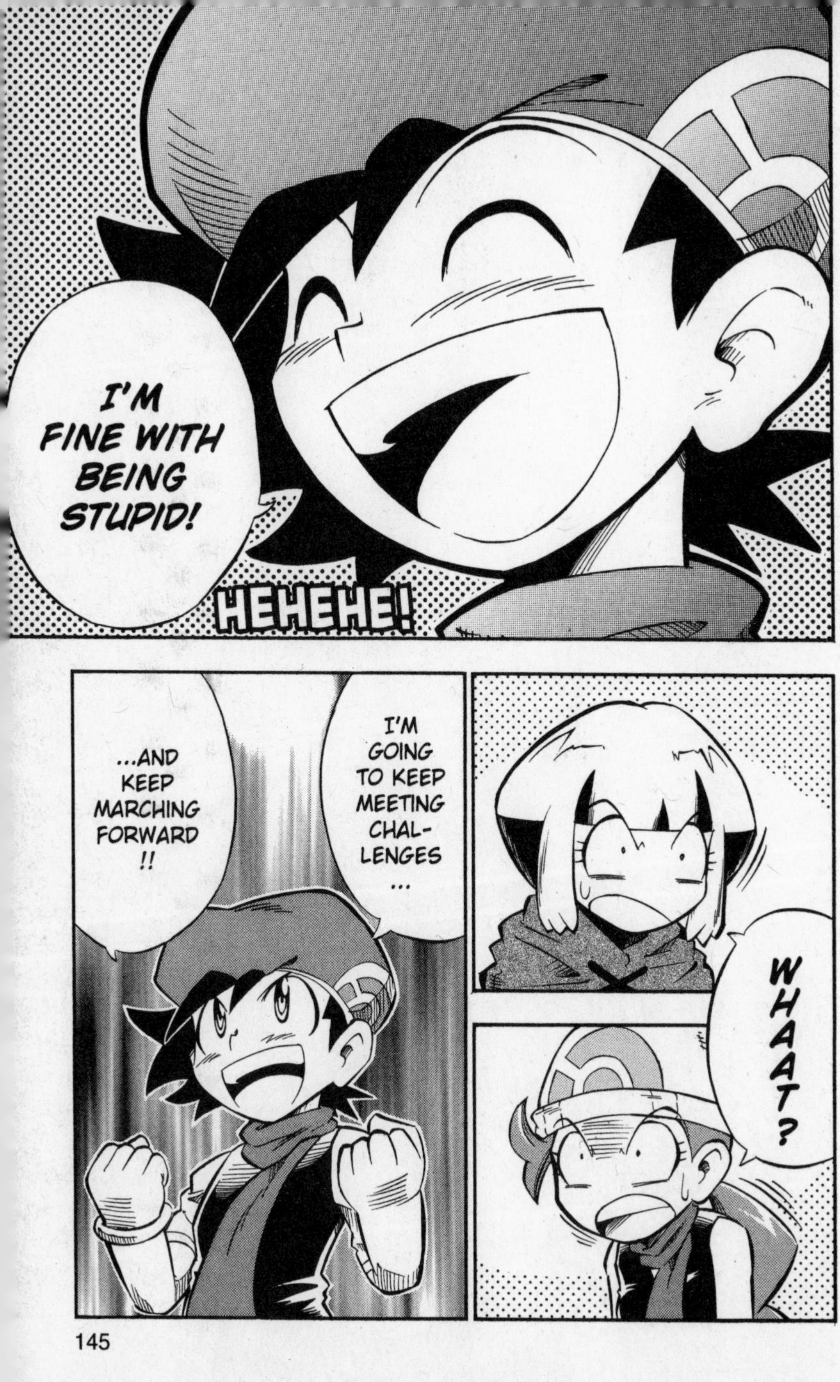
I'M FINE WITH BEING STUPID!
HEHEHE!
WHAAT?
I'M GOING TO KEEP MEETING CHAL-LENGES...
...AND KEEP MARCHING FORWARD!!

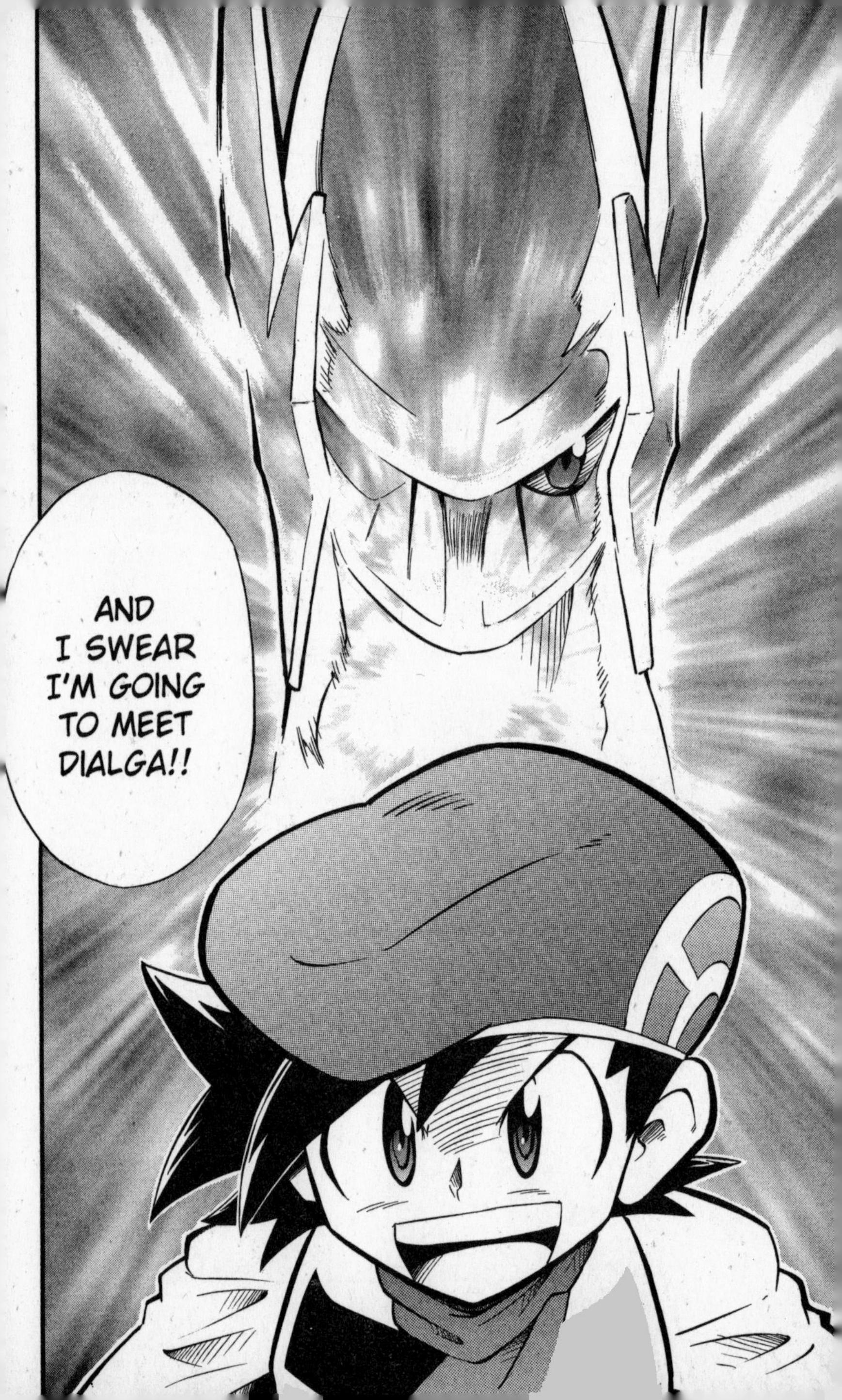
AND I SWEAR I'M GOING TO MEET DIALGA!!

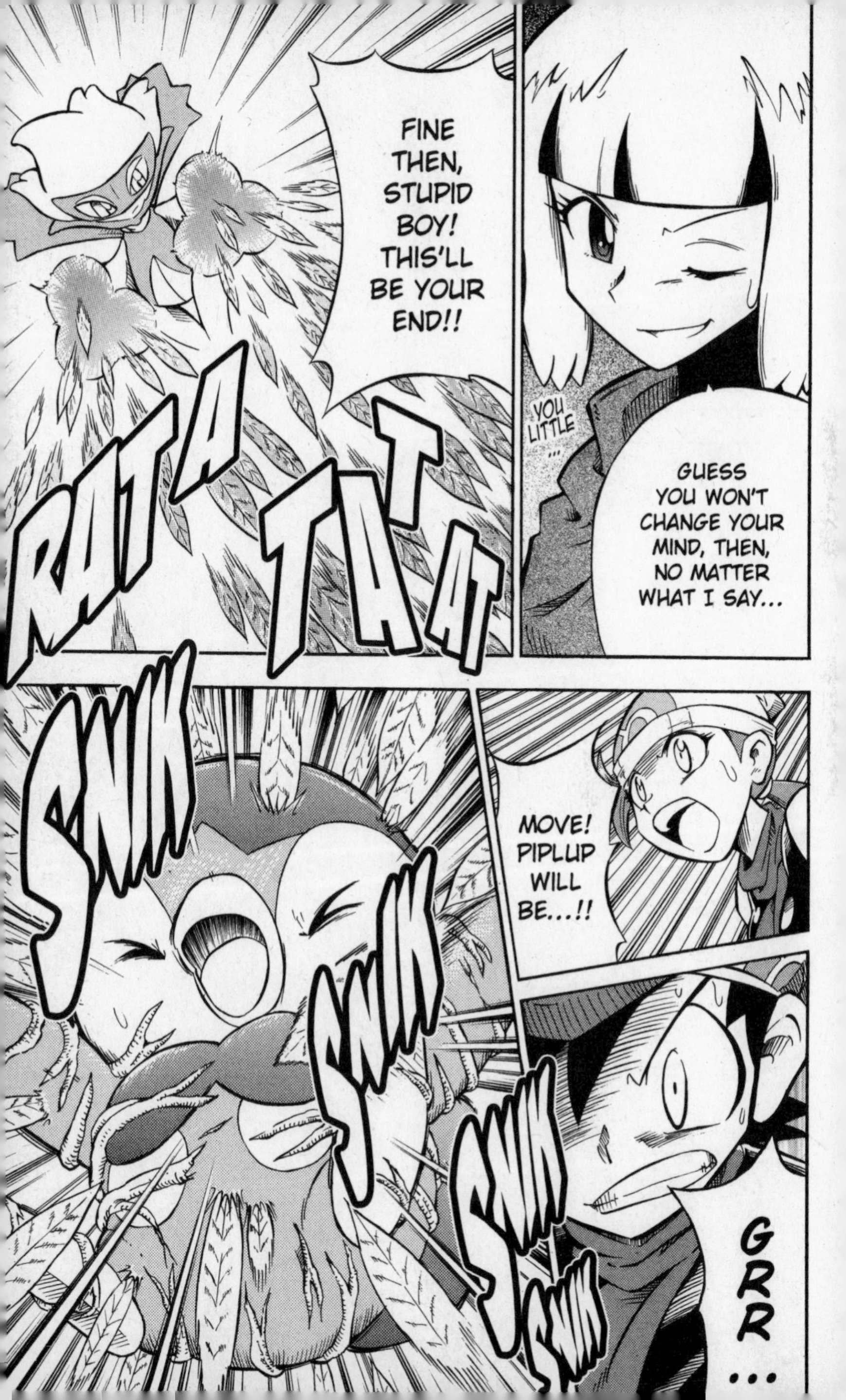
YOU LITTLE ...
GUESS YOU WON'T CHANGE YOUR MIND, THEN, NO MATTER WHAT I SAY...
FINE THEN, STUPID BOY! THIS'LL BE YOUR END!!
RAT A TAT TAT
MOVE! PIPLUP WILL BE...!!
GRR ...

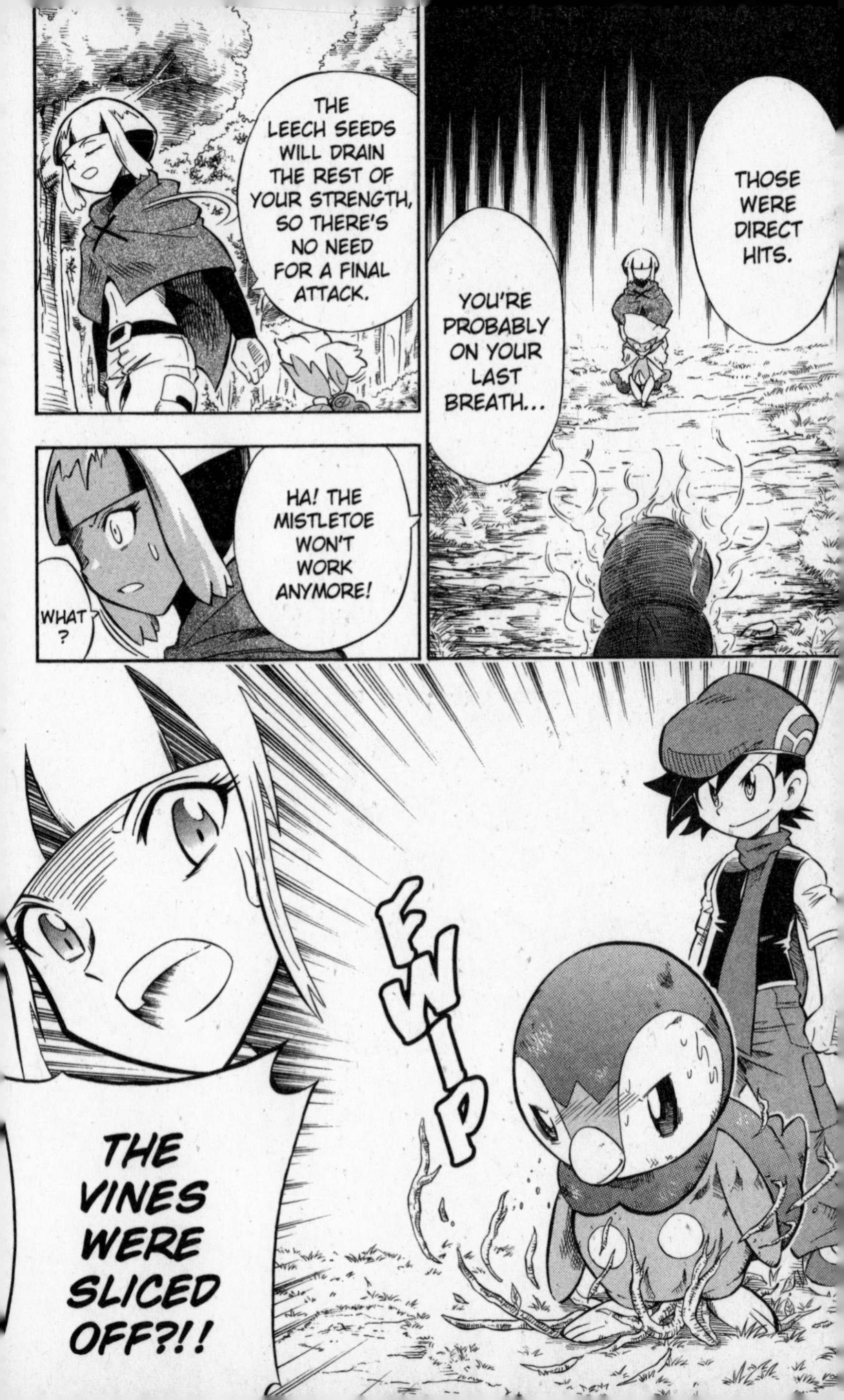
THOSE WERE DIRECT HITS.
YOU'RE PROBABLY ON YOUR LAST BREATH...
THE LEECH SEEDS WILL DRAIN THE REST OF YOUR STRENGTH, SO THERE'S NO NEED FOR A FINAL ATTACK.
HA! THE MISTLETOE WON'T WORK ANYMORE!
WHAT?
FWIP
THE VINES WERE SLICED OFF?!!

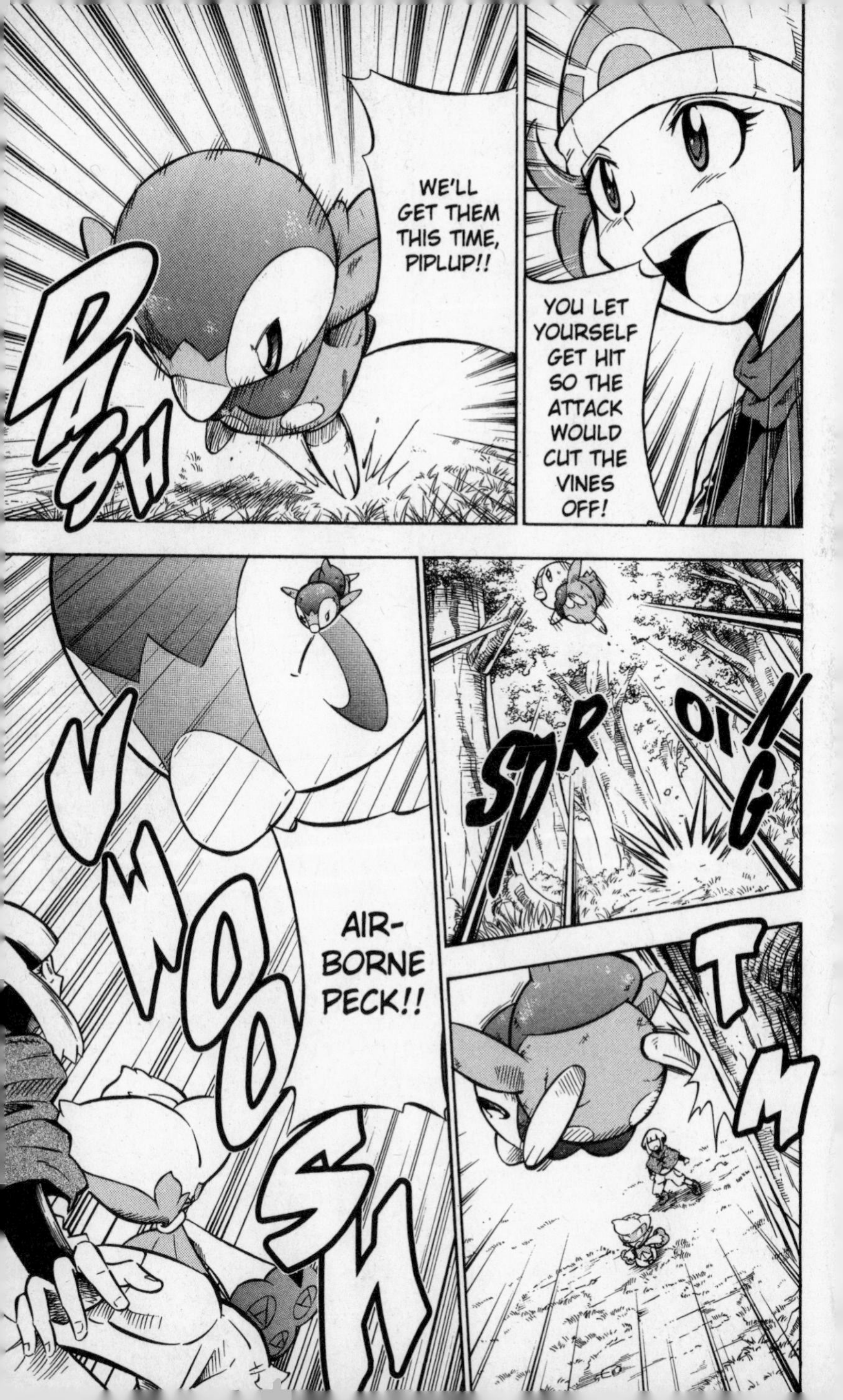
YOU LET YOURSELF GET HIT SO THE ATTACK WOULD CUT THE VINES OFF!
WE'LL GET THEM THIS TIME, PIPLUP!!
DASH
SPROING
TM
AIR-BORNE PECK!!
WHOOSH

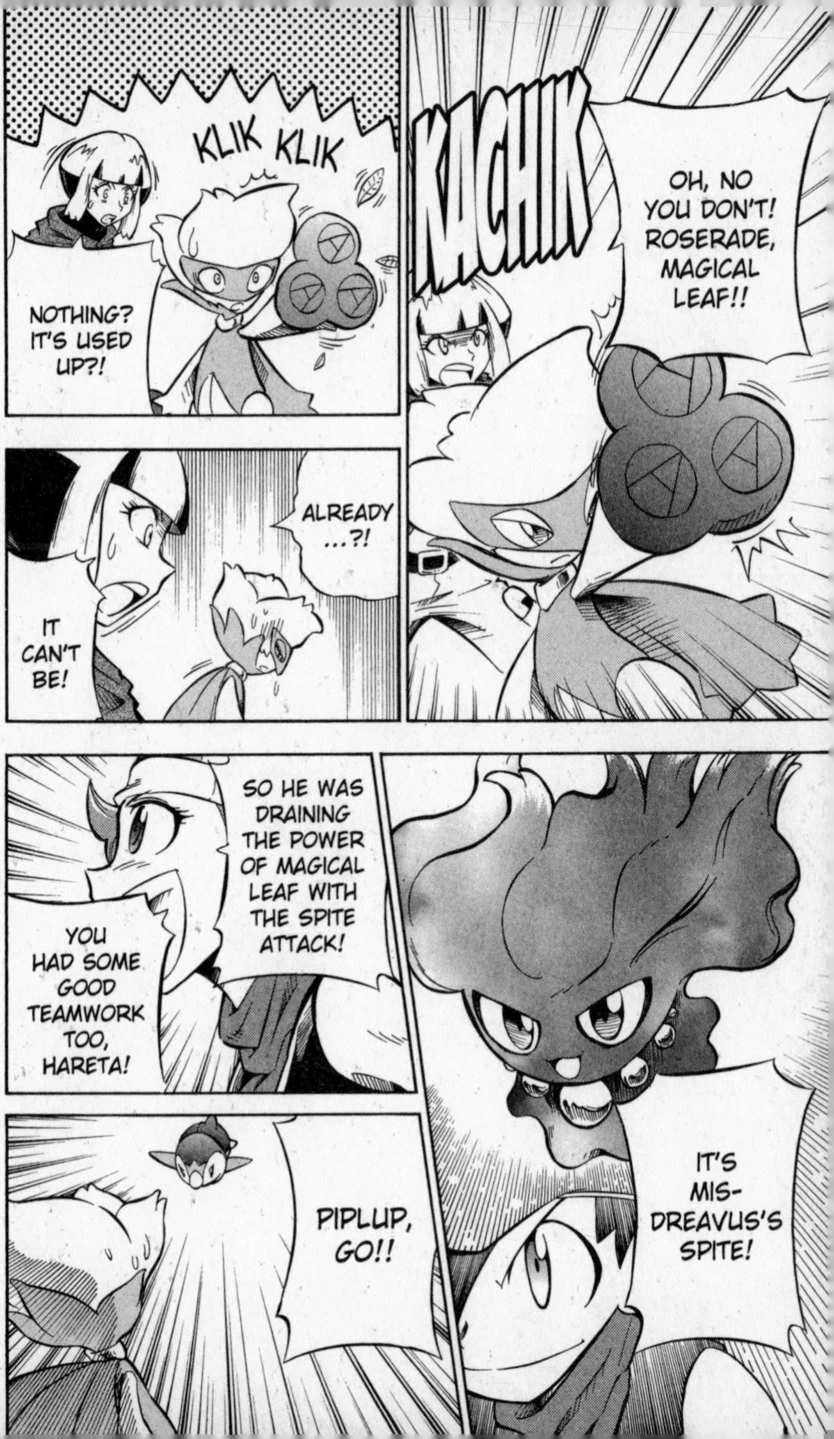
KACHIK
OH, NO YOU DON'T! ROSERADE, MAGICAL LEAF!!
KLIK KLIK
NOTHING? IT'S USED UP?!
ALREADY ...?!
IT CAN'T BE!
IT'S MIS-DREAVUS'S SPITE!
SO HE WAS DRAINING THE POWER OF MAGICAL LEAF WITH THE SPITE ATTACK!
YOU HAD SOME GOOD TEAMWORK TOO, HARETA!
PIPLUP, GO!!

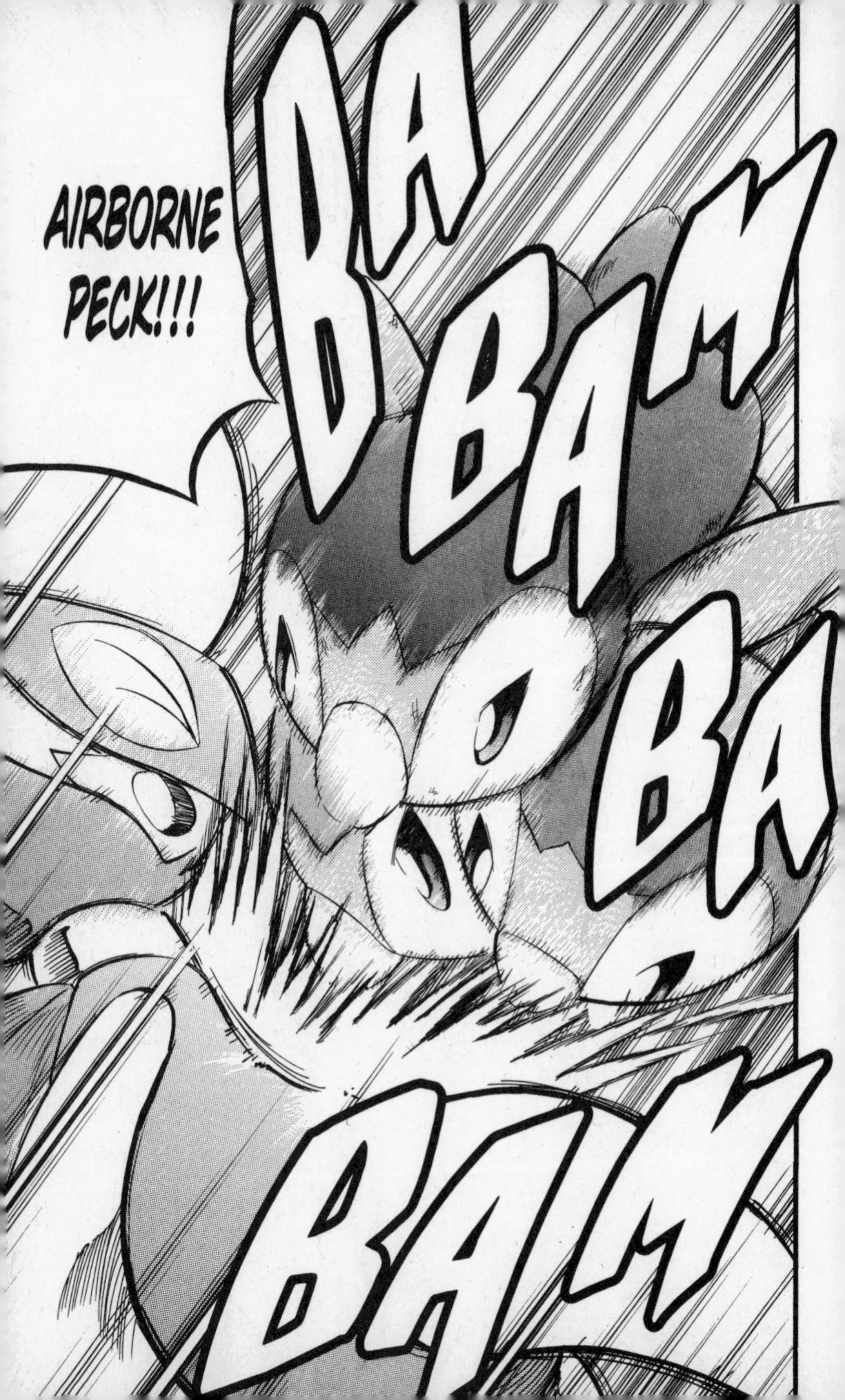
DA
AIRBORNE PECK!!!
BAM
BA
BA
BAM

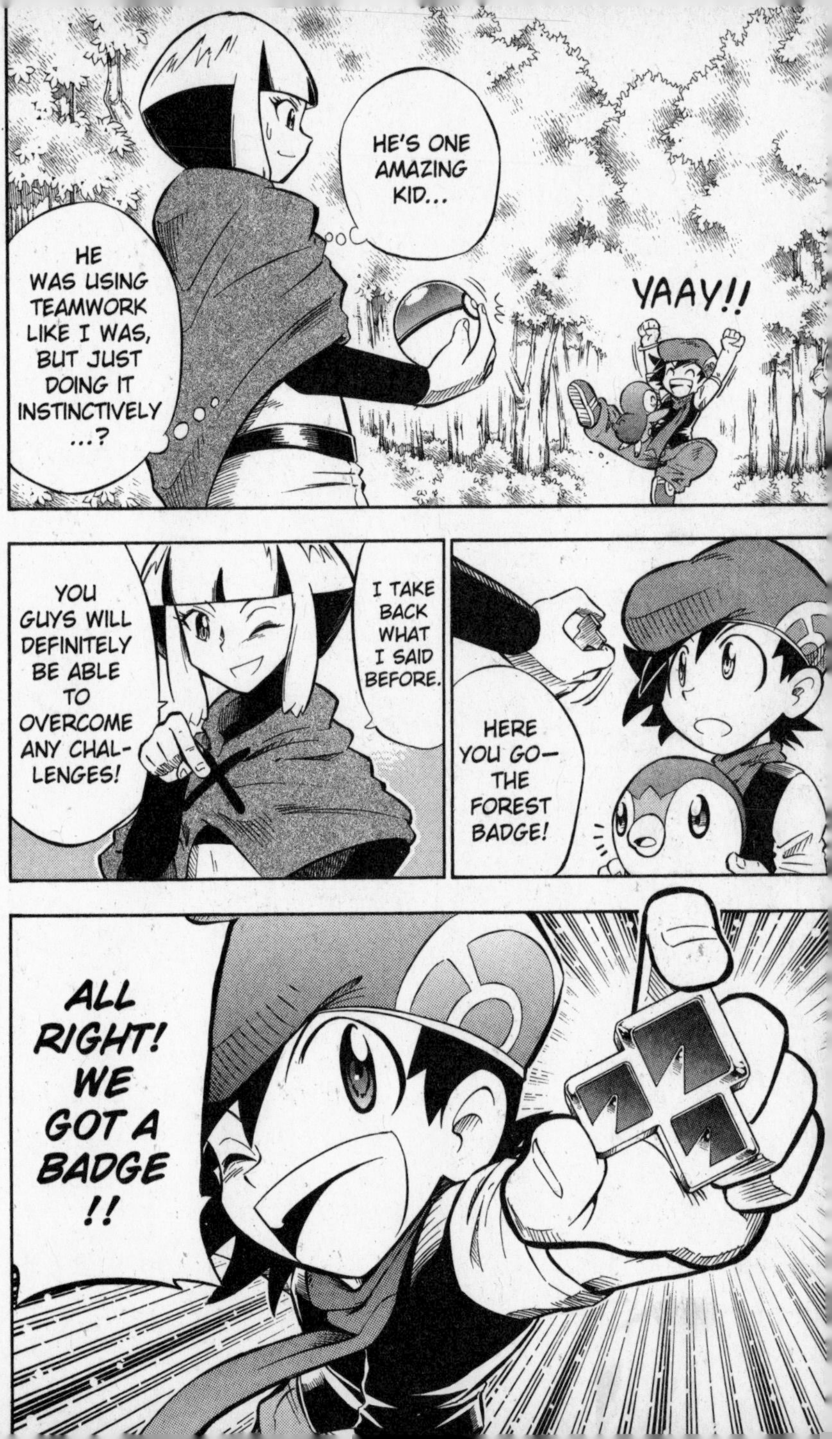
HE'S ONE AMAZING KID...
HE WAS USING TEAMWORK LIKE I WAS, BUT JUST DOING IT INSTINCTIVELY ...?
YAAY!!
YOU GUYS WILL DEFINITELY BE ABLE TO OVERCOME ANY CHAL-LENGES!
I TAKE BACK WHAT I SAID BEFORE.
HERE YOU GO— THE FOREST BADGE!
ALL RIGHT! WE GOT A BADGE !!

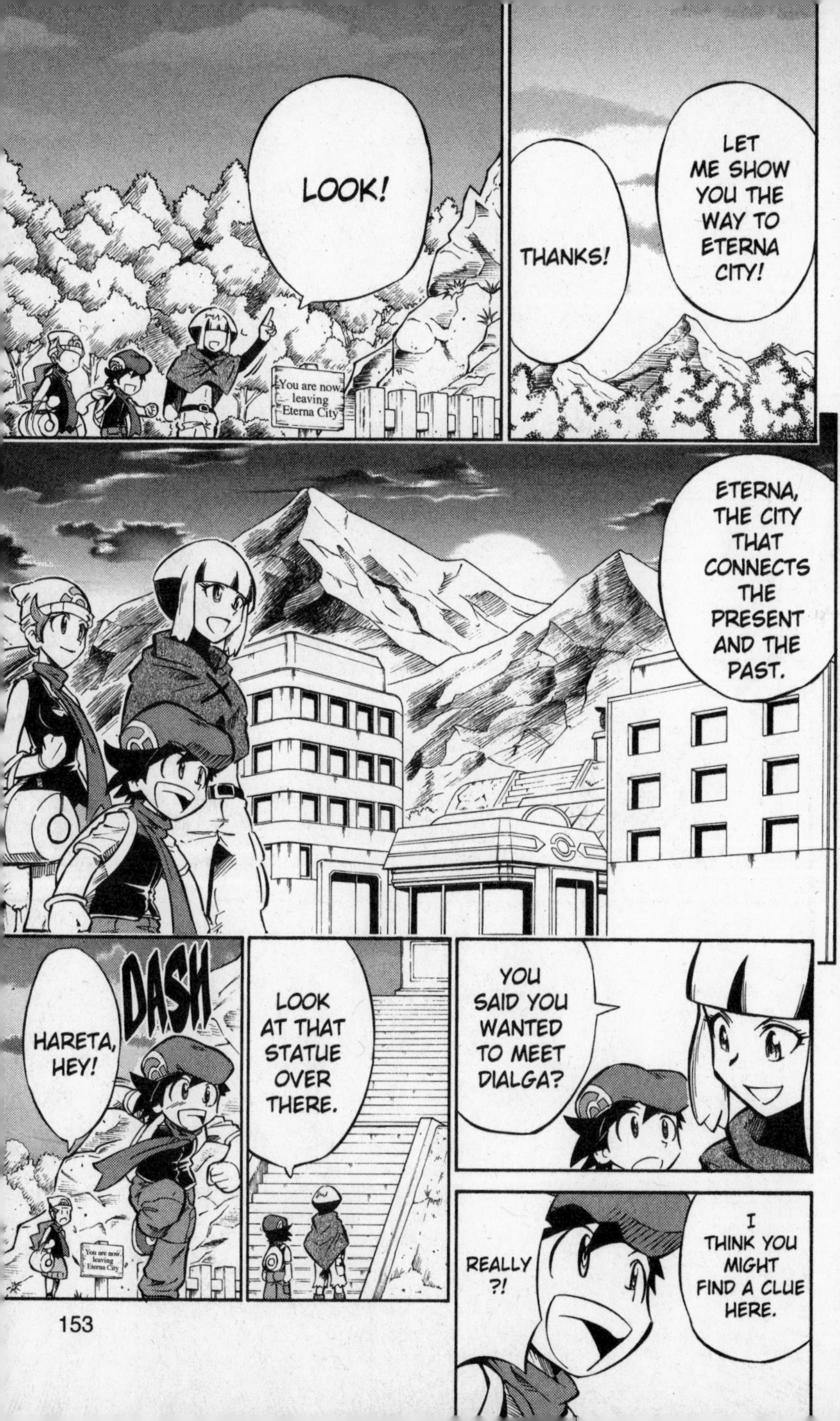

LET ME SHOW YOU THE WAY TO ETERNA CITY!
THANKS!
LOOK!
You are now leaving Eterna City
ETERNA, THE CITY THAT CONNECTS THE PRESENT AND THE PAST.
YOU SAID YOU WANTED TO MEET DIALGA?
I THINK YOU MIGHT FIND A CLUE HERE.
REALLY ?!
LOOK AT THAT STATUE OVER THERE.
DASH
HARETA, HEY!
You are now leaving Eterna City

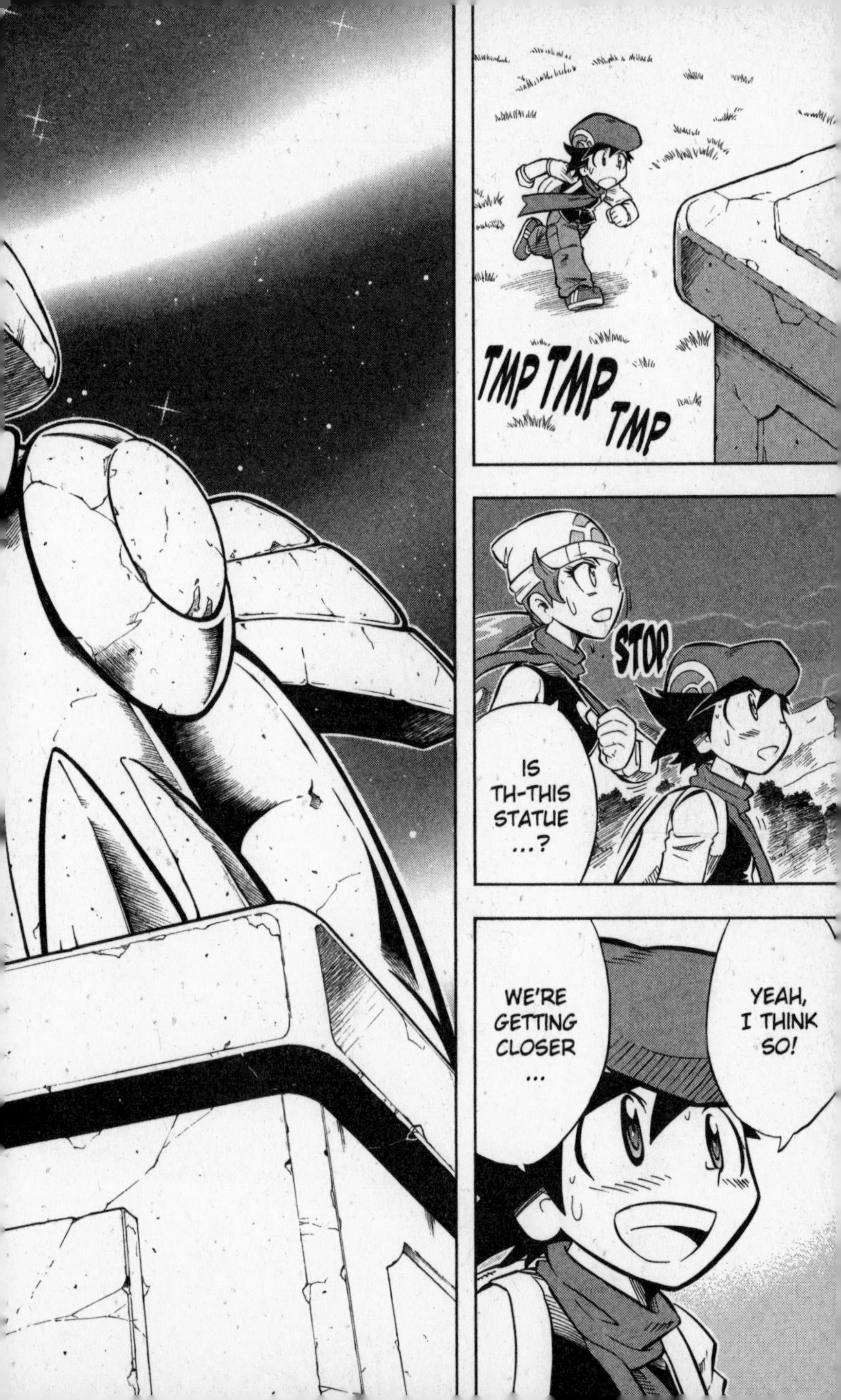
TMP TMP TMP
STOP
IS TH-THIS STATUE ...?
YEAH, I THINK SO!
WE'RE GETTING CLOSER ...

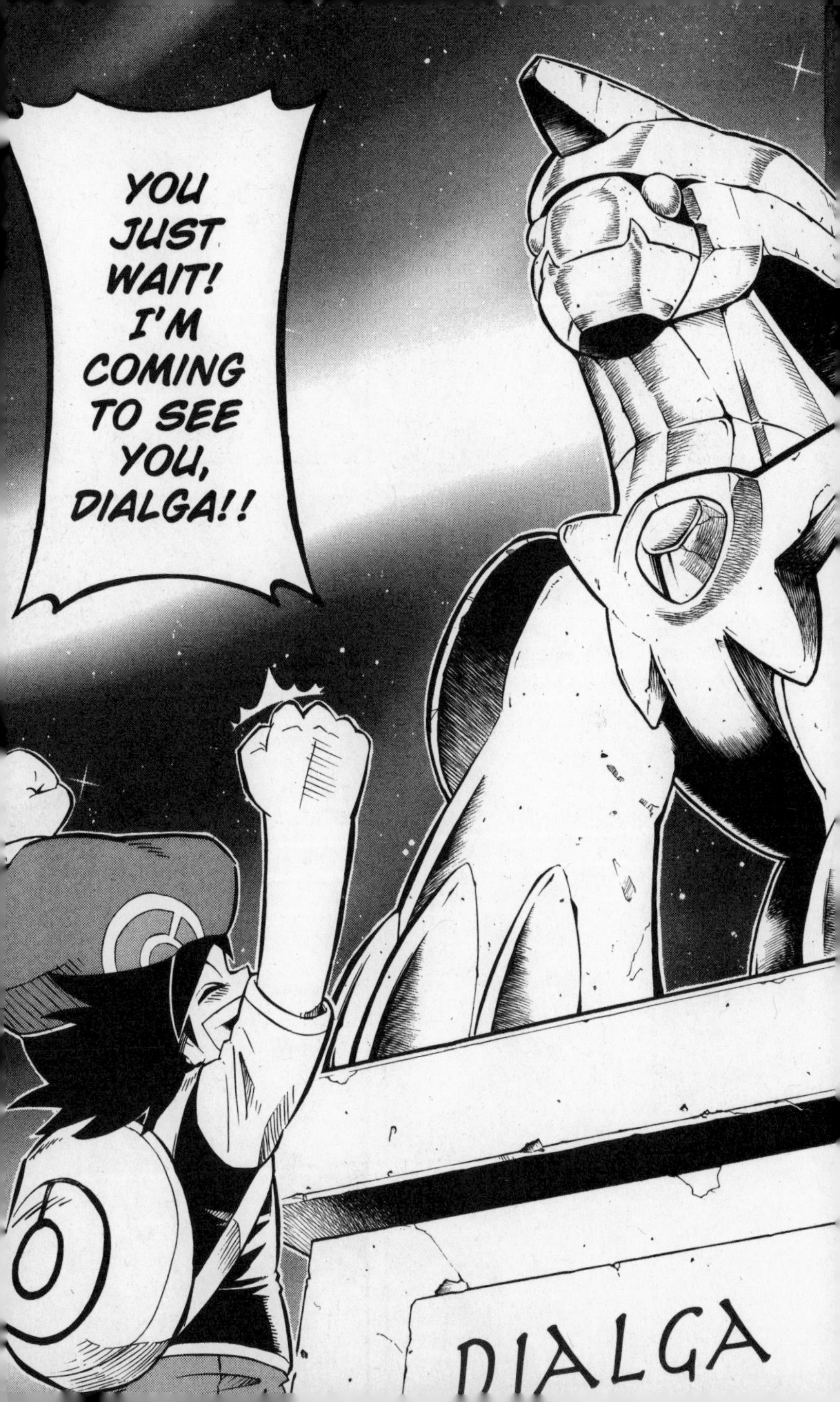
YOU JUST WAIT! I'M COMING TO SEE YOU, DIALGA!!
DIALGA

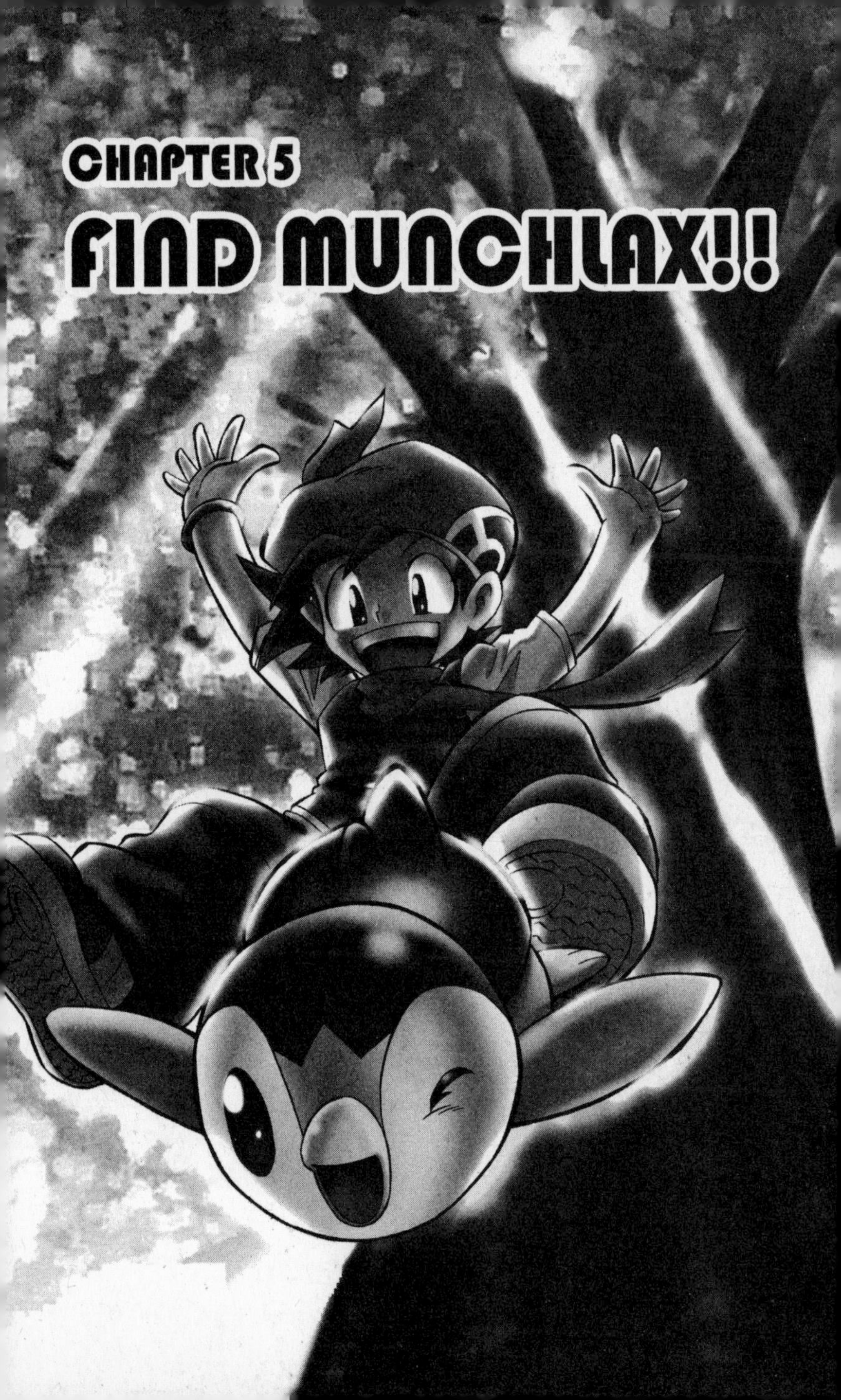
CHAPTER 5
FIND MUNCHLAX!!

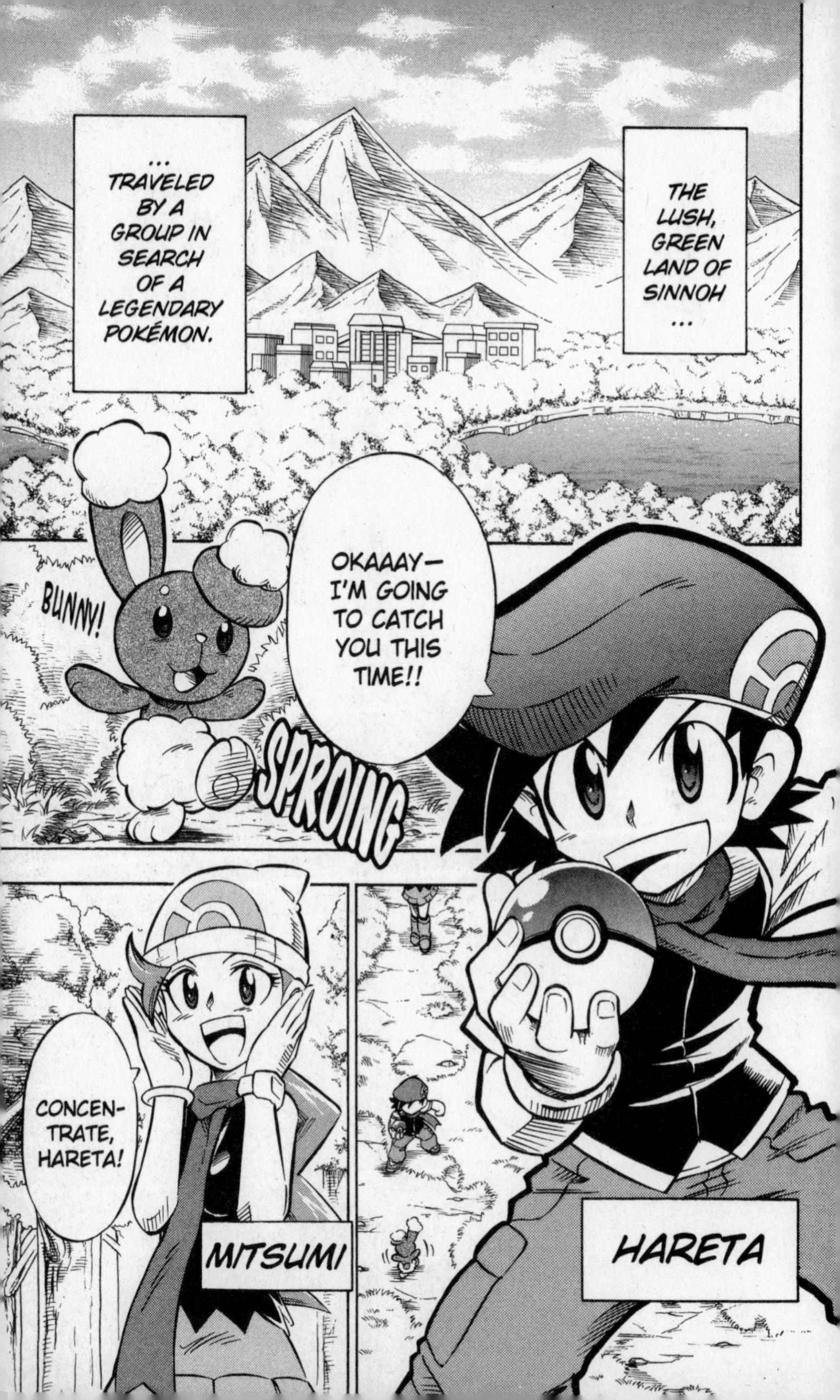
THE LUSH, GREEN LAND OF SINNOH ...
... TRAVELED BY A GROUP IN SEARCH OF A LEGENDARY POKÉMON.
OKAAAY— I'M GOING TO CATCH YOU THIS TIME!!
SPROING
BUNNY!
HARETA
CONCEN-TRATE, HARETA!
MITSUMI

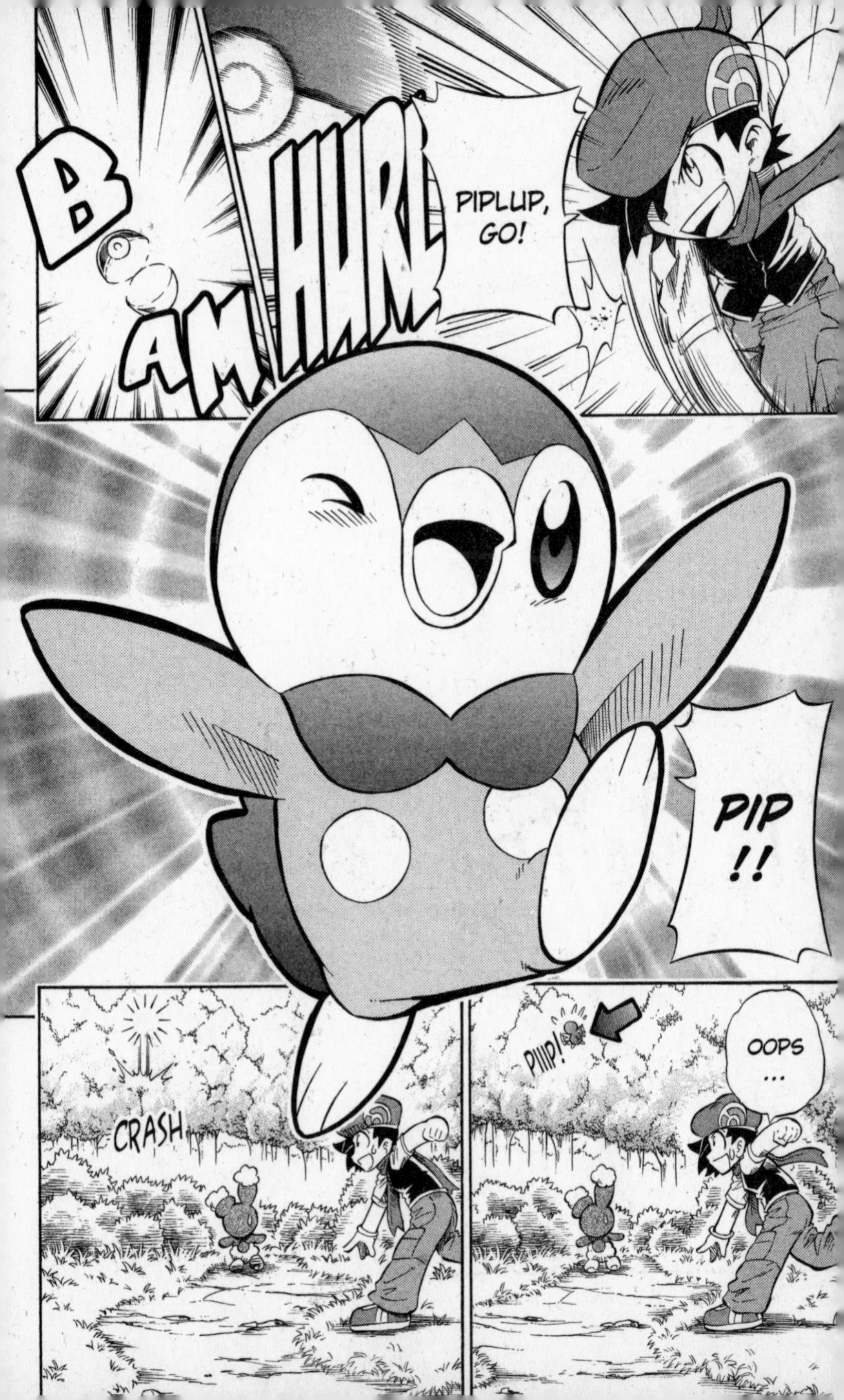
PIPLUP, GO!
HURL
BAM
PIP !!
OOPS ...
PIIIP!
CRASH

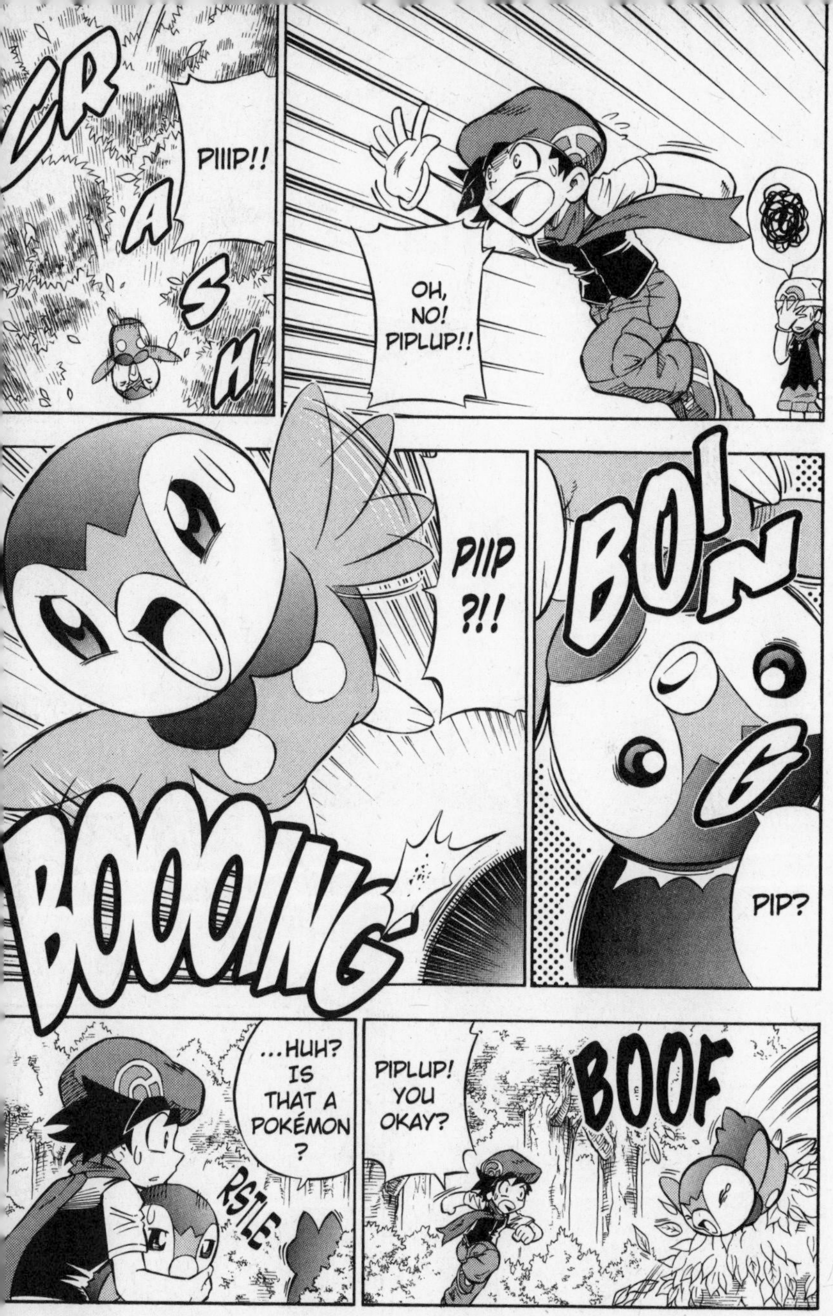
OH, NO! PIPLUP!!
CRASH
PIIIP!!
BOING
PIP?
PIIP ?!!
BOOOING
BOOF
PIPLUP! YOU OKAY?
...HUH? IS THAT A POKÉMON ?
RSTLE

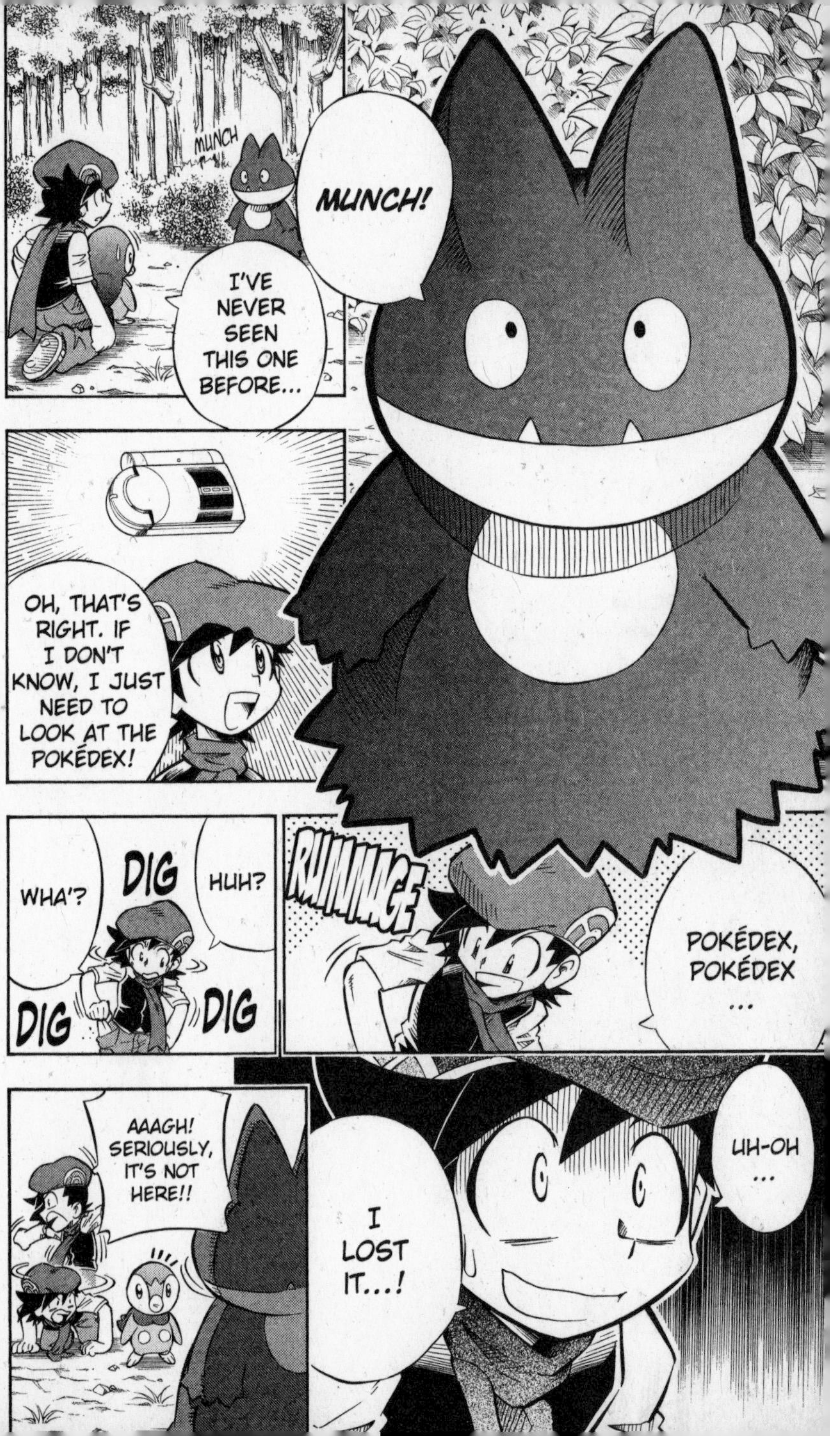

MUNCH!
MUNCH
I'VE NEVER SEEN THIS ONE BEFORE...
OH, THAT'S RIGHT. IF I DON'T KNOW, I JUST NEED TO LOOK AT THE POKÉDEX!
RUMMAGE
POKÉDEX, POKÉDEX ...
HUH?
DIG
WHA'?
DIG
DIG
UH-OH ...
I LOST IT...!
AAAGH! SERIOUSLY, IT'S NOT HERE!!

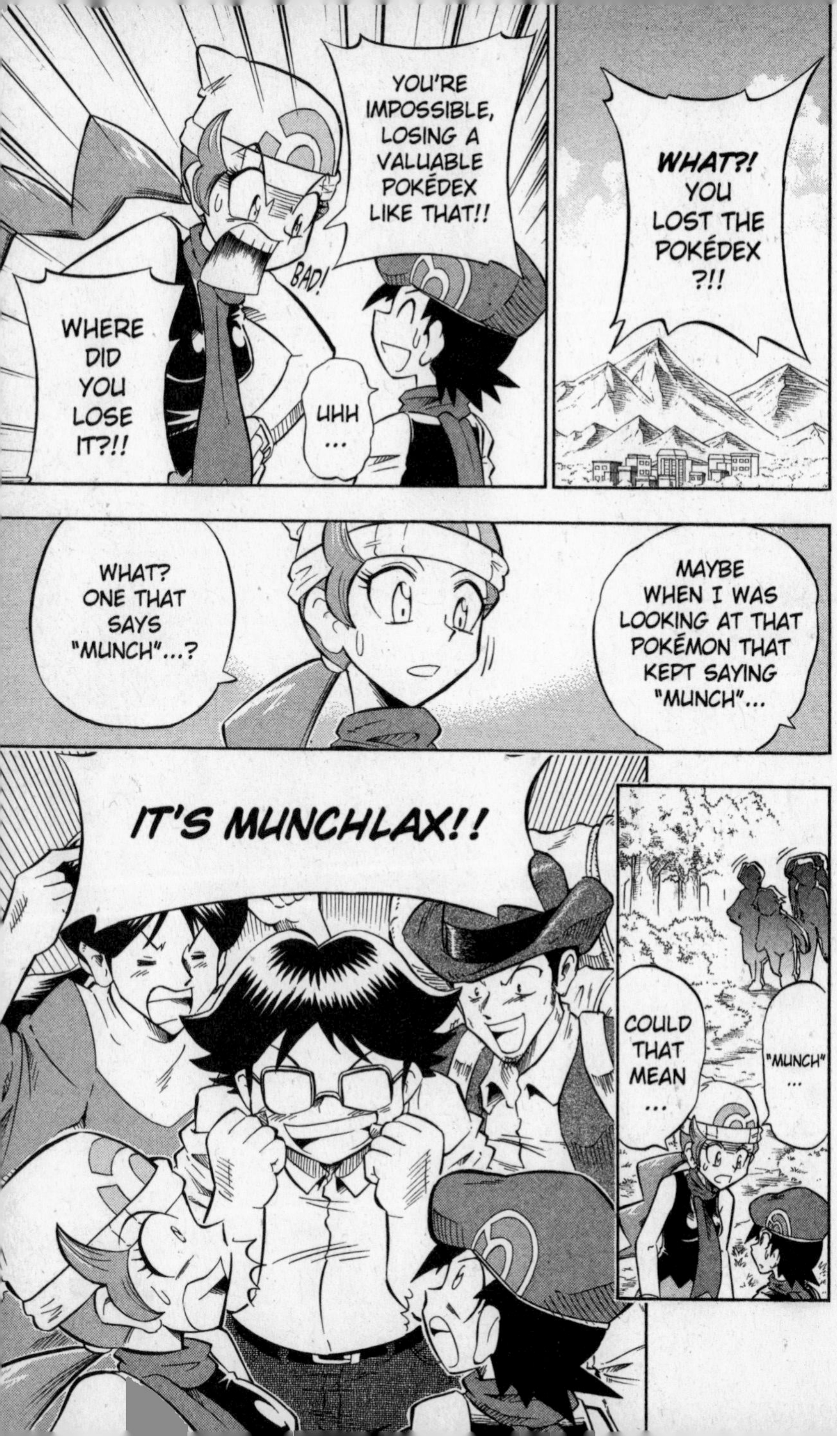
WHAT?! YOU LOST THE POKÉDEX ?!!
YOU'RE IMPOSSIBLE, LOSING A VALUABLE POKÉDEX LIKE THAT!!
BAD!
WHERE DID YOU LOSE IT?!!
UHH ...
MAYBE WHEN I WAS LOOKING AT THAT POKÉMON THAT KEPT SAYING "MUNCH"...
WHAT? ONE THAT SAYS "MUNCH"...?
"MUNCH" ...
COULD THAT MEAN ...
IT'S MUNCHLAX!!

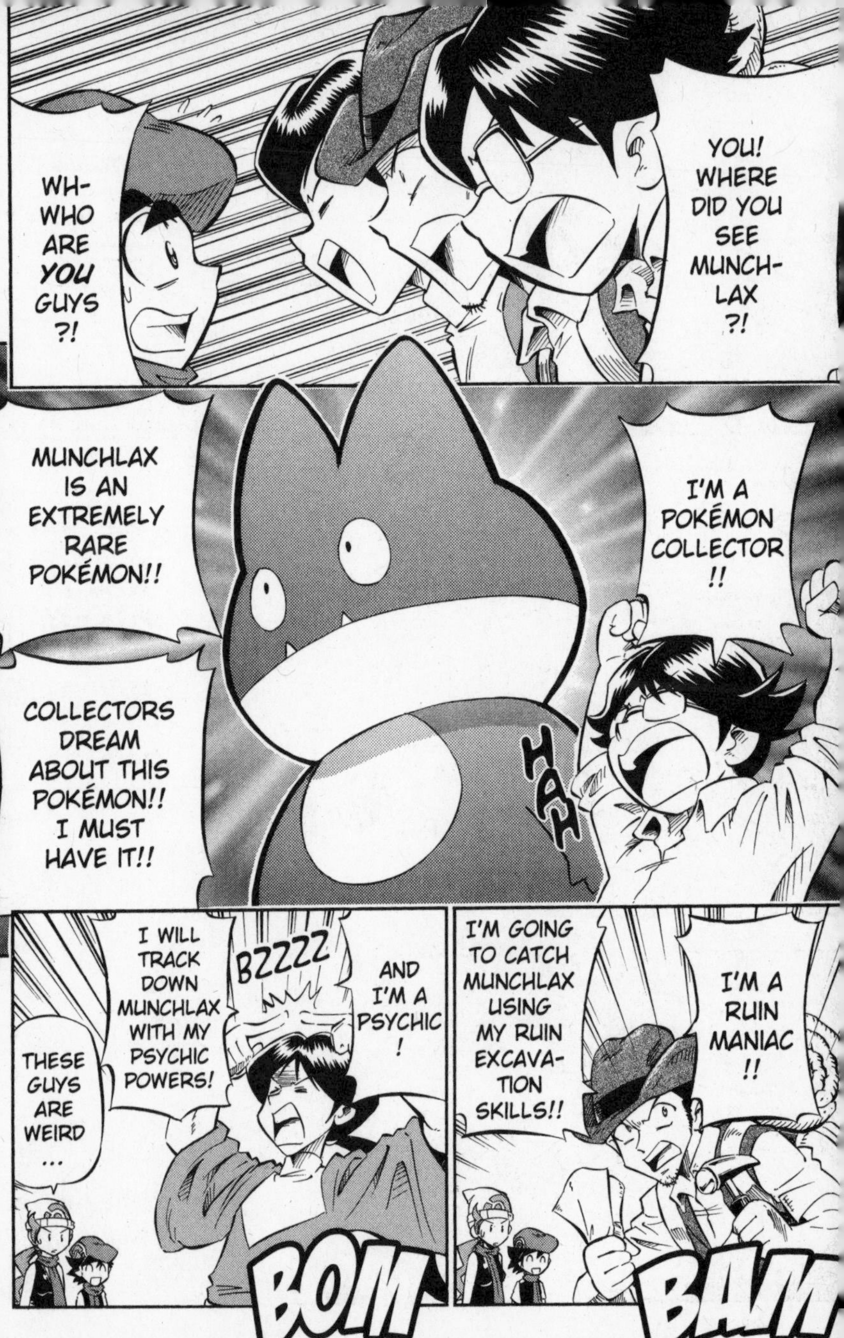
YOU! WHERE DID YOU SEE MUNCH-LAX ?!
WH- WHO ARE *YOU* GUYS ?!
I'M A POKÉMON COLLECTOR !!
HAH
MUNCHLAX IS AN EXTREMELY RARE POKÉMON!!
COLLECTORS DREAM ABOUT THIS POKÉMON!! I MUST HAVE IT!!
I'M A RUIN MANIAC !!
I'M GOING TO CATCH MUNCHLAX USING MY RUIN EXCAVA-TION SKILLS!!
BAM
AND I'M A PSYCHIC !
BZZZZ
I WILL TRACK DOWN MUNCHLAX WITH MY PSYCHIC POWERS!
THESE GUYS ARE WEIRD ...
BOM

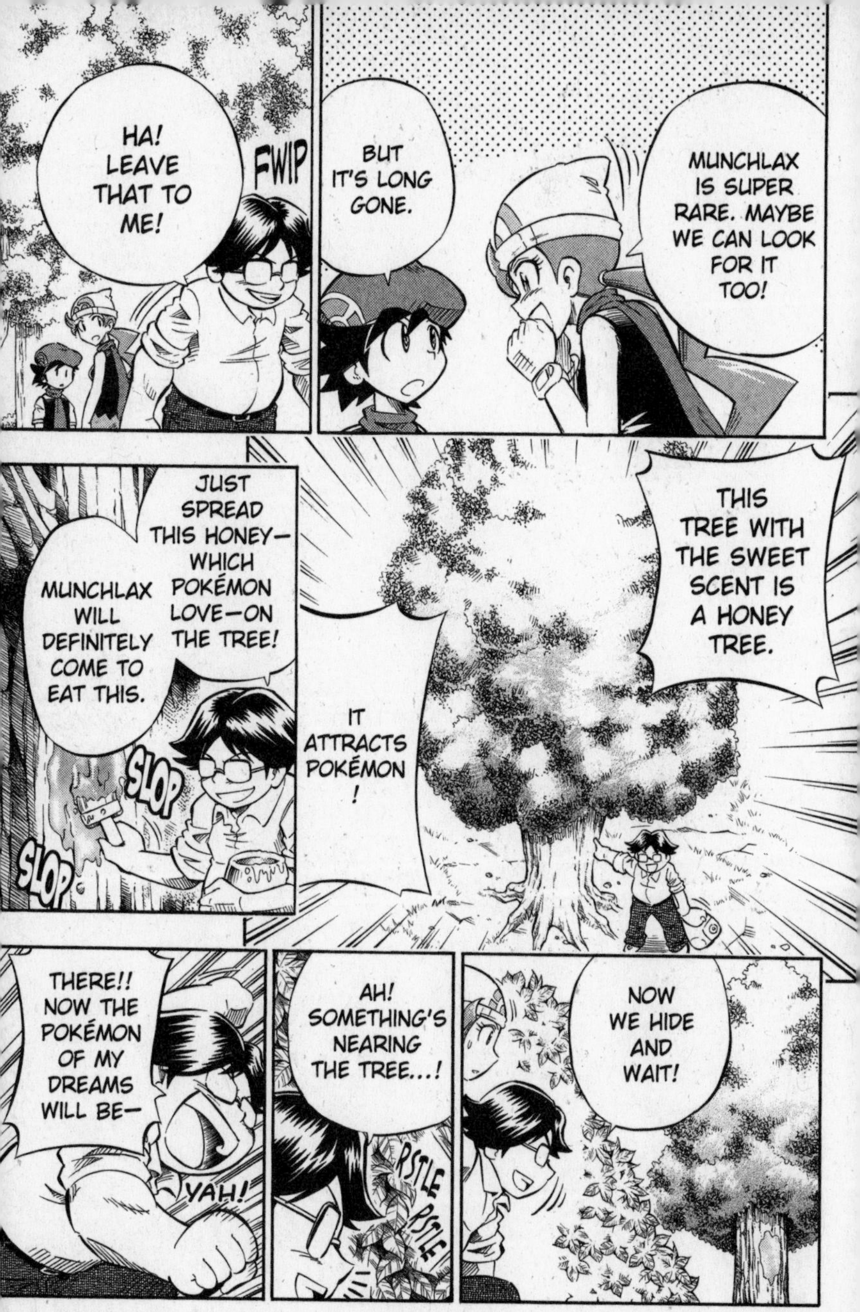
MUNCHLAX IS SUPER RARE. MAYBE WE CAN LOOK FOR IT TOO!
BUT IT'S LONG GONE.
HA! LEAVE THAT TO ME!
FWIP
THIS TREE WITH THE SWEET SCENT IS A HONEY TREE.
IT ATTRACTS POKÉMON!
JUST SPREAD THIS HONEY—WHICH POKÉMON LOVE—ON THE TREE!
MUNCHLAX WILL DEFINITELY COME TO EAT THIS.
SLOP
SLOP
NOW WE HIDE AND WAIT!
AH! SOMETHING'S NEARING THE TREE...!
RSTLE
RSTLE
THERE!! NOW THE POKÉMON OF MY DREAMS WILL BE—
YAH!

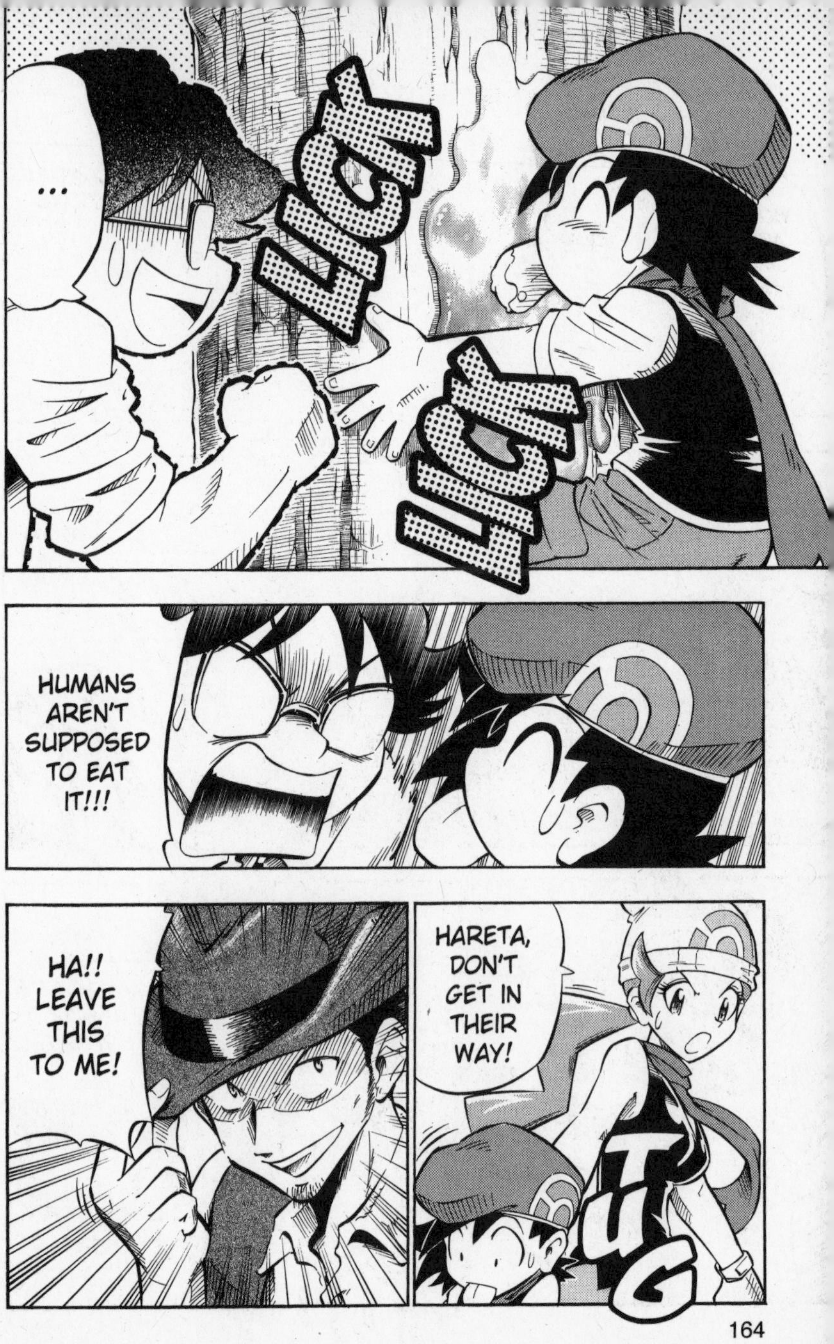
LICK
...
LICK
HUMANS AREN'T SUPPOSED TO EAT IT!!!
HARETA, DON'T GET IN THEIR WAY!
TUG
HA!! LEAVE THIS TO ME!

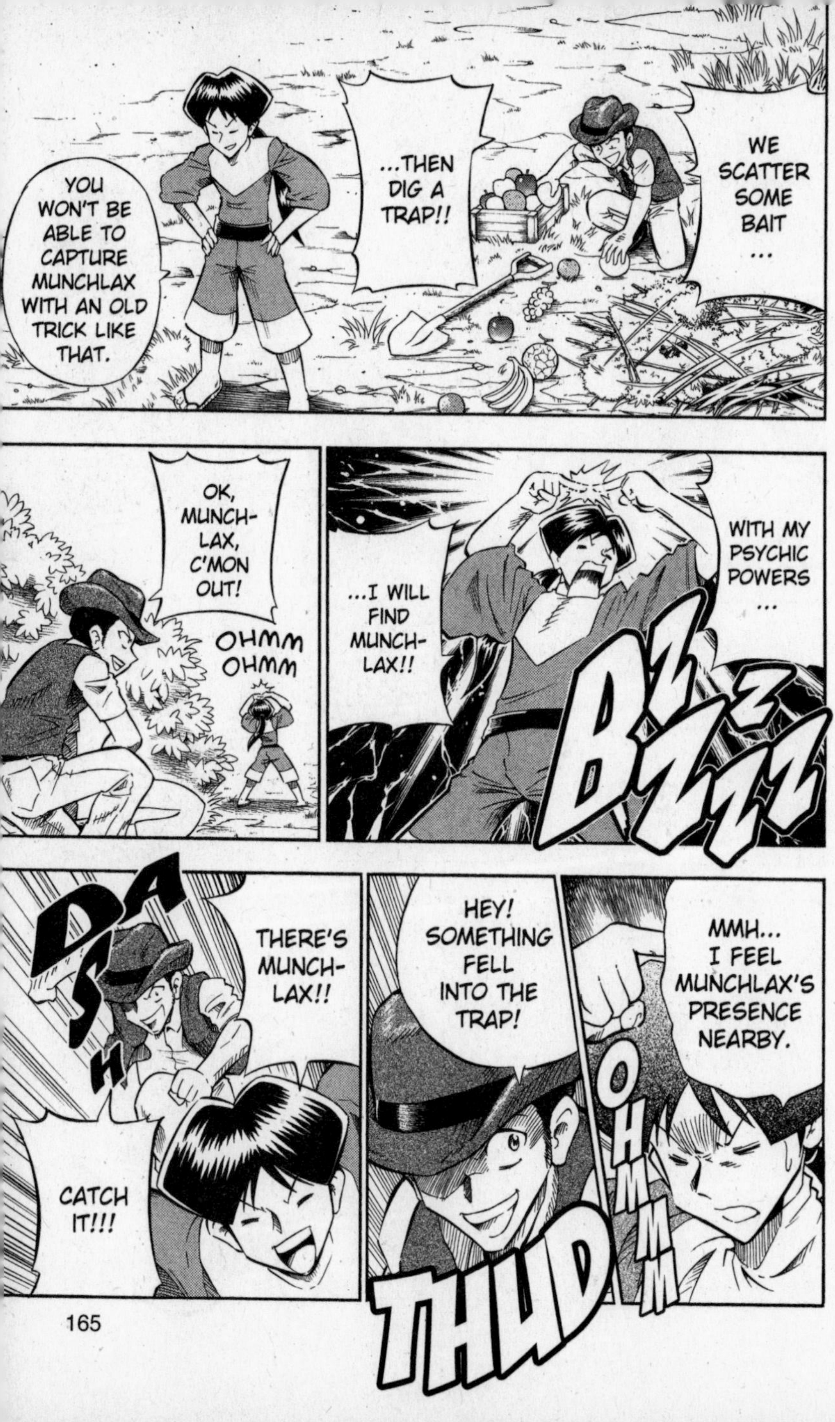
WE SCATTER SOME BAIT ...
...THEN DIG A TRAP!!
YOU WON'T BE ABLE TO CAPTURE MUNCHLAX WITH AN OLD TRICK LIKE THAT.
WITH MY PSYCHIC POWERS ...
...I WILL FIND MUNCHLAX!!
BZZZZ
OK, MUNCH-LAX, C'MON OUT!
OHMM OHMM
MMH... I FEEL MUNCHLAX'S PRESENCE NEARBY.
OHMMMM
HEY! SOMETHING FELL INTO THE TRAP!
THUD
THERE'S MUNCH-LAX!!
DASH
CATCH IT!!!

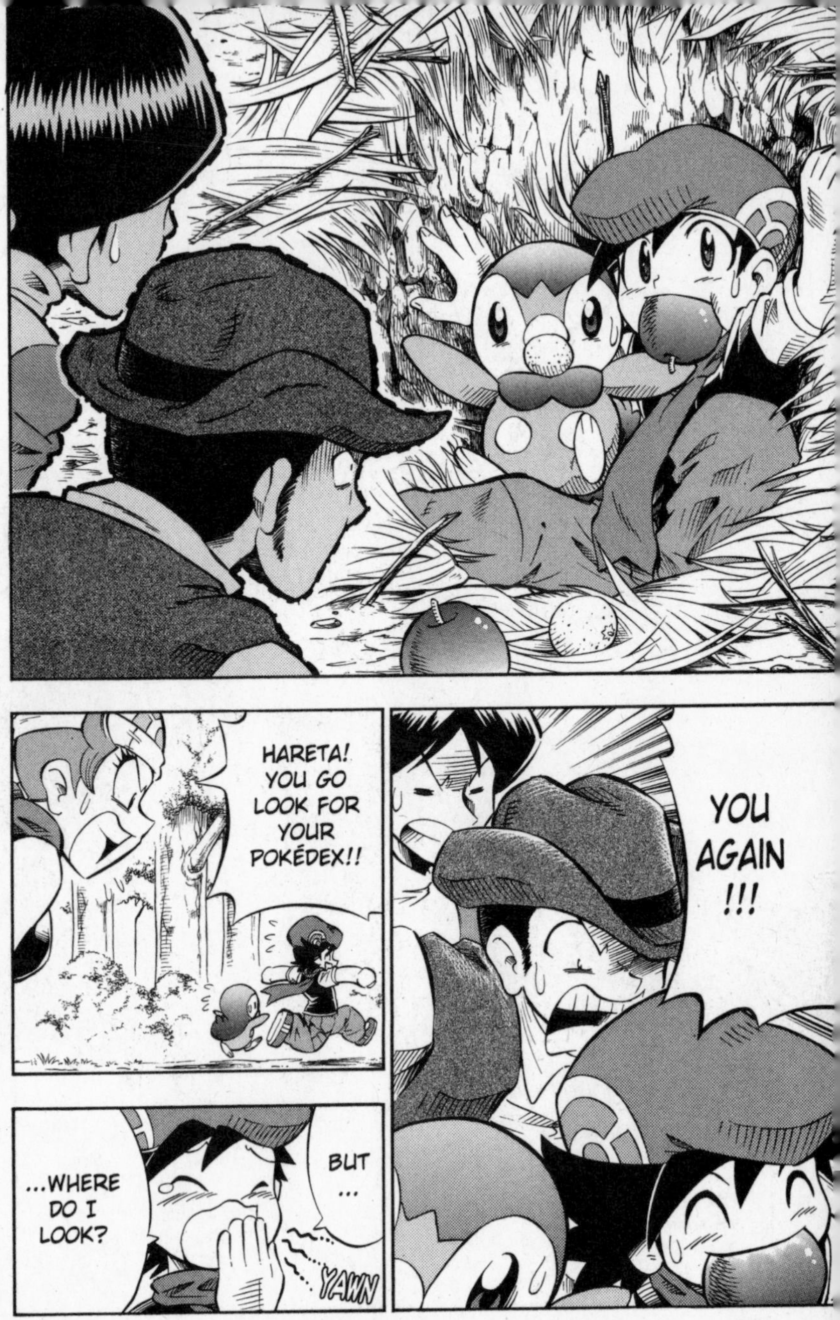
YOU AGAIN !!!
HARETA! YOU GO LOOK FOR YOUR POKÉDEX!!
BUT ...
...WHERE DO I LOOK?
YAWN

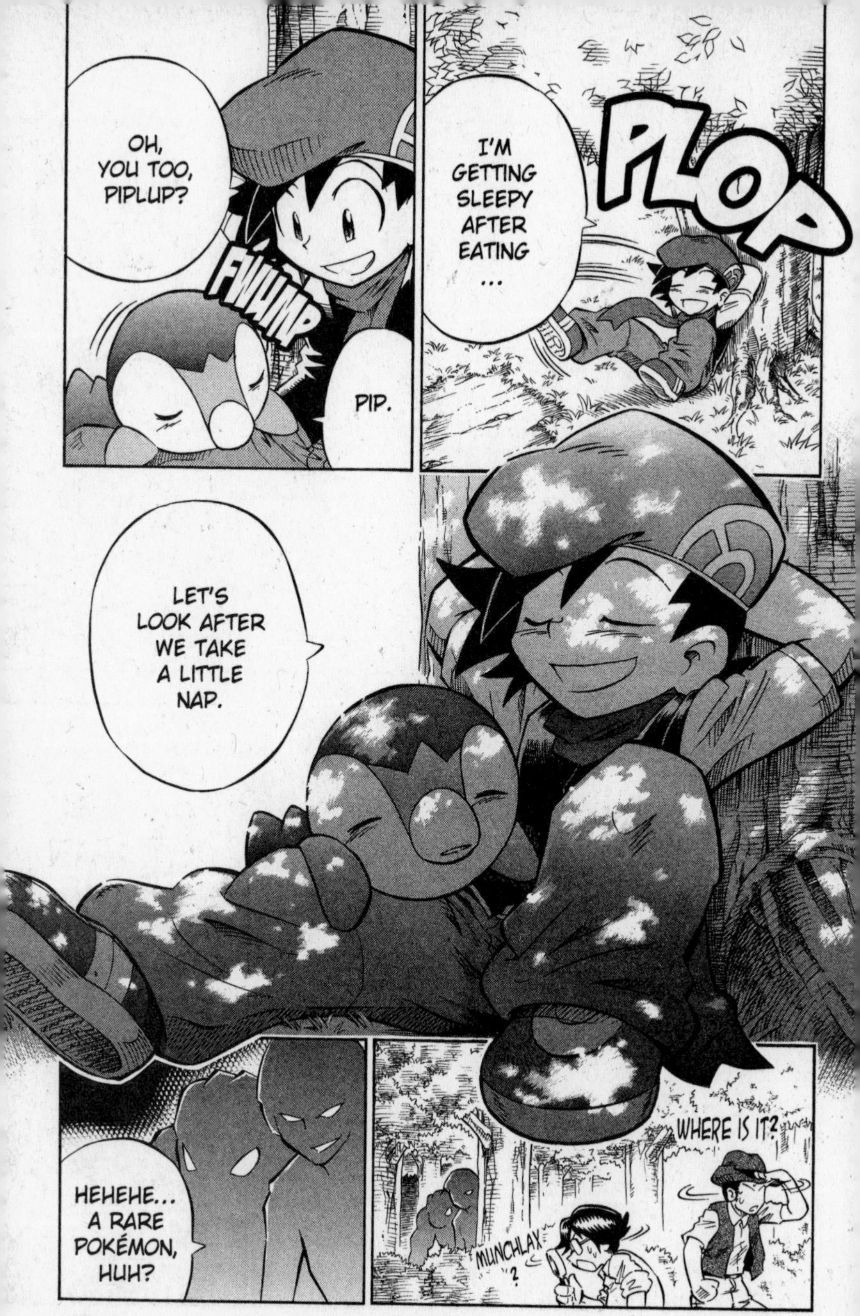

I'M GETTING SLEEPY AFTER EATING ...
PLOP
OH, YOU TOO, PIPLUP?
FWUMP
PIP.
LET'S LOOK AFTER WE TAKE A LITTLE NAP.
WHERE IS IT?
MUNCHLAX?
HEHEHE... A RARE POKÉMON, HUH?

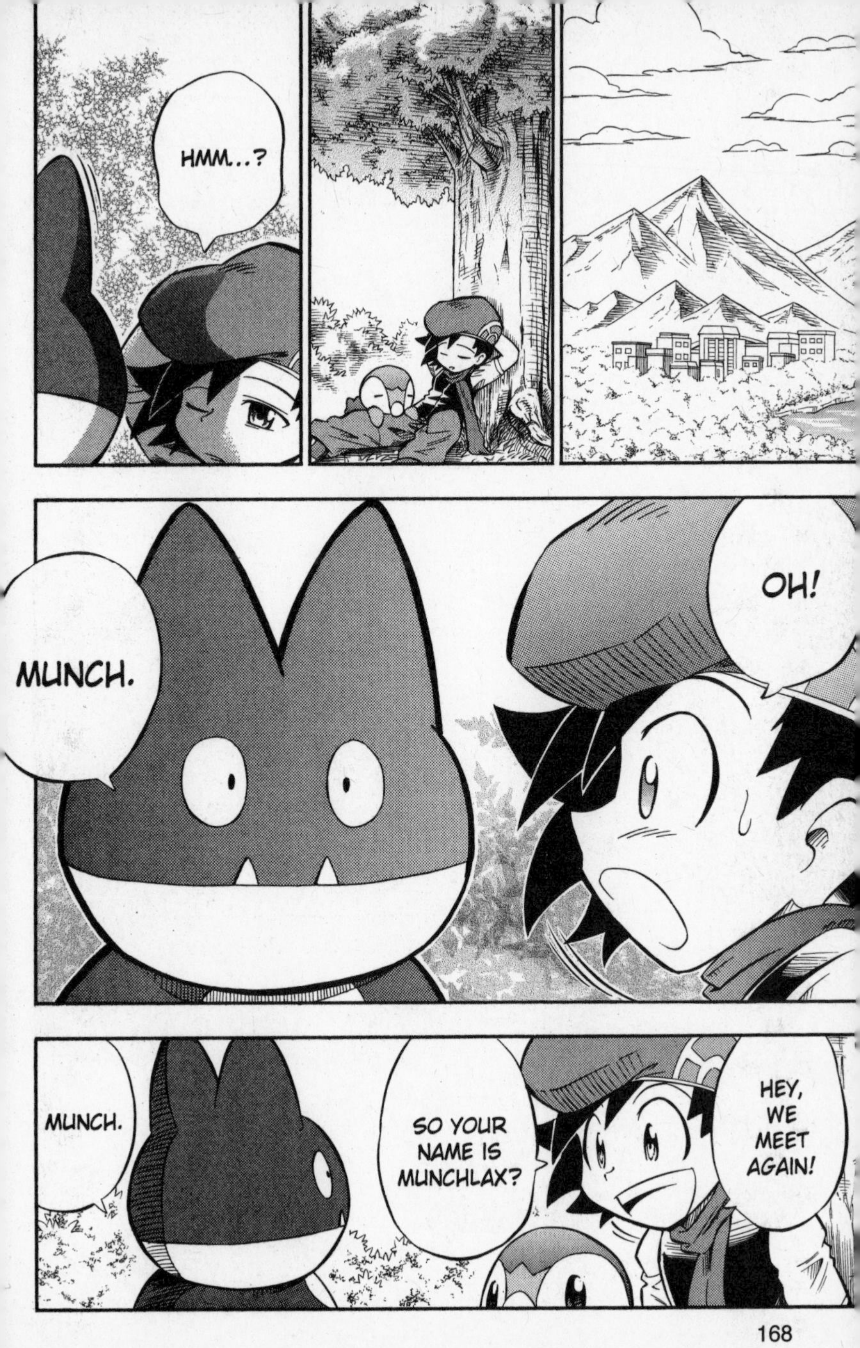
HMM..?
OH!
MUNCH.
HEY, WE MEET AGAIN!
SO YOUR NAME IS MUNCHLAX?
MUNCH.

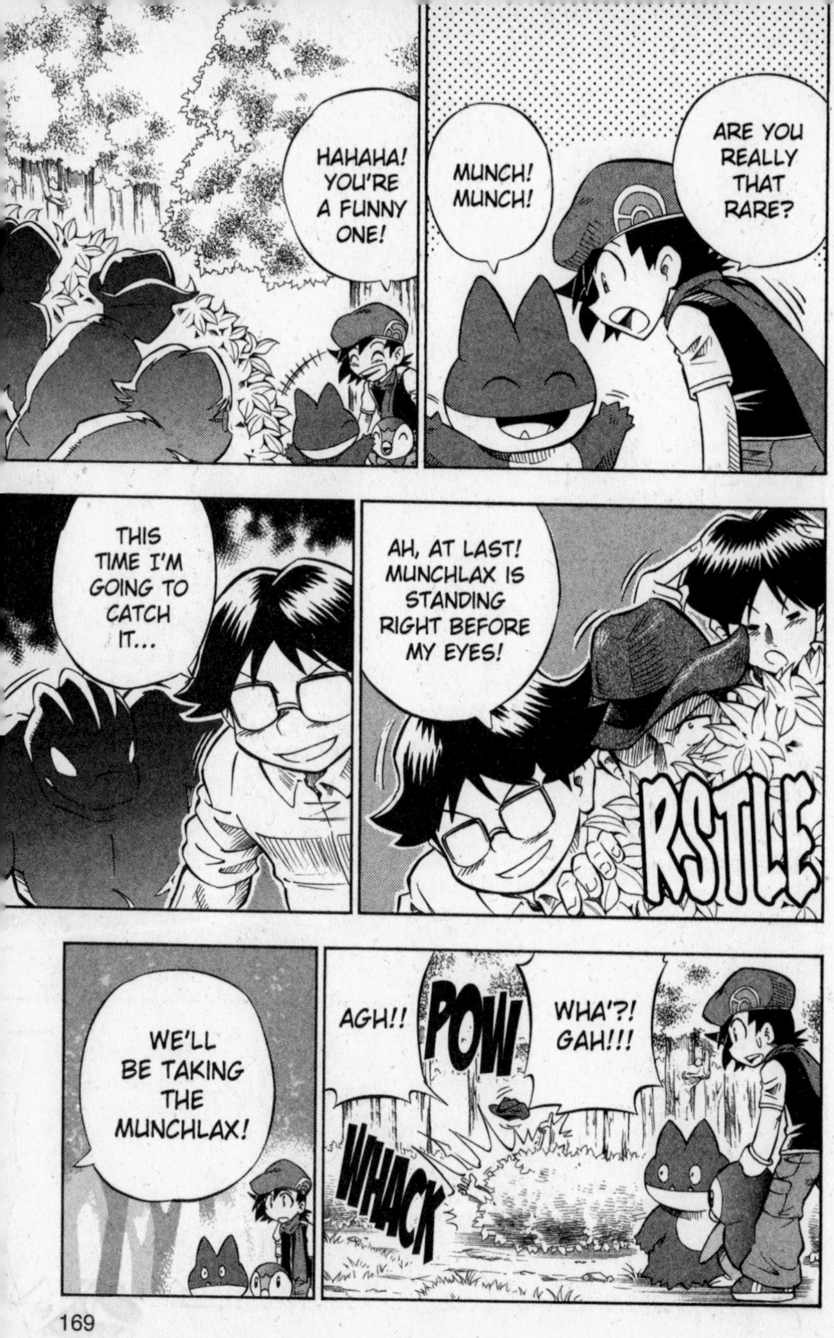
ARE YOU REALLY THAT RARE?
MUNCH! MUNCH!
HAHAHA! YOU'RE A FUNNY ONE!
AH, AT LAST! MUNCHLAX IS STANDING RIGHT BEFORE MY EYES!
RSTLE
THIS TIME I'M GOING TO CATCH IT...
WHA'?! GAH!!!
POW
AGH!!
WHACK
WE'LL BE TAKING THE MUNCHLAX!

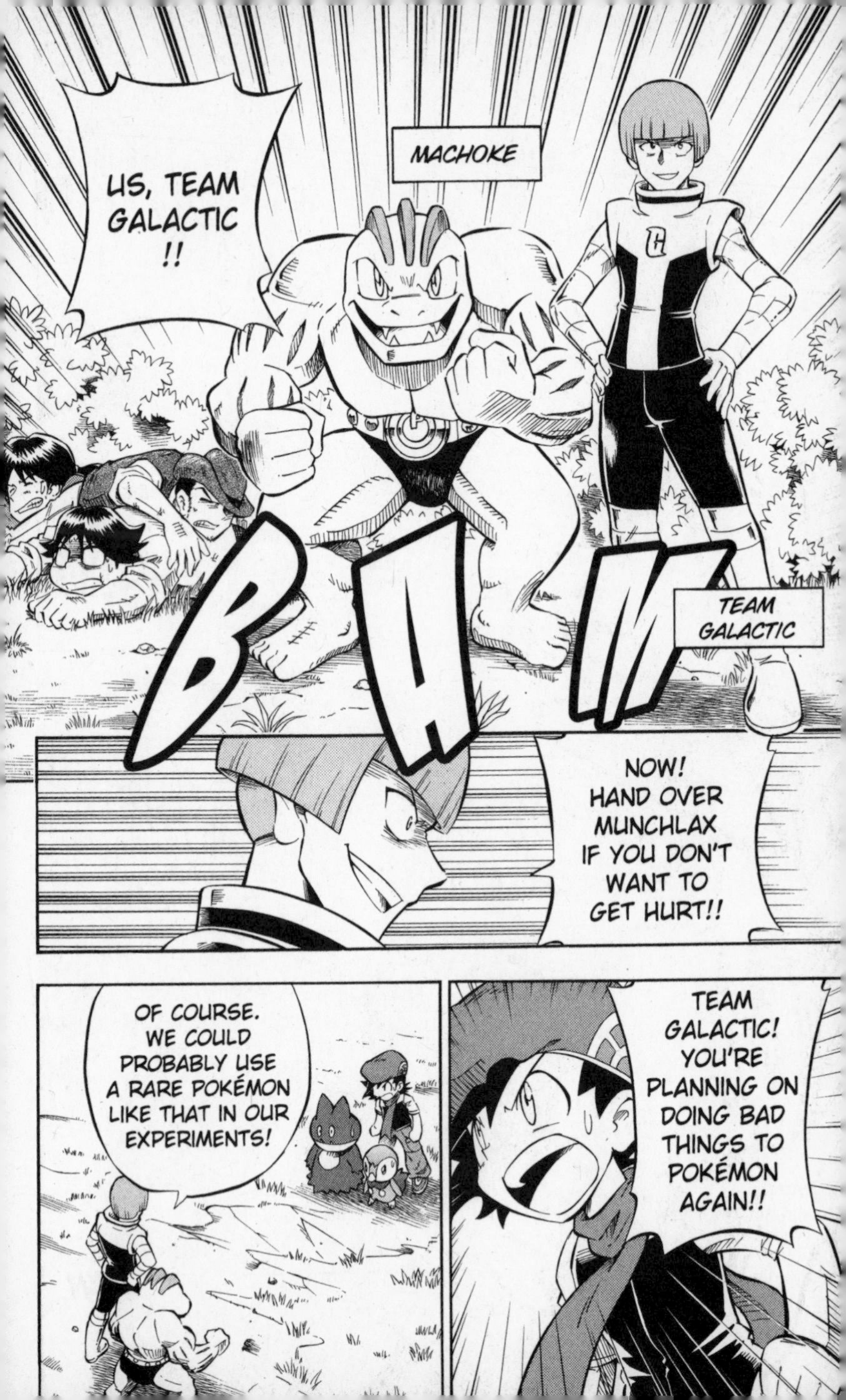

MACHOKE
US, TEAM GALACTIC!!
BAM
TEAM GALACTIC
NOW! HAND OVER MUNCHLAX IF YOU DON'T WANT TO GET HURT!!
TEAM GALACTIC! YOU'RE PLANNING ON DOING BAD THINGS TO POKÉMON AGAIN!!
OF COURSE. WE COULD PROBABLY USE A RARE POKÉMON LIKE THAT IN OUR EXPERIMENTS!

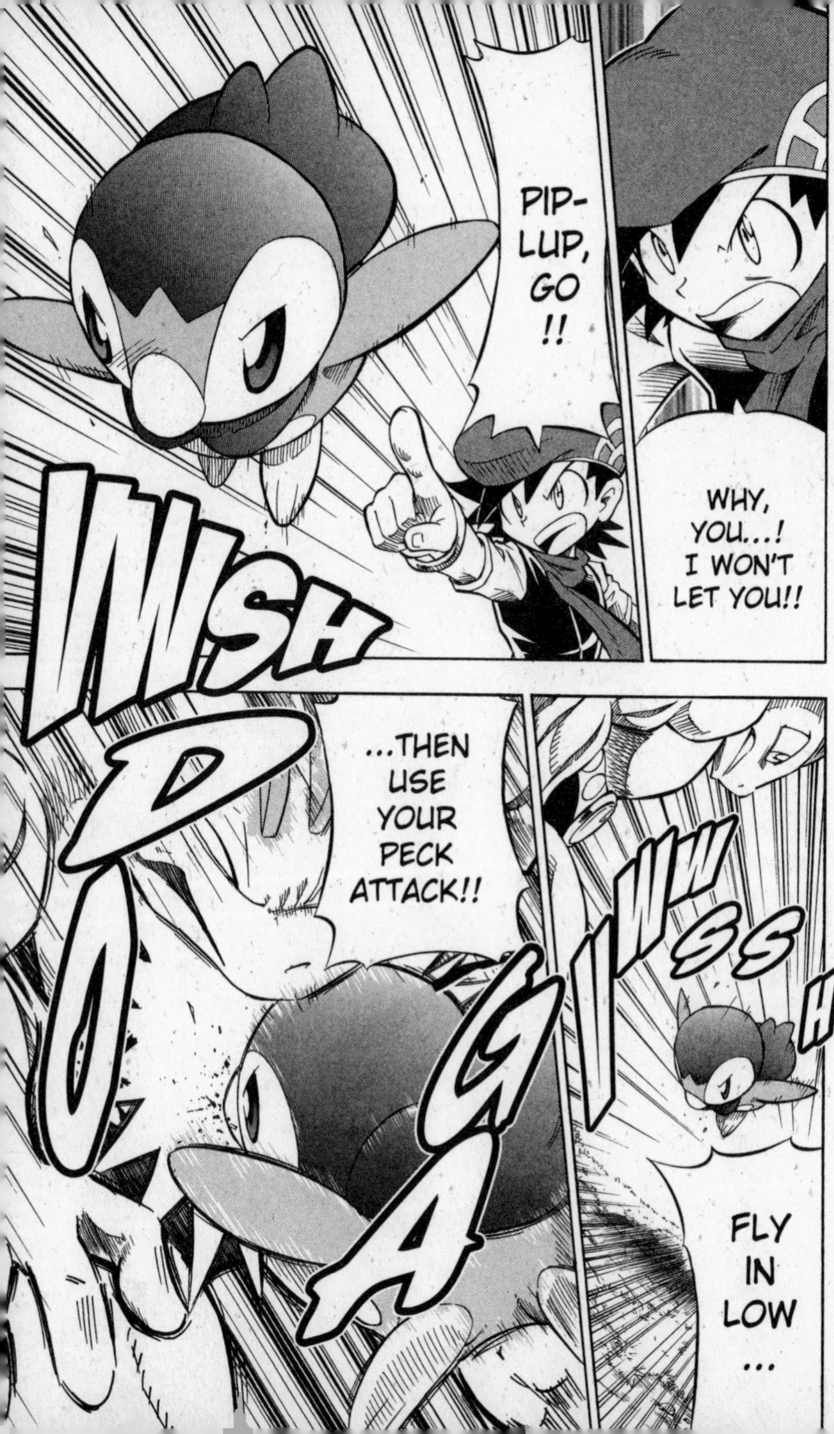
WHY, YOU...! I WON'T LET YOU!!
PIP-LUP, GO!!
FLY IN LOW...
...THEN USE YOUR PECK ATTACK!!

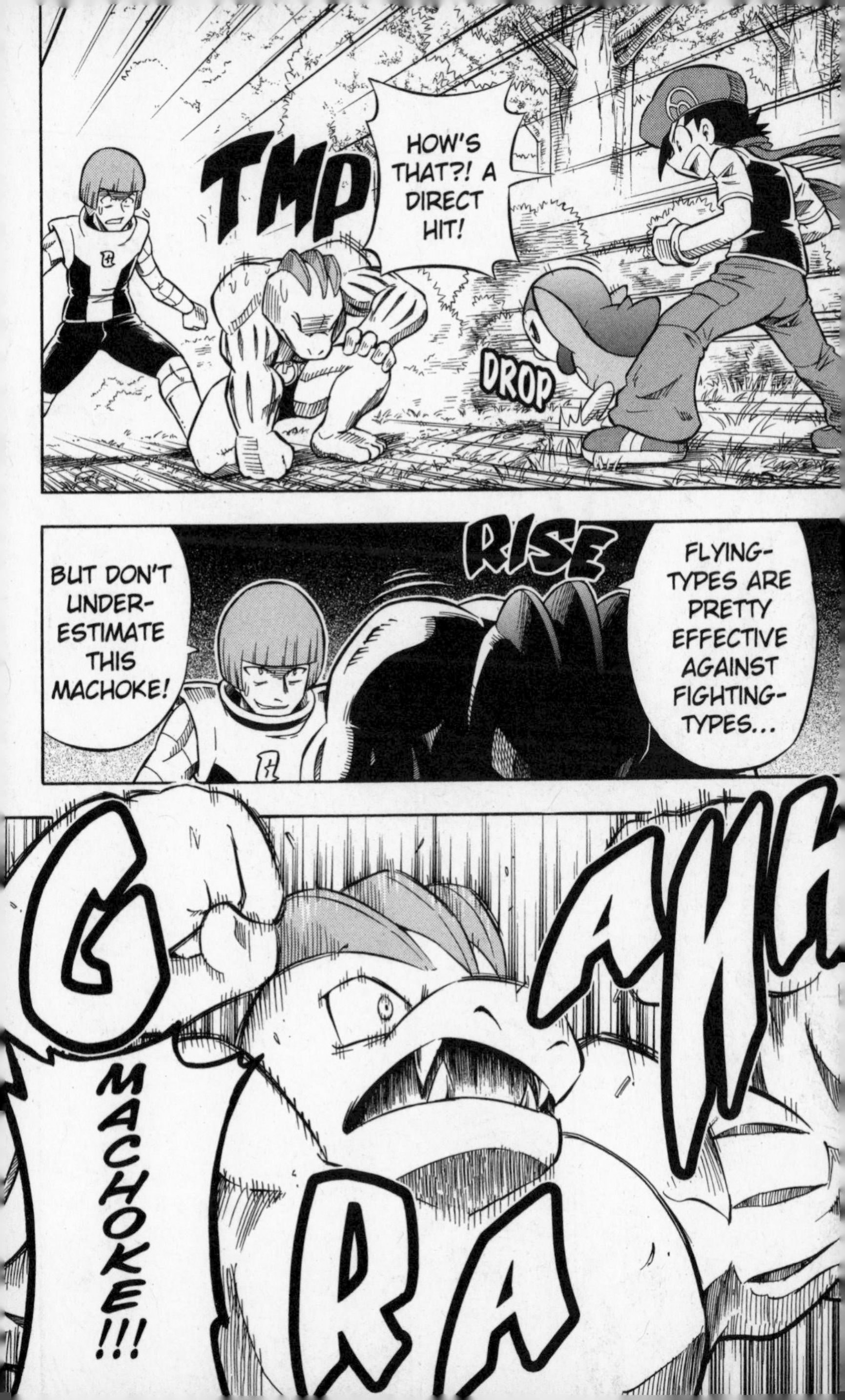
HOW'S THAT?! A DIRECT HIT!
TMP
DROP
FLYING-TYPES ARE PRETTY EFFECTIVE AGAINST FIGHTING-TYPES...
RISE
BUT DON'T UNDER-ESTIMATE THIS MACHOKE!
MACHOKE!!!
GAH
RA

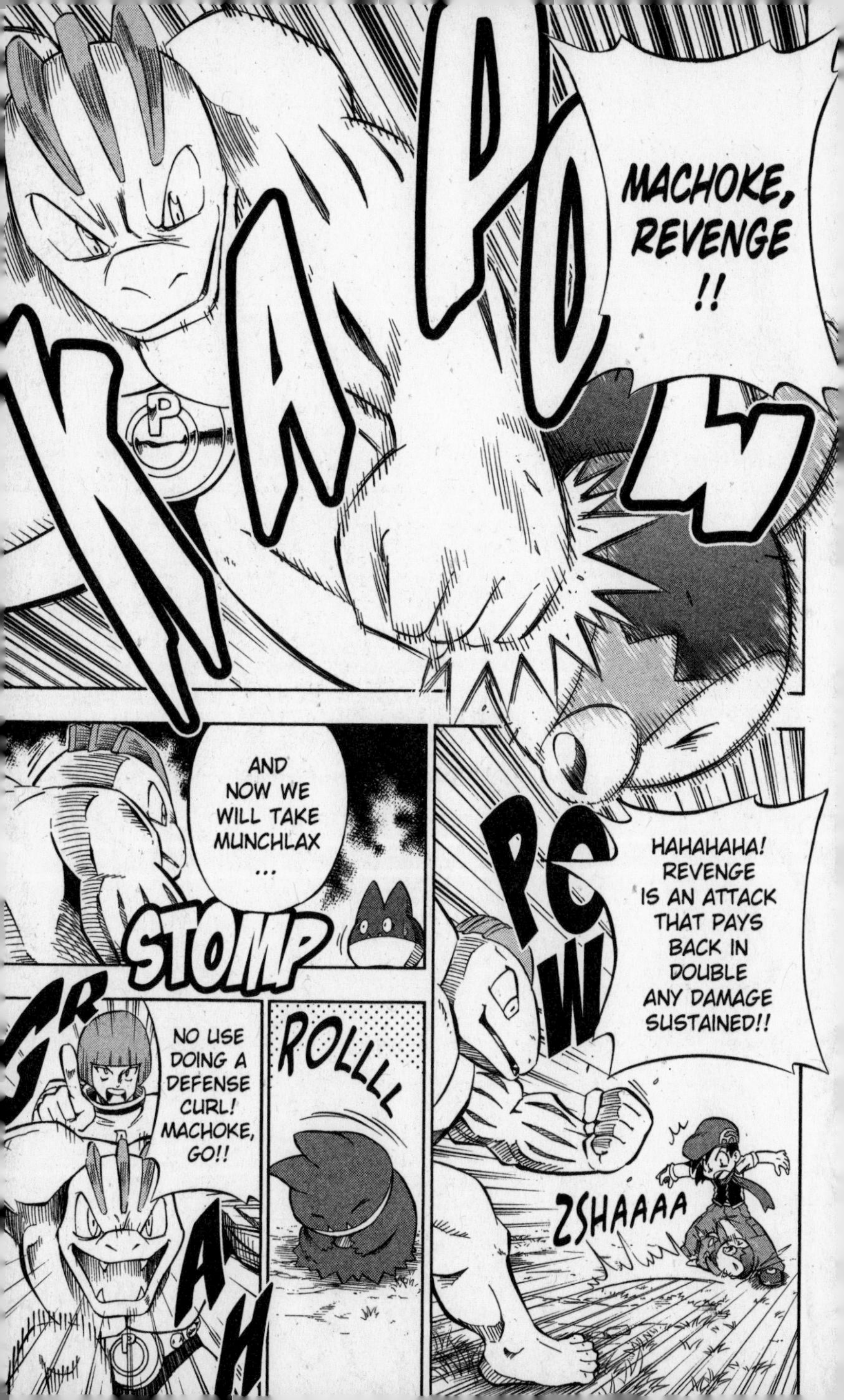
MACHOKE, REVENGE !!
KAPOW
POW
HAHAHAHA! REVENGE IS AN ATTACK THAT PAYS BACK IN DOUBLE ANY DAMAGE SUSTAINED!!
ZSHAAAA
AND NOW WE WILL TAKE MUNCHLAX ...
STOMP
ROLLLL
GR
NO USE DOING A DEFENSE CURL! MACHOKE, GO!!
AH

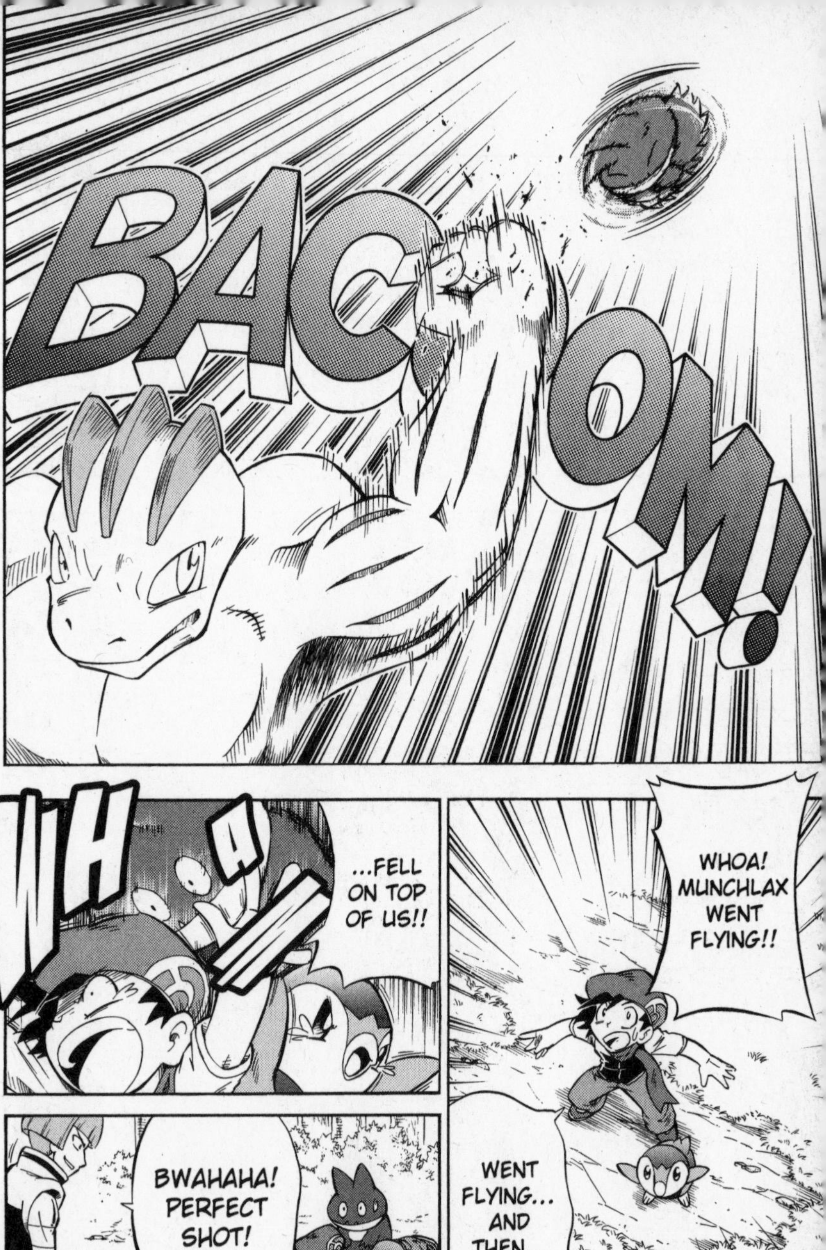
BAC OM!!
WHOA! MUNCHLAX WENT FLYING!!
WENT FLYING... AND THEN...
...FELL ON TOP OF US!!
WHA
BWAHAHA! PERFECT SHOT!

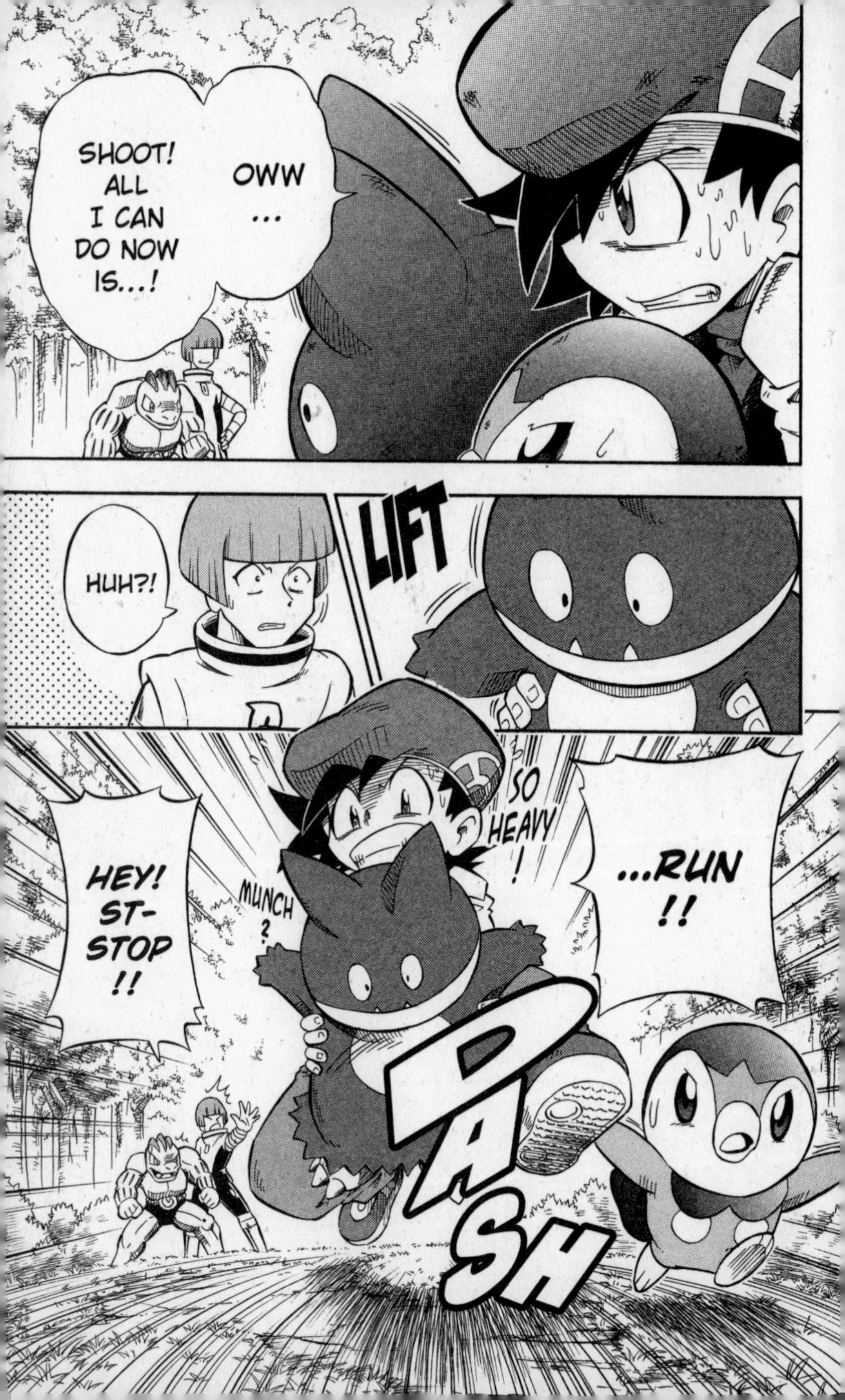
OWW ...
SHOOT! ALL I CAN DO NOW IS...!
LIFT
HUH?!
...RUN !!
SO HEAVY !
MUNCH ?
HEY! ST-STOP !!
DASH

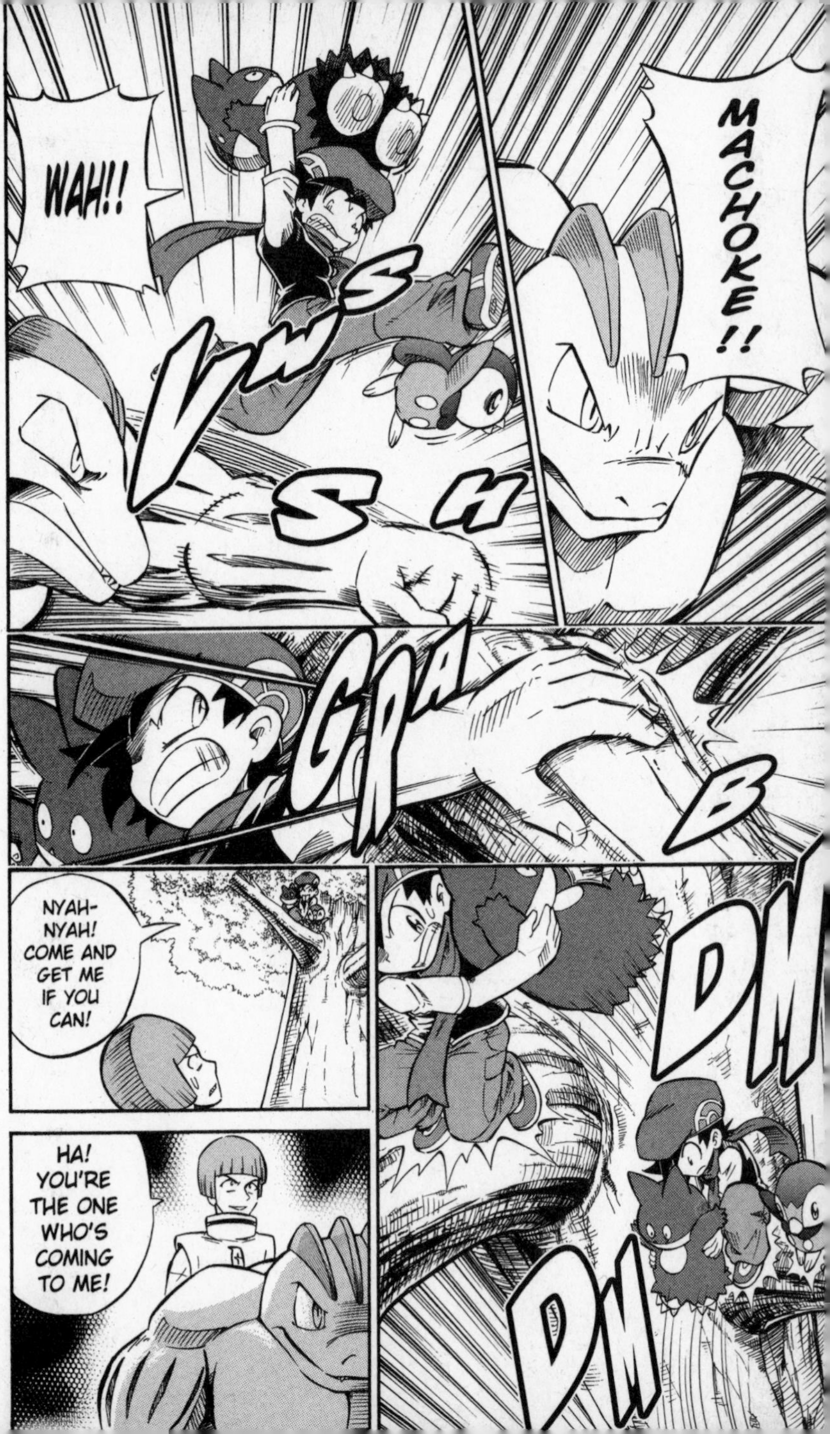

MACHOKE!!
WAH!!
VWSSH
GRAB
DM
DM
NYAH-NYAH! COME AND GET ME IF YOU CAN!
HA! YOU'RE THE ONE WHO'S COMING TO ME!

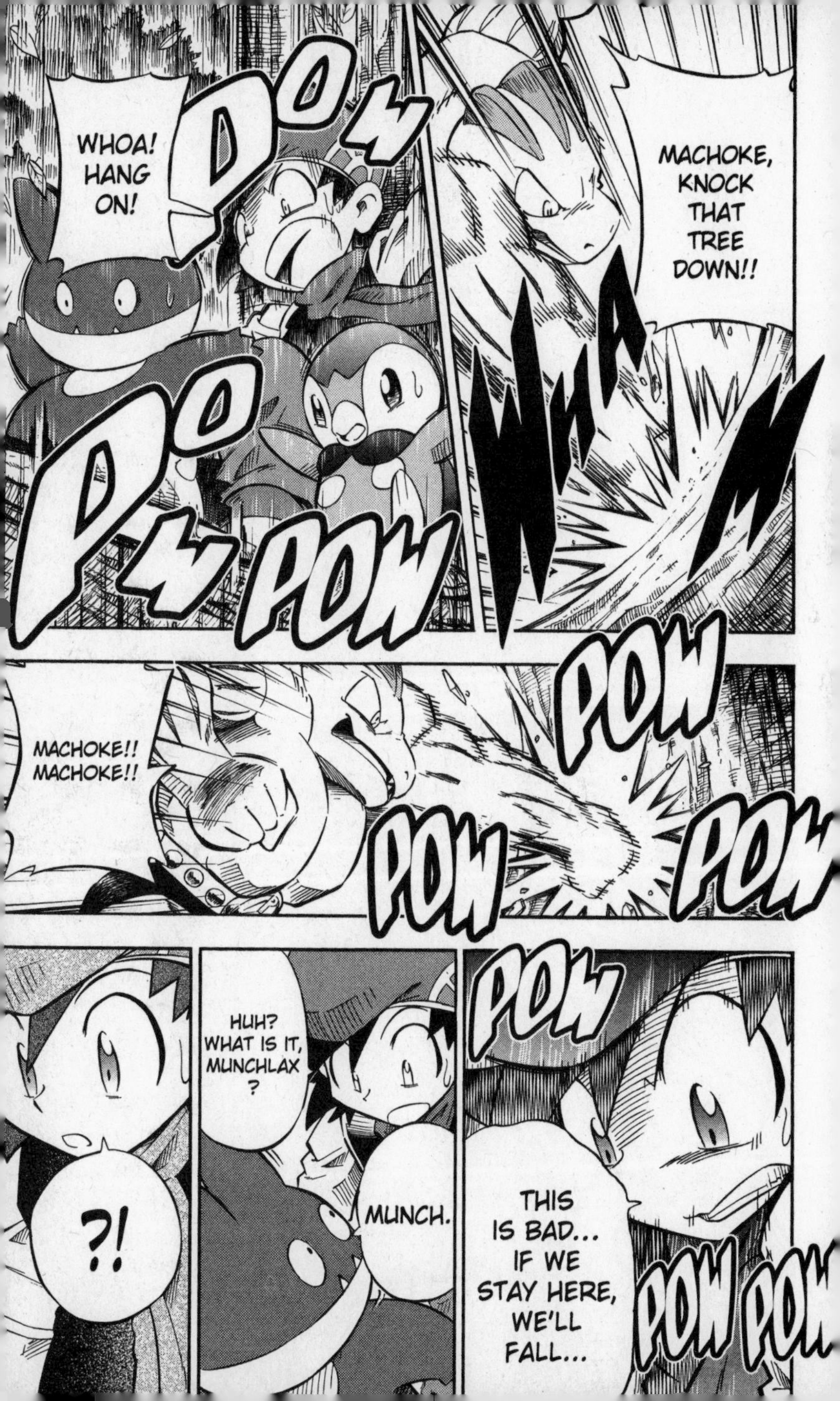
MACHOKE, KNOCK THAT TREE DOWN!!
DOOM
WHOA! HANG ON!
WHAM
DOOM
POW
POW
POW
MACHOKE!! MACHOKE!!
POW
POW
THIS IS BAD... IF WE STAY HERE, WE'LL FALL...
POW POW
HUH? WHAT IS IT, MUNCHLAX ?
MUNCH.
?!

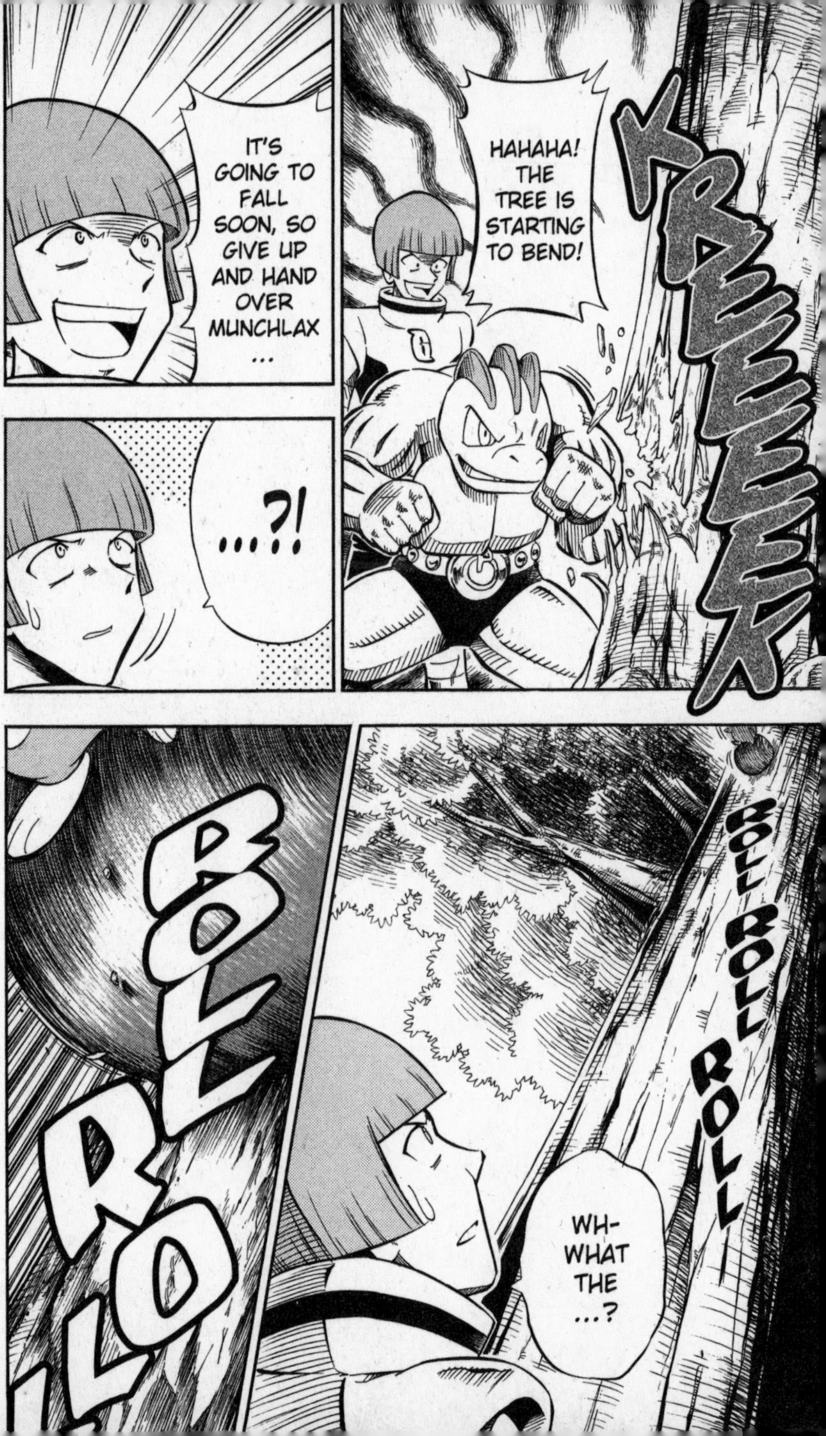
HAHAHA! THE TREE IS STARTING TO BEND!
KREEEEEK
IT'S GOING TO FALL SOON, SO GIVE UP AND HAND OVER MUNCHLAX ...
...?!
ROLL ROLL ROLL
WH-WHAT THE ...?
ROLL ROLL

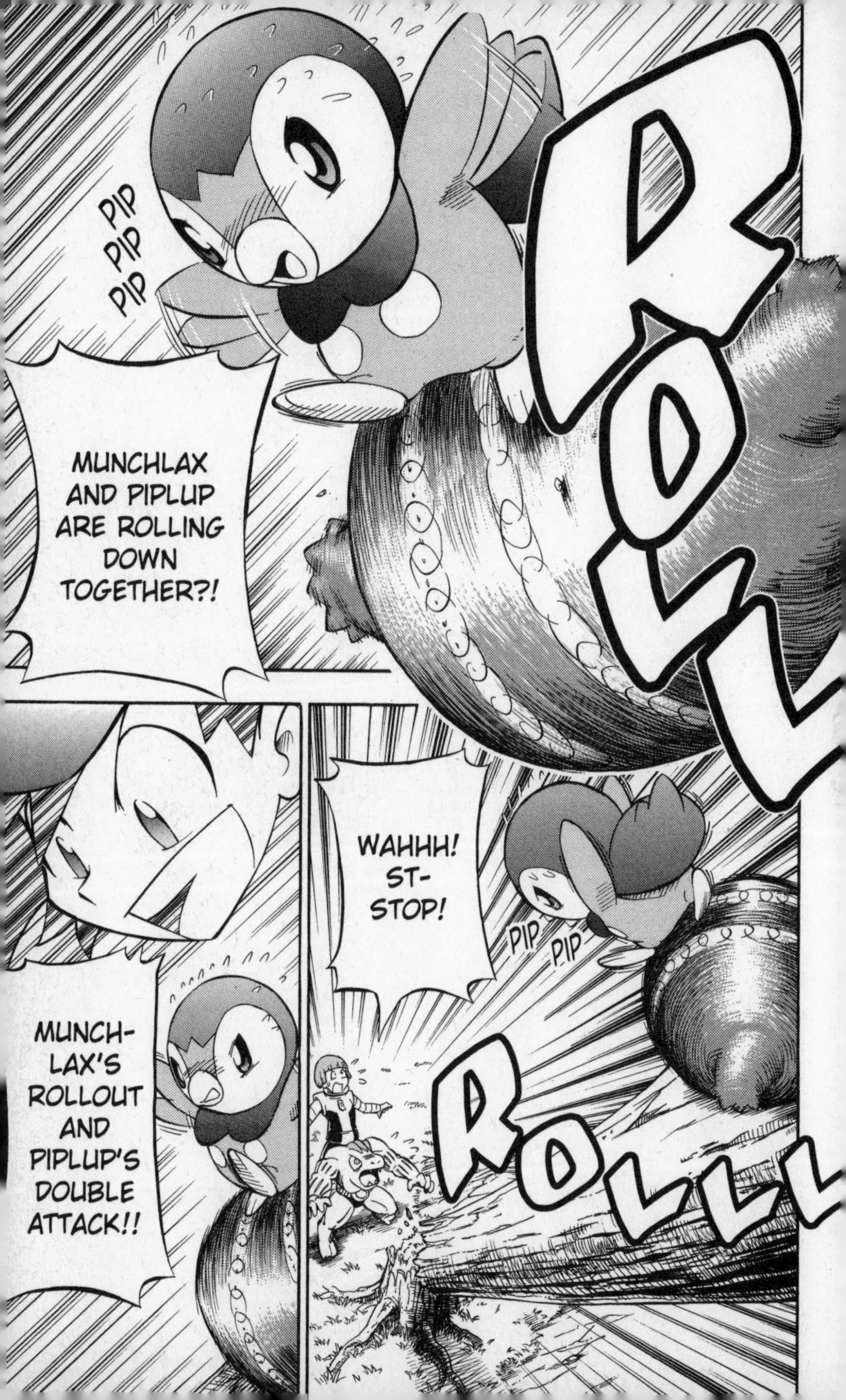
ROLL
PIP PIP PIP
MUNCHLAX AND PIPLUP ARE ROLLING DOWN TOGETHER?!
WAHHH! ST-STOP!
PIP PIP
ROLLL
MUNCH-LAX'S ROLLOUT AND PIPLUP'S DOUBLE ATTACK!!

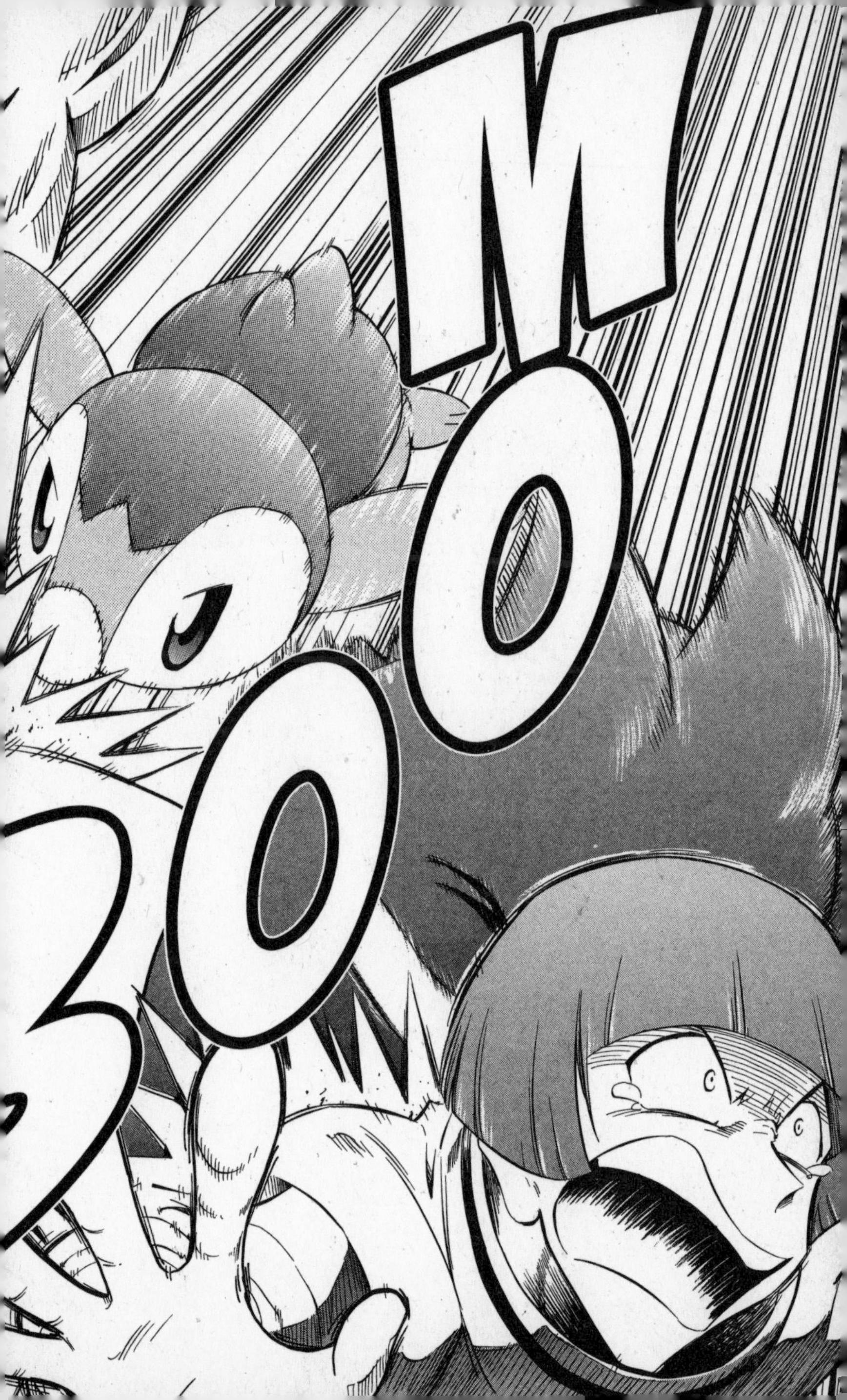
BOOM

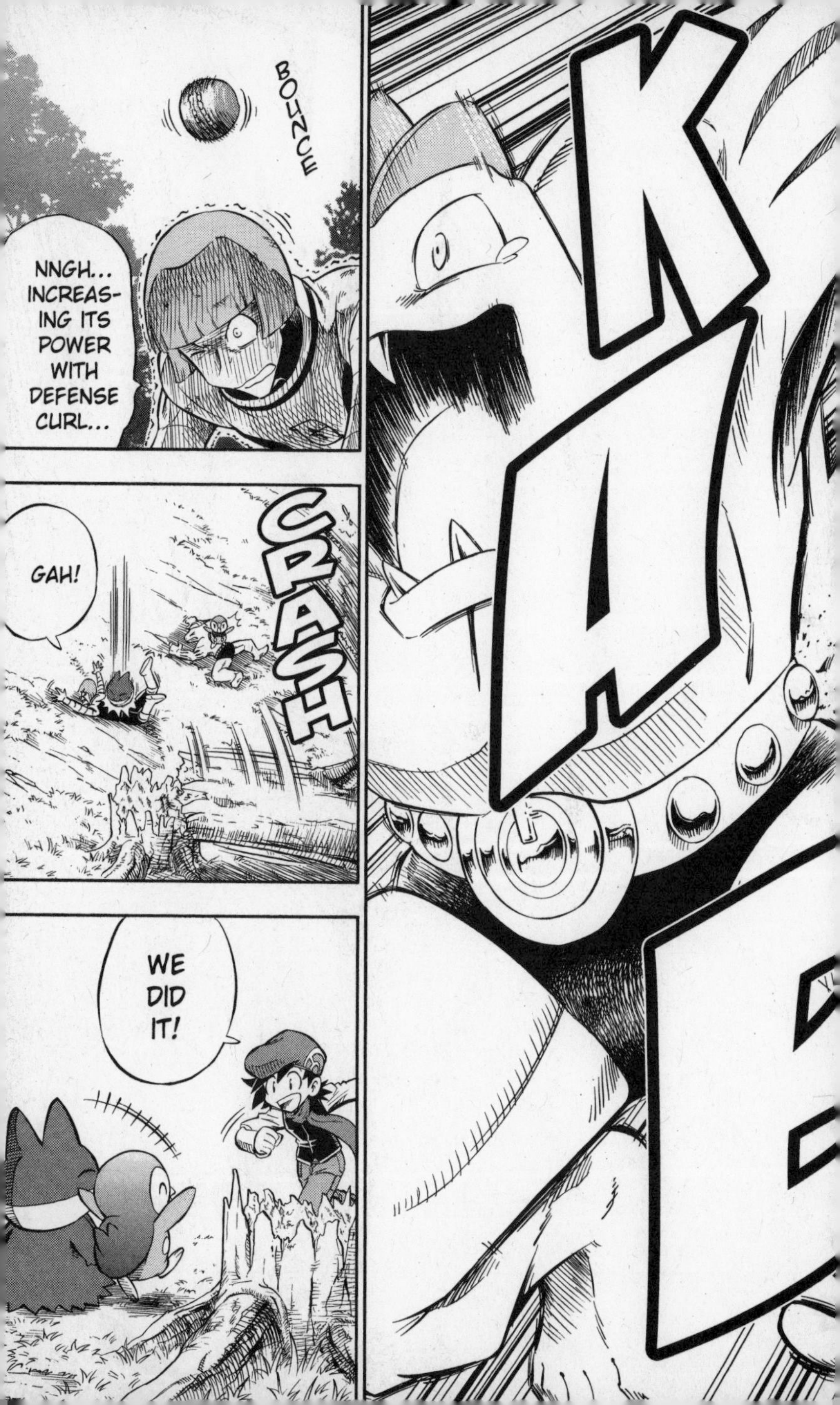
KA
BOUNCE
NNGH... INCREASING ITS POWER WITH DEFENSE CURL...
CRASH
GAH!
WE DID IT!

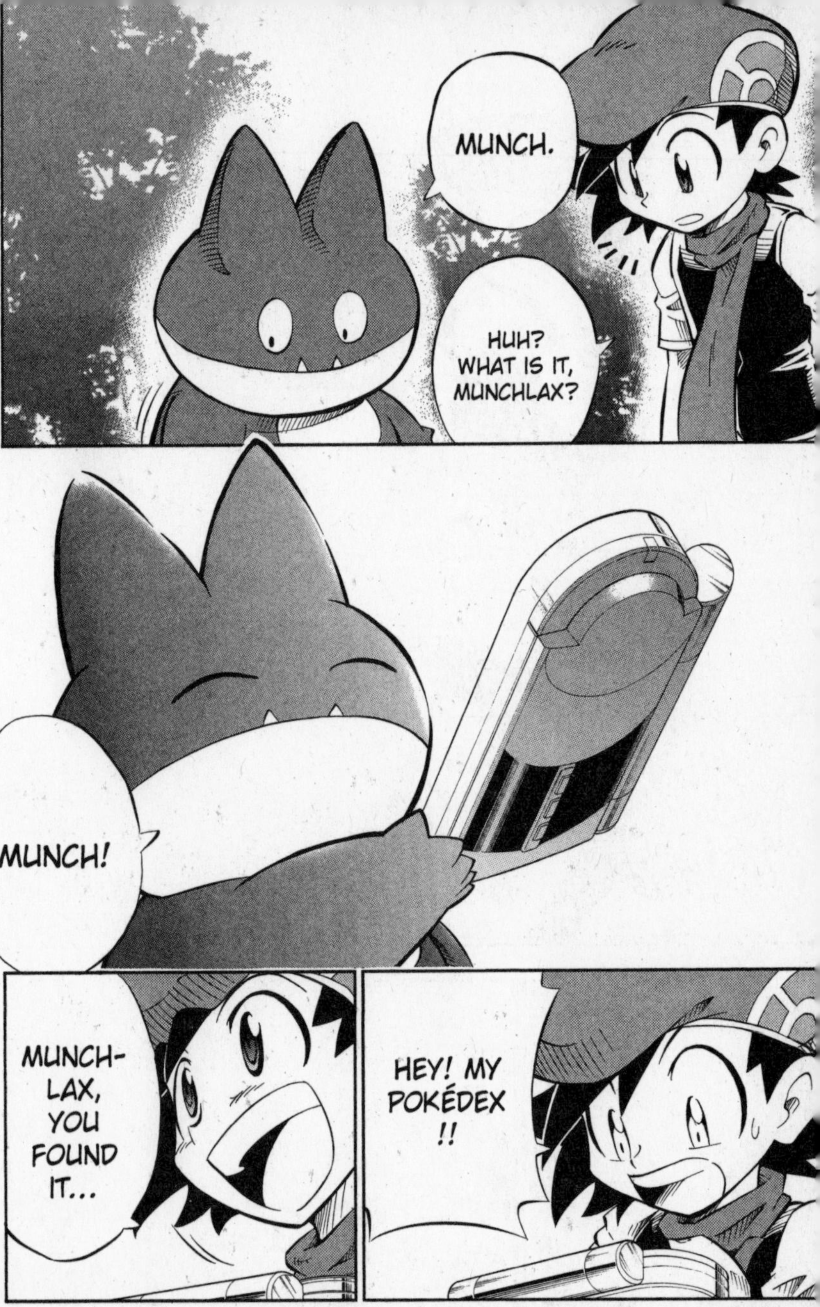
MUNCH.
HUH? WHAT IS IT, MUNCHLAX?
MUNCH!
HEY! MY POKÉDEX !!
MUNCH-LAX, YOU FOUND IT...

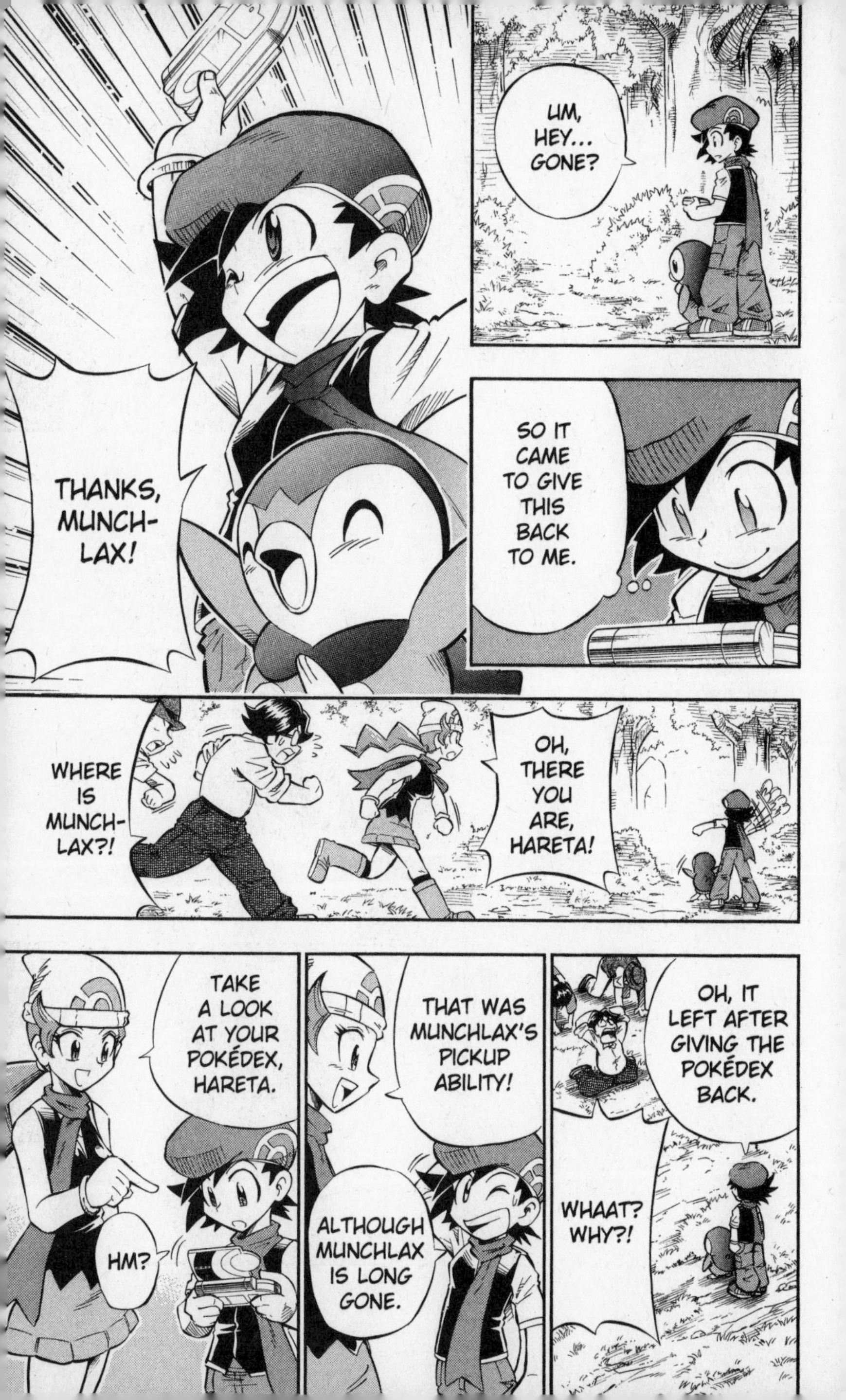
UM, HEY... GONE?
SO IT CAME TO GIVE THIS BACK TO ME.
THANKS, MUNCH-LAX!
OH, THERE YOU ARE, HARETA!
WHERE IS MUNCH-LAX?!
OH, IT LEFT AFTER GIVING THE POKÉDEX BACK.
WHAAT? WHY?!
THAT WAS MUNCHLAX'S PICKUP ABILITY!
ALTHOUGH MUNCHLAX IS LONG GONE.
TAKE A LOOK AT YOUR POKÉDEX, HARETA.
HM?

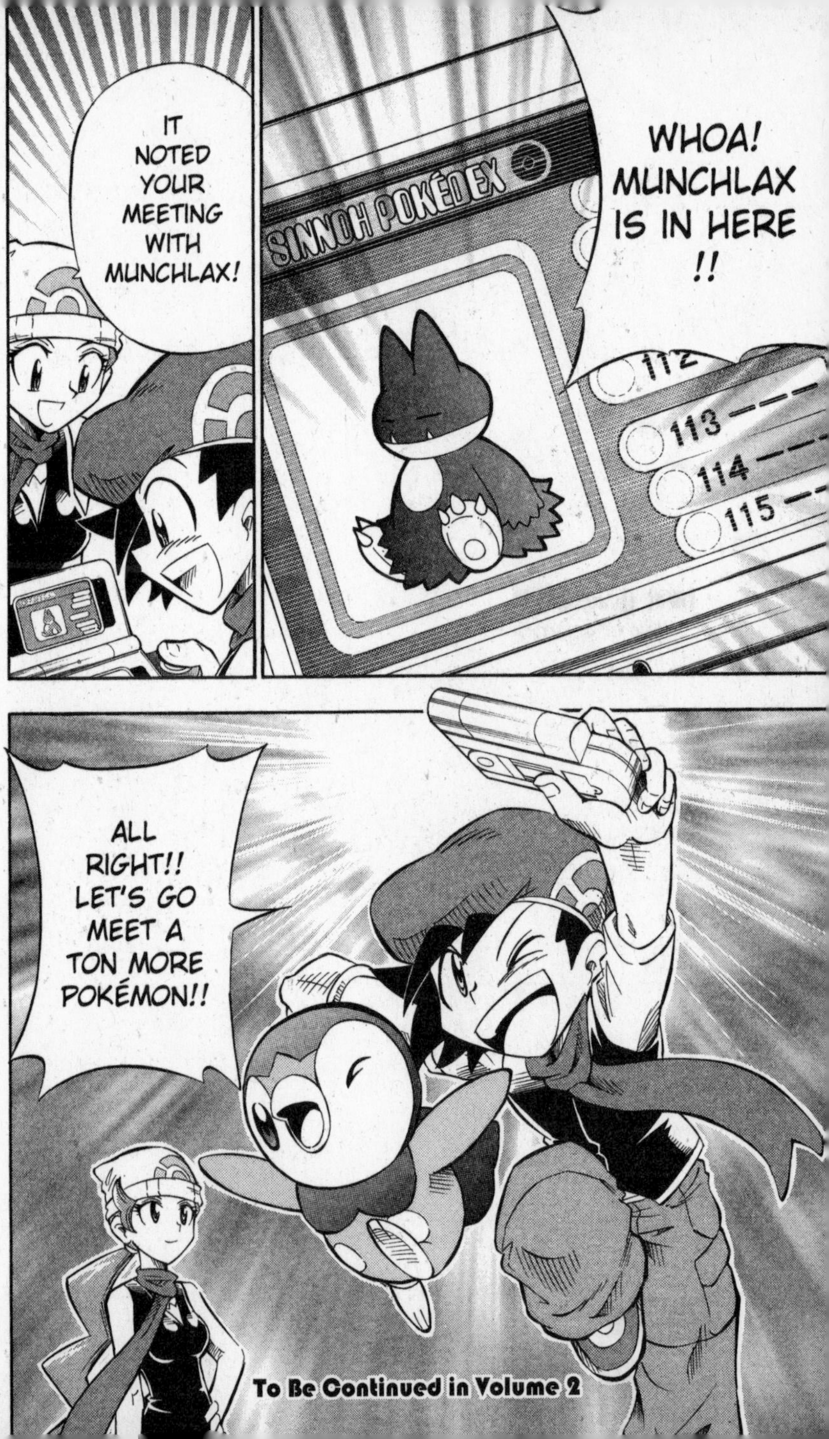
SINNOH POKÉDEX
112
113
114
115
WHOA! MUNCHLAX IS IN HERE !!
IT NOTED YOUR MEETING WITH MUNCHLAX!
ALL RIGHT!! LET'S GO MEET A TON MORE POKÉMON!!
To Be Continued in Volume 2

D·P SNAPSHOTS

SNEAKING A BITE

ROCK THE TARGET'S WORLD!

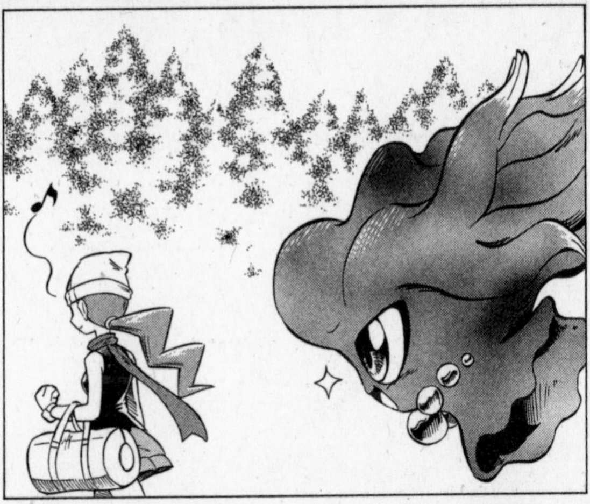

MISDREAVUS, ROCKING THE WORLD OF ITS ASTONISH VICTIM!

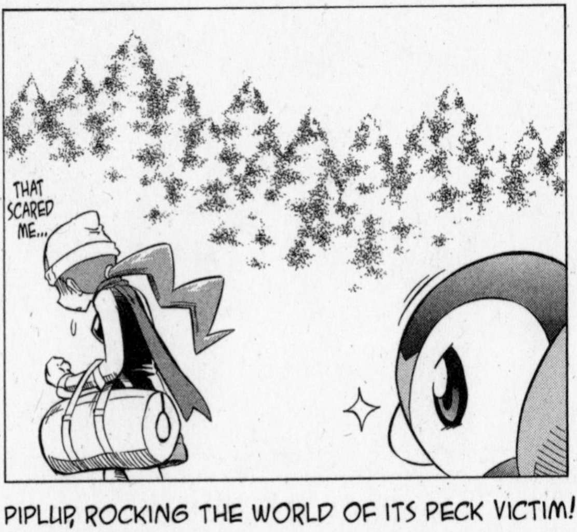
THAT SCARED ME...

PIPLUP, ROCKING THE WORLD OF ITS PECK VICTIM!

CHASE

FROM THE FRONT

FROM THE BACK

In-the-Next-Volume

Hareta, Mitsumi, and Jun—along with their Pokémon friends Piplup, Starly, and Turtwig—continue on their quest to find the Legendary Pokémon Dialga. But Team Galactic is still in the chase, and now their ultimate leader, Cyrus, is ready to make his move.

Available August 2008!

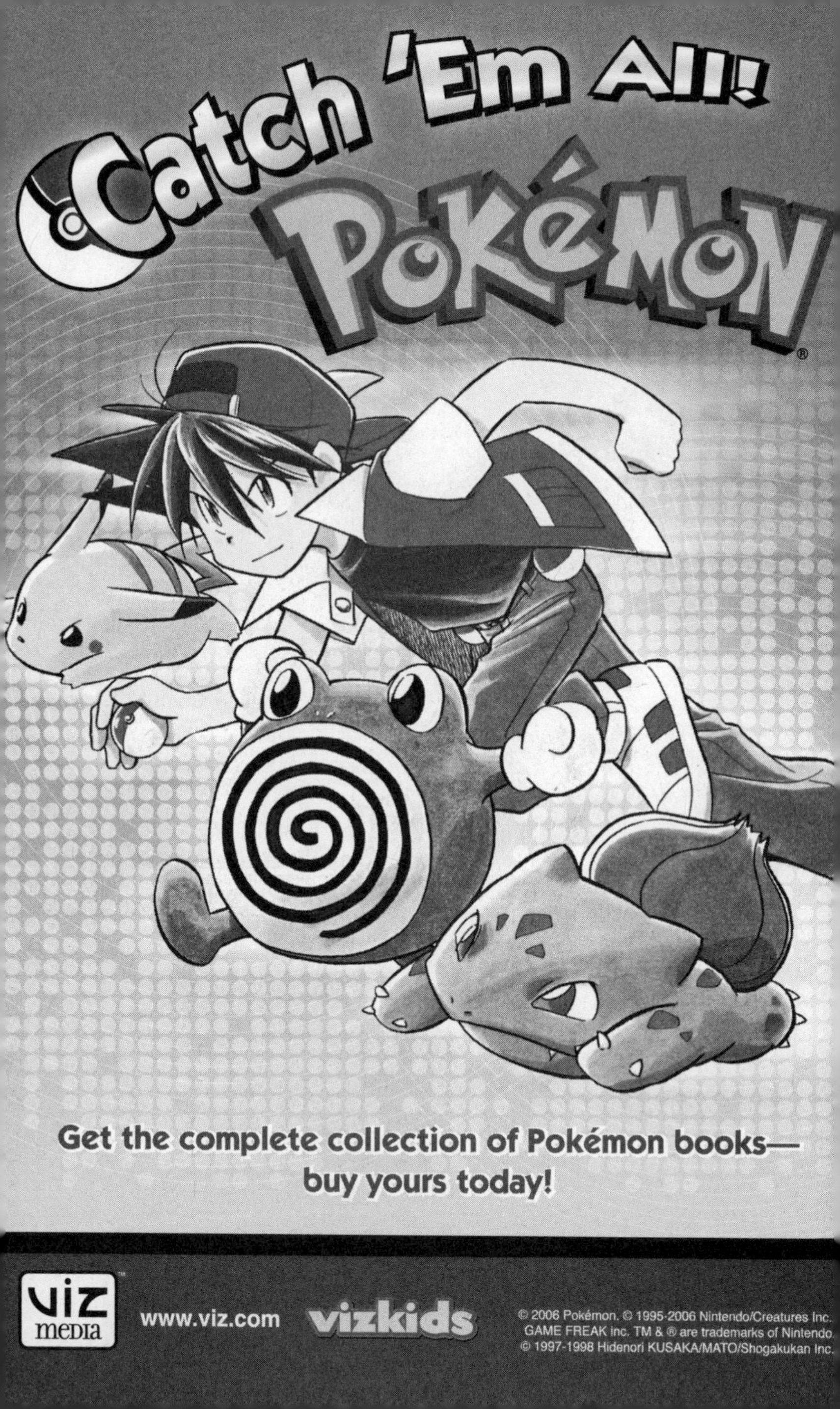
Catch 'Em All!
Pokémon®
Get the complete collection of Pokémon books—buy yours today!
viz media
www.viz.com
vizkids
© 2006 Pokémon. © 1995-2006 Nintendo/Creatures Inc. GAME FREAK inc. TM & ® are trademarks of Nintendo.
© 1997-1998 Hidenori KUSAKA/MATO/Shogakukan Inc.

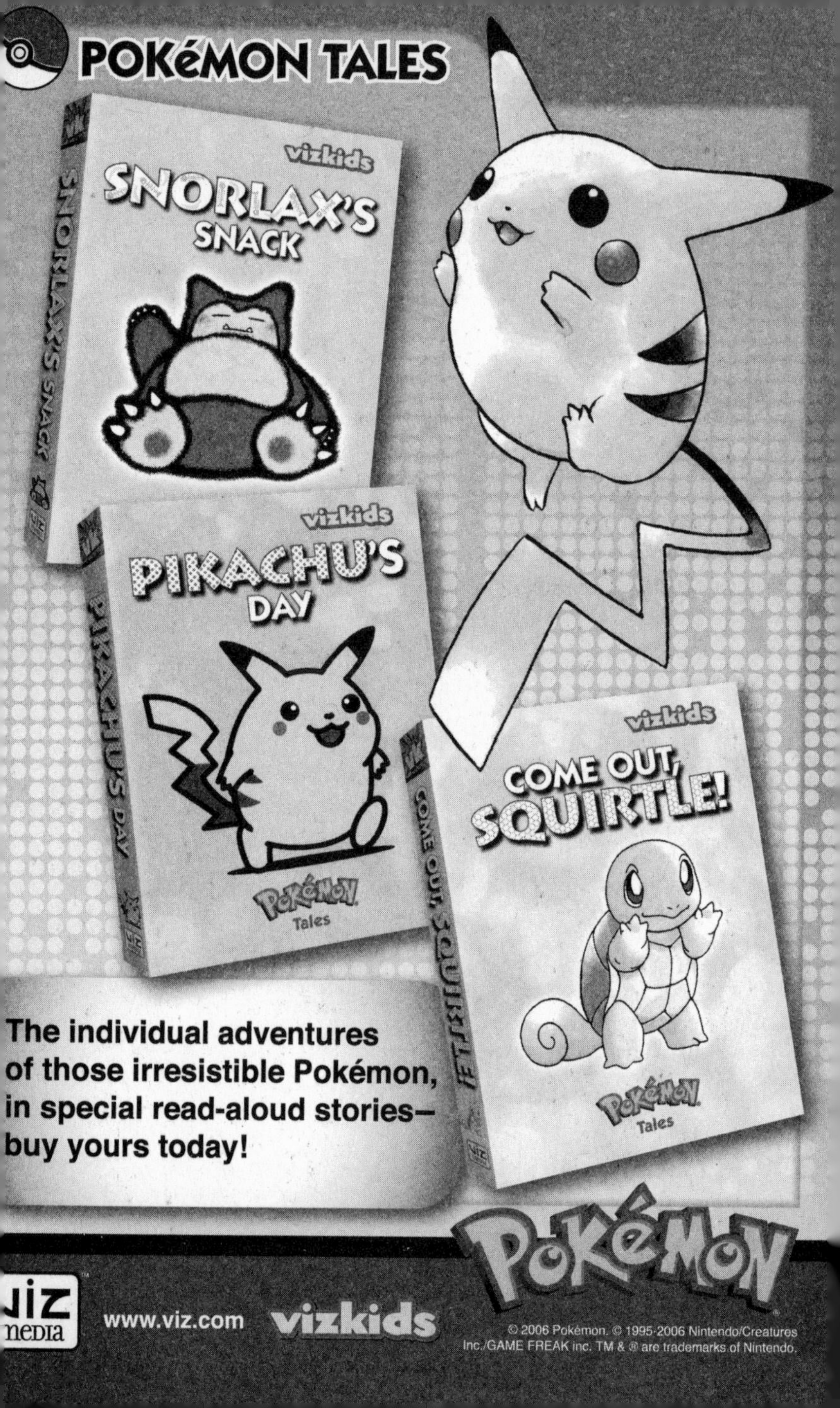
POKéMON TALES
vizkids
SNORLAX'S SNACK
vizkids
PIKACHU'S DAY
POKéMON Tales
vizkids
COME OUT, SQUIRTLE!
POKéMON Tales
The individual adventures of those irresistible Pokémon, in special read-aloud stories– buy yours today!
POKéMON
VIZ MEDIA
www.viz.com
vizkids
© 2006 Pokémon. © 1995-2006 Nintendo/Creatures Inc./GAME FREAK inc. TM & ® are trademarks of Nintendo.